O9-BSA-546

WITHDRAWN
No longer the property of the
Boston Public Library.
Sale of this material benefits the Library

SPIRAL

SPIRAL

A NOVEL

paul mceuen

THE DIAL PRESS | NEW YORK

Spiral is a work of fiction. Names, characters, places, and incidents are the products of the author's imagination or are used fictitiously. Any resemblance to actual events, locales, or persons, living or dead, is entirely coincidental.

Copyright © 2011 by Paul McEuen

All rights reserved.

Published in the United States by The Dial Press, an imprint of The Random House Publishing Group, a division of Random House, Inc., New York.

DIAL PRESS is a registered trademark of Random House, Inc., and the colophon is a trademark of Random House, Inc.

LIBRARY OF CONGRESS CATALOGING-IN-PUBLICATION DATA
McEuen, Paul.
Spiral / by Paul McEuen.
p.   cm.
ISBN 978-0-385-34211-7
1. Biotechnology—Fiction.   I. Title.
PS3613.C428S65 2010
813'.6—dc22
2010009768

Printed in the United States of America on acid-free paper

www.dialpress.com

2 4 6 8 9 7 5 3 1

FIRST EDITION

Book design by Steve Kennedy

To Susan (Willow)

■ PACIFIC OCEAN, MARCH 1946 ■

LIAM CONNOR WAS SICK TO SEE IT, STANDING ON THE DECK of the USS *North Dakota,* binoculars trained on the sea. The truth was clear, the truth he saw in the binoculars, the four American sailors in the bright red lifeboat, all young and alive, none older than Connor himself.

"TURN BACK," the commanding officer ordered through the megaphone.

"You can't do this!" screamed one of the Americans. "I have a son. I've never seen my son!" He had his shirt off, waving it frantically back and forth, a fluttering white bird over the blue water. Two other men rowed.

"TURN AROUND. *NOW.*"

Warning shots spat out of the Oerlikon twenty-millimeter deck cannons, the noise deafening, rapid-fire jackhammers, a strafe line between the lifeboat and the USS *North Dakota*. The men vanished behind a wall of sea spray.

The mist settled, the sea again quiet. The tall one jumped up and down, waving his damned white shirt, threatening to topple the small boat. "Stop firing!" he shouted. "We are *not* sick!"

"He's lying," said the Army general Willoughby. Willoughby was a few feet away from Liam on the foredeck, watching through his own field glasses, his lips drawn back, teeth clenched. "See the way he moves? He's jumping out of his skin."

On the bridge, the commanding officer of the *North Dakota* raised his megaphone. "TURN AROUND. THIS IS YOUR LAST WARNING."

Another spit of bullets from the guns, and the boat vanished again in a cloud of spray. This time the line was closer, near enough to soak the men. Connor saw fear clinging to their faces like the drops of water. If the gunner raised his sights by a few degrees, they'd be shredded.

The leader of the lifeboat sat down on the gunwale, the white shirt falling from his hands. The boat floated listlessly, slowly twisting while the four argued among themselves, their words carrying over the waves. The tall one pointed toward the *North Dakota*, shaking his head, mouthing the phrase *No other way.*

"The stupid bastards are coming," Willoughby said.

The tall one stood, facing the *North Dakota*, held his white shirt overhead. *"Go!"* he called out, and the rowers began rowing, plowing the sea as hard and fast as they could.

The commander of the *North Dakota* stood straight. The megaphone hung at his side.

He gave a slight nod.

It was over in seconds. Two Oerlikons fired simultaneously, and the sea erupted. The lifeboat exploded red, fragmented into an array of splinters and planks of wood. In an instant, both the men and the lifeboat were gone, nothing left but the mist and a stain of flotsam and debris on the water.

Liam saw something moving, flopping on the surface. At first he thought it was a dying fish. But it wasn't a fish. It was an arm, severed at the shoulder.

He vomited over the side of the ship.

LIAM CONNOR HAD SPENT FOUR YEARS IN THE BRITISH ARMY, but he had never seen men die like that. Liam was a small man, five-six, but strong-willed, wiry and tough. He was also Irish, with blond-red wavy hair and a complexion like putty stained with red ocher. He was tenacious, with a precocious, sharp mind and fast feet. He had started university at Cork at the age of fourteen and quickly established himself as a biology prodigy, on his way to a Ph.D. when the war intervened. He could also run a mile in just over four minutes fifteen seconds, making him the third fastest man in Ireland. He was a lieutenant, by the British Army's reckoning more valuable as a scientist than a bullet catcher. Barely twenty-two years old, he'd spent the past four years at Porton Down, in the southwest English county of Wiltshire, the center of British chemical and germ weapons research. His specialty was saprobic fungi, the feeders on the dead.

He was a scientist. He'd never seen men die like that, killed by their own brothers-in-arms.

TWO DAYS AGO HE'D BEEN IN GERMANY, AT A CHEMICAL FACTORY outside Munich. He was in the final weeks of his military service, a member of an Allied team conducting a postmortem of the Nazi chemical and germ warfare program. He expected to leave Germany within days, return to England and on to Ireland and his wife, Edith. They'd been married for almost three years, but in that time had spent less than ten days together. He missed her like he missed Ireland.

Thirty-six hours before, his plans had drastically changed. Liam was shoved on a troop transport plane in Munich with no explanation. Four flights later, he found himself halfway around the world, over the Pacific, circling a flotilla of U.S. Navy vessels. They'd strapped him in a parachute and ordered him out, the first parachute jump of his life. He'd been fished out of the sea and brought aboard the USS *North Dakota* just in time to see the slaughter of the four sailors.

The whole journey over, he'd been wondering why. They'd grabbed a lieutenant and shipped him across the globe. Now he was starting to understand. At Porton, they'd spent months preparing for what they believed inevitable, the use of germ weapons by the Nazis. The Germans had been the first to use poison gas on a large scale in World War I—few at Porton doubted that this time around, the Nazis would use germs. They'd been wrong. It was the Japanese.

. . .

LIAM'S POINT OF CONTACT ON THE USS *NORTH DAKOTA* WAS
a gangly major named Andy Scilla. He was a microbiologist from
Mississippi who'd trained at Harvard but kept his accent. Scilla
was from Camp Detrick in Maryland, the American center of
chemical and germ warfare, their equivalent of Porton Down. "I'll
be your date while you're here," he said, his drawl at first difficult
for Liam to follow. But he got used to it, got to like it. It reminded
him of some of the boggers back home.

Liam spent his first hour with Scilla in a small cabin three doors
down from the communications room. Here, Scilla said, they had
copies of the medical records of the men on the infected ship, the
USS *Vanguard,* along with a series of files they'd brought from
Tokyo, giving background on what was happening. They were
stored in a series of metal lockers to keep out the ever-present salt-
water. Scilla gave Liam the chain of events: "Five days ago, the ship
those men came from, the USS *Vanguard,* picked up a distress call
from the Japanese sub out there, the I-17. No one could figure it
out. Hell, it's been six months since the end of the war. Where's a
Jap sub been hiding all that time?

"Once the *Vanguard* arrived, they found the I-17 dead in the
water. They tried to establish radio contact, but they got zip. Absolutely nothing. But they could see a single Japanese soldier on the
bow of the sub. Just sitting there. They hollered at him, but he
didn't move a muscle. So they sent a team to board.

"What they found was a nightmare. The entire crew, maybe a
hundred men, sliced open like gutted fish. From the looks of it, they
had committed hara-kiri en masse. All except that one Japanese
soldier, alone on the bow of the sub. He looked catatonic, cross-
legged, back straight, staring forward like a statue. The leader of
the boarding crew, a chief petty officer named Maddox, thought he
was in traumatic shock. But that wasn't it. Not at all. He waited
until they were practically next to him. Then he sliced himself
open, shoved a grenade in his belly, and blew himself to bits."

"Suicide?" Liam asked. The Japanese were cultish about their
honor and death—surrender was a mortal sin.

"Not exactly. That took a while to figure out. Why blow yourself to bits right when the soldiers get there? If he was a kamikaze,
he would've attacked, thrown the grenade at the boarding crew.

Plus, they had plenty of weapons below, plenty of guns, lots of ammo. He could have killed quite a few of our men.

"No one really got it worked out for about twelve hours. The key was the boarding crew, the sailors that had been there when the bastard blew himself to bits. The leader, Maddox, took a pretty good whack to the head. He woke up two hours later in the *Vanguard*'s sick bay, asking about his men. Everyone was more or less fine. But eight hours later, in the bed next to Maddox, Smithson begins to display unusual symptoms. A depressed temperature, an unpleasant smell about him. An hour later, Smithson is scratching wildly at his skin and has to be physically restrained. He is incoherent, raving. Twenty hours later, Maddox is no better. He is certain that iron-skinned snakes are living in his belly, feeding on his intestines. From these two, it spread throughout the ship."

Liam understood. "The Jap was a vector. A germ bomb."

"Got it."

"And the rest of the boarding crew?"

"Maddox is dead. He got loose, grabbed a knife, and stabbed himself to death. Just kept shoving it in his gut again and again until he bled out. The doc on the *Vanguard* counted twenty-two separate entrance wounds. Smithson's still alive, but he bit off his own tongue. Spit it out on the floor in front of him, laughing madly the whole time. Reports say it's a complete nightmare over there. A day or two after infection, you begin to completely lose it. Go violently crazy. One guy seemed perfectly normal until he locked himself in the galley with four sailors, shot them in the guts, then stomped on their skulls until a few others broke in and put a bullet in him. Everyone is paranoid. As soon as you show any symptoms, they tie you down. They ran out of beds and are roping men to their bunks, to piping on the walls, everything."

"Holy Christ. How many are infected?"

"One hundred eighty-eight," Scilla said. "Of those, thirty-two have died. And they're losing a few more each hour."

"Clinical symptoms?"

"Their temperatures run a couple of degrees low."

"And their smell? You said there was an odor?"

"Yes. Sour."

"Ammonia? Like urine?"

"That's it."

"I'll tell you what it sounds like. It sounds like mycotoxin poisoning," Connor said. "Maybe *Claviceps purpurea*. Ergot. Or one of the species of *Fusarium*."

Scilla nodded. "That's why we brought you here. We're all germ people. Bacterial. But we got nobody with a background in fungi, so we called Porton. And they sent you."

"Anything else? Other physical signs?"

"A few of the men have spiral growths in their mouths."

"A pale white? Like candy floss? Cotton candy?"

"That's just the way they described it."

"How many are still symptom-free?"

"Less than forty now."

Liam tried to take it all in. He had never heard of virulence like this. The entire ship in four days?

Scilla grabbed a thick manila folder and dropped it on the table. The cover said TOP SECRET. "Read this. I'll be in the comm room when you're done."

LIAM READ.

Inside the folder was a twelve-page report issued by the U.S. Army Chemical Corps and under the signature of a Major General William N. Porter. The title was simple: *Summary of the Testimony of Hitoshi Kitano, Unit 731*. It was dated March 2, 1946. Liam had never heard of Hitoshi Kitano, but he'd heard rumors of Unit 731.

The report began with a short bio on Kitano. He was an officer in the Kwantung Army, the Japanese occupying force in north China. He was twenty-one years old. His uncle was a well-known lieutenant colonel, killed in the Philippines in 1944. His mother and father were killed in the atomic bomb explosion at Nagasaki. For the last two years of the war, Kitano was assigned to a biological weapons unit called Unit 731, in Harbin, China, a few hundred miles north of Peking, returning to Japan in the final days of the war. He'd been picked up by the British in Hirado, not far from Nagasaki.

From there, the report turned to Kitano's accounts of Unit 731.

The official title of Unit 731 was the Epidemic Prevention and Water Purification Department of the Kwantung Army, but its true mission was germ warfare. According to Kitano's account, Unit 731 was formed in the mid-1930s, the brainchild of a Japanese general named Shiro Ishii. He was unusually brash and aggressive by Japanese standards but undeniably brilliant, convincing key military officials that Japanese victory could be assured only by the development of new biological weapons.

Unit 731 grew into an enormous operation, Japan's version of the Manhattan Project, researching and testing every aspect of biological weaponry. Thousands of scientists, one hundred and fifty buildings, contained within a perimeter of six kilometers, all devoted to the perfection and refinement of biological weapons. They had collected pathogens from all over the world, tested them, refined them, coaxed out the deadliest strains. It dwarfed the efforts by the British at Porton Down and by the Americans at Camp Detrick.

They also ran field tests on the most promising weapons, according to Kitano. In Baoshan, in southern China, they tested "maggot bombs." These were ceramic containers dropped from planes that shattered on impact, spreading a gelatin emulsion filled with cholera bacteria and living flies. The flies survived the fall because of the gelatin, and then carried the cholera, landing on humans, animals, latrines, and cooking instruments, spreading the pestilence. Before the attack, Kitano said, cholera was unknown in Yunnan province. Within a month, cases were reported in sixty-six separate counties. Within two months, two hundred thousand were dead. All from a few bombs of jelly and flies, easily carried by a single airplane.

Liam was stunned. The British had run tests of anthrax at Gruinard Island off the coast of Scotland, tethering sheep and setting off anthrax bombs nearby. That seemed at the edge of what was too grisly to do. But field tests on humans? Entire cities? Hundreds of thousands of innocents killed? It was a terrible sin, far and away the most horrific germ weapons testing program in human history.

A medic knocked on the door, a tray of white tablets with him.

"What's this?" Liam asked.

"Penicillin," the medic said. "In case the sickness spreads here."

"It won't help," Liam replied. "It's fungal, not bacterial."

The medic shrugged. "I have my orders. We've got everyone on a regimen, a pill every eight hours. You want it or not?"

Liam passed. Nothing would help. The Scotsman Fleming's wonder drug was useless here. It would do absolutely nothing to stop a mycological infection.

The medic left, and Liam went back to his reading. The last ten pages were devoted to the crowning triumph of Unit 731, a fungal pathogen called the Uzumaki. Translation: spiral. According to Kitano, it was a doomsday weapon, to be used if the Americans threatened to overrun the home islands. Kitano was in charge of testing the Uzumaki on live subjects. It was highly virulent, spreading by the breath, spit, stomach juices, and fecal matter.

Kitano said that the latest version of the Uzumaki was kept in a sealed hinoki box, in seven small brass cylinders. A cylinder each for the seven chosen Tokkō. When the order came, each member of this elite suicide squad would board a submarine headed for their target. They would ingest the Uzumaki. Once it had taken hold, they would infect everyone they came in contact with.

The last section of the report was an evaluation of the likely authenticity of Kitano's testimony. There had been reports as far back as 1943 of a Japanese germ weapons program in Manchuria. Kitano's statements accurately matched descriptions of Unit 731 beginning to emerge from China. Shiro Ishii's testimony also dovetailed with Kitano's. The Japanese general was still alive and free, in negotiations with the Americans. He had offered to trade immunity for any war crimes in exchange for the records from Unit 731. Ishii did not know that the Americans also had Kitano, yet so far their stories matched quite closely. Overall, the likelihood that Kitano was telling the truth was judged to be very high.

Liam was dumbfounded, barely able to speak, when Scilla returned.

"Have any of the six other submarines been found? Any of the cylinders?"

Scilla shook his head no. "No one really believed any of it until the *Vanguard*. Until they found Seigo Mori on the deck of that sub."

"How do you know his name?"

"From Kitano. I interviewed him myself yesterday."

"Wait. He's on board?"

Scilla nodded. "Willoughby likes to keep him close. Kitano said Mori was plucked from the University of Tokyo, trained to be a torpedo kamikaze. But they changed plans on him. Sent him to Harbin, to Unit 731, to that psychopath Ishii. Said he was nineteen years old."

"Why attack now? Six months after the end of the war?"

"Maybe they didn't know it was over. Our best guess is that the sub had mechanical troubles, ran out of fuel. Kitano says it was headed to the Pacific coast, up near the Washington-Oregon border. Mori was going to blow himself up at a major water supply. Think about it, Connor. Instead of a boatload of people with the Uzumaki, there'd be a city full. Maybe the entire damn United States."

SCILLA LED LIAM TO THE COMMANDING OFFICER'S QUARTERS. Four men were inside: the commander of the *North Dakota*, Admiral Seymour Arvo; Major General Charles Willoughby; and two others that Liam had not met before. Willoughby, looking like a cadaver, ran the show. Liam had heard that MacArthur called him "my pet Fascist."

The other two men seemed familiar, but Liam couldn't place them at first. Then he realized the one with a narrow face and regal features was J. Robert Oppenheimer. The other, with a round nose and probing eyes, was Hans Bethe. Two of the greatest physicists the Americans had. Both key players in the Manhattan Project.

The men were crammed around a small map table, the surface covered with papers haphazardly arranged. Liam noticed what looked to be equations on many of the sheets. He knew enough physics to recognize Bernoulli's equation on one. Another had a sketch that looked like a shock wave.

Oppenheimer looked up. "This our fungal expert?"

"Liam Connor," Scilla said. "From Porton."

"Tell me," the regal man said, "what is the maximum temperature a fungal spore can take and still be viable?"

"Depends on how long it's hot," Liam answered.

"Say a fraction of a second."

"I'd say a hundred degrees."

"A hundred degrees. You sure?"

"No, I'm not sure. It could be more. Why?"

"What about a shock wave?" asked Bethe. His accent was German. "Acceleration of, say, thirty g's?"

"Probably wouldn't matter. It wouldn't affect the spore at all."

"What about radiation? Gamma rays?"

Liam realized what they had planned. "You're going to blow up the *Vanguard* with an atomic bomb."

"Unless you have a better idea," Oppenheimer said.

HITOSHI KITANO WAS HELD IN A SMALL CABIN THAT NORMALLY served as officers' quarters. Two sailors stood guard outside. Liam was accompanied by one of Willoughby's aides, a major named Anderson. He said few words but paid close attention, taking notes in a little red notebook.

Liam's nerves were on edge. Bethe and Oppenheimer had grilled him for an hour about fungi and spores, trying to decide if a nuclear blast would destroy the Uzumaki or merely launch its spores into the upper atmosphere, where the jet stream would spread them around the world. The odds favored destruction, but the verdict was still out. Liam, in turn, had warned them of the dangers of *not* acting. If, as he suspected, the culprit was a *Fusarium* fungus, there was a good chance it could spread around the world without the help of a nuclear blast. Many species of *Fusarium* could thrive inside the guts of migratory fowl. A bird could be infected and then be a thousand miles away in days. The feathers of birds were a huge risk. They were ideal for carrying spores.

Kitano stood the moment Liam entered. He was very thin, his clothes hanging on him, his skin stretched over the angular bones of his face. His hands were cuffed together. His right cheek was noticeably swollen. Scilla told him he'd had an infected tooth. He'd refused any treatment, any medications, finally acquiescing to letting them pull it, minus any painkillers. They said he'd barely flinched.

They introduced themselves politely, Hitoshi Kitano's English crisp and clear, accented but clearly understandable. Kitano sat with his back perfectly straight in his chair. Though no older than

Liam himself, he looked ancient in a way that Liam couldn't at first quite sort out. It was the eyes, Liam realized. His eyes seemed dead.

Liam had a number of questions for Kitano. Most prominent was how the Japanese would defend themselves against blowback from the Tokkō missions. Biological weapons were notoriously difficult to control. It was inconceivable to Liam that the Japanese would use a weapon as virulent as the Uzumaki if they didn't have a way of protecting their own people. If it was a fungus native to Japan, they might be naturally resistant, or have an old folk remedy. Alternatively, scientists at Unit 731 might have developed a preventative, or even a cure. There were no good antifungals, Liam knew. But if you are willing to kill people, you might be able to develop one. You infect a prisoner, you try out a cure. You fail, you try again. If such a program existed at Unit 731, Liam was willing to bet that Hitoshi Kitano knew about it.

"I am a scientist—a mycologist," Liam said. "I study fungi. Mushrooms. Molds."

Kitano nodded. "My father was also a scientist, an ornithologist. He studied magpies mostly, but he also kept pigeons. My mother said he loved the birds more than her."

"My wife has said the same sort of thing. About me and mushrooms."

Kitano smiled slightly.

"I was told that your parents died at Nagasaki. I'm sorry."

"Many died. On both sides." Kitano tilted his head like a bird. "I learned an interesting fact from Professor Oppenheimer. He said that Nagasaki was not the original target. It was Kokura. But it was cloudy in Kokura, so they went on to Nagasaki."

Liam tried to imagine what it must feel like to know that your family was dead because of the weather. War was a series of random catastrophes.

Liam got down to it. "At Unit 731 you worked on the Uzumaki. How did they create the different strains?"

"I am not a biologist. I was an engineer. I oversaw the tests. My understanding is they had some way to mix the traits. They could change the fungi. Make them adopt the properties of other fungi. They mixed the spores together with special chemicals. I do not know what kind."

"Was it acidic? Basic?"

"I don't know."

"Did you wear gloves?"

"Yes. Rubber gloves. And masks. After we made it airborne."

"How did you do that?"

"We would inject the Uzumaki variants into the *maruta,* wait for the madness to take hold."

"Maruta?"

"The prisoners were *maruta.* Logs."

"Logs? I don't understand."

"The official story is that Unit 731 was a lumber mill. We were cutting logs. We could have as many logs as we wished. We simply filled out a requisition form."

Liam tried to contain his loathing for the man in front of him. The bureaucracy of genocide. It was not unlike the German death camps, the experiments of Mengele. People became chunks of flesh to be manipulated, tortured, disposed of like rats.

Kitano continued. "After we infected them, we had them breathe on a glass slide. Then the doctors cultivated the spores on the slides. It took many tries, but finally it worked. A variant that was both highly infectious and could be spread by the breath. We called this *maruta* the Mother. The Mother of the Uzumaki."

"How many tries did it take?"

"Perhaps three, four hundred."

"You killed hundreds of people in the tests?"

"For the Uzumaki, we killed eight hundred and seventeen before we had the breather. But there were many programs like this. We downed approximately ten thousand *maruta* overall."

"Ten thousand? How could you stand it? It's inhuman. Monstrous."

"Perhaps. But the subjects at Unit 731 were well treated, well fed. Not like the other POW camps. Typically we injected them with the pathogen, systematically varying the dose. Then we watched as the disease progressed through them. It was very effective. Different strains could be crossed endlessly, the most deadly variants carefully selected by injecting them into prisoners and culturing the blood of those who died the fastest. After they began to show symptoms, we would take constant readings. Temperature, blood pressure, reaction times. Some we would dissect."

"After they were dead."

"No. While they were alive."

Liam was aghast. "Why in God's name would you do that?"

"To yield the most accurate picture. Anesthetic causes bio-chemical changes, affects the blood, the organs. As does death."

"It's murder. Sadistic, inhuman murder."

"Research, Mr. Connor. Very important research."

Kitano spoke as if he was describing the dissection of a frog. Liam took a deep breath, tried to keep his focus. "Who were the subjects?"

"Some were spies. Others criminals. The rest were Chinese civilians we took from the streets of the surrounding cities. The soldiers would unload the *maruta* and go back out again."

"And then you would kill them."

Kitano smiled condescendingly. "This was our task, Lieutenant Connor. Developing new weapons. Testing them. The scientists at Unit 731 were no different from your physicists developing the atomic bomb. Seigo Mori was no different than the American pilot that flew the mission that destroyed Nagasaki." Kitano leaned forward, cuffed hands on the table before him. "He was a gentle man, Mr. Connor. Everyone liked him. His father was a factory worker who died when he was only three. He often told me stories about his mother and older sister, how they both doted over him, the only man in the house. He wished to be a poet. But he was willing to die."

Liam asked the question he'd been waiting to ask. "You must have a way to stop the Uzumaki. To protect Japan."

"No."

"But if it found its way back to Japan, it would kill millions of your own people. How could you risk that?"

"We had no choice. The Uzumaki was the last resort. To be used when everything else was lost. When Japan had nothing left to lose. The Uzumaki is—how do you say it?—a doomsday weapon. Once released, it cannot be stopped."

A PAIR OF SAILORS ON DECK ON THE *NORTH DAKOTA* POINTED UP.

Liam followed the path of their gaze but saw nothing but clear blue sky. He was talking to Scilla about what he'd learned from Kitano. Scilla, in turn, was telling Liam about the latest developments on the *Vanguard,* and the news wasn't good. The captain was keeping everyone belowdecks to minimize the risk of the spread of the Uzumaki, but a group of sailors, almost certainly infected, had stolen guns and were holed up topside on the foredeck. They'd already killed three other sailors who'd tried to stop them. Liam was incensed that they were out in the open. Sooner or later, a spore would catch an air current, drift across the water, and infect one of the other ships.

Liam continued to study the patch of sky that the sailors were pointing to. It took a good minute before he saw it.

At first it was hardly more than a black speck moving slowly across the wide expanse.

"No," Liam said. "No. No. No."

Scilla grabbed a pair of binoculars. "It's a damned goose," he said.

They were hundreds of miles from any landfall. They could go days without seeing a bird. But the bastard was headed straight for them. "Go," Liam said. "Get out of here."

Liam looked across the open water to the USS *Vanguard.* On the foredeck, the siege continued against the sailors who'd broken free and come out into the open. A group from amidships launched an assault, the sailors firing back, screaming expletives. They were completely mad.

Scilla was dead still, watching the goose through the binoculars. *"Keep going,"* he said.

Liam could make out the goose's features now, the broad wingspan, the slow beating of the wings. Closer and closer it came, still high overhead but dropping slowly. Liam tried to will it away. "Keep going," he murmured. "Keep flying."

The goose didn't listen. It did the worst thing possible. It turned toward the *Vanguard,* then descended in spirals of decreasing radius, a narrowing gyre. Both men watched it drop, stall, and finally settle gently onto the deck of the USS *Vanguard.*

"Damn it!" Scilla said.

Liam watched through binoculars as one of the men on the *Vanguard* leveled a gun at the bird.

"No, no, no," Liam yelled, as if he could be heard across the expanse of ocean separating the two ships. "Get a tarp. Try to cover it."

The soldier shot, missed.

The goose flew away.

A FAST CRUISER AND A DESTROYER WERE DISPATCHED TO chase the goose, staying in continuous radio contact. They were barely able to match the bird's speed running wide open, thirty-five knots. The destroyer even fired its four-inch guns at the bird, a ridiculously futile effort, like trying to shoot a fly with a rifle. It would have been laughable if the stakes hadn't been so high. By the time they got the Vought OS2U Kingfisher scout planes in the air, the goose had disappeared into a cloud bank, and it hadn't been seen since.

A quiet descended over the ship. The chase boats plied the waters, searching for the errant goose, the Kingfishers buzzing overhead. Calls had been put out, scrambling planes from Tokyo to join in the search.

Willoughby was nearby, his face red, talking to a major. "Imagine if the Russians have this," he said. "The Russians were the first into Harbin. What if one of these cylinders ends up in Stalin's hands? You think Uncle Joe wouldn't use it?"

They were caught. If they did nothing, sooner or later the Uzumaki would spread beyond the confines of the *Vanguard,* either by a bird or spores carried by the wind. If they blew the ship up, they killed hundreds of men and ran the risk of spreading the Uzumaki even more widely. It was a devil's deal.

Liam stared across the half-mile that separated them from the *Vanguard.* The screams of the infected sailors carried over the water.

If the Uzumaki was a doomsday weapon, a single goose could be the beginning of a catastrophe on a historic scale. The world had just survived the most brutal, destructive war in history. Could the worst be yet to come?

No.

The Japanese must have a way to protect themselves. Liam couldn't believe otherwise. An entire nation doesn't commit suicide. And if they had a cure, Kitano knew about it. Kitano was hiding something—Liam sensed it. And he had an idea how to find out what it was.

He went below, to the room where Kitano was kept. Kitano

had been forgotten in the goose excitement, left with a lone guard outside his door.

The guard stopped him. "No one's allowed inside."

"I've got authorization," he lied.

"From who?"

"Willoughby."

"I wasn't told."

"Everyone's worried about the goose. It must've got dropped. You want me to—"

"No. It's okay."

LIAM TOOK A SEAT ACROSS FROM KITANO.

"A goose landed on the *Vanguard,* then took off again. There's a good chance it's infected. It was last seen going north."

No reaction. Kitano was exactly the same, the dead eyes, the even demeanor.

"Japan is to the north. That goose is headed toward Japan."

No reaction.

God damn it. Why wasn't he reacting? The goose could easily find its way to Japan, a thousand or so miles to the north. It would devastate Japan. Why wasn't Kitano upset?

Liam pushed him again about the Uzumaki, listened carefully as the grim-faced man told the same stories about the tests. At Liam's insistence, Kitano carefully described every experiment he saw or heard about at Harbin. It was grisly, horrifying, and useless. Kitano described nothing that sounded like a trial for a vaccine or a cure. Only death after death.

Kitano stopped. "You realize you are wrong. There is no cure."

"I don't believe you."

He saw something flicker in Kitano's eyes. "Let me tell you about our tests at Ningbo, on the eastern coast of China, south of Shanghai. We used low-flying airplanes that dropped wheat laced with bubonic plague. With standard bubonic plague, nine in ten who contract the disease die. With the strain released on the people of Ningbo, ninety-nine out of one hundred died."

"What is your point?"

"Seven of the team from Unit 731 were among the dead. The researchers contracted the disease themselves. They died. Ishii had no cure for bubonic plague. But that did not stop him. It did not stop us. We are not afraid to die, Mr. Connor. You must understand that, if you are to understand us."

Liam studied Kitano, tried to look into his soul. Kitano was right—the entire nation of Japan worshipped death. Glorified it. Maybe it was true. The Japanese had shown time and time again an utter insensitivity to losses on their own side. *Could* they have launched these attacks with no cure? The Uzumaki was the ultimate Tokkō mission. The suicide attack of a nation, in order to bring down the entire world.

He stayed after Kitano, asking more questions. "Did any of the Tokkō ever mention a name besides Uzumaki?" *No.* "Did you ever see them take any medication? Anything?" *No.* "Aspirin?" *No.* "A powder?" *No.* "Anything?" *No.*

Liam had asked all these questions before. He felt as though they were stuck on a wheel, spinning around and around, twirling questions without getting any closer to the answer.

He stared at Kitano, his thin features, cheek swollen from his removed tooth. Then, apropos of nothing, two separate images came to him. The first was of an autoclave, a machine for sterilizing biological equipment.

The second image was of the medic handing out the penicillin tablets. They were of no use. The Uzumaki wasn't bacterial. It was fungal.

A glimpse of the hem of the secret.

Liam chased the idea, followed it through. *Penicillium.* The most famous fungus in the world. In the early part of the war, thousands of soldiers died from bacterial infections. But after the Americans learned to mass-produce penicillin in 1943, Allied soldiers stopped dying. The antibiotic had an enormous impact on the war effort. Hardly an American or British soldier had not taken the drug by the time the war was over.

The Japanese had no penicillin. The Japanese died.

The Japanese had worked on it but had never gotten past the stage of producing the drug by the thimbleful. Probably not more than a handful of Japanese citizens had ever taken the drug.

What if that was the missing piece? The more Liam thought about it, the more sense it made. It was brilliant. Weakness to strength.

Liam met Kitano's gaze. He stared at him for maybe thirty seconds. Then Liam said, "Penicillin." He saw an involuntary flash of
recognition in Kitano's face. It was quickly gone, replaced by his
dead stare.

A tingling ran up Liam's spine. "You gave your test subjects
penicillin, didn't you?"

Kitano started to speak, stopped, faltered. Kitano's hand was
shaking. "I don't know what you're talking about."

Liam was on his feet. "You damn sure do, you bloody bastard."

THE ENGINES WERE RUNNING FULL TILT WHEN LIAM MADE IT
to the bridge.

Penicillin. That was the difference. The Allies had penicillin.
The Japanese did not. Penicillin was a miracle drug because it killed
deadly bacteria that led to infections. But after a regimen of penicillin, the human digestive tract was also wiped nearly clean of ben-
eficial bacteria. Yes, it killed off the problematic bacteria and saved
your life. But it also wiped out the natural bacteria in you, including the ones that kept fungal invaders at bay. Leaving a person sus-
ceptible to fungal invasion. Yeast infections, oral thrush—all were
common fungal infections that could flare up after a regimen of
penicillin. Without the right gut bacteria, the human body was defenseless.

Defenseless, Liam now understood, to the Uzumaki.

"Tell everyone to stop taking penicillin now," Liam yelled as
he hit the bridge. "The penicillin makes you vulnerable for God
knows how long." Everyone on the bridge was busy, serious, barely
acknowledging him. The USS *North Dakota* was turning away
from the *Vanguard*. All the other ships were doing the same.
"What's going on?" Liam asked. "Is it the goose?"

"No," Scilla said. "The goose landed on one of the chase ships.
A sailor tossed a tarp over it, then beat it to death." He handed
Liam his binoculars. "Look at the stern."

Liam took the binoculars, caught sight of the mayhem aboard
the *Vanguard*. A few of the sailors were strung up by their necks.
Others were beating them with bars of metal. Another was stab-
bing at the dangling bodies with a bayonet.

"It's all broken loose. They are completely crazy," Scilla said. "The captain of the *Vanguard* was screaming and ranting just before he cut off communications." Scilla opened the watertight door to the control room. "Willoughby called in the bomber two hours ago. It'll be here any moment."

AT FIRST THE PLANE WAS NOTHING MORE THAN A DOT ON the horizon.

"Are we far enough?" Liam heard a sailor ask nervously.

"We're at five miles," another said.

The plane grew larger, coming toward them in a perfectly straight line. Then the rumbling, the throaty burble of the props of the B-29 Superfortress.

Liam watched the B-29 pass directly overhead, impossibly high. A second dot appeared below it, separating, pulling away. It fell in a graceful arc, growing larger by the second, a stone tossed from heaven.

Bethe talked while it dropped. "Inside the bomb, a spherical shell of explosives will detonate. It is an implosion device, the explosives launching an inward shock wave, generating tremendous heat and pressure, compressing the plutonium encased inside, creating critical mass. It's not so complicated, once you understand. Dear God, a talented undergraduate could design one."

The bomb fell, a spear aimed from above. Just before it hit, a blinding flash. For the fourth time in human history, a nuclear chain reaction sparked into life, multiplied, and spread, vaporizing everything near it, pushing heat and air and dust into the heavens.

KITANO FELT THE PULSE RATTLE THROUGH THE SHIP LIKE A giant hammer blow. He was thrown back, knocking his head hard against the bulkhead. He shook it off, put his focus back where it needed to be. This was his moment. Connor knew Kitano's secret. He must act now.

His hands were cuffed together, but this was not an impediment. He took three sharp breaths, a Bushido technique to ready a warrior before a crucial act. Then he raised his hands and placed the middle finger of his right hand into his mouth. He set his teeth

precisely at the joint, just as he had practiced a hundred times before, on live prisoners. With a sudden violent chomp, he bit through
the meat, separating it at the gap between the proximal and medial
phalange, as cleanly as when he had practiced with the fingers of
prisoners.

The pain was nothing. Kitano was greater than pain.

He spit his finger out on the table, black spots before his eyes.

He focused on it, grabbed the bone and snapped it, using the
edge of the table as a wedge. A small brass cylinder, as thin as a
twig, protruded outward from the bone.

Kitano was bleeding profusely now. They could be here at any
moment. But no matter. He needed just a few seconds more.

He heard a click. The door opened.

THE FIRST THING LIAM SAW WAS BLOOD SPLATTERED IN DROPS
on the metal floor. He glanced around the room. It was empty.
Where was Kitano? Had he escaped?

Liam stepped inside, and Kitano blindsided him.

The impact drove Liam sideways into the wall. Liam felt something give in his shoulder and pain flared. He turned to fight, but
Kitano caught him with a head butt, blood erupting into Liam's
eyes. Blind, Liam managed to shove Kitano away, giving himself a
second to breathe.

But only a second. Kitano came at him, cuffed hands held over
his head like a club. Liam ducked low and drove a shoulder into
Kitano's midsection, sending them both to the floor.

They fought silently, viciously. They traded blows for what
seemed like hours but Liam would later estimate to be less than
thirty seconds. In the end, Liam delivered the decisive strike. He
got behind Kitano and ran him headfirst into the steel bulkhead ad-
jacent to the door. Kitano fell to the floor, dazed, barely conscious.

Kitano was streaked with red. Blood was everywhere.

Liam tried to catch his breath. His shoulder ached. "You knew
about the penicillin all along."

Kitano didn't answer. His eyes gave away nothing.

Liam looked around the room. Near his foot he saw a detached, bloody finger.

He grabbed Kitano's hand. The right one. It was missing the last two sections of the middle finger.

What the hell?

Liam nudged the finger with his foot. He bent over, studying it. Sticking out of the flesh was a small brass object.

He pulled it free, wiped the blood off with his fingers. It was perhaps an inch long, threaded at the middle. A small brass cylinder, a miniature version of the ones that Kitano had described, the ones carried by the seven Tokkō. Cylinders containing the Uzumaki.

"Jesus. You tell me everything, you bastard. Right now."

Kitano didn't speak, and in a fury now, Liam struck him again and again. It was strangely quiet in the room, no cries. Kitano took the blows silently.

"Tell me, you goddamn psychopath."

Kitano didn't answer. He was limp, his eyes half closed. Liam was holding him up by his collar. When he finally released him, Kitano fell to the floor. Liam stood over him, breathing hard, clenching and unclenching his fists.

Not moving, Kitano looked back up at him with glassy eyes.

Liam tried to calm down, sort it all out. He and Kitano were alone. The guard was on deck. Everyone was still on deck, Liam was sure, mesmerized by the size and spectacle of an atomic explosion.

Kitano stirred. He tried to stand but then fell back against the wall. He shook his head, trying to get his wits about him, attempted again to stand. He saw Liam, the cylinder.

Liam held up the cylinder. "It's in here, isn't it? The Uzumaki?"

Kitano slumped back, defeated. Neither spoke. Liam watched him, the man's hands still cuffed together, finger missing. The blood dripped steadily from Kitano's hand, forming a sticky pool on the floor. He was bleeding to death. Liam could stand here another five minutes and Kitano would bleed out. He would die. He should let him die. Liam wrapped his fingers around the cylinder, held it tight. "You goddamn bastard."

Finally Kitano said, "Kill me."

"What?"

"Kill me. I want to die. I failed. Please. Kill me."

. . .

LIAM WAS ALONE ON THE DECK OF THE USS *NORTH DAKOTA*.
It was past two a.m.

He looked down at the small brass cylinder in his hand.

He'd spent the last six hours in debriefings with Willoughby and
his lieutenants, helping them prepare a communiqué to MacArthur
describing the events leading to the destruction of the *Vanguard*. A
second communiqué covered everything that he had discovered:
that penicillin made you vulnerable to full-on infection. The vul-
nerability could persist for weeks, even years. Within hours, the
Uzumaki takes over your GI tract. Transmission by fecal matter or
stomach juices: vomiting, perhaps even spit. Once it is in your
lungs, the spores spread from your breath. No known cure. The
mycotoxins attack your sanity, producing mania, hallucinations,
then suicidal and homicidal urges. Later, they attack your organs,
causing internal hemorrhaging. Within a day, you are mad. Within
a week, you are dead. You live only long enough to infect those
around you, a walking biological time bomb.

He had told them about confronting Kitano after the explosion, finding him wounded, having bitten off his own finger, trying
to kill himself, trying to bleed to death.

They had fought. Liam had subdued him and then gone for
help.

That was the story he'd told.

He hadn't told them about the small brass cylinder in his hand.

Throw it overboard, he thought. *Toss it over. To the bottom of
the sea with it.*

Toss it, you dumb Irish bastard.

WHEN KITANO AWOKE, HE WAS IN THE INFIRMARY. HE WAS
strapped down. He was alone. His finger was bandaged, missing
the top two joints.

The cylinder was gone. He expected the MPs to come, interro-
gate him, torture him. Tear at his body until he'd told them everything about the Uzumaki.

But it never happened.

They questioned him about the penicillin for hours. But nothing more. Nothing about the cylinder that had been in his finger.

Over the next hours, his certainty grew until it was rock-solid. They did not *know*. They did not know what he had possessed. Liam Connor had not told them.

A few days after, he saw Connor briefly. They had brought him up for a few minutes of sunlight. Connor stood by the railing. Their eyes met. Connor shook his head almost imperceptibly. He glanced toward the sea. To say *I threw it overboard.*

Kitano nodded back, then turned and looked away, saying with his countenance that he understood, that it was over. That the Uzumaki was now at the bottom of the ocean.

But what Kitano thought was: *He still has it.*

■ SIXTY-FOUR YEARS LATER ■

DAY 1

THE CRAWLERS IN THE GARDEN

· I ·

LIAM CONNOR LOVED CORNELL. HE HAD TAUGHT AT THE university for more than half a century and expected full well to die shuffling between the Arts Quad and the Big Red Barn. Cornell was a chimera, both a member of the Ivy League and the New York state agricultural school. Nabokov wrote *Lolita* here, and Feynman started his scribbling about quantum electrodynamics, but Cornell was also a place where you could get your wheat checked for smut or your cow autopsied.

The campus was perched on a hill overlooking the city of Ithaca, population twenty-nine thousand, tucked between a pair of glacier-carved gorges. It was founded in 1865 by the millionaire and philanthropist Ezra Cornell, founder of Western Union and a freethinker who believed that the practical sciences should be taught with the same zeal as the classics. Cornell had made his money on the telegraph, the new communication technology that had remade society as fundamentally as would the Internet one hundred and fifty years later. He used his fortune to create a new kind of university, utterly different from the religion- and tradition-bound schools of the era: "An institution where any person could find instruction in any study," a quote that would become the school's motto. Coed and nondenominational from the day it opened, the university graduated its first female student in 1873 and its first African American in 1897. Liam was proud of the university's heritage—he had a deep appreciation and respect for the underdog. A person's value, he believed, was set by who they were, not by how others treated them. For eight centuries, the Irish had been treated as little more than apes by the British, and Liam never forgot it.

LIAM'S LABORATORIES WERE TUCKED AWAY IN THE BASE-ment of the Physical Sciences Building, a new glass, steel, and stone structure in the center of campus wedged between the old façades of Rockefeller and Baker halls. This evening he stood in the middle of his lab, a pair of silver, sharp-point #5 tweezers in his hand. The old Irishman was eighty-six years old, dressed in brown dungarees, a gray sweater, and old white sneakers. During his sixty years at Cornell, Liam had put together one of the most unusual and diverse collections of living fungi on the planet. The Gardens of Decay, as he called them, consisted of ten thousand postage stamp–sized plots of different mycological species laid out on a square grid, a mottled menagerie of yellows, greens, and grays, like farmland seen from thirty thousand feet. They occupied three large custom-built granite-topped tables, each almost nine feet across and weighing half a ton. To count all the species, ticking off one a second, would take hours, a testament to the power and fecundity of evolution.

Each of the tiny plots was labeled by a pair of letters and a three-digit number. Plot #HV-324 was *Hemileia vastatrix*, the rust fungus that invaded the British coffee plantations in Ceylon in 1875. Within a few years it decimated the crops and turned England into a nation of tea drinkers. A few rows over was *Aspergillus niger*, which was used for, among other things, the making of smokable *chandoo* opium during the height of the opium trade.

Next to it was *Entomophthora muscae*, the "fly destroyer" fungus, very tricky to grow in culture. It first invades the nervous system of the common housefly. Somehow—no one knew exactly how—*E. muscae* commands the fly to crawl to the highest place it can find and die there with its tail pointed skyward. After consuming the fly's innards for food, *E. muscae* uses the fly's lifeless husk as a launching pad, firing billions of spores skyward, each spore another fly massacre in the making.

Liam dug into one of the plots with his tweezers, uncovering a plastic bottle cap half covered with a grayish growth. He held it up to the light, his hand shaking slightly. The specimen was like most of the fungi in Liam's gardens: a saprobe, or feeder on the dead. They fed on the fallen, from plants to people, and Liam was expanding their definition of food. With a combination of trial, error, and genetic engineering, he was teaching them to feed on the detritus of modern society, to break down everything from credit cards to corn husks.

"Pop-pop?" Dylan said.

Liam looked up at his redheaded nine-year-old great-grandson. "Yes?"

"What's the difference between elephants and blueberries?"

Liam said, "Haven't a clue."

"They're both blue, except for the elephant. What did Tarzan say when he saw a thousand elephants coming over the hill?"

"Tell me."

" 'Here come the elephants.' What did Jane say when she saw a thousand elephants coming over the hill?"

"Enlighten me."

"She said, 'Here come the blueberries.' She was color-blind."

They both laughed. Dylan had a thing for elephant jokes. "Pop-pop? You know pretty much everything, right?"

Liam turned to face him. "I know a few things," he said.

"How do you know if a girl is . . . you know. Interested."

Liam raised his eyebrows. "A woman's smiles are hard to read, for a woman's secrets are many indeed."

"Come on. No rhymes."

He put down his tweezers. "Well. Let's see . . . How do you know? With your great-grandmother Edith, God rest her, it was simple. It was how she stood. She'd bend her leg, her right leg, so that her foot was on its toe. Then her heel would rotate in small circles. She claimed to find me as attractive as a spotted newt, but her heel said otherwise."

"You're making this up, aren't you? You're telling stories."

"If I'm lying, I'll hang in a tree, but her heel twisted for—"

"—none but me," Dylan finished, laughing.

Liam brightened, glad to see Dylan light of heart. Since the car accident with his mom nearly a year before, he'd had a tough time of it, brushing up against death at an age when he should be engaged with grasshoppers and multiplication tables. Liam fretted about him, picturing himself gone just when the boy needed him most.

But maybe Dylan was finally turning a corner.

In the gardens, a MicroCrawler came running, barely a blur as it zipped down one of the packed-dirt passageways between the rows of fungal plots. The Crawler stopped and used its razor-sharp silicon legs to slice off a sample of fungus. It headed for the corner of the table, where it loaded the sample into a device that analyzed it for RNA and protein expression. The spider-sized silicon-and-metal micro-robots called MicroCrawlers were tenders of the gardens. There were fourteen in all, each smaller than a dime, watched by a camera overhead and directed by a computer in the corner. Dylan was in love with the little robots, gave them all names.

Liam looked at Dylan. "Who's the girl?"

"Just someone. And I didn't notice anything with her heel."

"They're all different. But they all do something. When you look at her, what does she do?"

"Her eyes get funny. Like she's squinting."

"*Hmmm*. That could go either way. What else?"

"She makes fists."

"Are her thumbs on the inside or outside?"

"Inside."

"Well, then, my boy, you are golden."

Dylan smiled.

"Okay. Why do elephants paint the undersides of their feet yellow?"

Dylan worked it over. "You got me. No idea."

"So they can hide upside down in bowls of custard."

"That's stupid."

Liam shrugged. "Have you ever found an elephant in your custard?"

"No."

"Then it clearly works."

Dylan laughed, then focused on a spot a few feet away. "Pop-pop? Something's wrong with Mickey."

Mickey the MicroCrawler stood motionless a few rows over, frozen in place like a statue. Liam leaned over, nudged the Crawler with his tweezers. *"Hmmm."* Liam picked it up, acutely conscious of its tiny silicon legs, edges as sharp as a scalpel. He dropped the Crawler in his palm and poked it again with his tweezers. Nothing. He flipped Mickey onto its back and immediately saw the problem. "See that little black spot? The control circuit burned out. Jake said they'd had trouble with this batch."

"He can't fix it?"

"Nope."

"He's completely, utterly dead?"

"Afraid so."

Dylan's eyes narrowed. "I've never seen one die before."

"Crawlers are robust little buggers, but they're not immortal. Nothing is." Liam put a hand on the boy's shoulder. "What do you say we give Mickey a proper sendoff?"

Liam went to his computer, the Crawler still in hand. He clicked his way to iTunes and queued up the old Irish dirge "Lament for Art Ó Laoghaire." He gave Dylan a wiggle of his eyebrows, but Dylan suddenly looked serious.

The dirge picked up:

My rider of the bright eyes
What happened to you yesterday?
I thought you in my heart
When I bought your fine clothes.
A man the world could not slay.

"Let's find you a nice spot," he said to Mickey. He chose a diminutive patch of earth near the center of the gardens. He dropped the Crawler there, on its back, legs in the air. Liam noted the coordinates of the plot where he had placed Mickey and typed them into the computer.

Dylan watched closely. "What are you doing, Pop-pop?"

"Patience, little man. Some things can't be rushed."

Three MicroCrawlers appeared, zipping along the grid of passageways that cut between the plots like rows in a farmer's field.

They arrived at Mickey's location and immediately began tossing aside bits of dirt, digging a hole. Within seconds they had created a cavity large enough to hold their fallen comrade. Then they descended on him, tearing off his silicon legs, his head, ripping him thoroughly and completely apart.

Dylan was spellbound. "Oh, wow. This is so freaky."

"Keep watching." The Crawlers tossed Mickey's assorted bits into the tiny grave. Next came two more Crawlers, which disgorged their contents onto Mickey, vomiting up tiny water droplets filled with spores.

"Pop-pop? You made a fungus that can break down a Crawler? How?"

Liam smiled. "I borrowed genes from a bacterium that makes an acid. It can etch silicon." He used his tweezers to dig at a nearby plot. Inside was an older Crawler, half gone, covered with a thin film of fuzzy growth. "See? Not bad, eh?"

Dylan watched with a focus reserved for the weightiest of matters.

Back at the original site, the MicroCrawlers began filling the hole, and after a few seconds Mickey the Crawler was almost entirely covered. They patted down the earth with their silicon legs and skittered away. All that was left was a quarter-sized lump of soft earth and a solitary leg poking up like a tiny blade of silver grass.

"And that's that. Except it's not. A couple of months from now, Mickey will be thoroughly broken down to its atomic bits. Ready for another go."

"But he won't be Mickey anymore. He's dead."

"I like to think he's still alive," Liam said. "A bit of his aliveness in everything. Now. Back to boy-girl relationships. What's the latest with your mom's boyfriend?"

Dylan pulled his gaze away from the tiny grave.

"Mark? He's history."

Liam whistled. "That was quick. What happened?"

"She said he wasn't right."

"What do you think?"

"He wasn't right."

"Then off with his head."

Dylan turned and looked at his great-grandfather. "What about Jake?"

"For your mother?"

"Yeah. Why not?"

"*Hmmm.*" Liam placed his hands on the table. Jake. Jake Sterling. It was a scenario he'd considered many times. "I don't think he's your mom's type."

"Why not?"

"No reason. Just not."

He tried to be straight with Dylan whenever he could. Dylan was a smart kid, understood more of the world than most kids his age. But this was something beyond his reach.

TWENTY MINUTES LATER, THEY WERE WITH MAGGIE OUTSIDE of Clark Hall in the brisk autumn night. She stood waiting by her car, in jeans and a brown pullover sweater, looking lovely, as always, her blond-red hair framing bright, intelligent eyes, a small upturned nose, and pale lips.

"Mom, guess what? We had a Crawler funeral."

"Care to explain that one?"

Dylan told her about the fungus that could decompose a MicroCrawler. Then he jumped into the car, put in his earbuds, and turned up the music, a kid just like any other. Liam watched her reaction, taking joy at the flash of excitement in her eyes. "Let me guess: you stole a few genes from an archaeal bacterium?"

Liam nodded. "An alkaliphilic."

Maggie kissed her grandfather on the cheek. "Congratulations. Now come home with us. Have a late dinner. Tell me all about it."

"Can't. I have a northern blot running. And an RNA assay to finish."

"Pop-pop. Come on. You look like you're about to collapse."

"I always look like this. 'An aged man is but a paltry thing, a tattered coat—'

" '—upon a stick.' Don't be like this. It's late. It's almost nine."

Liam kissed her on the forehead. "Go."

. . .

LIAM RETURNED ALONE DOWN THE EMPTY HALLWAYS. MAG-gie was right. An eighty-six-year-old man should be spending every second he had with his family, not in a research lab alone, shuffling genes in and out of fungi. But this was the way it had to be. His work was not yet finished.

Liam stopped at the door to his lab and listened. No sound.

He was worried, not without cause. The woman, the one who had been following him, was getting more brazen, less and less worried about being seen. He'd had fame-struck stalkers like this twice before—an unfortunate side effect of the kind of notoriety Liam had achieved—but nothing had ever come of it. The police had talked to them, and they'd faded away. Liam had dutifully reported this one to the campus police, but they had yet to identify her.

Perhaps she was harmless, perhaps not. She was the right age, but she didn't move like a starstruck graduate student.

She moved like a professional.

Liam typed in a few commands and stood back to watch the Crawlers, then put his arthritic fingers to work at the thousand little tasks that the Crawlers still couldn't do. They couldn't, for example, set goals, choose which fungi to cull and which to propagate. They didn't have an agenda to guide their actions. Agendas mattered a great deal. Liam's agenda had been clear for more than sixty years, since that spring day in the Pacific. An agenda he kept entirely to himself.

Liam thought of Jake. On the pretext of showing Jake a rare herd of pure white deer that roamed the premises, Liam had taken him to Seneca Army Depot, an abandoned military facility thirty miles north and west. But the real reason for their trip was different. Liam had started to tell Jake things, peel back the layers. Jake was a student of war, he understood.

Liam's agenda was his own, except for the pieces he'd fed to Jake. Jake now knew that there had been a Japanese biological su-perweapon, destroyed by the fourth nuclear explosion in history. Liam had spoken the name: the Uzumaki. Liam had not said the word aloud for decades.

But Jake didn't know more still. He didn't know what that bas-tard Lawrence Dunne had started. Jake didn't know that Liam had in his possession one of the seven brass cylinders. Or that after over sixty years, he had finally found the Uzumaki's weakness.

Click.

Liam froze. The noise came from just outside the lab.

"Maggie?"

He wouldn't put it past her to come back and make another attempt to pull him away.

No answer.

"Jake?" He was a night owl, too. Liam often found him in his labs past midnight. "Jake?"

Liam listened. Nothing.

He looked around his lab. The Crawlers were in the gardens. The computer screen had put itself to sleep.

Nothing out of the ordinary.

Click!

The lights went out.

· 2 ·

TINK, TINK, TINK.

When Liam Connor came to, the sound was the first thing that broke through.

Tink, tink, tink.

He was confused, unstuck in time, flashes coming quick and disjointed. He was twelve, walking the green hills of Sligo, hunting new species of fungi. He was twenty-two, on a warship in the Pacific, contemplating a small brass cylinder in his hand. He was thirty-one, in their first house in Ithaca, watching his wife crawl out of bed, completely naked. He was fifty-nine, the king of Sweden hanging a medal on his neck. He was seventy-seven, seeing his great-grandson for the first time, Dylan's little beet-red face scrunched and screaming.

Tink, tink, tink.

After a moment, he settled down, becoming his current self. He was an old, old man, an Irish gnome. Eighty-six. Emeritus professor of biology at Cornell University.

He tried to move, but everything was wrong. He couldn't lift his arms. He couldn't open his mouth. He had the sense he was upright, but he couldn't be sure. His vision was blurry, smudges in black. He couldn't see anything, save for a faint glow coming from

behind him. It was a mix of yellow, green, and red, each color
ebbing and strengthening to its own rhythm.

Tink, tink, tink.

The sound was familiar. He knew the sound. What the hell
was it?

He tried to remember what had happened. He had been in his
lab, he was sure of that, tending to the gardens of decay. The gardens. He was fiddling in the gardens, then—then nothing. A blank
spot in his memory. Was it still the same night? Still Monday?

He couldn't move his head. He was upright, but he couldn't
move. Someone had struck him; he remembered that now. He
could still feel the blow.

He heard another sound. A rush of air, slight, gentle. Silence.
Then again.

Breathing.

He was sure of it. Someone was sitting right behind him. In the
darkness. Very close.

Tink, tink, tink.

He tried to open his mouth, to speak, but he couldn't move.
His mouth wouldn't open. Something was wrong with his tongue.
It was trapped against the bottom of his mouth.

He studied his surroundings, fighting a pain like a knife blade
between his eyes. He was in a huge room in the shape of a half-
cylinder. The concrete roof twenty feet overhead curved in a
smooth semicircle to the floor. He faced the back end of the cylinder, the flat, stained concrete wall no more than ten feet from
his face. Liam realized where he was: an old munitions bunker
on the abandoned Seneca Army Depot site, completely isolated
from the rest of the world. Liam had spent months at the depot
over the past four years, secretly toiling over his last great—and
highly secret—project.

A woman stepped in front of him, her face illuminated by the
dim, pulsing glow coming from behind. He recognized her immediately as the woman who had been following him. She was Asian—
Chinese, he was nearly certain. Somewhere between twenty and
thirty, wearing small, round glasses. She leaned forward, her face
no more than twelve inches from his, features illuminated by an
ever-changing mix of yellow, green, and red light. She was pretty,
made more so by the flaws of two thin, perfectly symmetric scars

that ran along her cheekbones. She wore all black, down to the gloves on her hands.

She flicked on a photographer's light, mounted on a stand beside her. He blinked against the sudden brightness, waited for the blotches of white to settle down into shape and color. He tried to speak but couldn't open his mouth. He felt as though his head were in a vise.

Once his eyes adjusted, she held up a small mirror so he could see himself. She adjusted the angle until he caught his reflection.

He was a shocking sight. His head was encased in a metal frame, with struts and bands holding his skullcase like a patient with a neck injury. A rubber-and-steel clamp held his jaw rigidly fixed. He looked old, incredibly old, even older than his eighty-six years. The wrinkles on his face were a cracked riverbed, and tufts of white hair stuck out every which way from his skull. He was a corpse, a ghost, strapped into headgear from a Frankensteinian nightmare.

She lowered the mirror. When she spoke, her English was excellent but still bore traces of her native land. "A mutual friend sent me," she said.

She was Chinese, from the north, he guessed. He felt a tremor at the base of his spine. What she said next nearly stopped his heart.

"I came for the Uzumaki."

Tink, tink, tink.

The sound. He knew the sound.

He looked down. A glass petri dish sat in her lap. Four sparkling objects were in the center of the dish, scurrying about, each no larger than a dime.

MicroCrawlers.

They skittered around in the petri dish with terrifying speed, colliding with the walls, *tink, tink, tink.* Their legs were segmented etched silicon, sharp as razor blades.

He closed his eyes, but he could still hear the *tink* of silicon against glass.

"I've taken this place apart. Where is it?"

He forced himself to focus. He hadn't yet seen a gun. If he could get loose, he'd have a chance. He was a small man, impossibly old, but he was still quick, and he could be brutally vicious when he needed to be.

Tink, tink, tink.

She reached toward him and touched a spot on his headgear. A whirring sound. The headgear pried open his jaw with a mechanical precision, rigid, like the door of a safe. The air was cold on the back of his throat.

Tink, tink, tink.

She lifted her right hand and closed her fingers into a fist. The Crawlers stopped their incessant scurrying in the glass dish. The sudden silence was jarring. Somehow she controlled the Crawlers with her gloved hand.

She picked up one of the Crawlers with a pair of tweezers. She placed the little robotic creature deep inside his mouth, on the back of his tongue. He had to fight not to panic, not to gag. The legs were like tiny scalpels, cutting into the tissue with even the slightest movement. He could taste droplets of blood rising up on the back of his tongue.

She touched another button and the piezo motors buzzed, closing his mouth for him, clamping his teeth together with an audible *tock!* She placed a hand on his mouth, sealing his lips. With two delicate fingers, she reached out and pinched his nose closed.

"Swallow it," she said.

The seconds ticked away, probably a minute, before he panicked. He struggled violently against his bonds, his body rebelling against the lack of oxygen. He felt as though he might break a bone at any minute. His will was strong, but he knew his body couldn't take this kind of punishment. He held out as long as he could, thrashing and pulling, but then his vision started to go.

You can't not breathe; breathing is involuntary.

You swallow.

He felt the Crawler progress down his esophagus, the sharp burning as the legs tore at the soft tissues. He tried to scream, but he couldn't move his jaw, couldn't lift his tongue. He was locked down, frozen, the sound of his scream trapped inside his head.

She removed her hands, and he gasped for air through clenched teeth, chest heaving. He tried to make sense of what was happening.

She pushed the button, and his mouth again opened. She used a small flashlight to look inside. "Good," she said.

She repeated this agonizing procedure three more times, until he had a total of four Crawlers in his belly. Liam fought to get control of himself, to quell the panic. He had to stay strong. He knew what she wanted. He couldn't let her have it. No matter what it took. No matter how much he would have to suffer.

She held her gloved hand up before him, fingers curled, as if her hand were a spider. "Ten seconds," she said.

She wiggled her fingers, bringing the Crawlers to life.

His entire body lit on fire, his teeth cracking together with brutal force. His stomach convulsed, twitching from the pain from a burning sun suddenly ignited inside him. His vision went white. He had never felt a pain like this, the twisting, roiling monster in his stomach sending out wave after wave of agony. Time slowed down.

He became unstuck, drifting in time. He saw birds, flying birds, chased by men with very large guns. A distant bell rang. He saw the ship, the line in the sky, the mushroom cloud, like it had happened yesterday. He saw thousands of tiny spirals spreading across the firmament like sparks from a fire.

Far away, he heard her voice, counting down numbers: "Three, two, one . . ."

The pain slowly subsided. It took what seemed like hours for his body to recover, for the convulsions in his stomach to fade. His eyes were squeezed shut. His cheeks were cold. He was crying.

He returned to himself. He opened his eyes. The woman was there, her gloved index finger tapping at her lips.

"TELL ME," ORCHID SAID. "BLINK TWICE IF YOU ARE READY."

She studied him, watching for the signs. The signs that he was breaking. She glanced at his hands. When they gave up, the hands relaxed, became dead fish. Connor's were clenched. Connor had not given up.

"Professor Connor, listen carefully," she said as she picked up the roll of medical tape. "You may think what just happened is the worst I can do to you. It is not. It will get much, much worse."

She taped his eyelids open, pulling the lids straight up. A powerful technique on many levels. The physical discomfort was excruciating as the eyes dried, but ever more critical was the denial of one more form of resistance. The stripping away of another layer. Removing the ability to block out visual stimuli, to make the outside world go away.

She snapped a photo of him in this state, then opened her satchel, removed a laptop computer. She typed in a few commands and then held the screen up before his face. She could tell from the twitches of his cheek muscles that his eyes were beginning to burn.

"I'm going to read you a list of names. Just listen. Just watch."

She opened a small flip pad and read the first name. "George Washington." An image of the first president appeared. "Charles Darwin." Darwin flashed up. His head was shaking. He could hardly see now, she surmised, his eyes drying inexorably.

She took a bottle of eye drops from the table, Murine, bought at a drugstore more than six hundred miles away. Never purchase anything local. No receipts. No remembered face.

Connor's eyes darted back and forth between the computer screen and her face. She felt it coming off him: the fear of knowing. He saw the infrared lasers and photodiodes mounted along the edges of the computer screen. He understood. Smart man, Liam Connor. She had never tortured a Nobel Prize winner before.

The computer was her truth detector. Advertising firms had developed sophisticated programs to monitor human reactions as people watched commercials on a computer screen. They traced eye movements. Pupil dilation. The blood flow in vessels in the sclera, the whites of his eyes. The military used the same technology for interrogations. She had adapted the technology for her own needs. She had found it effective.

Darwin stared up from the computer screen. Test names, these were tests. Calibrations. To see how Connor responded to stimuli, developing a map of his responses.

She started in on his colleagues. "Mark Sampson." A picture of his longtime scientific collaborator appeared. She had taken it from his website. No response. She continued reading, a new picture with each name. "Vlad Glazman." Nothing.

"Jake Sterling."

The little red indicator bar on the bottom of the screen flickered. A small signal but easily discernible above the noise. She made a note. *Good.* He was already high on her list—she had his home, his lab, his phone fully instrumented.

Now, she thought. *To the heart of it.*

NO, NO, NO, PLEASE, GOD, NO . . .

She worked her way through his colleagues, his friends, then finally his family. *Block your thoughts. Stop thinking. Stop feeling. . . .*

"Martin Connor."

"Ethel Connor."

"Arthur Connor."

"Maggie Connor."

The bar at the bottom of the screen jumped.

The woman glanced at him, then to the image of his granddaughter, Maggie, on the screen.

She made a note.

Liam was drenched in sweat. He shivered uncontrollably. He was freezing in his own sweat.

She leaned in until she was inches from his face. He smelled her. She smelled of wood and creosote. "Tell me where it is, Professor Connor. Quit fighting. You must already know how this ends."

She tapped the screen. "Your granddaughter," she said. "I will torture her right in front of you. Tell me or she dies."

Liam wanted to kill her. He wanted more than anything in the world to rip his arms free and strangle her.

She pushed a button and a new picture appeared on the screen. The little red meter spiked.

Dylan.

"When your granddaughter is dead, I will start on her son. Do you think you can watch that? Do you think you can be brave then?"

No, he couldn't be brave then. But he also couldn't give her the Uzumaki. The choice was stark, binary: watch them die or tell her.

She moved in close. "One minute. Tell me. Then everything will be over. You die. They live."

He refused to accept it. There *had* to be another way. He couldn't save them, he knew that now. No more than he could save himself. But there was something he could do. With his suffering, he could buy them a little time. If he was stronger than he'd ever been, Liam could do this one small thing.

They would have to do the rest.

"Ten seconds," she said. "Tell me now."

Liam readied himself. *With this suffering . . .*

The clocked ticked down. She held up her right hand, wiggled her fingers. The Crawlers came alive inside him.

Liam Connor screamed.

DAY 2

FUNGUS AMONG US

· 3 ·

MAGGIE CONNOR DOVE DEEPER UNDER THE COVERS. "NO ONE'S home," she mumbled.

The pounding on the door continued.

"Go *away*."

Silence.

"I'mmm stilll heeere. . . ." came the child's voice through the door.

She slowly pulled herself out of bed, reluctant to leave her cocoon. Goose bumps broke out all over her naked skin in the cool morning air. She threw on jeans and a thick-pile shirt, pale yellow, comfortable and concealing. At thirty-three, she still had it. But she didn't want her son to see it.

She shuffled to the door and cracked it open. Dylan peeked through.

"Fungus?" she said to her son in a mock-serious tone.

"Among us!" he answered back.

Maggie dressed and made her way down the long hallway, past Yvette's bedroom (a complete disaster), past Cindy's land of tie-dye, past Josephine's ever-so-spotless pale green sanctum, to the heart of the house, the kitchen. She took in the rich smells, the warmth. Along one wall, two ancient refrigerators stood side by side, the right one boasting a hand-painted yellow sun, the left one the multicolored handprints of her housemates. And, of course, there were the elves. The biggest stood in the corner, hand-carved in dark wood and nearly four feet tall. Several smaller ones peered down from the tops of the refrigerators.

When she and Dylan had considered moving to Rivendell five years ago, it was the elves that had closed the deal. "They come in from the forest," her prospective housemate Justin had told her son, then four years old. Justin was a graduate student in ecology and evolutionary biology, with an unruly dark beard and a shock of blond-brown hair that left the impression that he'd just emerged from the forest himself. "Be a good boy," Justin had said to Dylan, "and they'll watch over you, keep you in spices and glitter dust. But act badly—don't listen to your mom, yell too much, or leave your dishes unwashed—and they'll go back to the woods with the faeries, never to be seen again." Justin had finished his degree and moved to Yakima, Washington, a year later. Yvette had replaced him, leaving Dylan as the one and only man of the house.

Almost ten now, her son stood at the stove on top of a milk crate while tending a simmering pot of oatmeal, just big enough to see over the rim of the stainless-steel vessel. He twisted the spoon back and forth, keeping the oats from burning on the bottom. Turtle, their black Lab mix, was asleep at his feet.

Cindy Sharp, one of their housemates, a fifth-year art and architecture undergrad specializing in printmaking, sat at the kitchen table. Her hands were cupped around a large mug of coffee, and she looked as though she needed it. Cindy was twenty-three, still lost in the hedonistic newness of adulthood. She had curly hair, a slight overbite, and an eclectic taste in men that Maggie couldn't grasp.

"Out late?" Maggie asked.

"Visiting a sick friend," she said, using their code.

Maggie suppressed a laugh. "I hope he feels better."

Cindy grinned. "Oh, he does. He certainly does."

Dylan stirred the pot with greater alacrity. He must have broken their code. Cindy pushed back from the table and wandered over. "That stuff ready yet?" she asked. "I'm famished."

"Almost," Dylan answered.

"This boy," Cindy said, giving him a hug from behind. "So handsome, and he can cook, too." She looked to Maggie, chin resting on Dylan's head. "When he's older, he's mine."

"Hands off. There are laws." She pulled her son away, mussed his hair. Full-on red hair, nothing like his father's. More like Poppop's when he was younger. She wanted to squeeze him until her chest hurt, but she held off. He was nearing that age when boys begin to pull back from their mothers. She felt it, the way he twisted away when she touched him.

She elbowed her son in the ribs instead. "Fungus?"

"Among us!" he answered back.

THE SNOW OF THE PREVIOUS NIGHT HAD LEFT A WHITE blanket almost an inch thick on the grounds of the sprawling estate. An abandoned farm, it had been purchased for a song in the early seventies by a collection of back-to-the-earth types. They'd cleaned up the house, added more bedrooms, and built a large greenhouse out back to grow vegetables during the harsh Ithaca winters. Legend had it that while clearing brush, they'd found a shovel, its handle carefully and ornately carved with Hobbit heads, elves, and an angry orc. The residents had taken it as their totem. From then on, the place was known as Rivendell.

Maggie and Dylan bundled up before heading out the back door. The air was chilly cold, the skies relatively clear, a rarity for Ithaca this time of year. The sunlight was brilliant as they stomped a trail of footprints away from Rivendell, Turtle at their heels. Soon they were in shadows, beneath the canopy of a pine planted back in the 1920s, after the forests had been cleared for farming. Then the forest became more varied, more interesting. Larch mixed with hemlock; a grove of poplars surrounded a single, solitary oak. It was a stunning morning, a crazy superposition of fall and winter. Most of the leaves still clung to the trees, but they were giving up the ghost in droves, another batch cutting loose with every toss of the wind, falling to the bright snow.

Turtle stopped and sniffed near a log where the wind had scoured the leaves and snow. A late-season mushroom poked up through the exposed earth, the bright orange cap streaked with stains of brown. *That's strange,* she thought. She knelt down, inspecting it more closely, feeling the texture of its skin with her finger.

"What's that?" Dylan asked.

"I don't know. It looks like *Amanita jacksonii,* but see there? The color of the cap is wrong." She pulled a plastic Baggie from her pocket, along with a pocketknife. She dug the mushroom from the half-frozen earth and dropped it in the Baggie.

Dylan said, "Maybe another new species for the fantastic fungal forager?"

"You never know . . . ," Maggie replied, throwing an arm around her son. "If so, I'll be sure to give the dog the credit."

"*Fungus turtulus,*" Dylan said, smiling.

As they continued, the path was often obscured by leaves and snow, but Maggie and Dylan had no trouble finding their way. Nearly every morning, before Dylan went to school and Maggie to work at the Cornell Plant Pathology Herbarium, they walked a loop though the forest, tending to their Fungus-Among-Us projects.

It had started almost a year ago, a few weeks before Dylan's ninth birthday. On one of their off-trail jaunts through the woods, he had excitedly pointed to a patch of brown fungus on a tree, swearing that it looked just like Albert Einstein. Maggie hadn't seen the resemblance, but it had given her an idea. For his upcoming birthday, she hatched a plan to spell out DYLAN—9! on a log using fungus as living paint.

A week later, she was in the hospital with multiple fractures to her leg, the victim of a horrific crash with a pickup truck. On their way home from a hike, Dylan had been strapped tightly in the backseat when the out-of-control pickup T-boned their Volkswagen. Dylan was shaken up but not hurt, but the Ithaca College senior driving the pickup had been propelled straight through the windshield. He didn't make it to the hospital.

They talked about it many times afterward, the fragility of life. Dylan was having a hard time with it.

"You could have died, too, Mom," he'd said.

She hugged him. "I know, sweetie. But I didn't."

Fungus-Among-Us proved to be a helpful distraction. Figuring out how to do it turned into quite a project. Ultimately, she'd taken her cue from the waxy coatings that plants use to ward off bugs and fungi, making a stencil in wax paper and attaching it to a log. She'd carefully made the wax paper's edges flush with the surface of the wood, using candle wax to seal them. Then she'd liberally sprinkled on mold spores and left the whole thing alone for two weeks. The wax held, and the mold had grown on the exposed parts. The final result was striking, as if the woods themselves were wishing her son a happy birthday. Dylan had been giddy with delight, for the first time in too long. He'd started having nightmares a few days after the accident. They didn't come quite as often these days, but still with some regularity he'd wake screaming in the night, terrified that everyone he loved was dying.

Maggie and son had gone on to develop other approaches. A few brushstrokes of potato broth and sugar on a log would yield a healthy patch of *Aspergillus* in a couple of days. Sugar water brought the textured black of a sooty mold. With a million species to choose from, the possibilities were endless. They had a wonderful time with their joint project while her leg healed. Dylan still awoke from nightmares, thrashing and sweating, but not quite as often. Maggie had hoped that once the cast was off her leg, the last reminder of the accident, everything might go back to normal.

But then Dylan had his first panic attack.

A short spur trail led them to their major task this morning— the removal of the wax paper from their latest Fungus-Among-Us project. There were now bits of mycological art on trees and stumps all over Ithaca, thanks to the mother-and-son Connor team. They both loved the idea of unsuspecting travelers happening upon their creations, certain that forest sprites had been at work. Today's project was a triquetra.

It was as large as a pumpkin and chest-high on the trunk of a decaying spruce. The wax paper was still affixed to it. "You do this one," she said to her son.

"Really?"

"Go for it."

Dylan scrunched up his face and went to work, delicately tugging at the edges, peeling it bit by bit. Maggie had always loved the design, the interlocking strands. The triquetra was of Celtic origin, and only later was it appropriated by Christians as a symbol of the Holy Trinity. To the Celts, it represented the three phases of the feminine life cycle: the maiden, the mother, and the crone.

The removal step was tricky; sometimes pieces of the fungus would rip off and give the work a flawed, torn-edged look. But this time the wax paper came off perfectly, and the result was stunning. The ancient symbol melded elegantly with its surroundings, life growing out of the dead. She gave her son a squeeze. "It's beautiful."

"I don't know. There's a little spot at the bottom. . . ."

She mussed his hair. "It's *perfect*. Just like you. Now come on." She looked around. "Turtle?"

They met up with the dog at the top of a small rise. With the leaves half down, you could see the sharp lines of Rivendell in the distance. They started back, but they hadn't gone more than a few steps before Turtle stopped, cocked his head. Maggie picked it up a second later. Panicked voices.

"Maaaagggiiieeee!!!!!"

"Dylan!!!!!!!"

THEY WERE BREATHLESS BY THE TIME THEY MADE IT BACK.

Cindy was on the back porch, arms wrapped around her chest. Beside her stood the county sheriff, a shiny star of metal on his chest.

Cindy had tears in her eyes. "Oh, God. I'm so, so sorry."

· 4 ·

TWO HUNDRED STUDENTS WERE PACKED INTO SCHWARTZ AUDI-
torium for the nine a.m. lecture of Physics 1205, "Physics for Presidents." Jake Sterling was twenty minutes into the lecture. He'd
gotten off to a slow start—the long night before had seen too much
honesty, and the subsequent three a.m. end of a four-month relationship—but now he was hitting his stride.

The premise of "Physics for Presidents" was simple: assume
your audience was composed of future presidents of the United
States. You have them for one semester. What lessons would be of
optimal utility? Jake's answer was simple: he taught them the rules
of the world. What could and could not happen. We could build a
nuclear submarine but not a nuclear airplane. There was enough
sunlight to power the United States by solar, but only if we car-
peted a good chunk of Nevada with solar cells. His was an Army
man's approach, a presentation of options. Jake hadn't worn the
uniform for well over a decade, but he still had the no-nonsense at-
titude of a soldier.

"Isaac Newton was the tipping point—a solitary man standing
at the transition between the ancient world and the modern. Before
Newton, we were a civilization of superstitious craftsmen. We
could make plows and crossbows and trebuchets, but our under-

standing of the world—and our ability to control it—was something that we learned by experience, by trial and error. Or we were guided by 'experts' that had a line to a deeper truth. Religious leaders. Shamans. People who spent their lives waiting for the gods to reveal the mysterious forces at work in the universe. But no more. After Newton, you just sat down with pencil and paper and worked it all out. No magic. No mumbo jumbo. And no special training required, except a decent knowledge of mathematics."

Jake had taught this course three semesters in a row, a record for him in the eight years he'd been at Cornell. He typically switched teaching assignments as often as he could, preferring to wander the entire curriculum instead of digging deeper and deeper into the same hole. But he loved this course. His colleagues in other departments made noise about how art, politics, or the pen was a hammer to shape the world, but in Jake's estimation, technology was the biggest hammer out there.

Jake continued. "People wasted little time putting Newton's laws, and those of Maxwell, Einstein, and Schrödinger, to productive use. And since we had laws for everything, no matter how big or small, they allowed us to move beyond everyday human scales. The first great push was toward the ever bigger: mighty dams, great oceangoing vessels, and—perhaps the high-water mark of the big— venturing to the moon. Now we are in a second revolution. Question: what is it?"

The students looked bored. Their indifference surprised him. The discovery that the natural world was mathematically explicable was, to Jake, the single most significant development in the history of humanity. From this followed the obvious consequence: the world was controllable. The constituents of the world—radio waves, apples, or planets—did what the differential equations told them to do. You learn to perform some formal manipulations of symbols on a page, and the next thing you know, you're building radios that can communicate across oceans, or launching projectiles at your enemies with a precision that was terrifying to behold. It was that simple.

"What is it?" he repeated. "No guesses?"

"Nano," came an answer from the front.

"You got it. Nano. The realm of the ultrasmall. Small has replaced big as the terra incognita for techno-explorers. The nanoworld is the new frontier."

Jake clicked an icon on his computer and a color photo of an Intel Core 2 Quad processor chip appeared on the ten-foot-tall screen behind him. "A modern integrated circuit is the most complex and sophisticated piece of technology ever made," Jake said. He clicked again, and the view zoomed onto a single transistor within the circuit. "This transistor is a thousand times narrower than a human hair. It is as much smaller than you as the earth is bigger than you. Distances in this world are measured in nanometers. Nano—from the Greek *nanos,* meaning 'little old man,' indicating one billionth. That's small. One billionth of the population of the earth wouldn't even fill up the front row of this class.

"The power of nano makes it possible to construct an entire world in the space of a meter," Jake continued, as the image on the screen zoomed back out, the single transistor quickly lost in the rectangular maze of transistors, capacitors, and copper interconnects. "This computer chip is a world of doors and passageways for electrons, guiding them in a dance as intricate and involved as the daily movements of millions of people in any major city. An entire city for electrons can be built in a space smaller than a postage stamp." The image faded and was replaced by an aerial view of the gridlike streets of Midtown Manhattan. "A circuit as complex as Manhattan could fit on the tip of my finger," he said. "And unlike a real city, there are no traffic jams, no gridlock. All of it works flawlessly. Not a single packet of electrons out of place.

"In a computer chip, time is also miniaturized. Your computer can do operations—multiply two numbers, or communicate with its neighbors—about once every nanosecond. A one-gigahertz processor makes roughly a billion computations a second. Think about it. A billion in one second. You only live for, at most, three billion seconds. In only three ticks of the clock, a computer has as many thoughts as you will have in your whole life." Jake stopped to let that sink in. "So every three seconds, your computer is like the entire population of Manhattan living a lifetime. And people wonder why it takes so long to boot up."

A few laughs rippled through the students.

"Miniaturization was the most revolutionary force in the second half of the twentieth century. From Bill Gates to Gordon Moore, empires have been made constructing and controlling tiny electron cities that have lifetimes of thoughts in seconds. Computers, in effect, miniaturized our thoughts. But humans do more than think. What else do we do?"

"Sleep," someone called from the back. More laughs.

"True enough. What else?"

"Move. We walk around."

"Right. We walk. But walking is a pretty sophisticated form of locomotion. Let's start with something simpler. What about crawling, for example? Can we make machines that crawl?

"Let me introduce a couple of my graduate students," Jake said. He waved, and they came up on stage. "This is Joe Xu and Dave Gruber. They've got something to show you."

Jake kept going while Dave and Joe set up. "How many of you have heard of DARPA?"

A few hands went up.

"DARPA stands for Defense Advanced Research Projects Agency. It's a kind of military venture-capital firm—always on the lookout for the Next Big Thing. The Internet, the global positioning system, and the Predator Unmanned Aerial Vehicle, those were all DARPA projects. Most sink like a stone, but those that succeed can change the world.

"In 2004, DARPA hit upon a new way to drive innovation: the DARPA Grand Challenge competitions. These are open competitions where DARPA sets a goal and teams of scientists and engineers from around the country try and tackle it. The first one was to create a car that could navigate a desert racecourse without a driver. First prize was two million dollars. In 2004, nobody succeeded. In 2005, five crossed the finish line. By 2007, the challenge had moved from the desert to city streets, and people are now seriously talking about driverless cars on America's highways. The lesson was clear: you throw money and talent at a problem, spice it up with a little head-to-head battle, and it's incredible how fast innovation can happen.

"For their next competition, DARPA went small," Jake continued. "The Grand MicroChallenge was to develop a robot smaller than a dime that could survive on its own in a woodland environment, without external guidance or power, for a month. The 'woods' consisted of a giant terrarium DARPA set up in a storage hangar at Fort Belvoir, near Mount Vernon in Virginia. The first year was a bust. Nobody got close, including our team. All the entrants ran out of juice long before the month was out. But the next year, with Liam Connor's help, we won it running away." This got their attention. Liam was a legend—the old man's wrinkled face was easily the most recognized on campus.

Joe and Dave were nearly ready, and Jake retreated to the edge of the stage. Joe, whose real name was Xinjian, was a classic physics grad student, tall and thin, with wide eyes and a love for detail. He was in his fifth year, finishing his thesis on the mechanics of micro-robot locomotion. He already had an offer for a permanent position in Hong Kong but was holding out for a Millikan Fellowship at Caltech. Gruber was a little more unusual, a third-year muscular fireplug with a flair for public speaking—he'd done some acting as an undergraduate at Yale. Each had their part down pat: Dave handled the audience, and Joe handled the Crawlers.

Joe sat at the microscope set up on the corner of the stage. The scope's video camera was hooked up to the overhead projector. Joe flipped a switch, and several in the class gasped. A giant creature appeared on the screen: a robotic spider-monster. It scurried to the left, then stopped, turned one hundred and eighty degrees on its six legs, and took off in the opposite direction.

"Say hello to a MicroCrawler," Dave said. "Arguably the most advanced miniature robot in the world. And don't worry, it won't hurt you. The image is magnified a thousand times. It has jointed silicon legs that propel it forward, and a small microprocessor in its body that controls its movement. This one here is our smallest— about the size of a mustard seed. We have models ranging up to the size of a quarter. We build them at the Cornell Nanofabrication Facility using the same patterning, depositing, and sculpting techniques people normally use to make computer chips."

Jake watched as the students stared at the Crawler, rapt. He smiled at Dave and Joe—the three of them had been through this routine dozens of times, but the spark hadn't faded. Jake was proud of them. Jake had designed the Crawlers and oversaw the project, but Dave and Joe had done most of the painstaking detail work needed to make the designs a reality. Thousands of hours of struggle, failure, and more struggle. The three of them had gone through years of engineering, design, tweaking, and redesign in creating these little beasts. Doing something that had never been done before was brutally hard, like assembling a model ship in the dark. Make that a ship in a *very small bottle* in the dark. But they had done it. And—the glory of technology—done once, it could be done again, by anyone, anywhere. All you needed were the fabrication recipes and the right tools.

Joe adjusted the microscope's optics, zooming out so the students could see the entire petri dish that corralled the tiny robots. Ten Crawlers scurried around while dozens more lay motionless, littering the miniature landscape. One hopped in a tight circle, like a fly with a wounded wing.

"What's wrong with that one?" a student in front asked.

Joe said, "On this batch, we had a bad liftoff during step twenty. When we put down the piezo actuators."

"Step *twenty*?"

"It takes forty-seven separate fabrication steps to make a Crawler," Dave said. "Forty-nine for ones with a full communications system. It rivals Intel's most complex computer chip. Five weeks of twelve-hour days to get through the entire process, assuming nothing goes wrong."

"And something always goes wrong," Joe added with a pained laugh. "It's like walking a tightrope. Each step must be perfect. Make one little mistake, it's all over." He picked up a pair of tweezers and guided them toward the tiny creatures, the tips appearing enormous in the microscope's field of view. He carefully brushed away the dead Crawlers until only the scurriers and the circler remained. "Let's put you out of your misery," Joe said as he grabbed the circler with the forceps. He applied pressure, and its body shattered into a hundred pieces. The students cringed.

A student in the second row raised his hand. Dave called on him.

"They seem like they're looking for something."

"They are."

"What?"

"Lunch."

Joe opened up a little box marked CRAWLER FOOD, removed a handful of corn kernels, and placed them on the glass slide. First one Crawler, then another, descended on the kernels, scissoring their scalpel-sharp legs, slashing through the kernels' fibrous skin to the soft flesh inside. Joe zoomed in on one Crawler as it stuffed bits of shredded corn into the small feeding portal on its front. "We've made ones that can feed on almost anything you want," Jake said. "Corn. Grape juice. A packet of sugar can keep one going for days. Each one's got a genetically modified fungus that lives in its belly and converts a sugar source into ethanol fuel, courtesy of Liam Connor."

"The issue with microbots has always been power," Jake said, stepping back to center stage. "Quite a few teams built little robots like these for the first Grand MicroChallenge, but they all had the same weakness. They were powered by onboard batteries—tiny cells that run out of juice after a couple of minutes. And you can't load them with more batteries—they'd be too heavy to move. It was a showstopper. Everyone was stuck.

"Enter Liam Connor. He said to me, 'No problem, my boy. You just have to teach the little fellows to eat.' "

Jake let that settle in before continuing.

"His idea was to create a fungus that could serve as a digester and convert food to energy. He started with something called *Ustilago maydis*—a fungus that lives on corn, and he added some genes from brewer's yeast—the stuff that converts sugar to ethanol when you make beer or wine. The Crawler eats by shredding bits of food with its legs and stuffing them into a feeding portal. That portal—its mouth—leads to its stomach—a little chamber filled with the fungus. The fungus breaks down the food and voilà! Fuel. The fuel powers the Crawler, and the Crawler eats some more. It can keep going as long as the food holds out. We call them HungryCrawlers. And they are champions."

"So what did you do with the DARPA prize money?" a student called out.

Jake laughed. "I still have my share, sitting in the bank. Joe?"

"I bought a house for my parents in China."

"Dave?"

"I bought stock. Mostly Google and Intel. And a Segway."

Jake said, "It's a hazard. He rides it up and down the halls."

A hand went up, a student down in front, wearing a red Windbreaker and matching high-tops, no more than eighteen years old. "What about intellectual property?" he asked.

"We've got seven patents filed," Jake said. "Three have already been granted." Jake was always amazed at how quickly the thoughts of today's students went to the business side. Fifteen years ago, when he was an undergraduate, no one thought about IP, about patents. Now it was different. Kids saw dollar signs everywhere.

"Anyone license it yet?"

"Quite a few. A start-up in Boston wants every home in America to have MicroCrawler mini-Roombas running around. On countertops, walls, ceilings, cleaning away everything from crumbs to cobwebs. A medical technology company in North Carolina hopes to use them as remote surgeons that can work on a patient from the inside, excising tumors or clearing blockages without the need for incisions or the risk of infection. But our biggest suitors are a couple of military contractors. Micro-robotics is going to be the next big thing in warfare. That's why DARPA ran the Grand MicroChallenge. Small spies, tiny assassins, things like—"

A cellphone went off. Jake was annoyed but not surprised. This happened at least once a class. Jake spotted the culprit fishing the phone out of his pocket. He did his best to shame him with his stare.

The student didn't notice, fixated on the screen of his phone, an expression of shock on his face. What he did next surprised Jake. He whispered to his neighbors, got up, and headed for the door.

As he was working his way down the row of seats, another student pulled a phone out and started working it with his thumbs. He looked around, whispered to his friend, pointed to the door.

That's when it really got going. Two more cellphones started ringing. Five times that number silently fished phones out from bookbags, pocketbooks, and knapsacks. More people began to leave. Jake had never seen anything like it.

He glanced at Dave and Joe. Both shook their heads, not knowing what was happening. Dave flipped open his own phone.

A couple of students near the back got up, talking louder now. "It's Liam Connor," one of them said, loud enough for everyone to hear.

"What? What about Liam Connor?" Jake asked.

"They just found a body in Fall Creek Gorge," the student said.

"And?"

Dave closed his phone, face white. "Jake, this can't be true. They're saying that the body is Liam Connor's."

· 5 ·

THE HILLS ON WHICH CORNELL UNIVERSITY STOOD WERE
the remnants of the glacial moraine left over from the last ice age.
Streams cut through this loosely packed earth and shale until they
reached older, solid rock, carving the dramatic gorges and water-
falls for which the campus was famous. Fall Creek Gorge was the
deepest, a huge gash in the earth defining the north boundary of
campus. It was spanned by a narrow suspension footbridge linking
the central part of campus to the houses and dorms farther north.
From its midpoint, it was a two-hundred-foot plunge to the rushing waters of Fall Creek below.

Jake always brought the students here later in the semester
when he taught "Physics for Presidents." They stood on the bridge
and stared at the water below while Jake gave them a rundown on
the geology, describing the advances and retreats of the glaciers
that carved out the gorges. Then Jake would give them a little
demo. He would take a watermelon and drop it off the bridge.
They'd all time it with their watches, the seconds ticking by until it
burst on the stones below. Three-point-two seconds was the aver-
age answer. They'd compare it to what Newton predicted.

But the real lesson wasn't Newton's laws, the acceleration due
to gravity, $v^2 = 2gh$. That was a cover. Jake had worked up this field

trip after he had lost a student to suicide. Jake knew the statistics. Over the past twenty-eight years, sixteen students had jumped from this bridge. It was a painful fact about a pressure-cooker school like Cornell, but it had hit Jake hard. He still couldn't forget the parents at the funeral. No parent should ever have to go through that. No kid should ever put their parents through that.

The real lesson of the watermelon was about the violence of falling. The melon splattered, bits of red flesh streaking out like the sun from the point of impact. Potential energy turned into kinetic, velocity growing with every second of the fall. He brought the class here every semester to see what would happen when you went over. Cut through the romanticism and get down to the reality. You jump, you fall, you hit.

Three-point-two seconds. *Blam.*

MORE PEOPLE WERE ARRIVING BY THE SECOND, MORE STU-dents, more faculty, more police. They were coming from all across campus. Jake had joined the rush, running over from the Schwartz Auditorium lecture hall. If it truly was Liam Connor, Jake didn't think it would stop until the entire campus was clustered up against the gorge.

Liam Connor was an icon. He'd been at Cornell for sixty years, was known to every student, faculty member, and alumnus. He was in many ways the face of Cornell, the last of the pivotal scientists—people like Hans Bethe, Richard Feynman, Carl Sagan, and Barbara McClintock—who had turned a sleepy central New York town into one of the most important centers of science in the world.

Jake kept flashing to the last time he'd seen Liam—yesterday, lunch at Banfi's. They were both in a hurry. They'd chatted about a recent experiment; a guy at Caltech had come up with a way to make a strand of DNA assemble itself into a smiley face only fifty nanometers across. Not just one but billions and billions, all floating around in a single little test tube. "The most concentrated solution of happiness ever made," Liam had joked. Liam was beaming. His own discovery, someone else's, Liam barely seemed to notice the difference. He loved every new development, every step up the scientific ladder.

There was no way that Liam Connor had jumped from that bridge.

DOZENS OF PEOPLE PUSHED AGAINST HIM, CROWDING FROM all sides. Jake's stomach churned. He hated death, despised it. Not in the way most people did, ones who mostly feared it. Jake hated it as an enemy. Hated what it took, what it left behind. Jake was in the Army for four years, a time that included the First Gulf War. No soldier spends time in a war zone without getting to know death's sight and smell. But familiarity had bred contempt. Jake found death to be a colossal waste. Someone's alive, and then not. It was sudden. Stark. Irreversible.

An unmarked helicopter swept in from the west, dipping down over the dorms of West Campus and pulling up directly over the gorge, hovering dead still. The door was open, and Jake saw a cameraman hanging out on the skids, lens pointed straight down. The local station must have hired the pilot to bring them over.

"Check this out," said a student to his right. He had his phone out, showing it to a friend. "It's on CNN."

Jake took out his iPhone, carved himself out a little space up against a parked car. He pulled up the CNN website, found the footage rolling. The view was from directly overhead, the suspension footbridge maybe a hundred yards below, a thin ribbon of blue metal hanging over empty space. The bridge was empty except for a lone policeman. Crowds on either side were held back by yellow police tape and a phalanx of officers.

The camera view zoomed into the gorge. Jake counted seven people: an officer taking pictures, two more watching, two EMTs, and two more in plain clothes that Jake guessed were also police. Their movements were choreographed, professionals going about their jobs.

The view from the camera pulled back, then panned over to the waterfall upstream from the rescuers, the remnants of an old hydroelectric station clinging to the walls of the cliff. The water was running hard, plunging over the waterfall, cascading downward.

The sound of the broadcast was inaudible in all the noise around him. Where the hell was the volume? It was a new phone; he hadn't had it more than two weeks. He found the volume, turned it up. Nothing. The mute? Where's the mute? The itchy dread in Jake's stomach was building, his initial disbelief eaten away by the acid of information coming in. If this was on CNN, then—

The camera swung back, zoomed in on the accident scene. In close on the victim.

There.

The image was grainy, but there was no doubt. The old brown coat. The shock of white hair.

Jake felt as though he'd been punched in the chest. He lowered his phone, hardly believing it. He looked up to the helicopter suspended in the sky.

Around him, people were yelling, struggling to be heard over the noise of the helicopter. Everyone was packed in tight, jostling him, elbows in his sides. The crowd surged, knocking Jake against an empty police cruiser. He barely noticed. All he could see was Liam and Dylan a week before, laughing their heads off, running Crawler races in the gardens of decay.

· 6 ·

AT THE POLICE STATION, MAGGIE WAS FURIOUS. THEY KEPT saying her grandfather killed himself, but she was certain they were wrong. "It's impossible," she said for the tenth time, pacing the room.

"I know this is a terrible shock. I'm very sorry. But please try to calm down, Ms. Connor," the police chief said. His name was Larry Stacker. He was neatly dressed, short brown hair, a blue tie over a white shirt. Maggie thought he looked like a banker.

"No way," she said, shaking her head. "He had no reason. He was healthy. He was—" She looked away, trying to regain control. The office was modest, the painted concrete walls bare, save for a couple of diplomas and a picture of the Cornell campus from above. She expected the head of the Cornell police to have fancier digs. She wanted him to have a palatial office. She wanted to believe that he had every resource in the world at his disposal.

"When did you last see him?" Stacker asked.

"Last night. Around nine p.m. Outside the Physical Sciences Complex. He was fine. Making jokes. He and Dylan were going letterboxing this afternoon."

"Dylan? Who is Dylan?"

"My son. His great-grandson. Please listen to me. There was

absolutely nothing wrong with Liam. He loved Dylan. He loved me. He loved his work, his friends—everything. He was the most goddamned content person I've ever known. He had a big talk coming up next month at the AAAS meeting. He was getting ready for it. Why do all that if he was about to kill himself?"

Stacker was silent. He was waiting her out, Maggie thought, wearing what must be the face he used for the bereaved, projecting equal parts steadiness and sympathy.

"There's no suicide note, right?"

"That's correct. But most suicides don't leave a note."

She shook her head. "I don't care. I'm telling you, he *did not* jump from that bridge."

"Ms. Connor. I know this is very difficult to accept. But there's no question. Your grandfather jumped."

"How could you possibly say that? How could you know? Were you there? Did you see it?"

"In a manner of speaking. We have a security camera on that bridge."

Maggie was stunned. "Oh my God. You're serious."

"I'm so sorry, Ms. Connor. There were witnesses as well. They saw a woman on the bridge with your grandfather. We're looking for her now." He opened a manila file, removed a printout, and passed it over. "Do you recognize her?"

Maggie studied the image. It was grainy, a pixilated image of the woman from the waist up, clearly a blowup of a longer shot. It caught the woman in profile, dark hair pulled back, long forehead, thin cheeks. Asian. She looked to be in her mid-twenties. She wore a black coat and gloves.

Maggie shook her head. She was fighting back tears. "I've never seen her before. You don't know who she is?"

"Not yet. But your grandfather had said a woman that matches her description was following him. He'd reported it a week ago."

"*Following* him? Why?"

"We don't know."

"Could she—"

"She wasn't close to him when it happened. Professor Connor seemed to run ahead of her."

"Did she try to stop him?"

"It's hard to say for sure."

"Let me see the video."

"I don't see what good that will do, Ms. Connor."

"I don't care. Show it to me."

After five minutes of fighting, Stacker reluctantly opened his laptop.

Maggie watched, her heart pounding. The scene was grainy. The bridge was empty, swaying ever so slightly in the wind. A time stamp at the bottom said nine-thirty-two a.m.

"Oh, God. There he is." The tears ran down her cheeks. She fought the urge to cry out loud.

Liam was slowly shuffling along, the unknown woman beside him. He had on his old brown overcoat, the one with the big wooden buttons. She could barely make out his face. "Oh, Pop-pop." She put a hand to her mouth.

He continued to progress along the bridge, the woman beside him. She couldn't tell if they were talking.

They approached the middle of the span.

It happened so fast. One minute he was shuffling along. The next minute he was running. Fast. Then he was up and over.

Gone.

FOR JAKE, THE NEXT FOUR HOURS WERE A LONG, SLOW WALK underwater. The first stop was Barton Hall, home of the Cornell police department. A lieutenant named Ed Becraft had led Jake to a dingy little room with plastic chairs and a white table. He looked to be in his late forties, with a wrinkled brown suit and tired blue eyes. He had a soft, high voice, incongruous, given his bulk and his job. When he told Jake the video camera on the bridge had caught Liam jumping, Jake was stunned.

Becraft showed Jake a picture of the woman who'd been with Liam on the bridge. "You recognize her?"

Jake shook his head.

Becraft nodded, then stood. "I need a minute," he said. He gave Jake a voluntary statement form and asked him to fill it out, then left him alone.

Jake tried to get his head around it, but the whole episode didn't register as real. Like a string of words said over and over until they lost their meaning and became just a stretch of sound: *Liam Connor is dead.*

He picked up bits of conversations in the hallway. Rumors were spreading, speculation about what could have made Liam kill himself. The leading theories revolved around an incurable disease, cancer or incipient Alzheimer's, affecting either his health or his judgment. It was all noise, Jake knew—the desperate attempt of people's brains to adjust to a suddenly shifted reality. Whenever something big happened, there was always a great deal of *Sturm und Drang*. Jake was trying to see through it. To pick the signal out of the noise. To understand why one of the greatest biologists of the twentieth century, a man surrounded by family and friends, all of whom adored him, chose to kill himself. And why would he do it in such a sudden, dramatic, out-of-character way, with absolutely no explanation?

When Jake was done filling out the form, he poked his head into the hallway. Becraft saw him and came back, a mug in hand. "You okay? You want coffee?"

"No, thanks. I'm fine."

"Tea?"

"I'm fine," Jake said.

"Let me just say again, I'm sorry for your loss."

Becraft settled into his chair, picked up a pen. He made a couple of notes on a pad before looking up. When he did, it was all business, the questions coming fast. "Any reason you know of why Connor would want to end his life?"

"No."

"Was he depressed?"

"No."

"Was he sick?"

"No."

"Any unusual behavior?"

"No. Nothing."

"Was he tired? Slowing down?"

"You have to be kidding. He worked twelve-hour days. Nights and weekends, he'd be there, fiddling in the gardens."

"Gardens?"

Jake gave him a quick rundown on Liam's fungal research, the granite-topped tables in the Physical Sciences Complex. Becraft took copious notes. The interview went on for another ten minutes, but the only thing that Becraft reacted to was the information about Liam's labs. He'd grabbed his superior, a police chief named Stacker, and they dispatched a team to seal it off.

Then they'd asked Jake to wait.

He drifted up to the main part of Barton Hall, a cavernous space so big you could park a 747 in it. In addition to housing the Cornell police, Barton was also the home of the ROTC, as well as an indoor running track. It had been an airplane hangar in World War I, an armory during World War II. At the time, it was the largest freestanding enclosed space in the world. Now undergraduates took final exams there en masse, row upon row toiling under the watchful eyes of TAs and professors. When Jake taught Physics 1112, this is where they took their final.

Jake stared out over the hall, imagining Liam running the track, eight times around for a mile. Liam had been a dedicated runner when he was younger, a good one. He'd gotten within fifteen seconds of the world record for the mile in the early fifties. Jake ran a bit himself, but he was more of a lifter. He liked the clarity of weights. The steel went up or it didn't. Success or failure. With running, you were never done. You could keep going forever.

Jake tried to get inside the old man's skin. How many times had Liam stood in this hall over the years? The *New York Times* did a survey, asking where the greatest Grateful Dead show ever was. The answer was Barton Hall, 1977. Liam would have been what? In his fifties then?

Liam listened almost exclusively to old Irish folk tunes, sad, sonorous ballads about lost love and delayed revenge, but he and Jake had once talked about the music of the sixties and early seventies. Jake had been surprised by Liam's encyclopedic knowledge of everything from Bob Dylan and the Greenwich Village folk scene through the Byrds, the Beatles, and the Grateful Dead. Jake had said it was a revolutionary time, but Liam had a different take. He said it wasn't a revolutionary period in music at all. Rather, it was a reactionary one—a throwback to when the popular art of a society was a dialogue about the issues of the day, not simply bread and circuses.

Liam's take on things always made you think, whether you agreed with him or not. Jake rarely emerged from their wide-ranging discussions with his initial perspective intact.

Jake was going to miss him like hell.

A voice behind him: "Professor Sterling? You ready?"

. . .

BECRAFT LED THE WAY AS THEY WALKED DOWN EAST AVENUE toward Liam's laboratory in the Physical Sciences Complex. The air was crisp and cold, carrying the scent of autumn leaves. The sun was out, normally a cause for celebration in perennially cloudy upstate New York, but today it seemed garish.

To their right was the Andrew Dickson White House, named after Cornell's first president, followed by Rockefeller Hall, built in 1906 with $274,494 from John D. Rockefeller. To their left was the Arts Quad, a large open space overseen by a statue of Ezra Cornell. It was surrounded by a mix of old and new buildings, some dating back to the university's founding in 1865.

Below the Arts Quad and past the library was the "Libe Slope," a steep hill that ran from the edge of the library down to the West Campus dorms. This was the site of the traditional end-of-the-year blowout party that invariably filled the Gannett Health Services center with overindulgent undergrads. Beyond Libe Slope and the dorms was the eclectic mix of buildings and houses that made up downtown Ithaca, and beyond that the wide, flat expanse of Cayuga Lake.

They turned right, toward the stone-and-steel façade of the Physical Sciences Complex, tucked in between Baker, Clark, and Rockefeller halls. Five minutes later they arrived at Liam's lab. A uniformed officer stood guard outside. Technically, B24F was one of Jake's labs, but in practice it was Liam's domain. Jake had arranged for the space, saving Liam the trouble and paperwork. Liam was never an empire builder, always preferring to keep a low profile. He'd never bought into the science-as-industry model, where progress came by having a swarm of students and post-docs toiling away, picking a field clean like locusts. Even at the height of his career, the world's leading expert on fungi was a perennial outsider, always preferring to work with just one or two students, lost in the unknown, tracking the craziest, most interesting idea he could find. His was so different from Jake's way. Liam threw the long ball. Jake ran it right up the middle, making a few yards each carry.

Becraft said, "Professor Sterling, is there anything in here that could be dangerous? Anything potentially explosive? Any chemicals we should be aware of?"

"No, nothing beyond the usual."

"Usual?"

"Bottles of reagents, maybe some syringes, things like that."

He nodded. "Okay, then go ahead. Open the door."

Jake slid his ID through the reader, and the door clicked open. Becraft flipped the switch, illuminating the rectangular space, twenty feet wide and twice that deep. The room was orderly and deathly still. There was a laptop on the desk in the corner, the screen blank. The opposite wall was lined with three lab benches, the shelves packed with pipettes, flasks of reagents, and sample cuvettes. And in the center of it all, the three huge mandalas of the gardens of decay. Jake always thought they looked like a giant painting by Klee, a spellbinding tapestry of complex mixtures of greens and yellows tucked between the narrow passageways down which the Crawlers ran.

"That's what you told me about?" Becraft asked. "The gardens of . . ."

"Decay. That's them. Each square is a different kind of fungus. Genetically engineered to cause the decay of one kind of trash or another."

"Incredible," Becraft said. But then Jake saw his gaze change. "Professor Sterling, speed is important in a case like this. If there's something to be found, we want it now instead of later. Understand?"

"Sure. Of course."

"What I want you to do is this: Walk slowly through the lab and carefully examine every little thing. Is there anything out of the ordinary? Anything odd? I don't care how small a detail it is. If it strikes you as wrong in any way, speak up." He handed Jake a pair of powdered gloves. "But don't touch anything without asking me first."

Jake pulled the gloves on and circled the perimeter of the lab while Becraft went to work. Jake watched Becraft quizzically as he turned over the trash can and laid the contents out on a small white sheet he had brought with him in a translucent bag. "What are you looking for?"

"Draft of a suicide note. A paper cup with a good print. You never know. When I was with the Rochester PD, I once found the credit card receipt from the purchase of a murder weapon in a trash can not ten feet from the victim. The husband had dropped it there."

Jake returned to his searching. The door to a metal cabinet was slightly ajar. He glanced inside: a half-empty bottle of whiskey sat on the shelf. Next to it were two tumblers, a trace of brown in the bottom of each. Liam marked every important event, good or bad, with a shot of whiskey.

A memory bubbled up from a few years back. Jake had returned from a morning run to find Liam sitting in the hallway of his apartment complex, cross-legged on the floor outside his door, a paper bag at his side. "Is that the human snail?" Liam had said.

"Snail?" Jake smiled. "You're just jealous."

Liam scanned Jake up and down, taking in his running shorts and sweatshirt, the sweat dripping. "Of you?"

"Of my knees."

"That is, in fact, true," Liam said. His knees had forced him to give up running almost two decades ago. "Which route this morning?"

"Cayuga trail. Up by the lake, then along Fall Creek to Route Thirteen."

"Time?"

"Today? Hour forty-five."

"When I was your age, I could have shaved thirty minutes off that."

"When you were my age, the gorge was buried under an ice sheet."

"You are funny. A human tortoise, but funny."

Jake offered a hand. Liam took it, pulling himself up from the floor, a clinking sound coming from the paper bag in his other hand. He stood, all five and a half feet of him, head high. Jake was nearly a foot taller. It was an odd feeling, to be physically so much larger than this man Jake viewed as a giant.

Once inside, Liam pulled a bottle of Cooley whiskey and two tumblers out of the bag. He poured two fingers into each tumbler.

Jake said, "To what do I owe the visit?" Though he knew.

"Thought you might want a drink. Given all that's happening today."

"All" being Gulf War II.

Jake had tried to avoid the TV, the images of missile assaults on Baghdad, banners in blue and white along the bottom, but Liam flipped it on. "Shock and awe," Liam said. "Wars have taglines now." Jake barely heard him. The visuals were enough to set the triggers snapping inside him, the trip wires of an ex-soldier. The itchy feeling, dread and adrenaline. The sense that he should be there, a part of it, good or bad. The ground incursion had started up a few hours before, a massive wall of steel and ordnance grinding forward out of Kuwait. It was going even easier than the first round, thirteen years before. No columns of Iraqi soldiers to plow under. They had learned. They stayed out of the way of the grinding monstrous machine. The real fight would come later, though no one knew that then.

Liam took a drink. "May it be short, and then may it be over."

JAKE CLOSED THE CABINET DOOR, LETTING THE MEMORY GO. He looked around the lab, trying to focus on his task. *Anything out of the ordinary.*

A lab notebook lay on the bench, facedown. He glanced at Becraft.

"Can I?" Jake asked.

Becraft nodded.

Jake picked up the notebook by the edges, turned it over. He touched a finger to the mottled red cover. Liam had written his name on it, along with the start date, March 23. No ending date. Most everyone used computers for lab notebooks these days, but Liam stuck to paper and pen.

Jake opened it and scanned the entries. Most of it was standard stuff—descriptions of experiments, names of data files, and lists of protocols. But there were other items, too:

> Mountain chickadees can lose 10% of their bodyweight overnight in winter and face certain death if they don't get food every 24 hrs.

Liam's notebooks were famous among his colleagues and students. Everyone liked to sneak a peek at them. He kept everything in them, seeing no clear separation between a genetic sequence and an aphorism.

Jake flipped through the pages, coming across a series of comical drawings. A bumblebee wearing glasses and smoking a cigar. A spider blowing bubbles. Liam had rendered them in exquisite detail and with considerable skill. Jake flipped forward, the dates in the notebook approaching the present. He stopped on October 25, yesterday. The last entry was a series of numbers, column after column, rendered in Liam's careful handwriting.

"Anything?" Becraft asked.

"Not so far."

"Can you take a look at this?"

The investigator had Liam's Internet history up on his laptop.

http://www.msnbc.msn.com/
http://www.google.com/
http://www.msnbc.msn.com/
http://gene.genetics.uga.edu/
http://www.msnbc.msn.com/
http://www.letterboxing.org/
http://www.amazon.com/
http://www.rawstory.com/
http://www.nytimes.com/
http://www.msnbc.msn.com/

Jake scanned through the list: MSNBC. Amazon. All mundane entries. Apparently, before you leap off a bridge you read the news and go shopping for a book.

Bullshit.

"A couple of these stand out to me," said the investigator. He clicked on http://gene.genetics.uga.edu. The page popped up.

"It's a fungal genetic database," Jake said. "See? Click on an organism, choose a chromosome, and up comes the genetic sequence." Jake hit a few keys, and an almost endless string of genetic letters appeared.

GACTAGCCATTTAACGTACCATTACCTA . . .

"So this is a website he'd go to as part of his work?"

"All the time. He was genetically engineering fungi. Shuffling genes in and out to get what he wanted. That's what the gardens are about."

They kept at it, but all of the other websites appeared equally benign. No sites about suicide. Nothing about cancer, or depression, or anything else indicating that Liam was sick or distraught in any way. No sites about God or death or love. Just the normal detritus of the day.

Jake felt trapped, wanted to crawl out of his skin, see it from a different angle. He just couldn't make it work. He simply could not reconcile the man he knew with the action he'd taken. No one commits suicide out of the blue like that, not without hinting at it first, not without showing some kind of sign. There was something he wasn't seeing, but what?

Jake looked again around the room. The neat stacks of papers. The notebook on the lab table. The fungi in the gardens of decay. It was Liam's world. Nothing different than any other day.

He stood over the gardens, stared down at the even rows of squares. He couldn't escape a small itch, a sense that something was awry.

When it hit him, he couldn't believe he hadn't seen it before.

Jake turned to Becraft. "Did you do something with the Crawlers?"

"Crawlers?"

"The ones he used here in the garden. There should be ten or twenty of them. Maybe a few more over there on the table."

"What are you talking about?"

"MicroCrawlers. They're little robots—they look sort of like spiders. The devices allowed Liam to tend to thousands of different fungal samples, all by himself. They were like his graduate students."

"How big?"

"Each is about the size of a fingernail. Your men didn't take them?"

"No."

"Maybe when they came earlier? To secure the room?"

"No. No one else has been inside. Nothing was touched."

"You're sure."

"Yes."

"Well, they're gone. Someone must have taken them."

"Why would someone take them? Who else had key access to this room?"

"Just me, Liam, and a couple of my graduate students. I don't get it. If someone wanted Crawlers, they wouldn't come here first. They would go to my lab. We've got hundreds of them."

"Could some of yours be missing, too?"

Jake thought it through. "I need to talk to Dave and Joe."

· 8 ·

DUFFIELD HALL LOOMED OVER THE ENGINEERING QUAD, A blocky monolith of glass and steel glowing in the darkness. Inside was the Cornell Nanofabrication Facility, or the CNF, as it was known to three decades of students. Jake checked his watch: ten-fifteen p.m. More than twelve hours had passed since they'd discovered Liam's body.

Jake entered Duffield Hall through double doors on the north end of the building. This led into a huge atrium that extended nearly a hundred yards. On a typical day, sunlight poured though the translucent skylights in the high ceiling above, and students and faculty would be everywhere, chatting, ordering drinks at the coffee stand, and lounging in chairs along the walls. Even at this hour, a handful of students and faculty would typically be about, but tonight the space was eerily quiet, as if life itself had been drained out of the campus with Liam's death.

To the right was a series of windows opening into the CNF labs. Joe and Dave were inside, looking for any sign of the missing Crawlers and double-checking that their own stocks were untouched. A careful check of Liam's records, plus information Maggie had given the police about a Crawler funeral, had put the total number missing at thirteen. Jake and his students had been at it for more than six hours, searching for them everywhere, brainstorming about where they could be or why someone would have taken them. Maybe they'd been stolen by undergraduates as a prank, or Liam had locked them away for safekeeping somewhere? So far, they were in the dark.

Jake's phone went off. He checked the area code—California—and let it go. His phone had not stopped ringing—colleagues, reporters, friends—everyone wanting to know what had *really* happened. Jake had called back only a select few people. He had called his DARPA grant manager, a Stanford professor on loan to DARPA in Arlington, Virginia, and told him about the missing Crawlers. Since DARPA paid the bills, Jake thought they deserved to know. He'd also tried to call Maggie Connor—to offer his condolences and ask how Dylan was holding up—but the phone had been constantly busy.

Jake stared into the glass that separated him from the rarefied environment inside the CNF. This is where Dave and Joe made the Crawlers, carving them out of silicon wafers like Michelangelo finding the David inside the stone. The room before him was filled with GCA projection steppers, wafer coaters, and an old EV620 contact mask aligner, all part of the assembly line of the microworld. This entire section of the CNF was standard computer-chip technology—furnaces for growing oxides, acid baths for etching, and evaporators for depositing metal films. Enough sheer miniaturizing power to write the *Encyclopaedia Britannica* on the head of a pin.

A young woman entered, dressed in a light blue jumpsuit, blue booties, and a white headcovering. She looked a little like Beth, his ex-wife. They'd married young, then grown apart after he had come back from the war. She lived in Phoenix now, was remarried, with a kid, a little girl named Olivia. Once a year they talked on the phone. There wasn't much to say. Beth had a new life. She was doing okay.

Jake watched the woman work, movements deliberate as she dipped a silicon wafer into a beaker, holding it carefully with specialized tweezers. She clicked the button on a stopwatch, swishing the wafer in the liquid. After a time, she lifted it out and dipped it into a water bath. Jake recognized the procedure, the ritual. The removal of every speck of dust and dirt, leaving behind nothing but the pure silicon crystal underneath, every atom locked in its place relative to its neighbors. The elimination of everything that did not belong, so she could begin her work on a perfect canvas.

She glanced up, saw him watching. He smiled politely, turned away.

Liam's death was bringing back the black empties. It was just like it had been with Beth—he couldn't fully connect with her. Jake felt detached, slippery, as though his insides and outsides were disconnected.

He returned his thoughts to Liam. Though Liam was a biologist, he loved the wonderful precision of all this technology, the miniature landscapes of almost impossibly intricate detail that were created. Liam had been there in the beginning, at the birth of the first information revolution. He was friends with all of the big players: Alan Turing, von Neumann at Princeton, Weiner at MIT. The ideas were there by the fifties—the vision of machines executing algorithmic programs stored on some kind of linear tape. It was increasingly clear that life worked that way, with DNA as the tape, and cells as the machines that executed the programs. It was also clear that electronics could be made to work that way, with magnetic bits or packets of charge as the data and computer chips as the processors.

Shockley, Kilby, Moore—they took up the challenge. Liam knew all of them, right up to Bill Gates and the Google guys. He'd said he had a front-row seat for the information revolution and he wasn't going to waste it. He'd studied the growth of the semiconductor industry like he studied fungi, following each step in the evolution of this new technology, and watching, in turn, how the world adapted to it.

And he'd loved the Crawlers. While the military saw the Crawlers as potential spies, Liam saw them as soldiers in a new revolution. Liam believed that a second wave was coming—one even bigger than the information revolution. When the technologies of the information age were applied to biology, life would become an engineering discipline. Using tools such as microfluidic labs-on-a-chip, PCR machines, and assemblers such as the Micro-Crawlers, you'd be able to make living cells the way you made computer chips, process DNA like so many ones and zeroes. He was incredibly excited. He thought that in five years he'd be making fungi from scratch. Design their genetic sequence on the computer, push a few buttons, and there they would be. A genome as easy to write as a string of computer code. A new fungus as simple to construct as an integrated circuit. He maintained that the Crawlers would be the foot soldiers in the revolution.

Jake still couldn't believe that Liam wouldn't be there to see it happen. Wouldn't be there when someone managed to boot up the first artificial cell. When kids started to post their favorite genomes on their MySpace pages. When the cell nucleus replaced the computer chip as the symbol of technological sophistication.

When Dylan built his first bacterium.

Liam thought the technologies of synthetic biology would be a tsunami, one that would make the electronics revolution seem like ripples in a pond. Jake could barely imagine it. What would it be like when companies manufactured creatures instead of products? When disaffected kids used the tools of the synthetic biology revolution to hack into life instead of into computers?

Jake felt himself sagging. He tried to shake off the exhaustion. All he knew for sure was that the new revolution would be messy. There were no simple equations for something like life. It was a completely different kind of problem. A random mutation and the smallest player could suddenly take down the largest, multiplying again and again, growing exponentially. A virus jumps from a monkey to a human and you have the AIDS epidemic. Ebola escapes the jungles of Africa and a hundred million could die. A dominant player like Homo sapiens could be laid low in an instant. It was madness, a wild, crazy war with billions of warriors, millions of different sides. No one could predict the outcome, not even Liam Connor.

Joe emerged from the CNF, looking beat.

"And?" Jake asked.

"We checked everywhere. We opened every storage bin. Every wafer cassette. Looked in every sample box."

"And you found?"

"Not a Crawler out of place."

JAKE WAS JUST ABOUT TO DISMISS ANY SINISTER SIGNIFI-cance to the missing Crawlers. No matter how he turned it over in his head, no matter what angle he looked at it from, he couldn't see how the missing Crawlers could be connected to Liam's death. And Jake had a rule: never blame conspiracies when mischief or happenstance would suffice.

But then came two new pieces of information.

The first came from Vlad Glazman, Jake's friend and scientific colleague, a fifty-two-year-old Russian émigré and tenured professor of computer science. Vlad had asked Jake to stop by his lab. "For a drink," he said. "In honor of our lost friend." He wouldn't say more, but Jake knew there was more. Vlad knew Liam as well as Jake did, maybe better.

Jake arrived at Vlad's lab just after midnight to find the Russian working his way through a bottle of Gorilka Nemiroff—"a nice Ukrainian vodka," Vlad said. He was a squat man, with a square head and broad shoulders, as if he'd been compressed by a vise. His hair was dark, like his eyes, and his lips were surprisingly full, almost sensual. He was married to a woman he'd met at a conference in Europe, as blond and tall as he was dark and squat. They were having problems.

Vlad poured Jake a drink and said, "You think Connor was sick?"

"I don't know what to think."

Vlad grunted. "He was not sick."

Jake took a swallow and found the vodka pleasantly harsh, the burn on the back of the throat a welcome fire. He let his gaze walk around the room. Vlad's lab was a mashup of science, with UNIX boxes and Cat5 cables next to PCR machines and rows of thumb-activated pipettes. Nearly every bit of available counter space in Vlad's lab was covered by stacks of papers. He had cleared them off a spot, carefully allocating the displaced papers to other piles.

Vlad lifted his glass, took a drink. "You know what I think?" Vlad said.

"Tell me."

"He knew secrets."

"What kind?"

"Secrets they didn't want him to tell."

" 'They'?"

"They."

"Vlad the Paranoid," Jake said. Which was true. Vlad saw

darkness everywhere. In Moscow, he'd spent his nights building CPUs out of salvaged parts while toiling away during the day
as a low-level technical staffer for Directorate T—Scientific and
Technical—a part of the First Chief Directorate of the KGB. Vlad's
status as a Jew kept him from achieving a formal position of any
significance, but he got out, and the West had no such restrictions.
Since coming to Cornell, he had become a major player in asyn-
chronous information processing, writing code that kept different
computer processors happily talking to one another. Five years
ago, Vlad had switched fields to synthetic biology, drawn by the
promise of programming in the code of life. He plied his trade with
money leaking across the dark boundary of classified research. He
had contacts throughout the military-funding universe: at ONR,
AFOSR, DARPA, you name it. He had never lost the sense from
his days in the Soviet Union that someone was looking over his
shoulder.

Jake thumbed a paper on a pile next to him, something on
micro-RNA gene regulation. The piles looked haphazard, but Vlad
knew exactly what was in every one of them. Jake had seen it many
times: He'd reach into a pile, pull out the exact article from *Science*
or the *Proceedings of the National Academy of Sciences* that they'd
been discussing. "The fossil record," Vlad would say.

Jake said, "You're saying someone killed him? But the video
showed him jump."

"I'm saying nothing. I am letting vodka talk."

"Let it talk more."

Vlad took another sip. "I had conversation with friend at
DTRA."

"Ditra?"

"Defense Threat Reduction Agency. The go-to agency for
anti-WMD." Vlad closed one eye, thinking hard. "Located in
Virginia—Fort Belvoir. Couple thousand employees. Budget two
billion a year."

"And who is this friend?"

Vlad waved him off.

"Okay. So you had a conversation. And?"

"He wanted to know what happened."

"To Liam? What did you tell him?"

"I told him what I know. Which is nothing."

"And *why* was he asking?"

"You liked Liam, right?"

"You're kidding? I would've killed for him. Why?"

"He was smart, Liam Connor. Complex. Playing games on many levels."

"Make your point, Vlad."

"All I know is this. Not everyone liked our sweet old Irishman. I was told he sometimes played hardball. That a year or two back he had fight with head of Homeland Security. And deputy national security adviser. The delightful Mr. Dunne."

"About what?"

"Don't know. But my friend says Connor wasn't happy. He said Connor was . . ." He struggled for the word. "Like *liver*. Livid."

"You really don't know what it was about."

"Boy Scout honor."

"So? What happened?"

Vlad considered his empty glass. "From what I hear, Dunne threw Connor out of his office. Told him to go to hell."

Vlad poured them both another shot of Gorilka. "Just be careful. My friend sounded nervous. And these people do not play games."

"Meaning?"

Vlad looked thoughtful. "Meaning I feel more at home in your country all the time. Understand? Rules are different now. Times are—what did man with bad voice say? Times they are a-changing."

"Bob Dylan."

"That is him. Smart man. You should listen."

THE SECOND PIECE OF INFORMATION CAME AS A CALL TO Jake's cellphone. It was after two a.m. and he was on his way home. He was on foot, walking the path through the old graveyard that separated Cornell from the neighborhoods below, weaving among the gravestones like a ghost.

The caller ID said "Cornell PD."

"Professor Sterling? Sorry to call so late. It's Lieutenant Ed Becraft, Cornell PD. We met earlier today." Jake heard a tapping, like a pencil on a desk.

"Is there something new on Connor?"

The pencil taps kept up a steady rhythm. "Not exactly. My chief just got a call. From the office of a Major Elber at Fort Detrick, Maryland."

"Fort *Detrick*? What did they want?"

"Between the two of us, Elber is the chief bioterrorism investigator at USAMRIID." Becraft spoke the acronym like a word, *you-sam-rid*. It stood for the U.S. Army Medical Research Institute of Infectious Diseases. "He wanted to know where we were on Liam Connor's death. And if we'd learned anything about the missing Crawlers."

"Why?"

"He said he couldn't say. That it was classified."

"What did you tell him?"

"That the investigation was ongoing. And the MicroCrawlers are still missing." The pencil was tapping faster now. "Professor Sterling, I gave Connor's grants a closer look. One jumps out at me. The principal investigator is listed as Vladimir Glazman. Connor is listed as co-PI. It's got your name on it, too. DARPA project 54756/A00."

Jake recited the title from memory: *"Crawlers in a Box: A Revolutionary Approach to Bioterrorism."*

"Care to explain?"

"That's going to take some time."

"Well, let me ask you this: the fungi in Professor Connor's lab? Could they be dangerous?"

"I don't think so," Jake said. "His lab wasn't rated for anything dangerous—it was BSL-1. Biosafety Level 1. It means that nothing in there was a significant health risk."

"That's odd."

"Why?"

No more pencil tapping. "Elber, this fellow from Detrick? He told me to seal off Connor's lab. No one gets in or out. He said they would have a team here in the morning. Does that sound like BSL-1?"

"No, it doesn't," Jake said.

"Well, then, we need to talk."

9

ORCHID HELD THE STEERING WHEEL AT TEN O'CLOCK AND two o'clock, her hands wrapped in skintight black Forzieri gloves. She stared at her hands. The hands that had failed her. She still had a hard time accepting her failure. She'd known all his pressure points. She had researched his habits, his family, everything. But Liam Connor had tricked her.

When he had finally confessed, he was barely alive. The Uzumaki, he'd said, was hidden in a stretch of forest at the edge of the Cornell campus. She had taken him there, followed him across the bridge.

And then Liam Connor had jumped.

She took a hand from the steering wheel, began to strum her fingers on her thigh. No nervous habit this; she was typing. Her gloves had a piezoelectric material woven inside that generated a tiny electrical signal with the movement of each finger. The words appeared as ghostly green letters along the top of her glasses: EN ROUTE TO MESSENGER.

She needed time. The Messenger would give it to her.

She touched index finger to thumb, and the tiny camera in her glasses took a picture of the road ahead. As stipulated, Orchid provided complete documentation: detailed notes combined with time-stamped photographs, from the beginning to the end. No detail escaped documentation. The client had demanded it.

The old Camry plowed on. A few puddles of weak light thrown down by street lamps lining the road were all that interrupted the inky blackness. The I-Deal self-storage facility came into view. She turned off Route 79, the gravel crunching under her tires, and pulled the car to a stop two rows away from the unit she had rented two days previously and outfitted for her needs.

She gave herself two minutes. She closed her eyes, folded her hands together, thumbs touching lips. She started the process, the calming, the stabilization that placed her where she needed to be.

Two minutes later, she was ice. She reached over the seat and grabbed her backpack. She unzipped the top and checked the contents:

1. D-321G infrared goggles.
2. Pen-style X-Acto knife.
3. A pair of eight-inch pruning shears.
4. Blazer butane microtorch.
5. 100cc syringe loaded with LSA-25.
6. Johnson & Johnson rolled medical gauze, stored in a Ziploc sandwich bag.
7. Ziploc freezer bag filled with ice.

She stepped out of the car, smooth and calm, backpack draped over her shoulder. The night was cold, the asphalt mottled with patches of light snow. She walked through the silence, mind empty, letting doubt remain in the car, fingers typing on thigh: APPROACHING MESSENGER.

She stopped before I-Deal unit #209. A few careful twists of the dial and the combination lock clicked open. She rolled the sliding door up two feet, bent down, and stepped under. She slid the door closed behind her, disappearing into the pitch-black darkness. Inside, she paused, taking in the smell. Wood and metal and a vague chemical odor. That would be the plastic. She had lined the walls, floor, and roof with plastic sheeting because of the inevitable spray.

And another odor, stronger than the rest. A scent that was her stock in trade.

Terror.

Working by feel, she removed the Night Optics D-321G night-vision goggles from her pack and pulled them down over her eyes. The darkness was no longer darkness. The goggles were Gen 3, equipped with an infrared flashlight invisible to human eyes but not the gallium arsenide photocathode and microchannel plate detectors in the 321. The room was empty, save for a small satchel in the corner and a single nylon rope dangling from the ceiling, taut from the weight it held.

At the end of the rope, hanging in a prone position in the center of the empty space, was the Messenger. He was a human cocoon, wrapped in cloth so only his face and chest were exposed, and supported knees to shoulder by nylon webbing. She had hunted him hours before, taking him in a stairwell in the Bronx. She used the Paxarms Mark 24B pistol projector with a dart equipped with fentanyl, to be followed by the M-5050 antidote. Fentanyl had the bonus that, should the target get away before the antidote was administered, the target would die.

The Messenger twisted slowly in the darkness, fear in his eyes, mouth stuffed with cotton matte and taped shut, dramatically dulling his ability to make any kind of sound. It had been a simple hunt, too simple to be truly enjoyable, even if he was Japanese. He was completely unsuspecting. If asked, he would say he had done nothing to make one of the highest-paid killers in Asia hunt him. It was true. The Messenger's only crime was his name.

He couldn't see her but sensed her coming closer. She could tell by the heightened wriggling.

She gave him the injection first, then went to work on his chest with the X-Acto knife, cutting the Chinese characters with quick, sharp strokes. He was Japanese, so there was little hair to contend with. And he was young and fit, so the skin was smooth and taut. Blood popped up like fallen raindrops.

She finished the lettering, snapped a photo of her work, then mopped up the excess blood with a bit of gauze. She replaced the X-Acto knife and took out the clippers. When she had bound the Messenger, she had taped down all the fingers on his right hand save the middle one, as if he was giving her the finger. She placed the blades of the shears at the juncture of the knuckle.

She squeezed hard.

Snap!

He fluttered, grunting and moaning, dangling at the end of his rope. The blood spurted down on the plastic sheet below, the flow making a central puddle surrounded by little circular swirls, the sound like rain.

She took out the torch, fired up the flame, and cauterized the wound. The smell of burned blood and flesh was sharp in her nostrils.

She picked up the severed finger and wrapped it in gauze, then put it in the Ziploc freezer bag filled with ice and stored it in her pack. She waited for three minutes, then checked again that the bleeding was stanched.

She put away her tools, then typed on her leg: MESSENGER READY.

He wriggled in his cocoon, rotating slowly. "Don't worry," she whispered, stopping his motion with a hand on the side of his head. "Tomorrow is your big day."

DAY 3

■ WEDNESDAY, OCTOBER 27 ■

LETTERBOX

10

JAKE COULDN'T SLEEP. HE TOSSED AND TURNED, THEN FINALLY
gave up. He rose and made a pot of coffee, then set to pacing his
apartment, the windows outside black with night. A niggling memory kept at him, a certain conversation with Liam as they had
walked among the abandoned concrete bunkers of Seneca. At the
time, Jake had thought that it was just an old man unburdening
himself.

The two-lane road was empty as he drove through the predawn
darkness, only the occasional farmer's pickup passing in the opposite direction. Before the sun rose, he was thirty miles northwest of
Ithaca on Route 96A, in the middle of a bucolic landscape of hills
and farms. He topped a small rise and spotted his destination. It
looked like an abandoned prison in his headlights; triple fencing,
like layers of an onion, enclosed the ten-thousand-acre wasteland
that was once the Seneca Army Depot.

Liam had told Jake the history. The Seneca Army Depot had
been built on Roosevelt's orders in the run-up to World War II,
when Liam was still a student in Ireland. By the time battleships
were aflame at Pearl Harbor and Liam was queuing up to enlist in
the British Army, the Seneca Depot had more than five hundred

concrete bunkers storing armaments, helping to feed the war machine.

After the war, new, larger bunkers were built to store nuclear weapons. Liam was in Ithaca by this time, starting the work that would make him famous. The depot acquired a fame of its own. At its peak, the depot was a small city employing more than ten thousand people, one of the largest facilities of its kind in the country. Jake remembered the newspaper photographs from later in the 1980s, when Dr. Spock, cheered on by thousands of anti-nuke demonstrators, climbed these fences to draw attention to the nuclear weapons inside.

Now no one was watching. With the fall of the Soviet Union, the depot was shuttered, officially decommissioned in 2000. It had been left to the deer, the willows, and the geese. A few chunks of real estate had been bitten off: a prison along one edge, a youth center on another. But the core of the depot was a ghost town, a concrete mausoleum, eight miles long and four miles wide, nothing but neglected roads and bunkers. It was one of the most isolated, least-trafficked spots in the state.

After parking outside the fence, he got out and sat on the hood of his Subaru. Half freezing, he watched the sun creep over the rows and rows of munitions bunkers. Every four hundred feet was another eerie concrete monolith, all long out of use. Beat-up roads cut between them, all slowly succumbing to weeds and grass. Jake had been inside one of the bunkers, a dank and musty place filled with mold and decaying leaves. They'd once stored nukes inside, Liam had said. The triggers to set them off were kept in a separate unit, hidden underneath a white building made to look like a guardhouse.

Liam had connections with the current keepers of the depot, a consortium of businessmen planning to use the bunkers as ultra-secure housing for computer servers. He had finagled a key to one of the gates, even gotten permission to come anytime. He was running a biology experiment with the herd of rare white deer trapped inside the fences, a test of genetic variability in a confined population.

Liam had told Jake he could think clearly here, sheltered from his schedule's more immediate demands. Still, Jake thought the weight of the past was heavy in this place, banishing the trivial. At

Liam's urging, Jake had accompanied him here many times, the two men shooting the shit as they walked up and down the rows of concrete bunkers.

Their talk often turned to war, what they'd experienced and what the future held. Neither liked what they saw when they peered into their crystal balls. They discussed the arc of technology, how the last fifty years had seen a revolution of the small. With new levels of information command and control, this revolution was changing warfare. It was also changing the tools of battle themselves. Small was the new big, and the generals were finally getting the message.

The era of tanks and fighter jets battling on land and in the sky was drawing to a close. The wars of the future would be fought on small battlefields by tiny weapons striking from a thousand directions at once. The fight would take place inside computer networks, inside human bodies. Cyber-warfare. Swarms of semi-autonomous robots, such as the Crawlers. Biological weapons.

It was on one of these trips that Liam told Jake about the Uzumaki.

Jake had been stunned when Liam recounted the tale of the seven Tokkō with their deadly cylinders. About the Japanese submarine carrying one of the seven, its discovery by the USS *Vanguard*. Liam's eyes had burned fiercely bright when describing the horrendous nuclear blast that had instantly destroyed the Uzumaki along with two hundred thirty-seven men.

"Bastards," Liam had said. "Willoughby. MacArthur. They wanted it, the Uzumaki. And they got it. Kept it secret all these years. Covered the whole thing up, right along with the atrocities at Unit 731. Now that pisspot at the NSA, Dunne, has Detrick working on it again."

Liam had given him an ironic smile. "Hell of a thing, isn't it? A little fungus, more dangerous than all the weapons once stored here, a little bit of growth you could carry in a thimble."

Jake now stared out over the bunkers.

· II ·

LIAM CONNOR, RENOWNED BIOLOGIST, ONE OF THE LAST LIVING FOUNDING FATHERS OF MOLECULAR BIOLOGY, DIES AT 86

By Benjamin D. Ludgate

Liam Connor, Nobel laureate who unlocked the secrets of selective adaptation, died Tuesday morning in Ithaca, New York. His death was announced at Cornell University, where he worked and taught for sixty years. His body was found at the bottom of a gorge on campus. The circumstances of his death are under investigation.

A contemporary of James Watson and Francis Crick, the scientists who revealed the structure of DNA, Connor was best known for his work on mobile genetic elements, and for establishing that DNA resided not only in the nucleus but also in various other compartments in the cell. These ideas revolutionized cell and evolutionary biology.

Liam Connor was born in County Cork, Ireland, in 1924, the sixth child in a shopkeeper's family. As a young boy, he was fascinated by plants and fungi, and he developed an encyclopedic library of these organisms based on his own classification system. When he was fourteen, his father took him to University College Cork (then Queen's College), where he studied under the tutelage of Professor Seamus Bailey. Within a few years, he was considered the most promising young biologist in the country. In 1943 he married Edith Somerville, a poet and essayist to whom he would remain married until her death in 2004.

In 1942, Liam Connor enlisted in the British Army. For four years he served at Porton Down, the British chemical and biological weapons center, working on countermeasures to potential Axis weapons, including a brief period in Japan after the end of the war. In 1946, Connor emigrated to the U.S., spending three years doing classified work at Camp Detrick (later Fort Detrick) in Frederick, Maryland, on biological weapons countermeasures.

He moved to Cornell University in 1950, taking a faculty position in the College of Agriculture. He first embarked on a fungal taxonomy project, creating what would become the 400,000-specimen Cornell Plant Pathology Herbarium, a collection now managed by his granddaughter, Margaret Connor. Throughout his life, he would continue to travel the globe, looking for specimens for the herbarium, especially those from northeastern China and South America.

In the early fifties, he had his first major breakthrough. Building on the work of Barbara McClintock, he studied transposons, sections of the genetic code that could move around within the genome. Connor showed that these transposons could turn genes on and off, and correctly postulated that retroviruses were specialized forms of transposons. Even more revolutionary were his experiments on endosymbiosis, an idea first proposed by the Russian botanist Konstantin Merezhkovsky in 1909. Connor, together with biologist Lynn Margulis, showed that key cell components such as mitochondria were originally bacteria that were engulfed by the host cell. Controversial when it was proposed, endosymbiosis is now accepted as a major cornerstone in the evolution of complex organisms.

Connor was elected to the National Academy of Sciences in 1960 and was awarded the Wolf Prize in 1972, the National Medal of Science in 1978, and (with Barbara McClintock) the Nobel Prize in Physiology or Medicine in 1983. He received honorary doctoral degrees from seventeen institutions worldwide, including Queen's College, Beijing University, and the University of Chicago. He was voted one of the ten most influential biologists of the twentieth century by the American Association for the Advancement of Science.

In addition to his academic duties, Connor was a founding member of JASON, an academic think tank providing classified advice to the FBI, the CIA, and the military. Said John Rand, assistant secretary of state in the Nixon administration, "Connor was the one. He convinced Nixon to renounce offensive biological weapons in 1969." He was also a major force behind the 1972 Biological Weapons Convention. Connor remained active on the issue, arguing vociferously against the buildup of the U.S. defensive bioweapons program over the last few years.

At the same time, Connor was a tireless advocate for the constructive uses of biotechnology. He became a major supporter of the field of synthetic biology, writing opinion pieces and lobbying Congress. His book *Merge*, describing the coming symbiosis between cells and microelectronics, is considered a classic in the field.

He is survived by a daughter, three grandchildren, and a great-grandson. He remained an active scientist to the end. Last year he was part of a team that won the Defense Advanced Research Projects Agency (DARPA) Grand Challenge competition for autonomous microbots. Said his colleague on the project, Jake Sterling, "There's no other way to say it. He was a pure genius." In an interview three years ago, Connor was asked to name his biggest breakthrough. He replied, "I am still hoping to make it."

. . .

MAGGIE PUT THE PAPER DOWN, TEARS IN HER EYES. CINDY'S hand was on her shoulder. The breakfast table was quiet, just the two of them. Everyone else was still in bed.

Maggie tapped the article. "It's very respectful."

"Of course."

"Most of it was probably written years ago."

"I'm sure."

Maggie folded the paper carefully, laid it on the table. The front-page piece was less flattering, filled with speculation about why he had killed himself. The picture they'd used was an aerial shot of the Fall Creek Gorge, with literally thousands of people clustered around both ends of the suspension bridge.

"Maggie? You all right?" Cindy asked.

Maggie realized she was holding her head in her hands, staring down at the table. "I keep thinking of the video of Liam jumping." She rubbed her hands across her face. "That woman that was on the bridge with him. She has to be the key. Liam wouldn't jump without a reason. He wouldn't do that to Dylan."

"Still no word on her?"

"No. I called the police twenty minutes ago. Nothing."

Maggie was exhausted. She was up a half-dozen times the night before, struck with an irrational need to check on Dylan to make sure he was safe. She glanced toward the bedroom where her son was still sleeping. The last twenty-four hours had been tough on him—Dylan idolized his great-grandfather. Maggie had separated from Dylan's biological father, Arthur Mix, six months after Dylan was born. A professor of operations research at Harvard, he had shown no real interest in staying in close contact, and Maggie had long ago given up trying to force it. They would see each other once or twice a year, but Dylan treated Arthur more like a distant uncle than a father.

Dylan was a great kid, but this was way beyond what any nine-year-old should have to handle. Maggie had been devastated when her father had died of pancreatic cancer and her mother passed away later the same year. She was twenty when it happened. Dylan was half that age. And he was having panic attacks. She had to come get him in the middle of the day at school just last month. He said his chest hurt. He said that he was sure he was going to die.

Dylan was seeing a child psychologist, a woman about Maggie's age with children of her own, but it was slow going. If Dylan's fears grew worse, she said drugs might be an option, but Maggie hoped it wouldn't come to that.

A knock at the front door. "Who is that?" Cindy asked, surprised. Visitors had to call to get through the police guard at the top of the road. The press had been relentless.

"I'll get it," Maggie said. "It's probably Mel, Liam's lawyer. He called a few minutes ago."

She opened the door to find Melvin Lorince waiting, a large collapsible file under his arm. She'd last seen Mel at his wife's funeral four months ago. Nearly as old as Liam was, Mel was remarkably tall, even with his stoop, with hands like giant spiders.

"Maggie, forgive me for intruding."

"You know you're never intruding. Please. Come in."

"I won't impose. I wouldn't have bothered you, except I promised your grandfather." He handed her the collapsible file.

"What's this?"

"Papers to sign. Copies of his will. Deeds to the house. A few other things. Some of them might surprise you. Liam had made a few investments."

"What kind?"

"Just take a look. There's a ledger that gives a full accounting. There's also a letter inside. Addressed to you."

"A letter."

He nodded.

"When did he give this to you?"

"Two weeks ago. He told me that as soon as possible after his demise, I should deliver this to you. Personally. Made me promise out loud."

She felt the tears starting again. "Two weeks ago? Are you serious? How did he seem?"

"His normal self. Making jokes about it. I remember he said, 'Only a precaution. In case I'm hit by a bus. I've no intention of going anywhere just yet.' "

"Did he sound sincere?"

"I thought so then. Now—I don't know, Maggie. I can't make any sense of this. He loved you and Dylan so much. He talked about you all the time. He was so proud of you. . . ." Mel paused. He was losing it, too.

Maggie rubbed her eyes. She made herself say it. "You think he was . . . preparing for this?"

Mel shook his head. "I truly don't know. I'm pretty good at reading people, but your grandfather? I could never tell when he was having me on. He could tell me the moon was made of ice cream and I'd believe him." He looked down, as if he'd find the answer in the baseboards of the floor. "He was a proud man. A gifted man. Age takes your gifts from you." He shook his head again, touched his hands to his face. "Being old is . . . *difficult*. You slowly begin to fade. And at some point, there's not enough left."

"So you believe it was suicide?"

"Maggie, I'm sorry." He put a hand out, touched her arm.

SHE TOOK THE FILE TO HER BEDROOM, PLACED IT IN THE center of her unmade bed. She stepped back, gathering herself up. Pop-pop had prepared this for her. Before he died.

He might have known he was going to die.

She found the letter right away. The envelope was white, blank except for her name, MAGGIE CONNOR, written in her grandfather's familiar scrawl.

She ran her fingers across his handwriting, smearing the pencil strokes across the white paper. She could almost see him, hunched at his desk. He was a champion letter writer, practically wrapping himself around the words. He would go on for pages, including scientific ideas, snippets of words from anyone from Yeats to Beckett, little drawings. His letters were a wonder.

She didn't want to look inside. It was likely the last physical object she would ever receive from her grandfather. It marked a kind of peak, a divide separating a past where Pop-pop was alive from a future where he wasn't. She didn't want to cross that divide.

She set the letter aside, just for a moment, and sorted through the rest of the folder. Inside was a stack of legal documents, nothing more personal than a property deed. She found the ledger Mel had mentioned. A spreadsheet on the opening pages listed Liam Connor's stock holdings, including dates the stocks were purchased, the price, and annual tallies of liquidation value.

Maggie was shocked. Liam was not just a brilliant scientist—he was a brilliant investor. Starting with twelve hundred dollars in

1950, he had slowly built his portfolio with purchases of IBM, Intel, Apple, right up through Google. If she understood the numbers, Liam Connor's estate was worth millions.

Maggie set the ledger on the bed. Is that what this was about? Money? She didn't care about money. She didn't want her grandfather's money.

She didn't care if he was worth ten billion dollars. She'd trade it all in a second to know *why*.

Maggie flipped through the rest, but there was nothing else that mattered.

Nothing but the letter.

She carefully unsealed the flap, her hands shaking. She took a few deep breaths, trying to steady herself. She couldn't believe how afraid she was to open it. How afraid she was to find out if he really *had* planned to jump.

Calm down, Maggie. Buck up.

She removed a stationery-sized sheet of thin yellow paper from the envelope.

> Maggie—
> Tell Dylan that it's one last trip to the moors.
> Jake knows the territory.
> Ask him where the elephants perch.
> I love you so—
>
>   Pop-pop

· 12 ·

"MY BOSS IS UNDER TREMENDOUS PRESSURE TO BRING THIS
case to a close," Becraft said as he and Jake rode up the elevator in
Weill Hall, the brand-new, two-hundred-sixty-thousand-square-
foot behemoth in the heart of campus. "To declare it a suicide and
move on. You saw the reporters camped outside his office. And the
provost is calling him almost hourly. We're all working double
shifts, trying to put it to bed, but the chief is resisting. Said it
doesn't smell right."

Becraft was here to learn everything he could about the Crawlers
in a Box project. He was talkative, his weariness opening him up.
Jake decided to take advantage. "Does it smell right to you?" Jake
asked.

"It stinks. We can't find the woman on the bridge. We can't find
the Crawlers. And now we've got people from Fort Detrick on the
way, unwilling to tell us anything."

THE ELEVATOR DOORS OPENED TO THE THIRD FLOOR OF
Weill Hall. They went past the atrium and down a corridor painted
antiseptic white. Jake stopped at a door with a sign that said SYN-
THETIC BIOLOGY—V. GLAZMAN above a series of standard yellow-

and-black warning stickers about the dangers found inside. He pushed open the door. "Vlad?"

The Russian appeared, chomping on a mouthful of gum. Since he'd quit smoking, Vlad was an inveterate gum chewer, stopping only when he was drinking.

Jake did the introductions. Vlad pulled a box of Chiclets from his pocket, offered some to Becraft. He shook his head no. "You sure?" Vlad persisted. "Fruit flavor." Rejected, Vlad tossed a handful in his mouth. "Come," he said.

They passed lab bench after lab bench, each set up with the necessary tools for DNA synthesis, gene sequencing, plasmid transfection, and genome design. They followed the squat Russian until he stopped at a long table in the corner.

With great fanfare, he pulled a Plexiglas box from his pocket, the size of a pack of cigarettes. He held the plastic box up for Becraft to see. It was filled with computer circuitry and complex miniature piping, like a tiny factory. "Meet NEWTON," he said. "It is acronym. Stands for Needle Electrowetting Technique for Oligonucleotide Nanogenotyping."

Becraft shook his head. "Come again?"

"Have you ever seen BSL-4 diagnostic lab? Where they handle the most dangerous pathogens? They are monstrosities, with air locks and doors and pressure suits. It is like working at the bottom of ocean. There are maybe ten in the entire country. Even a small one costs tens of millions.

"This," he said as he tapped the box, "can replace them. Squeeze a BSL-4 lab down to a room six inches long, four inches wide, and two inches tall. Less than a thousand dollars, total cost."

Vlad picked up a glass slide. He handed it to Becraft. "Spit," he said.

"On the slide? Why?"

"Humor me."

Becraft spit on the slide. Vlad took it and placed it under a microscope hooked up to a video monitor. "Let's say I worry you have smallpox virus. What do I do? I have you spit on slide. Then I put NEWTON to work."

Vlad put the NEWTON box near the glass slide, then took out a laser pointer and his BlackBerry and started working the keys. As they watched, a little door opened on the front of the NEWTON box. A Crawler skittered out and ran across the table. Becraft took a half-step back.

"It's controlled by microwave signal," Jake said. "Basically like a cellphone, but working at a different frequency." Vlad aimed the laser pointer at the Crawler. A red dot appeared on the table. The Crawler sensed the beam, ran sideways toward it. It followed the red dot as Vlad moved the beam along the table.

Becraft watched, amazed. "It's following the light?"

"The heat," Jake said. "The Crawler has a bolometric heat sensor. It can even pick up the thermal signal given off by your hand."

Vlad led the Crawler across the Formica bench, up and onto the glass slide. Then he hit a key on his BlackBerry and the Crawler stopped.

The Crawler's image filled the monitor, enlarged fifty times. The Crawler was supping at Becraft's spittle like a deer at a stream.

"There you go," Vlad said. "The Crawler has sample. Now we just send it home." With his BlackBerry and the laser pointer, he led it back to the box. The door opened, and in it went. "If this were real threat, we could be doing this from the next room. Or next state."

Vlad picked up the box, placed it under the microscope. "Now it gets interesting." They watched on the monitor as the Crawler walked in and regurgitated the droplet back up out of its proboscis, creating a cloudy spherical orb of liquid on a transparent piece of plastic. The Crawler retreated to the corner of the box.

Vlad pushed a button, and the droplet was sucked in, down into a tiny tube, disappearing into an array of tiny channels. "Preprocessing," Vlad said. "Separating DNA from drool." A minute later, the droplet reappeared on what looked like a shiny field of silver grass, clearer now. Underneath the grass, the outlines of electronic circuitry were dimly visible.

"Our test sample," Vlad said, gesturing to the nearly perfect orb on the screen. "Droplet is sitting on special computer chip. The surface is array of tiny vertical needles etched in silicon. Each less than one hundred nanometers in diameter. The needles are hydrophobic—water hates them—so droplet floats on surface."

"It looks like it's glowing," Becraft said.

"Fluorescence," Vlad said. "Dye molecules are in droplet that stick to DNA. Make it glow."

Vlad adjusted the microscope, and the image zoomed out; the field of grass became a perfectly square miniature lawn. Next to the lawn was a label—fifteen letters etched in silicon: AAACGACTTACGTAT. Vlad zoomed out farther to reveal an array of square lawns, each labeled by a different set of fifteen letters but always a combination of A,C,T, and G, the letters of the genetic alphabet.

Vlad worked his BlackBerry, and the droplet suddenly flattened, penetrating down into the field of needles. "With simple voltage pulse, I make the water droplet stick itself on needles."

"Vlad the Impaler," Jake said.

Vlad glanced at Becraft. "He thinks he is clever." He hit a key on his BlackBerry. "Okay—up!" The droplet was once again a perfect sphere on top of the needles.

"I don't get it," Becraft said. "What does this have to do with detecting a biopathogen?"

"The droplet is like a tiny test tube," Vlad said. "Each patch tests for different pathogen. I make the droplet sit. . . ." Vlad made the droplet move to the next patch and descend again, impaling itself on the needles. "The needles have oligos bound to it—short strands of single-stranded DNA. Each is a genetic sentence taken from different pathogen. If the DNA in droplet matches the DNA stuck to needles, they bind together. Two single strands of DNA link up to form double helix. If the sequences don't match, they won't." He hit a key, and the droplet popped back up.

The droplet suddenly took off, running along the grassy patches like a crazed mouse in a maze. The watery orb ran to another patch, descended, then popped back up. "We do it over and over, testing for each pathogen," Vlad said as the droplet ran around on the chip, flattening and popping back up at a dizzying pace.

Becraft pointed to a square. "Wait. That spot is glowing."

"DNA found a match there. Its complementary strand. It bound to DNA on square like lover, staying behind when droplet went away."

"And so that square glows."

Vlad nodded. "It tells you the pathogen." Vlad checked the sequence written on the chip next to the glowing patch: CACGT-GACAGAGTTT. "*Hmm.* Human parainfluenza virus."

Becraft stepped back.

Vlad put an arm on his shoulder. "Common cold."

Becraft said, "What was Connor's part in all this?"

Vlad nodded. "This chip works with viruses. They are easy—a virus is nothing but genetic material and a protein shell. A few reagents release DNA or RNA, then we run a few steps of PCR to amplify. But bacteria, fungi, they are different. Their genes are locked up inside nucleus, which is inside membrane, which is inside cell wall."

Jake said, "Connor was developing protocols. Using the Crawlers to collect the samples, slice open the cells, extract the DNA, all the preparatory steps. The gardens of decay were his testing ground. He was teaching Crawlers to conduct every kind of genetic test you might imagine. It was easy for him to adapt his work to this project."

"And provide advice," Vlad said. "Say a topic, he'd tell you everything about it. What it linked to. Fungi, bacteria, viruses. The whole history of pandemics, their use as biological weapons."

Becraft looked to Jake. "I thought you told me Connor didn't work with anything dangerous."

"He doesn't. When you are developing the protocols, you can use anything. Liam worked with whatever benign fungi he happened to be growing in the gardens."

"So I ask you again. He didn't work with any dangerous pathogens?"

"No," Jake said.

Vlad jumped in. "Neither do I. We develop technology on harmless stuff. Cold rhinoviruses. *E. coli.* Nothing that is not in you already."

Becraft looked unsatisfied. "Could the Crawlers be used for something dangerous?"

"Like what?"

"I don't know. Could they be used to *make* a pathogen instead of test for one?"

"No," Vlad said. "You would need more than just Crawlers. You would need an entire lab."

The inspector rubbed his eyes. "So. Let me be clear. A few missing Crawlers by themselves would be completely harmless."

Jake started to answer, but Vlad got there first. "Well. No. Not necessarily."

Becraft stared at the Russian.

Jake knew what was coming. He and Vlad occasionally strayed into this kind of territory in their late-night drinking-and-tale-spinning sessions. Wars fought by insect robot proxies. A disgruntled kid crossing a rhinovirus with smallpox and killing off half the country.

Vlad said, "What if you already *had* pathogen? You could store it inside Crawler. Then you could carry Crawler around in package of Chiclets. Shake it out, it could find its way anywhere. Crawl into a ventilation duct. Slip under a door. The Crawler could even *bite* someone. Inject pathogen into wound. You have a pathogen you want to get out? A Crawler would make *hell* of a vector."

Jake's phone buzzed in his pocket. He fished it out, surprised by the name on the screen.

"Yes?"

"Jake. It's Maggie Connor. Can we talk?"

· 13 ·

TIMES SQUARE WAS A CACOPHONOUS SYMPHONY. ADVERTISE-
ments screamed down from the JumboTrons. The streets were
packed with city buses and yellow cabs. The occasional bike messenger ducked though cracks in the traffic. Pedestrians ran, walked,
shuffled, and backtracked.

Officer James Ostrand loved the place. He had loved it for the
twenty-two years he'd been a cop. He'd watched it evolve from grit
to glamour, from strip joints to the advertising center of the universe. His wife was always after him to move, leave the city, maybe
down to Pennsylvania, where her sister lived, but Ostrand would
never do it. He loved the mix of rich and poor, the debutantes and
the destitute. He loved Times Square. You stand here long enough,
you'd see every kind of person that God ever made.

Unfortunately, that included crazy freaks like this one.

"Jesus Christ, stop squirming!" Ostrand yelled as he struggled
to get the cuffs on the Japanese kid. He'd spotted the guy two minutes ago, shirt half off, running past the TKTS booth at the north
end of the square, screaming his head off about dragons, blood,
and darkness. His right hand was wrapped in gauze, bloodstained
and half unraveled.

The psycho had knocked over a couple of tourists, pushed an

old lady to the side, leaving a trail of mayhem until Ostrand got to him. The guy's eyes were wide, his pupils the size of quarters. He looked to be in his mid-twenties, relatively clean cut, which was a surprise. You get one of these every now and then—someone off their meds or on a bad acid trip. This guy was the latter, he was pretty sure. He had every indication of being blown out of his mind. Not unusual in itself, but this one looked like a business-school kid. It was nearly five p.m. on a Wednesday. Maybe on a Saturday night in the Village, but a Wednesday afternoon?

Ostrand took a closer look at the gauzed hand. The bloodstains were centered at a spot where his middle finger should have been. *Shit.*

"Can you hear me?" Ostrand asked once he had the guy cuffed and sitting up, being careful of his injured hand.

"I am the blood," the guy said, eyes rolling back in his head.

"What is your name?"

"I am the blood. My lady can see in the darkness."

Jesus. Look at that. Ostrand pulled back the unbuttoned oxford shirt. His chest was a mess. Some kind of symbols carved into the flesh.

七三一

鬼子

"Hey, Officer?"

Ostrand ignored the voice behind him, mesmerized. Blood was caked around the edges of the cuts. What did he do this with? A knife? A razor blade?

"Officer?"

"Get back."

"Hey man, I got a picture."

Ostrand turned to face the guy. He was skinny, maybe twenty-five, with a shaved head. A crowd had started to form behind him.

"A picture of what?"

"The woman. The babe that dropped him off."

"Dropped him off? You saw it?"

The kid nodded. "He was in the trunk, man. She just popped the lid, he jumped out, and she took off. Right over there." He pointed.

"What kind of car?"

"I don't know. Red." He held out his phone. "Check it out. It's a good shot."

Ostrand took the phone. It *was* a good shot. Broadside, catching her in profile. Mid-twenties, Asian, pretty face. A gray jacket, green cap on her head.

Ostrand held up the phone to the crowd, a bad feeling rising up his spine. "Anybody else see this woman?"

14

JAKE BROUGHT HIS SUBARU TO A STOP IN FRONT OF MAGGIE
Connor's place. He glanced down at the letter. It was a single sheet
of blank yellow paper, no letterhead, no date, only six handwritten
words. Liam Connor's lawyer had delivered it to him twenty minutes
before. After talking to Maggie, he'd gone to his office and found
the lawyer there, a tall, silver-haired man Jake had never met.

He gave an envelope to Jake. No explanation, just an envelope.
The letter inside was to the point: *Jake, Please watch over them.*
—Liam.

The sun was playing hide-and-seek with the clouds, stippling
the walkway with light and shadow as Jake approached the front
door. He had never been to Rivendell before. Liam had introduced
him to Maggie years ago, and he'd felt an immediate attraction.
They'd seen each other at one function or another, and once or
twice in the lab when she came to see Liam. She was very attractive, that was certain, in the casual, no-makeup-and-old-jeans
Ithaca way. And wicked smart. She'd left her mark on the mycological literature, with a citation record that would be a ticket to a faculty job at most any institution in the country. Liam was forever
going on about her encyclopedic knowledge of everything from
hockey to Hockney. But she'd stepped off the academic fast track,

more interested in making fungus art with her son than winning at the publish-or-perish rat race. Jake respected her for that. He definitely had a thing for her, and he thought she knew it. Yet Maggie was always reserved around him.

About a year ago, one hot day in July, Jake stopped in at Liam's lab after a run, sweating like a river. July 23, he remembered. Maggie and her son Dylan were there, visiting Liam.

Jake also took an instant liking to the boy.

Dylan was a fanatic for the Crawlers, immediately hitting him with question after question. *Why six legs and not eight?* Answer: six was enough; you don't put in more than you need. *How much does each Crawler cost?* The first one? Millions. But if put in full production, a Crawler should set you back no more than a mocha Frappuccino. They'd kept going like this for half an hour, talking shop, until Maggie dragged him away.

By that winter, Jake was spending time with Dylan almost weekly. He showed him the tools of the trade, the scanning electron microscopes and confocal imagers, the micromanipulators and optical tweezers that were a scientist's hands and eyes in the nanoscale world. Dylan soaked it all up. He possessed an intimate grasp of things mechanical that Jake wished more of his students had. Jake also knew of Dylan's troubles. Once, after Jake had left him alone in the lab, the boy had a mini-meltdown. Jake was sympathetic. From the war, he had his own bad dreams. They talked about fears, of getting past them and feeling safe. Jake wasn't half bad at calming the kid down.

Jake also began to piece together a more complete picture of Maggie, from both their brief meetings and his conversations with Dylan and Liam. In addition to her job as the curator of the Cornell Plant Pathology Herbarium, she volunteered for something called Cayuga Dog Rescue. He'd thought seriously about asking her out, but he'd always held back. He told himself it was because she was the granddaughter of Liam Connor. He respected the old man too much to risk a mess. But down deep there was something else.

THE RIVENDELL KITCHEN WAS LARGE AND MESSY, WITH POTS and pans hanging from the ceiling haphazardly and two big old refrigerators flanking the stove. Most notable were the statuettes: funny little creatures, some with pointed ears. A big one carved in wood in the corner, almost four feet tall. Two smaller plastic ones on top of one of the refrigerators. The clock was a little blue man in white gloves, pointing out the time. Jake let his gaze wander over the room. The place was a stark contrast to his Spartan two-bedroom apartment.

She saw him glancing at the statuettes. "Rivendell," she said. "Elf city."

"Got it." He pointed to the clock. "But technically, that one's a Smurf."

Maggie tried to smile.

Jake said, "I'm still in shock. Devastated is a better word. He was . . . he was the most amazing man I've ever known."

"He cared about you a great deal."

"He wouldn't shut up about you."

Dylan emerged from the dark hallway.

"Hey," Jake said. "You okay, big guy?"

"I'm sad."

"Me, too. You'd be crazy if you weren't."

Jake pulled Liam's note from his pocket, handed it to Maggie. "I got this a half-hour ago."

"Who gave you this?" she asked, after taking a look.

"Liam's lawyer."

"Melvin?"

"I don't know. He just used his last name. Lorince."

"He was here, too." Maggie handed Jake her own note. He recognized the stationery and the handwriting, both the same as the note he'd received. Her note said: "Tell Dylan that it's one last trip to the moors. Jake knows the territory. Ask him where the elephants perch."

"Liam put it in with a bunch of legal papers," Maggie said. "To be delivered on his death."

"But why?" Jake asked.

"He's leading us. The *moors* reference—"

"Pop-pop said it all the time," Dylan interjected. "When we were about to go on a letterboxing expedition."

"Letterboxing?"

"It's a kind of treasure hunt," Maggie said. "A combination of hiking and puzzle solving."

Dylan scrunched up his face. "How 'bout a trip to the moors, laddie?" he mimicked, in a surprisingly good rendition of his great-grandfather's intonation. "Letterboxing was invented in the moors of England."

"So Liam was into letterboxing?" Jake asked.

"Pop-pop and I did it together," Dylan said. "It was my idea—I read about it online. But Pop-pop loved it, too."

"He and Dylan went all the time. I tagged along once or twice, but I thought it was better to let the boys have it to themselves."

Jake said, "And I know where an elephant perches."

"Anywhere it wants to," Dylan answered.

Jake smiled. "Why shouldn't you sit under an elephant's perch?"

"Because of the elephant," Dylan said.

Maggie looked to Jake. "What are you two talking about?"

"The elephant's perch. It was something I told Liam. I know where the elephant's perch is."

"Where?"

"The Sawtooth Mountains. Near Stanley, Idaho."

"I don't understand."

"The Elephant's Perch is an eight-pitch rock-climbing route. I almost got killed there. The woman I was dating at the time took me up it. A rope got stuck, a storm came in. The lightning nearly nailed us before we got down. Liam turned it into one of his elephant jokes: 'Where does an elephant perch?' "

"How did Liam know about it?"

"From one of our bull sessions. Talking about brushes with death. First war stories, then outdoor disasters. I told him about Elephant's Perch, he told me about nearly drowning in a box canyon in China."

"What does this have to do with letterboxing?"

"I don't know."

"Dylan? Do you have any—"

But Dylan was gone.

. . .

THEY FOUND HIM IN HIS ROOM, SEATED AT HIS LAPTOP, FIN-
gers flying over the keyboard. Jake watched, the back of his neck
tingling. He was at a site called Letterboxing North America.

Maggie said, "A letterbox is—it's kind of hard to explain. It's
usually a small box of some sort hidden in the woods, with a notebook and a rubber stamp inside."

"There's one on the desk, Mom. Over there. Pop-pop and I
were going to put it out near Lucifer Falls."

It was a cigar box. Inside was an inkpad in a thin snap-shut
metal case, a logbook, and a little wooden block with a rubber
stamp on one surface. Maggie picked up the logbook. "People who
visit the letterbox will make their own personal stamp inside, a
record of their visit, that they found the letterbox."

She took the stamp and inked it, then stamped it on the page.
The image was a spiral.

"That's Liam's letterboxing stamp. That swirl."

"I don't understand."

"Everyone has their own stamp. Liam's is a spiral. Mine's a
mushroom. Dylan's is an arrowhead."

"What's the purpose?"

"Nothing. It's just an adventure, a treasure hunt. You follow
clues to find the letterbox, and stamp the logbook inside the box."

"So you hide these. How do people get the clues?"

Dylan said, "The instructions on how to find letterboxes are on
this site. There are thousands of letterboxes listed."

Jake watched over his shoulder and quickly began to understand. They entries were organized by geography, by state and region, followed by city. Dylan was on the central Idaho list.

"I think Pop-pop might have been playing. That the elephant stuff
was part of the riddle. There are four letterboxes near Stanley, Idaho."

Maggie nodded. "I knew it. I knew he wouldn't leave us without an explanation. I *knew* it."

Dylan clicked on one.

The Spiral   LbNA # 23877

Placed by: FungusAmongUs
Placement date: October 17

State: Idaho
County: Tompkins
Nearest city: Stanley
Number of boxes: 1

"Look who placed it: FungusAmongUs," Maggie said. "Click on the directions."

Dylan clicked on the icon.

LETTERBOX CLUES

The hollow hides a footpath, follow it you must,
to the settler's creek that dances across the land held in trust.

After spotting a ship, veer left and keep going,
to water and up is a tree pregnant and showing.

After making a choice, move up toward the left,
then seek among fallen one whose life's long bereft.

A new kingdom you seek, so continue the fight,
to a marriage of royals, darkness and light.

Can't find them here, this geezer and hag?
Then seek among stones, don't dally or lag.

Though comes the darkness, though the cold winds blow,
This will banish the worst, set the whole world aglow.

"You think Liam wrote this?" Jake asked.

"It sounds like him," Maggie said. "He often wrote his clues as silly poetry. But why would he give us clues to a letterbox in Idaho? He wants us to go to *Idaho*?"

Dylan stared at the screen. "What land in trust?"

"Oh my God," Maggie said. Her eyes were on fire. She reached over her son's shoulder, hit print. An inkjet in the corner sprang to life.

"What?" Jake asked.

"This letterbox isn't in Idaho. It's a couple of miles from here."

. . .

THEY PARKED IN A LITTLE LOT OFF ELLIS HOLLOW CREEK
Road, next to a sign that said FINGER LAKES LAND TRUST PRESERVE.

"Did Liam come here with Dylan a lot?" Jake asked.

"We both did," Maggie said. "Liam's on the board of advisers
of the Finger Lakes Land Trust. And Dylan and I did a couple of
Fungus-Among-Us art projects out here. It's a beautiful area,
mostly forests, gorges, and streams, all owned by the Finger Lakes
Land Trust. Over a hundred acres total. It used to be a hunting
ground for the Cayuga Indians."

The sun was low, the trail cut by long, dark shadows, as they
worked their way through the brush. Maggie read the second pair
of lines: " 'After spotting a ship, veer left and keep going/to water
and up is a tree pregnant and showing.' There's a rotten old rowboat near the trail juncture," she said. "It's about a quarter of a
mile up. Dylan loved to play in it when he was younger."

"He seems to be holding up pretty well."

"He puts up a good front—it's a Connor trait. But Liam's death
has been very hard on him, I can tell. He's hurt, and he's confused.
Just like me." Dylan had fought to come with them, but Maggie
wasn't having any of it. She didn't know what they were going to
find, but she didn't want her son to see it until she knew what it was.

A slight breeze was in the trees, setting off the eerie squeaking
of tree branches rubbing against one another. They half walked,
half ran down the trail. On the way over, Jake had told her about
his conversation with the Cornell police, that people were coming
from Fort Detrick to investigate Liam's death and search his labs.
And about Vlad's comment that a Crawler would make a great vector for a pathogen.

"You think he would've kept any dangerous fungi in his lab?"
Jake asked.

"It's possible. There are thousands of deadly strains. Fungi are
mostly feeders on the dead, but more than a few are willing to
speed up the process and create their own food. There it is," she
said, spying the broken-down rowboat in the shadows on the side
of the trail. Maggie had a flashlight with her, played the beam up
and down the rotting boards. The trail forked, one part continuing
straight, the other dropping off to the left. Maggie veered left, Jake

behind her. A few hundred yards later was a stream. From there, the path went up a small rise, a larger ridge to the left. She stopped and flashed the beam around, the woods swallowing it. She reread the note.

"Pregnant tree?"

"Up there. You see that?" Jake said. "Partway up the hill. There." He took off, running up the rise toward a strange-looking tree, its trunk bent. In profile, the bend looked like a protruding belly.

Maggie was right behind him. "It has to be it. The 'tree pregnant and showing.' " She read the next lines: "then seek among fallen one whose life's long bereft." Just downhill from the pregnant tree was a fallen trunk, well on its way to total decay. She made her way over, palms sweating now. She ran her fingers over the green and brown moss clinging to the exterior of the trunk, tapped on it with her knuckles. It responded with a soft *thunk*.

"It's hollow," she said. She knelt down and aimed the flashlight inside. The core of the trunk was completely gone. Diffuse light filtered partly down the hollow horizontal shaft, but the trunk bent and the deepest reaches were hidden in darkness. She felt her way along the soft, wet, decaying wood.

"Ahh!" she yelped, and whipped her hand out.

"What?"

"Something moved in there."

"What?"

"I think it was a worm or a bug or something." She put her arm back in, shoulder pressed hard against the opening. "Nothing."

Jake read the next lines.

*"A new kingdom you seek, so continue the fight,
to a marriage of royals, darkness and light.*

*Can't find them here, this geezer and hag?
Then seek among stones, don't dally or lag."*

"Wait," she said. "I think I get it now."

"What?"

"How much do you know about the kingdoms of life?"

"There are six, right? Plants, animals, bacteria, fungi. And the other ones."

"Archaea and protists. Now. Look what Liam said. A marriage of royals. Different kingdoms. I think he meant a lichen. A lichen is a symbiote, part fungus and part algae. The fungus gives the algae water and minerals, like a gardener. The algae, in turn, produce food for the fungus by photosynthesis. A symbiotic relationship between different *kingdoms*."

Jake finally got it. "A marriage of royals."

Maggie nodded.

Jake shook his head. "You're telling me Liam wanted you to look for a *lichen*?"

"I think so."

ONCE THEY HAD THE IDEA, IT TOOK LESS THAN FIVE MIN-utes to find it. Maggie squatted before a collection of rocks arranged in a loose pile. She lifted one off the top and showed it to Jake: a mottled, crusty growth on the rocks, like old paint, some patches reddish and the others yellow. Separating them was a twisted pattern of cracks, like dried mud.

"It's two species of crustose lichen," Maggie said. "When they meet, they put out chemicals that repel each other, form a kind of barrier. The black sections are the no-man's-land. They both agree to stay off each other's turf. They're intertwined but two distinct organisms."

She picked up the lichen-covered stones until she found a square metal box below.

She stood, the object cradled in her hands. Jake held the flashlight on it. It was a rusted lunchbox, Scooby-Doo on the outside.

Tears came to her eyes. "I haven't seen this in years."

"It was yours?"

Maggie nodded. "Pop-pop bought it for me when I was maybe six."

Maggie unfastened the latches, her fingers trembling.

Inside was a plastic Baggie containing something hard and disk-shaped. She stood, holding it in her palm gently. She could make out three luminescent smears on the disk, each a different color. "Turn off the flashlight," she said.

"Wow," he said. "It's glowing."

The glowing slowly pulsed, brightening and fading, almost like breathing.

She carefully opened the Baggie. Inside was a round piece of wood. On it were three patches of fuzzy fungal growth, like mold on bread, except that each was glowing a different color, one red, one green, one yellow. Three distinct patterns. A yellow mushroom. A green arrowhead. And a red spider-creature that looked, Maggie realized, like a MicroCrawler.

Maggie understood.

The symbols for her. Dylan.

And Jake.

She looked to Jake. Tears welled up in her eyes.

The three symbols pulsed with life.

Though comes the darkness, though the cold winds blow,
This will banish the worst, set the whole world aglow.

"Jake?"

"I don't understand. The colors."

"Green fluorescent protein. It's a gene extracted from a jellyfish. The red is . . ." She stopped, too choked up to speak. She turned to Jake, then looked back down at the three symbols. Her tears were flowing now, buds of rain sliding down her cheeks.

She looked again at the piece of wood. "Why?" she said, her voice cracking. She started to quiver, as if the pent-up grief was about to burst through her skin. "This is all you left us, Pop-pop? You shove a few genes in a fungus, make it glow? Why?"

"I'm sorry, Maggie."

She looked out at the woods as though Liam was there, waiting. "This is your goodbye? This is it? This is all you have to say?"

15

TISH PAIGE WAS PASSED-OUT TIRED. THE ER HAD BEEN RELA-tively quiet, but she'd been on duty for twelve hours straight. And before that, a marathon clubbing stretch followed by maybe the best sex she'd ever had. A speed-freak boyfriend was proving to be hard on her. If he wasn't so damned cute, she'd toss him out. She'd get off shift, he'd be at her flat, one day naked, the next day dressed to the nines, but always with an agenda that would sweep her away from all the blood and broken needles. Didn't matter the time—she typically dragged in around two a.m.—because as far as she could tell, he never slept. She was beginning to think that was what he saw in her—the odd hours of an ER resident. Someone to be up with him while the rest of the world slept.

"Dr. Paige? We got an odd one."

She pulled herself to her feet, entered the staging area. The patient on the gurney was an Asian male, strapped down at the waist. An intern named Kaster was working him over.

"What is going on with him?"

"We don't know exactly yet. A woman dumped him off in Times Square. Had him in the trunk. He was screaming in the ambulance, so they sedated him. Said it took their entire stock."

Paige looked him over. *Japanese,* she thought. His right hand was bandaged, bloody.

"What's the deal there?"

"Missing his middle finger. Recent. Last forty-eight hours. Someone cut it off, then crudely cauterized it."

She scrunched her nose. A strong odor, like urine, was in the air. "You smell that?"

"Yeah. He stinks. It's coming off him. Like it's in his sweat."

"Vitals?"

"Reasonable, except his temperature. It's low—96.5. Don't know why. We've started standard toxicology tests, but nothing definite yet. I'm betting it's one of the new designer drugs gone bad. Whatever it was, it packed a punch. Look at this."

Intern Kaster pulled open the gown, revealing the strange symbols on the man's chest, some kind of Chinese lettering. What looked like a lowercase *t,* followed by three horizontal dashes, then a single dash.

Kaster pointed. "See the crusts of blood around the wound? Dried. It's been there for a while. You think he carved it himself?"

"No," said Paige. "The cuts are remarkably clean. Someone took some care here. He looks way too messed up to do that. You know what it means?"

"We got Yasuki, the X-ray tech, up here. He said the first part is a number—731. The second line is Mandarin for *Devil.*"

Paige frowned. "You said a woman dropped him off. Maybe some kind of S-and-M thing?"

"If so, count me out."

She started a physical investigation of the man. Young, fit. No needle tracks. None of the loose skin or bruises she normally found on a drug addict, even functioning ones. Paige nervously tapped a fingernail against her front tooth.

She wasn't sure what, but something about all this struck a chord. Especially the number. She looked at Kaster. "Google *731.*"

"Why?"

"Just do it."

She checked his pulse. It was slow, steady. Then the pupils. They were saucers, and completely unresponsive to light. But she couldn't be certain if it was because of what he'd taken or the sedatives the paramedics had loaded him up on. She glanced at Kaster. She was bent over the computer, clicking on the keys. Kaster said, "Oh, wow."

"What?"

"There was something called Unit 731. During World War Two." She went quiet, scanning the screen.

"And?"

"It was some kind of bioweapons research facility. Japanese." She kept reading, her face going slack. "Jesus. Listen to this. They used Chinese civilians as test subjects. Some American and Russian POWs, too. The guy who ran it, Shiro Ishii? They say he was the Japanese equivalent of Josef Mengele."

Paige froze. "They used people as guinea pigs? For biological weapons testing?"

She nodded. "It gets worse. There's a big warning on this page—saying that the pictures on this site are *extremely* graphic. Don't go any further if you are easily upset." Her fingers clicked on the keyboard. "Oh, Jesus."

Paige looked over her shoulder. On the screen was a black-and-white photo of a Japanese doctor next to a metal autopsy table. The man on the table was sliced wide open. "Look at the caption," Kaster said. "The guy was alive when they did this."

"*Live* autopsies? How come I've never heard of this?"

"I don't know. But apparently these guys were working on everything. Anthrax. Black plague. Everything."

"He's moving!" Paige said. He'd gotten the strap off his waist and had lifted himself up on one arm, turning sideways. They grabbed him, and he fell back down on his stomach. In a few seconds, he was limp again. "Come on," Paige ordered, all the weariness gone. "Let's get full blood panels on this guy."

Kaster whistled. "Look at that."

A number was freshly tattooed low on his back, across the lumbar region.

800-232-4636

Paige was in hypervigilance mode now. Every nerve was standing on end.

"What do you suggest we do?" Kaster said.

"Call it."

Kaster picked up the phone on the far wall, punched in the number. A second later, she lowered the phone, looking ashen.

"And?"

"It's the Centers for Disease Control and Prevention."

Paige snapped up straight. "No one leaves. Seal off this room. *Now.*"

16

JAKE AND MAGGIE STOOD ON THE BACK PORCH, LEANING ON the railing and watching the darkness. When they'd returned from Ellis Hollow, Maggie had shown the glowing fungi to her son. Dylan had been solemn, watching the red, green, and yellow fungi slowly pulse and fade. Two months ago, Dylan said, Pop-pop had been telling him about the latest Nobel Prize in chemistry. It was for the use of fluorescent proteins, how the genes for them could be inserted into any organism, and that organism would glow. He'd promised Dylan a demonstration. Apparently, this was it.

Maggie, with an assist from Dylan, had convinced Jake to stay. Her housemates were there, along with two boyfriends: Josephine, Eric, Yvette, Cindy, and Bryan. Yvette and Josephine had dinner going; everyone drank wine from old jelly jars. Jake was completely taken in by the conversation, the mix of warmth and humor, sadness and hope. The quiet but steadfast sympathy they all expressed to Maggie and Dylan. Jake had the strong sense of family, even if no bloodlines were shared. He knew that Maggie's parents were both dead, and her aunt and cousins were not due until the funeral.

Afterward, Jake and Maggie had drifted away from the rest, onto the back porch, winter coats on and holding steaming mugs of tea. They'd swapped stories about Liam for the better part of an hour, missing him more with each one. The last story had been Maggie's, about the time Liam had taken her fungus hunting in Treman State Park, a few miles to the west. "I was six," she said. "Believe it or not, I found a new species. He named it after me."

"Really?"

"*Cordyceps margaretae.* It makes an immunosuppressant that is sometimes used in transplant surgeries. I still get a little in royalties." She laughed. "It was a setup, I'm sure. But he always denied it. Said I was the luckiest little girl he'd ever seen."

The back door opened and Dylan came out, Turtle trailing behind. The two dissolved into the darkness of the yard, barely visible in the spare moonlight. Dylan stopped under the lights at the door to the greenhouse, then cupped his hands together and blew into them. He held his hands out, as if he was ceremoniously letting the breath go. After a few seconds, he dropped his arms and continued on inside the greenhouse.

Maggie saw Jake watching, puzzled.

"The spreading of the breaths," she said.

"What is that?"

"An interesting little fact. How every breath contains every other one."

"I'm not getting it."

"Do you know how many gas molecules are in a breath?"

Jake started working on it. "Let's see. Air is about a thousand times less dense than water. So—"

Maggie smiled. "Wait. I'll tell you. About ten to the twenty-second power. And that's about the same as the number of breaths in the world."

"Okay . . ."

"It means that once Dylan's breath spreads out, when someone, anyone, anywhere in the world takes a breath, it'll have one molecule from that breath Dylan just released."

Jake inspected the idea, looking for threads. "It must work the other way, too? Every breath we take in has a molecule from every breath anyone else ever took?"

She nodded.

"That's disturbing somehow."

"It can be."

"You taught Dylan this?"

"Liam did."

Jake heard a band of geese flying overhead. Heading south. "He was a helluva man, your grandfather. One of the few people in the world I truly looked up to."

She turned to face him. "He really respected you, Jake. He thought you were a very decent man."

"It's an ex-soldier thing. Different armies, different wars, it doesn't matter. There's a bond."

"It was more than that."

Jake didn't know what to say to that. Instead he watched Dylan at work in the greenhouse, a watering can in his hand.

"Can I ask you something?" Maggie said tentatively. "Something I always wondered?"

"Shoot."

"Why did you join the Army?"

"You want the real answer?"

She laughed. "No. Give me the fake one."

"Okay, I will. The fake one is that I needed money for college."

"And the real one?"

"I thought it was the right thing to do."

She took it in, nodding. "That's more or less what Pop-pop said. Why he joined during World War Two. The Irish hated the British, had been under their thumb for eight hundred years. Some people called him a traitor." She glanced at him. "What was it like?"

"The Gulf War? The thing I remember most is the sand. It got in everything, in your hair, in your bed, in the guns, in the food. You got used to the grind of it between your teeth.

"We spent six months in the desert, waiting, in the sand. I was a combat engineer. In the Forty-sixth Battalion. We were in support of the First Infantry Division. We made the bridges. The camps. The roads. We had it best, the engineers. We had something to do. We were always at work, putting up new forward compounds, improving the roads, clearing them after the sandstorms would sweep through. The combat grunts had it worse. They just sat. Waiting to fight. Digging foxholes, the sand filling them, digging them again. It was hell on them, you could tell. They got crazier, weirder."

"How long were you there?"

"Almost six months. It was so damned hot, and as the invasion got close, every couple of days the bioweapons sirens would go off and we'd have to suit up. Everybody was sure Saddam had anthrax weapons, God knows what else. So we'd put on these full-body suits, gas masks, and sweat it out. You wanted to rip the damned thing off and at the same time you worried that some little microbe was going to sneak through a faulty seal and kill you.

"Then, boom, the orders come down. We're on the move, going in, crossing the border into Kuwait. Our orders are to blast forward, destroying everything in our path. But the Iraqis have all these trenches dug, these bunkers of sand pushed up. It was a total pain in the ass. You could blow them up, but there weren't enough bombs to do the whole thing. So the plan was send in the armored bulldozers, create a breach, then we'd send in mechanized units to get in behind them, then attack from the rear.

"But then someone had an idea. Use bulldozers."

Jake looked up. "It was one of those ideas that had a kind of rough elegance. Why the hell not? Who needs to kill them with bullets when you can bury them in sand? All you need is a big shovel. The idea floated up through the chain of command, then came back down again. *Get your bulldozers ready.*"

Jake shook his head. "You know, we engineers, we're one step away. We just built the roads. It's different, building the roads."

"It sounds terrible."

"It was. The Iraqis didn't have a chance in hell. Some saw us coming and ran. Others stayed, just disappeared as the sand swept over them, like a crab on the shore when the tide pushed in. The worst were the ones halfway between. They'd finally get what was about to happen, and they'd pop up, maybe thirty yards in front of the blade. But it was too late. Our orders were clear. Keep plowing.

"One guy I'll always remember. He charged me. He couldn't have been more than fifteen years old. He had this stupid sidearm, he was running at the bulldozer, firing into the blade. He wasn't even trying to hit me. He just kept firing into the blade. He was screaming. You couldn't hear it, not for the engines, all the other crazy shit happening, but he was screaming, yelling, charging. Then he went under, like all the rest. He was gone." Jake shook his head. "Can we talk about something else?"

"Sorry. Of course."

But they didn't talk about anything. They just watched the night, listened to the bits of conversation drifting in from the kitchen.

Out in the darkness, the slap of a closing door. Dylan emerged from the greenhouse, Turtle at his side. Jake watched closely as the boy crossed the distance to the house. "How are the tomatoes doing?" Maggie asked as he stepped up on the porch.

"Almost ready. I think I can pick them pretty soon."

She pulled him close, kissed him on the forehead. "Good. Now go get ready for bed."

Dylan turned to face Jake. He held out a hand. "Good night."

The two shook formally. Dylan ducked his head and disappeared inside. Maggie watched her son go, took a breath, and looked gratefully at Jake before glancing away, suddenly embarrassed.

Jake smiled. "A question for you."

"Shoot."

"The spreading-of-the-breaths thing. How long does it take for the gas molecules all around the world to mix? How long until a breath makes it to, say, China?"

"Ten years. It takes about a decade for the air on the planet to get stirred completely." She looked down at the deck, put her arms around herself. "So right now, Liam's last breath is still mostly right here. Right around us."

Jake nodded. "But less so with each day."

They were silent after that, watching the darkness. Jake glanced over, catching her in profile, the slight subtle motion of her hair in the breeze. When someone died, all the relationships surrounding that person were shaken, had to be rebuilt in new ways to help fill the void. That's what grief helped you do.

He wanted contact, to feel the warmth of her. He leaned toward her, and their shoulders touched. She kept looking at the woods, but he felt her body relax. On the railing, he placed his hand over hers, let it rest there. "You know," he said, "it's not just Dylan."

"I know. But listen—"

Jake's cell went off in his pocket. "Sorry," he said.

She pulled her hand in. "It's fine. Go ahead. Take it."

He fished it out, and his pulse jumped a notch. "It's Becraft," he said to Maggie. He accepted the call. "Yes?"

"Professor Sterling? We need you to come down. Right away. It's about the missing MicroCrawlers."

"Did you find them?"

"Some of them, yes. The Onondaga medical examiner's office just called." Becraft paused. "Look. I'd prefer it if you came down."

Jake looked to Maggie. "Tell me where you found them."

"We just got Liam Connor's autopsy report. They found four in his stomach."

· 17 ·

LAWRENCE DUNNE MADE HIS PLAY. CHOOSING ONE OF THE small black stones from the wooden bowl, he placed it with a sharp click onto the Go board. He tried to project authority, but it was a desperation move.

His opponent bit her lower lip, studying the pattern of stones arrayed in a gridlike pattern on the board. They were alone in a Motel 6, the yellow walls adorned with paintings of ducks and dogs. She was naked, sitting cross-legged on the bed. He sat across from her, as naked as she.

She clicked her piece down, smooth and white.

"Shit," Dunne said.

Her wide smile lit up the generic room. "You're mine." She dove for him, knocking him backward onto the bed, scattering the stones.

Dunne wrestled her onto her back, enjoying the view. He allowed himself two indulgences, games he enjoyed whether he won or lost. The first was Go, the second this woman. Her name was Audrey Candor, née Pister. They'd met at Yale ten years ago, when she was an undergraduate student sitting in on his course on game theory and geopolitics. She was from Long Island, her father a Wall Street financier and her mother a minor movie star in the eighties.

Audrey was married to the son of a rich diplomat from France, but Dunne and she had kept up their trysts over the years. She was smart, devilish, and unbelievably gorgeous. Dunne wasn't an unattractive guy—he had a rakish charm—but she was in another category altogether.

He bent over her, staring down at smooth white skin and coal-black eyes. She wore a pale red lipstick, the kind he liked. Picking one of his black stones off the mattress, he balanced it on her nipple. She giggled.

"Run away with me," he said. "We'll crash a plane into a small Pacific island, live off fruit and berries. I'll rig snares to trap wild boar."

She laughed. "You'd better crash into an island with a Whole Foods."

"You underestimate me. I can be a beast."

"Show, don't tell," she ordered, pulling him down.

An unwelcome knock on the door.

"*What?*"

"Mr. Dunne? You don't seem to be answering your cell. There's a call from your assistant."

"Get lost," he said. His ringer had been very purposefully turned off. "I'll be free in twenty."

"Sir? He said Lancer absolutely needs to talk to you."

"Holy Christ," Dunne said, thoughts of the deserted Pacific isle long forgotten.

OUT FRONT A BLACK LIMO IDLED, TWO SECRET SERVICE AGENTS at the ready. Three minutes later, Dunne was on the vehicle's secure line with the President of the United States.

"Lawrence?"

"Yes, Mr. President?"

"You need to get to Manhattan. Now."

DUNNE WAS EDGY AS HE RODE IN THE SPEEDING LIMO, THE police escort's horns blaring as they headed for Reagan National Airport. The President had sounded rattled, his trademark confidence shaken. The two men knew each other well. When the POTUS had started his improbable run at the White House, Dunne had been one of his earliest supporters and his primary foreign-policy adviser on Asian affairs. When he'd won in a landslide that surprised even his dedicated supporters, the President had rewarded Dunne with the position of deputy national security adviser. He'd offered Dunne the national security adviser job, but Dunne preferred to stay out of the media spotlight, where he could focus on policy rather than polish.

Now Dunne was on the phone with the deputy director of the FBI, William Carlisle, who described the situation with the Times Square victim: "Twenty-three years old, Japanese. Recently had his middle right finger chopped off, the wound crudely cauterized. He was incoherent, raving, clearly under the influence of a hallucinogenic, as yet unidentified."

"What do we know about him?"

Carlisle sounded as though he was reading. "Undergrad at Columbia, art major. Specializes in sculpture, small pieces made from bits of wire. Originally from Tokyo. Nothing else in his background is unusual. Father is a low-level diplomat at the Japanese embassy in Ottawa, mother a poet. A team's interviewing them now. So far nothing remarkable about him, save one thing. You ready? The kid's name is Hitoshi Kitano."

For a second, Dunne thought he hadn't heard right. He thought of the eighty-five-year-old man with the same name rotting in jail. "*Hitoshi Kitano?* You gotta be kidding me."

"Nope."

He still couldn't believe it. For reasons unknown to Carlisle, Dunne had hoped the name Hitoshi Kitano would be forever relegated to the roll at Hazelton prison. He cleared his throat. "Any relation?"

"None. Nothing that we can find. There's no connection. It's either coincidence or—"

"Or it's a goddamn message."

· 18 ·

JAKE UNLOCKED THE DOOR TO HIS APARTMENT AND STEPPED into the darkness. He stood in the entryway for a moment, listening. The steam pipes of the old building clanked. The compressor on his refrigerator turned on with a click and a hum. Everything was just as it always was. Except that it wasn't.

The autopsy report was clear: Liam Connor had been tortured. His tongue had been glued to the bottom of his mouth. Fibers consistent with a straitjacket were on his shirt. And they'd found four MicroCrawlers in his stomach, along with thousands of tiny rips to the tissues, a lot of internal bleeding. The pathologist said that Liam would probably have died from the internal bleeding, had he not jumped.

This was now a whole other kind of nightmare. The FBI was taking over, the search for the woman on the bridge going national. They were even going to put out an APB on the nine Crawlers still unaccounted for. Finding them was no longer the job of a couple of graduate students and campus police but of the entire law-enforcement apparatus of the country. The FBI was worried that the Crawlers might be a part of a larger plan, might be used as a vector for a biological attack. Becraft had also talked to the man at

Fort Detrick, General Arvenick. He said they'd be sending more people in the morning.

He and Maggie had barely talked on the drive back from the police. She was too upset. She was crying most of the time. "Who would do that?" she'd kept saying. "Torture a sweet old man?"

It killed Jake to see her so upset. He could barely stand it.

Rivendell had been dark when they'd pulled up the long gravel driveway. Jake had walked her to the door. "Maggie, I'm going to stay here tonight."

"No. I'll be all right. I need some time alone. To think about what I'm going to say to Dylan."

"I can sleep out here in the car. Keep watch."

She forced a smile. "Jake. Thank you. You've done a great deal already. There's a police car at the head of the road. I'll be all right. Go home."

"You sure you don't want me to—"

She gave him a kiss on the cheek. "Go home. We'll talk in the morning."

JAKE TURNED ON THE TV, WENT TO CNN TO SEE IF THEY'D picked up on any of this yet. He found nothing but a weather report—it was snowing farther north.

He went to the bedroom, flicking on lights as he went. He pulled the sheet of paper from his pocket, the one Liam had left for him. "Jake, Please watch after them. —Liam."

Jake could see it now, in hindsight. Liam had been gently pushing Jake and Dylan together since at least the summer. He would bring Dylan over to Jake's labs, leave the two of them alone together. He was setting Jake up to step in.

"Please watch after them." What the hell does that mean? Look after them? Protect them? From what? Did he know someone was after him? And if so, why didn't he tell someone?

Jake went to his closet and pulled out something he hadn't touched in a couple of years. His soldier's pack. He dragged it out. It left a trail of sand. You could never get the sand out of things. It was everywhere.

What Jake hated most was its mutability. You dig a foxhole,

the walls would cave in. The wind comes up, the sand comes in, pulling down and down on you. Jake had read a book once, two years after the war, that had caught it right. *The Woman in the Dunes,* by the Japanese author Kōbō Abe. Jake had dreams of the sand walls coming down, burying him. You dig and dig, and every day the sand is still there. That's what Jake felt like. Like he was being buried.

A crazy idea was forming, taking slow shape in Jake's mind. He kept thinking about what Liam had told him, the superweapon the Japanese had developed. The sinking of the ship in the Pacific, all those soldiers killed. It was conceivable that all this—Liam's death, the stolen Crawlers—was connected to the secrets that Liam had told him, his stories about the Uzumaki. Liam had sworn Jake to secrecy, said it was still classified, one of the last great secrets of that long-ago war. At the time, Jake had thought that Liam was just an old man unburdening himself. But was there more to it? Did the woman torture Liam to find out what he knew?

MAGGIE COULDN'T SLEEP, EVEN THOUGH THE HOUSE WAS pin-drop quiet. It had taken her an hour before she settled down enough to even think straight. She kept being assaulted by images of her grandfather in pain. Her grandfather writhing in agony. Her grandfather screaming . . .

Why had she sent Jake away? The feelings he aroused disturbed her, kept her off-balance. He was great with Dylan, but still she was nervous around him. She needed to keep her distance. She hoped she'd be strong enough.

She tried to calm herself, tried to think it through. On the table before her was the folder Mel Lorince had left. Beside it were the directions to the letterbox. And next to that the disk with the glowing, pulsing fungus shapes: the mushroom, the arrowhead, and the Crawler.

He hadn't committed suicide, she knew that for sure now. He had jumped, but it was to get away from the woman. At least that made sense. Horrifying as it was, at least that *made sense*. But what about the letterbox, the glowing fungi—what were they about? It couldn't be a coincidence that he had left this trail for them to follow right before he died. They must have missed something. Liam had left something else behind for them to find.

But what? She went back through the materials in the envelope that Liam's lawyer had left. Nothing unusual besides the note about the letterbox. *Then what? Logic, Ms. Connor. Think it through.* If Liam had left them something else, reason said it would have been something at the end of the trail they'd already followed.

The end of the trail was the piece of wood with the glowing fungi.

She held the piece of wood up to the light. Her grandfather had drilled holes in the side of the piece and inserted three glass lyophil straws, each containing cultures of the fungus in case the stuff on the outside died. That was odd, now that she thought about it. Why was he so interested in making sure she had a living batch of the fungus?

The three symbols glowed, pulsing. She studied them closely, looking for watermarks, secret writing, she didn't know what. He must have worked very hard to get them to turn on and off like that. It was a biological feedback loop, she knew. Express the green fluorescent protein pathway from the *Aequorea victoria* jellyfish, then have that expression induce the creation of a suppressor that would turn it off. Similar for the red and yellow fungi, using different proteins. Liam had played these games before. He was a master at genetic modification.

She stared at the green arrowhead. Her son's letterboxing symbol. It pulsed, one long, one short. The pattern was irregular. Something must have gone wrong in Liam's genetic circuit.

No. Not irregular. A pattern.

A repeating pattern.

A memory came to her, when she was a little girl. She and Liam played a game called telegraph. They tapped out messages using Morse code. She'd played the same game with Dylan, teaching him to spell out his name.

The red. A long pulse, then two shorter.

The green one. A long pulse, then short.

The yellow. A short pulse, followed by a longer one.

Oh my God.

The Morse code symbols were all letters in Dylan's name—was that it? Then the series of dots and dashes became clear to her:

```
—  • •    = D
—  •      = N
•  —      = A
```

She picked up Liam's fungus disk. *DNA.* The idea hit her like a lightning bolt. She grabbed the instructions:

> *The hollow hides a footpath, follow it you must,*
> *to the settler's creek that dances across the land held in trust.*

The first letter of each line throughout the entire message was an A, C, or T. Written altogether, they spelled out: TTATATATCT. The last letters were all G's and T's: TTGGTTTTGG.

The first and last letters spelled out two short genetic sequences.

Primers. They were primers. The beginning and end of a genetic string.

She stared at the glowing fungi, her skin electric. She was as certain as she'd ever been of anything. Liam had hidden his message inside the fungus. He had written it into its genome.

JAKE WOKE ON THE COUCH, FULLY DRESSED, HIS CELL RINGing. His sleep had been black, devoid of dreams. He fished the phone from the coffee table. It was six-thirty a.m. He didn't recognize the number, but the area code was 202—Washington, D.C.

"Yes?"

A woman's voice was on the line. "Professor Sterling? Can you hold? The deputy national security adviser will be with you in a moment." Then she was off the line.

Lawrence Dunne?

Dunne was a foreign-policy wunderkind, one of the few to predict both the spectacular fall of the Soviet Union and the equally spectacular rise of China. Jake had met Dunne once, at a Defense Science Board reception, before Dunne was promoted to deputy national security adviser. Dunne knew how to work a room, had struck Jake as fiercely intelligent, but that didn't mean Jake liked him. He didn't. Jake's general experience was that those on the civilian side of the national security establishment were dangerously untempered, playing games with knives when they had never been cut. Dunne was no exception.

"Professor Sterling?"

"I'm here."

"Lawrence Dunne. I've a lot on my plate right now, so I'm going to get right to it. You worked closely with Liam Connor, correct?"

"Yes."

"Did he ever mention a man named Hitoshi Kitano?"

"The billionaire? No. Why?"

Silence. "We need you to come in. To Fort Detrick. Right away."

"Why?"

"I've no time for explanations right now. One of our staff will call and arrange transport."

"All right. But what is this—"

"Professor Sterling. I must go, but I personally wanted to stress something to you. At this point, any conversation you may have had with Liam Connor is classified information and should only be discussed with someone in an official capacity. Do you understand?"

Jake heard a knocking at his door.

He started toward it, phone still to his ear.

"No, I'm not entirely sure that I do. Why do you—"

Dunne said, "Please, Professor. Save the talk for later, when we meet."

The phone went dead.

Jake opened the door.

Maggie was there, the glowing fungus and the letterbox instructions in her hands. She looked exhausted, cold, and scared.

"I need your help," she said.

DAY 4

■ THURSDAY, OCTOBER 28 ■

KITANO

19

LAWRENCE DUNNE NODDED TO THE NYPD OFFICER ON THE
line as he passed, flanked by his Secret Service detail and a small
cluster of aides. The police had set up a multiblock perimeter
around Bellevue Hospital, east to west from Second Avenue to the
East River and north and south from Twenty-fifth to Thirtieth
streets. He checked the time on his BlackBerry: six-forty-nine a.m.
The first morning sunlight was just starting to hit the upper floors
of the Midtown skyscrapers. Dunne had just arrived from City
Hall. The mayor, his staff, and the Office of Emergency Management were doing their best to keep the panic under control and set
contingency plans in the event of the worst. Dunne had gotten
away as soon as he could.

He'd made the call to Sterling on the trip over. On Dunne's rec-
ommendation, the FBI had kept tabs on Connor after their confrontation two years previously, checking to see if the old man was
talking out of school about the Uzumaki. They found no evidence,
but the profilers said one of the most likely conduits would be Jake
Sterling. They'd get the truth later, he thought, once Sterling was at
Detrick. Now if they could just find the other likely conduit, Maggie Connor.

A tighter, tougher cordon awaited him a block in, this one controlled by the Army. The spotlights had everything lit up like noon. The Chemical Biological Incident Response Force (CBIRF) worked it by the book, sealed off the ward, made it airtight, and then placed the entire hospital under quarantine. Operational procedures were in place to handle an Uzumaki outbreak, thanks in large part to Dunne. Before he'd taken his position at the NSC six years before, the government had taken a hands-off approach to the Uzumaki. The fungus had been locked up, the spores sealed away in 1972 after Nixon renounced the offensive use of biological weapons. In 1979, Jimmy Carter put it further out of sight, in the hands of that woman Latterell, buried in the chain of command of the USDA, an agency with no military mission. The spores were kept in a sealed, cooled vault for the next twenty years.

After persistent lobbying by Dunne and a few key bioweapons experts and political heavyweights, the seals on the vault had been broken, the Uzumaki brought back to life. It was cultivated, its DNA sequenced, all in the first class-4 facility that the USDA weed people ever had. Upon hearing of this, Connor had been furious. He showed up in Dunne's office, literally screamed at him, said that a countermeasures program was a Pandora's box. If the Chinese caught wind, they would be furious beyond belief. The Uzumaki could, Connor said, set off a biological arms race between the two nations, potentially more paranoia-inducing, dangerous, and ultimately destructive than the nuclear arms race with the Soviets decades before.

But Connor was wrong. China could never be trusted; of this Dunne was sure. The case for a crash countermeasures program was a slam dunk. Two of the original seven Japanese subs carrying the Uzumaki cylinders were never found. One was believed to be sunk in deep water somewhere between Hawaii and California, unrecoverable, but the last one was a giant question mark. And who knew what the Chinese might have dug up at Unit 731? All it took was one hardy little spore. Growing a fungus wasn't like enriching uranium: no high-tech centrifuges needed, no yellowcake imports, no production facilities to show up on satellite photos. The Chinese could have the Uzumaki, and the United States would never know. Not until it was used. Until the Chinese handed it to the North Koreans, the North Koreans sold it to al-Qaeda, and al-Qaeda released it in a major U.S. city.

The most devastating terrorist attack in human history.

. . .

THE HUEY'S BLADES WHERE CHURNING TO LIFE AS DUNNE approached alone, ordering his retinue to stay behind. The makeshift helipad was set up in the middle of the FDR Drive, the chopper fueled and ready to take off for Fort Detrick. The airspace had been cleared within fifty miles of their flight path, and fighters scrambled to escort them.

Dunne spotted Sadie Toloff, the chief scientist of the USDA's Foreign Disease–Weed Science Research Unit and the leader of Fort Detrick's Uzumaki countermeasures program. Dunne knew Sadie very well. She was attractive, with short blond hair in a pageboy cut, though her features were a bit too quirky to be considered classically beautiful. She was wiry, almost nerdy, but very fit—she was a middle-distance runner in college. She completed her Ph.D. twenty years ago, on host-pathogen coevolution in cereal crops. He had known her for years, had personally approved her latest promotion, had even been her lover for a brief stretch four years ago. A mistake, they both agreed. Each was incapable of fealty to anything but the job. When a few spores from a citrus blight blew across the Atlantic on the African winds, Toloff and her team were the first responders. She was also known within a small, elite circle as Queen of the Uzumaki.

Yelling to be heard over the noise of the rotors, Toloff kept it all business. "That's a triple-sealed Hazmat container with blood, saliva, and stool samples from the Times Square victim, along with breath samples for airborne spores. The individual containers are locked inside a steel-molybdenum vault that can withstand anything short of a nuclear blast. If the chopper goes down, that container will not, under any conceivable circumstances, breach."

Toloff pointed to the team of four men handling the container. "Those two are from USAMRIID and the other two from my team at USDA." She frowned. "They think us weed folks are pansies. Can't stand that this is my show."

Dunne nodded. USAMRIID dealt with the high-profile killers, human pathogens, such as smallpox and Ebola. The USDA team handled invasive pathogens. It wasn't often the two organizations worked together closely, but the Uzumaki had something for everyone. "So far no fistfights?" Dunne asked.

"You wait," she said. "Blood will flow."

"You look beat," Dunne said.

"I'm fine. But I'll be better once we're back at Detrick." She rubbed her forehead with her palm. "What is happening, Lawrence? Some psycho woman kills Connor, then loads a Japanese kid up with what looks to hell like the Uzumaki and dumps him in Times Square? Where could she have gotten it?"

"No idea. We don't know who she is yet. Could be the Chinese are backing her, or she could be an independent operator."

"But why kill Connor?"

"Connor knew a lot about Uzumaki. Maybe she tortured him for information—how it could be used, what countermeasures we had."

Toloff shook her head. "This is such a clusterfuck. Has anyone talked to Connor's granddaughter?"

"You know her?"

"The fungus world is tiny, Lawrence. We all know each other."

"Well, we haven't located her yet. She left her house this morning, and no one has seen her since."

The pilot came over. "Sirs? We leave in two."

Dunne looked at the copter, the blades spinning up. He needed a chance to think. Away from the conference calls, the briefings. "How long's the flight?"

"Maybe an hour and a half. You looking for a ride?"

20

JAKE DROVE FAST AS THEY SKIRTED THE MAIN CORNELL CAMPUS, the snow-laced streets and sidewalks eerily empty, the entrances blocked off by local police. It was eight-twelve a.m.—the first classes of the morning should be under way.

He continued on, going east on Route 366, past the Cornell orchards and their rows of apple trees. The fields were decorated in frost, the plants glistening white in the car's headlights. It was arresting, the pastoral normalcy, as if this morning was like any other.

Maggie was in the seat beside him, the glowing fungus in her lap. She was all business, focused and determined, but also distant, as if a wall had gone up around her.

Vlad Glazman was in the back, the last bite of a jelly doughnut forgotten in his right hand. He preferred to ride in the backseat, for reasons he couldn't or wouldn't say. Jake had practically dragged him from his bed ten minutes earlier, filled a Mason jar with the lukewarm coffee he found on the stove, and grabbed the jelly doughnut from the fridge. Vlad, to put it mildly, was not a morning person, unable to function without a massive dose of caffeine and sugar. He refused to teach any morning classes. He considered it a sin to be up before eleven.

Jake waited until Vlad was tanked up, his neurons firing. Then he told him everything.

Vlad didn't respond for what seemed like forever. Finally he sucked down the last of the coffee and leaned forward from the backseat. "Let me get this correct. Connor told you about a Japanese superweapon called—"

"The Uzumaki."

"Right. Carried by seven Japanese soldiers. In little brass cylinders. A fungus that could end the world."

"You got it."

"Then Dunne calls you personally—about the Uzumaki, you are certain. But you didn't mention to him about *other* fungus, the glowing fungus. The one you found under a pile of rocks."

"That's right."

"*That* fungus that *might* have a secret message in its genome." Vlad licked the last of the jelly off his fingers. "This is crazy. Like the clocks with little birds."

"Vlad, come on. This woman tortured Liam to find out what he knew—"

"I know, I know. But he jumped first." Vlad rubbed his temples with his palms. "You believe this?" Vlad asked. "*Really* believe it?"

"Yes."

He took a deep breath, nodded slowly. "Then I suppose I believe it, too."

DECIDING TO PULL VLAD INTO THIS MESS WAS NO EASY choice, but Jake and Maggie needed someone with access to a genetics lab. With the campus closed, they couldn't get to the Cornell BioResource Center, the genetic sequencing facility that Maggie normally used. But Jake remembered that Vlad had a friend that ran a backyard genetics lab.

From the backseat, Vlad said, "My friend at DTRA—who said Dunne and Connor fought? He heard rumors about secret bioweapons project run out of USAMRIID and the USDA. Very tightly held. Now it makes sense. Maybe this is what Connor was so angry about. Must be some sort of countermeasures program."

"Why would Liam be so upset about that?" Maggie asked.

"That is obvious," Vlad said. "The principle of defensive asymmetry. Connor's law, as invented by your grandfather in the fifties: you create a cure, you create a weapon."

"I still don't get it."

"During the Vietnam War, we—meaning, the U.S. military—considered the covert use of smallpox on the North Vietnamese in Laos. Why? The Americans were vaccinated, the North Vietnamese were not. Smallpox was a viable weapon because we had the cure and the Vietnamese did not."

Jake said, "Same with the Uzumaki. When the Japanese had it, before there was penicillin in Japan, they were safe. The Americans were not. But later, when the entire world used penicillin, everyone was vulnerable and the Uzumaki was no longer a weapon."

"Correct," Vlad said. "But if our scientists come up with a cure at Detrick—"

"Connor's law," Jake said. "It's a weapon again. But this time a weapon controlled by us. As long as we are the only country with the cure."

"Correct. Locked and loaded."

Maggie shook her head. "This is insane. You really think Liam was worried about the U.S. using a biological weapon?"

"Absolutely," Vlad said. "Connor saw it all, from the fifties to now. Not just Vietnam. One of plans for the invasion of Cuba called for a botulinum biological attack. At the time, chairman of the Joint Chiefs—Lyman Lemnitzer—argued like a madman for it. There were plans to get Castro with toxic fungus in his wet suit. We had a hundred operational scenarios."

"But that was decades ago," Maggie said.

"The world repeats. Strong becomes weak. Weak becomes strong. When scared, you do what you have to."

"But who is strong enough to scare *us*?"

"If you are Lawrence Dunne?" Jake said. "China. Dunne is a right-wing nut. His entire reputation is based on the Chinese threat. He's convinced half the current administration that the Chinese will surpass us militarily by 2015."

Maggie sat back, frowning. "But even if Liam knew all about the Uzumaki, he was opposed to Dunne's scheme. It doesn't tell us why that woman tortured him. What good would that knowledge do *her*?"

"Maybe she works for the Guoanbu—Chinese security," Vlad said. "They'd have no trouble believing the U.S. is developing a biological first-strike capability."

"But we're the good guys," Maggie said, "aren't we?"

Vlad grimly smiled. "We are supposed to be. Not everyone is."

Maggie took a right turn and pulled into the parking lot of the Cornell Plant Pathology Herbarium.

"My home away from home," Maggie said. "We used to be on the main campus, in the Plant Science Building, but we got pushed out. Hardly anybody cares about physical specimens anymore. It's all about genomics."

Jake got out and scanned the area as Maggie unlocked the front door. The building was set along a gravel road, surrounded by fields on three sides and woods behind. The isolation made him nervous. The soldier in him said that this would be a hell of a place to launch an ambush.

Vlad rolled out of the backseat. He lifted the cuff of his left pants leg and pulled out a snub-nosed pistol. "I'll wait out here," he said. "Put an eye out."

THE RECEPTION AREA WAS BRIGHT AND FRIENDLY, WITH chairs and couches for visitors.

"Through here," Maggie said, leading Jake to a door at the back. It opened into a large space, maybe forty feet wide and a hundred deep, filled with rows of dull brown metal cabinets. The place had a cold, industrial feel, with concrete floors and an odd smell.

"Homey," Jake said.

"It wasn't designed for this," Maggie said. "They used to raise raptors in here. Last year, workmen came in and cleared out the cages, sandblasted the floors, and moved us in." She knocked her knuckles against one of the cabinets, the sound echoing in the large space. "Each one of these contains thousands of fungal specimens, categorized by type. We've got over four hundred thousand overall."

"A fungal mausoleum," Jake said.

"That's one way to see it, I suppose."

Maggie led the way to a small lab equipped with microscopes

and equipment for sample preparation and inspection. On a piece of white filter paper, she scraped off a few flecks of the luminescent fungus.

"You know how this goes? Do any molecular biology yourself?"

"Not really. I'm a silicon man."

"It's pretty straightforward. This is a commercial kit for extracting DNA. First I grind the fungus up in some buffer," she said, using a mortar and pestle, "to break down the cells. Then I treat it with a series of chemicals that will strip off the proteins and release the DNA.

"We're going fishing for what we call the GOM, or genetic owner's manual, of the fungus," Maggie said. "It's an artificial stretch of DNA inserted into the genome. Liam always used GOMs when he tinkered with an organism—to tell you what genetic modifications were made, what they might do, and who made them. If you are going to mess with the molecular programming of an organism—"

"—you better be willing to sign your work," Jake finished.

"So he told you about GOMs."

"Only the basics."

"Well, here's the advanced course. All you need to recover the information are the short genetic sequences at the beginning and the end of the GOM, called primers. Which Liam hid in the letterbox instructions, the first and last letters. Once you have those, it's easy," she said. "Even a physicist could do it."

Jake watched as she worked her way steadily through the extraction process. Her movements were spare and precise, nothing wasted. Jake got a strange feeling watching her, a kind of echo. Liam had worked exactly the same way.

"I've been thinking," she said. "This Uzumaki fungus that the Japanese weaponized. It had to come from somewhere."

"Meaning?"

"The Japanese didn't just whip it up from scratch. They must've found it somewhere."

"Maybe it was regional?" Jake said. "Endemic to Japan."

"Not likely. Hosts and parasites evolve together. Liam said this was a corn fungus, correct? So if you want to find a corn fungus, you go to where corn came from—Mexico, South America. Now, here's something interesting. My grandfather spent a lot of time in those areas. He was studying whether fungal spores could be spread by bird or butterfly migration—for example, monarchs fly thousands of miles from the U.S. to as far south as Mexico every year. But he never published anything on this. It always struck me as quixotic, all those trips. But maybe he was looking for something he wasn't telling me about, something related to the Uzumaki."

"So if he found something, you think he might have left the information about what it was encoded in the DNA here."

"It's possible." Maggie held up a small microcentrifuge tube full of transparent liquid. "Done," she said. "Ready for sequencing."

MOMENTS LATER, THEY WERE BACK OUTSIDE. VLAD WAS WAITing by the car, gun in hand. "Anything?" Jake asked.

"A pheasant attacked, but I fought him off."

Maggie handed Jake the tube with the DNA. "You two go. You don't need me. I'm staying here."

"What? Why?"

"I want to check the USDA APHIS alerts, to see if anything matches the description of the Uzumaki. If they're worried about a pathogen, they'll put out a notice. I also have all of Liam's field notebooks in the back of the herbarium, the notes he took on his trips. I want to check the ones that cover his trips to South America. Especially Brazil."

"I'm not leaving you here alone," Jake said.

"The woman who hurt Liam is long gone. New York City, Bellevue."

"I don't care. You're not—"

"Stay with me if you want. Help me look. Vlad can take the DNA."

Vlad shook his head. "*Nyet.* I don't drive."

Jake said, "He can barely take riding in a car. Won't go near a plane. Come with us."

"Jake, this place is like a fortress. There are only two doors, and they're both steel-reinforced."

Jake didn't like it, but he could see Liam in her eyes, that unwavering determination. If Jake wasn't willing to throw her bodily into the car and sit on her the whole ride, he was going to lose this one.

"Give her your gun," Jake said.

Vlad handed his pistol to Maggie.

"Are you kidding? I've never fired a gun in my life."

"Don't worry," Vlad said. "It is like camera. Just point and shoot."

21

THE HELICOPTER CARRYING THE POTENTIALLY CATASTROPHIC payload flew at three thousand feet over the outskirts of Frederick, Maryland. Through the Huey's window, Dunne watched the rows of houses and crisscrossing streets jammed with morning traffic pass underneath them. He checked his watch: eight a.m.—rush hour. Dunne couldn't help think about the madness of Fort Detrick's location. Ground zero for biowarfare—the place that kept the most dangerous agents ever devised by man or nature—should be off the map, housed somewhere in the desert or the badlands of South Dakota. Instead it was in the middle of the second-largest city in Maryland, a mere fifty miles from Washington, D.C. If the Uzumaki got out, Detrick would be the command center for the fight to stop it.

The Huey banked as they crossed the north entrance guard shack. Dunne watched the Eight Ball, the four-story steel globe used during the fifties and sixties to test the efficacy of bioweapon dispersion and aerosolization, pass beneath them. Since the forties, Detrick had been the focal point for U.S. chemical and biological weapons efforts, but had fallen on hard times after biological weapons were banned in 1972. Now she was in the middle of a new growth spurt, due in no small part to his efforts. The one-two punch of September 11 and the anthrax attacks had put bioterrorism back at the center of the national security agenda. Buildings were going up as fast as they could be slapped together on the twelve-hundred-acre site, creating the largest concentration of class-3 and class-4 biohazard facilities in the United States. This included Toloff's dedicated and highly secret facility for Uzumaki research and countermeasure development.

Toloff was up front, making arrangements with the ground crews for their arrival. The copilot unstrapped himself and came back to Dunne's seat. He knelt next to Dunne, yelling to be heard over the noise of the rotors. "Sir, I've been told to deliver you a message from the national security adviser's office. I quote: 'Get your ass to the White House.' "

Dunne couldn't help smiling. His superior, National Security Adviser Marvin Alex, was an old Washington hand who'd done stints at State and Defense for both Republican and Democratic administrations. His salty language was SOP.

"Should I send a response, sir?"

"Tell him I'll be there to help him hold hands inside of two hours."

Dunne had already triggered the U protocol, a series of escalating steps to be followed in case of a potential Uzumaki outbreak. They were at level 2 until the Uzumaki infection in the Japanese kid could be verified. At level 2, the CDC, USAMRIID, and all the various alphabet soup of federal agencies quietly started procedures to ready themselves for full-blown response, like a giant beast awakening for the final battle at Armageddon.

Dunne pulled out his laptop and brought up the two photos of the young Chinese woman: one taken by the security camera on the bridge at Cornell, the other by a passerby in Times Square.

Who the hell are you?

Two years ago, Dunne had led a small team of bioweapons experts and epidemiologists through a series of worst-case scenarios for the Uzumaki: a terrorist group gets ahold of one of the missing cylinders, or the Chinese dig it up at Harbin and decide to use it in a preemptive attack. Without an effective treatment or a vaccine—both of which were months, if not years, away—the number of dead from even a single-point-of-dispersal event could be in the millions. A lone actor could single-handedly trigger a disaster of cataclysmic proportions.

DUNNE WAS OUT OF HIS SEAT THE MOMENT THE HELICOPTER sat down on the helipad next to the main USAMRIID building. Toloff was already on the tarmac, barking orders at the ground crew. Dunne watched as the Hazmat container was wheeled away, then followed Toloff as they jogged along Ditto Avenue through the heart of Detrick.

Toloff pointed to the red-brick building up ahead. "In under an hour we'll know exactly how much shit we're in. We'll crack open the vault in a class-3 area, move the sealed biosafety containers into class-4. I'll run everything from there."

Dunne grabbed her arm. "I'm going to be talking to the President in a few minutes. He's going to want an answer, good or bad."

She didn't have to reply. Her anguished face said it all.

22

JAKE AND VLAD DROVE PAST ONE DILAPIDATED HOUSE AFTER another, their yards filled with cast-off farm equipment, auto parts, and washer-dryers. Buffalo Road was only ten miles from downtown Ithaca but a world away. Central New York was mostly rural poor, dotted by old industrial towns. Ithaca was an anomaly, an educational mecca with twenty thousand or so overeducated academics and artists plunked down at the northern edge of Appalachia.

Vlad leaned forward. "Slow down," he said. "I want to live to be an old man."

"We're fine," Jake said. He glanced at the speedometer—seventy-five. Fine, unless they crested a hill and found a tractor coming the other way.

"Please," Vlad said. "I am convinced I will make a very good old man."

Jake kept the gas on as they passed an abandoned farmhouse, the roof swaybacked and peppered with holes, the windows covered in rotting particleboard. A stack of rusted wheel rims in the yard had fallen over, spreading across the yard like poker chips on a blackjack table. An old grain silo stood in the field behind it, the front gone, save the metal staves like the rib cage of a long-dead animal.

"Why would anyone live out here when they don't have to?" Jake asked.

"He likes a place to shoot his guns." Vlad also had a thing for guns. The Cornell police arrested him once after they'd received calls of a strange man firing a pistol into Cascadilla Gorge. "What the hell are you doing?" the arresting officer had asked.

"Shooting at rocks."

"Why?"

"Rocks don't shoot back."

Vlad tapped Jake on the shoulder. "Okay, slow down. There."

JAKE PARKED BEHIND A BRAND-NEW JET-BLACK CADILLAC Escalade, and they started up the walk. Uncut weeds poked up between the stepping stones. At first glance, Harpo's place blended in with the rest. The yard was full of junk like all the others, but this junkyard was more of a high-tech graveyard. Computer servers. Broken monitors. Various things Jake couldn't identify for sure, but they looked like burned-out versions of what he saw in bio labs: centrifuges, hot plates, PCR cyclers. There was even a DNA synthesizer.

"We don't tell him anything about why we want this," Jake said. "We agree?"

"Don't worry. He will not ask."

The door to the house was new, with the flat brown paneling that Jake recognized as the vinyl covering of a reinforced steel door. There were two dead bolts in addition to the knob, and a small security camera above the door encased in a little black cage.

The front door opened before they could knock. A big man stood there, maybe six-three, two-fifty. Thick through the waist and even thicker through the chest. He wore sweatpants, orange Crocs on his feet, and a T-shirt advertising a Cambridge bar called the Plough & Stars. He had a Snickers bar in his hand.

It wasn't hard to see where he got the name Harpo. On his head was a shock of curly white hair, almost like a fright wig. "This Jake?" he said to Vlad. "The Crawler guy?"

"He is the one."

He welcomed them in, gregarious and open, a contrast to all

the security measures. He threw an arm around Jake. "I love your little robots, would kill to get my hands on a few. You might sell me some? Been trying to pry some loose from Boris Badenov here," he said with a glance at Vlad, "but he ain't biting." He let go of Jake, turned serious. "Think about it. I could make you good money—two hundred bucks apiece, easy. Conversation pieces for technophiles. You teach it to dance the Macarena to an MP3, I bet we could get five times that. What do you say? You interested?"

Jake passed, a bit too gruffly. He was already antsy. He just wanted to get the DNA sequenced and get back to Maggie.

Harpo took it gracefully. "Come on."

The interior of Harpo's house was a total contrast to the outside. The living room was well lit and relatively clean but completely devoid of furniture. Instead it was full of computer servers, most of them dark. "You want an HP BladeSystem c7000?" Harpo said, patting one of the silent server stacks. "I'll sell it to you cheap. Got no use for them now. I ran a data-mining service for a while. We generated customer profiles based on Web surfing patterns, but now everyone's gotten into that game. You want easy pickings, you gotta be in at the beginning. Selling something no one else does." He smiled. "Like I'm doing now."

"What do you sell?"

"You ever heard of vanity publishers? You write a book and the big houses won't buy? For a fee, a vanity publisher will print your book for you, churn out a hundred copies, a thousand, whatever you pay for. Enough copies to give to your friends and pretend you're a big-time author. Well, I'm a vanity publisher, too. But I publish in DNA."

"Meaning?"

"Meaning DNA publishing is your chance to expand your print run to astronomical scales. Any message you want, I'll encode it in DNA, run PCR on it, and send you a *billion* copies." He held up a small vial of clear liquid. "This one's shipping today."

"You're kidding. Who buys this stuff?"

"You name it. Frustrated poets. Novelists. One woman had me make six billion copies of her poem, one for every human on the planet. It stank, by the way. All about calla lilies. Another guy, some religious nut, wanted the Sermon on the Mount. He carries a little mister with him, like for perfumes? Everywhere he goes, he gives a little squirt. Says he's spreading peace and joy. But it pays the bills."

He led them down the hall, past a door that opened to the bathroom, then on to another room, what Jake surmised had once been the master bedroom. The door had been taken off the hinges. In its place was a series of plastic transparent curtains. "Keeps the dust down," he said as he pulled them back. "Here it is. My manufacturing facility."

Jake was taken aback. He had expected a few beakers and gels, but nothing like this. The onetime master bedroom was a full-fledged biotech lab. Along the wall were black-topped lab benches with overhead cabinets, all of it new and shiny. On the countertops were the standard fare of a modern biology lab: centrifuges, pipettes, shakers, and row upon row of reagents. Except for a few odd-looking pieces that were clearly homemade, Jake could have been in any of a hundred research labs at Cornell. It was as if a crane had plucked a room from the Life Science Technology Building and plopped it down on Buffalo Road.

"How much did all this cost you?"

"Not more than forty K. I got most of it on DoveBid—it's an industrial equipment online auctioneer. Wait for a biotech firm to go belly-up, you can get deals. Not like the deals I did a few years back during the telecom bust, but not bad. The rest I made myself. This stuff ain't rocket science. What's a PCR cycler but a fancy Crock Pot?" He turned to face Vlad. "Okay, you Russian piece of shit, I'm assuming you didn't bring Captain Robot Bug here so I could bring his prose to life."

"You ready for challenge?" Vlad held up the tiny vial with the DNA from Liam's glowing fungus inside. "We need sequence."

"Concentration?"

"Unknown."

"How homogeneous?"

"Don't know."

"How long is the strand?"

"Don't know."

"But you have the primer sequence?"

Vlad nodded.

"And when do you want it?"

"Now."

Harpo took the vial. He turned to Jake. "Here's the deal, sport. Two hundred bucks an hour, plus supplies. And I keep the time sheet in my head. Cash only. No checks. No Visa, no MasterCard. And no American Express."

· 23 ·

THE FIRST ENTRY MAGGIE FOUND ABOUT THE UZUMAKI WAS in Liam's journal from 1953. She sat on the concrete floor in the back of the herbarium, her grandfather's notebooks scattered around her. She'd retrieved them from a storage room where the notebooks of many of Cornell's most famous mycologists were kept. The cardboard boxes were stacked floor to ceiling, the air awash in the aromatic compounds created during the slow, steady breakdown of the pages. She'd found her grandfather's, dragged them out of the storage room, and dug through them, looking for trips to South America and Brazil, her nerves on edge. The notebooks were out of sequence—she had to go through them one by one.

Surrounding her as she worked were the rows and rows of seven-foot-high metal cabinets filled with fungal specimens. The smell of mothballs was strong, the naphthalene a poison to the cigarette beetles that were the archivist's bane. Her grandfather loved rummaging through those cabinets, had worked among them for half a century. All of his finds, the hundreds of species he had discovered and classified, were there. He had traveled across the globe in search of new species. In almost any corner of the world, he befriended the local experts on fungi, whether they were academics or farmers. But he had made a particularly large number of trips to Brazil. Maggie had traveled with him once, when she was seventeen. She was amazed at the people he knew. He had friends all over the country, in almost every province, it seemed, people who knew everything about the local fungal populations.

And there was something else about Brazil that she remembered. São Paolo had more than a million residents of Japanese descent. She remembered especially one neighborhood, called Liberdade, where she suddenly felt as though she had been transported to the Far East. Liam had explained why: the Japanese and Brazilians had signed a treaty in 1907 to encourage the immigration of poor Japanese peasants to Brazil to work the coffee crops. These were the descendants of those workers, the largest population of Japanese outside of Japan.

The entry that had grabbed Maggie's attention was on page thirty-two of Liam's 1953 field notebook. Her grandfather's handwriting was controlled and confident, showing none of the shakiness that would come to him in later years. She felt a knot growing in her stomach as she read the description of her grandfather's find:

8/28/53

Swirl-like morphology, attacks during Oct./Nov., taking root on the corn stubble left in the field after harvest. Farmers fear it. Say it causes spirits to come inside. "Spirits?" I ask. They explain: hallucinations, madness.

This must be it. Tentative name: *Fusarium spiralis*.

She read on, skimming her grandfather's careful phenotype description and attempt at taxonomy, placing it in the proper place in the fungal kingdom. Then came a section of text that tied it all together.

I asked about Japanese. Had they been here? An old man from a small village outside Porto Alegre said that a small Japanese contingent had come there in 1939. They circulated among the Japanese migrant community, offered money for unusual or dangerous organisms, particularly crop pests. They claimed to be from the Japanese agricultural ministry, but no one believed them.

The villager said the Japanese knew nothing about maize or farming. Nor were they interested in techniques for growing. Only in whether people got sick.

The rumor was they were military. I asked, "Did they take samples of the fungus?" He nodded. They left with an enormous chest full of samples. Hundreds of species. They seemed pleased. He said, "I hated them. They were cruel, heartless men."

Maggie was completely immersed, her universe reduced to the page of the notebook before her. She nearly jumped out of her skin when her cell rang.

It was Jake.

She told him what she found. He said that Harpo and Vlad were working on the sequence and should have it in about an hour. He said he'd check back in later.

MAGGIE TURNED TO THE FUNGAL REGISTRY DATABASE, TYPING the specimen name, *Fusarium spiralis,* into the computer in the prep room. She found nothing: the database had no record of a species by that name. Liam always said that one of his greatest joys was the discovery of an interesting new species, the fun of sharing it with the rest of the fungus community.

But he'd kept this one a secret.

She took a different tack, looking to see if it had been listed by anyone else. It didn't take long. She found it listed under *Fusarium spirale.* The fungus was registered in 2002 by a Brazilian scientist, Dr. Alberto Chagas of the University of São Paolo, along with Dr. Sadie Toloff of the USDA.

Sadie Toloff?

Maggie wouldn't call Sadie a close friend, but the two women knew and respected each other. They had consulted each other on both scientific and bureaucratic issues that had arisen over the years. Toloff had never gone in for species chasing, an obsession among some mycologists. So what was she doing in Brazil searching out obscure fungi?

The answer was obvious. She was looking for the same thing Liam had been looking for.

She heard a sound, practically jumped out of her skin, then

realized it was the heater starting up. She didn't know if it was the adrenaline or the fear, but she was sure someone was watching her. She picked up Vlad's gun, then set it back down.

Come on, girl. You've got work to do.

Maggie read the descriptor for *Fusarium spirale*. It was native to northern Brazil and infected corn and cereal substrates. It produced a pair of nasty mycotoxins, a common fumonisin called B1, a nephrotoxin that affected kidneys, and another one similar to the LSA compound found in *Claviceps,* aka ergot. If ingested, these mycotoxins caused symptoms ranging from mania and hallucinations to constricted blood flow in exterior appendages that led to gangrene. From what she read, all the local farmers had a mantra: stay away from the spiral.

It was a nasty fungus but no worse than dozens of other mycotoxin-producing species. What was special about this one? According to what Jake had told her a few hours before, Liam maintained that the Uzumaki was the most dangerous biological pathogen he'd ever seen. So how did it get that way? How had the Japanese changed it when they knew next to nothing about genetics at that time?

A few more clicks gave her the first clue. *Fusarium spirale* was an unusual bugger: it was dimorphic. Dimorphic fungi could exist in two completely different morphological states, with utterly different phenotypes—like a caterpillar and a butterfly. You'd never know by looking at them that they were the same species.

Depending on its environment, *Fusarium spirale* could be the spiral that attacked and devoured corn in the fields. This form produced toxins discouraging predators and reproduced sexually, sending billions of spores skyward to be spread by the wind and rain.

The second form was much simpler, a single-celled yeastlike organism. It grew in hot, moist conditions, such as inside the bodies of warm-blooded mammals. It would take up residence in the digestive tract of either humans or birds, reproducing asexually, by simple division. It would grow quickly but was relatively harmless, producing none of the poisonous toxins that were present in the spiral form. Its goal was simple—to ride along with the mammal, not causing it too much discomfort, until it dropped out in the fecal matter of the host and would begin life again in its spiral form.

Maggie struggled to piece it all together. She stared down at the pictures of the little spiral growths. So how had the Japanese turned fungus into a weapon?

Dimorph. Two forms. One kills you, the other doesn't. She was beginning to get an inkling about how it would go. How you could turn this fungus into a killing machine.

Maggie decided to take a risk and call Sadie Toloff. She looked up the number in the old, beaten address book she still kept. She hadn't talked to Sadie in a couple of years, since a conference in Toronto. But she thought she could trust her.

Maggie opened her cellphone and dialed the number. It rang once, then went dead.

She hung up, tried again. The result was the same. What was wrong with the damn lines? Maybe the circuits were overloaded because of the events at Bellevue.

She decided to try the landline in the reception area. She dialed Toloff's cell. This time it rang four times, then clicked to voice mail.

Maggie kept it short. "It's Maggie Connor. I'm okay. In shock about Liam. I need to talk to you about *Fusarium spirale.* Give a call and I'll explain everything."

She hung up the phone.

The heater chugged, turned itself off. The room was deathly quiet.

All of a sudden, she felt very alone. She wished to hell Jake would get back.

· 24 ·

HARPO'S NEAT AND ORDERLY LAB WAS A WRECK. USED PIPETTE tips littered the countertops, and gels were everywhere. Vlad and Harpo had finished the PCR, and now they were running a Sanger gel, counting off bands. They were doing it retro, using two-decade-old technology. Jake knew the basics of what they were doing, but it was another thing to watch them going at it. Like sitting in the corner of an old-time editing room in Hollywood, bits of film taped to the walls, the director and his assistant trying to piece together the story hidden in the images.

Vlad dropped a cuvette, cursed in Russian.

Jake watched them, outwardly calm but inside twisted up with worry. "What's the problem?"

"Something went wrong," Harpo said. "All we got was a fragment. But I think I know what the problem is. We just have to lower the cycling temperature."

"How long?"

"Another hour. At least."

FRUSTRATED, JAKE PACED THE HOUSE. HE STOPPED AT THE back window, looking out at the forest that picked up right behind ·

Harpo's yard. A dog loitered, a handsome old hound with huge ears and black eyes. He stood in front of a fancy doghouse with the name DUKE over the door, his tail raised and watching Jake. He started barking, then thought better of it, sat down, and scratched his ear.

Jake wondered whether the NSA people were looking for him. They had made reservations for him on a flight out of Ithaca that had left hours ago. Jake guessed that if he called his voice mail at home, there would be messages asking what the hell had happened. He decided to leave those messages unchecked. At least a little while longer.

To his right, behind a glass case, was Harpo's collection of guns. Mostly hunting rifles but with a few military pieces thrown in. Jake recognized the sleek lines of the M16 and, below it, an M9 pistol in a black holster. It was the civilian version of the sidearm Jake had carried when he was in the service. He still had it, tucked away on a high shelf in the closet of his apartment. He took it down, cleaned and oiled it, every few months, not because he thought he'd ever use it but out of a sense of respect. The special burdens of soldiers.

Three days.

Three days ago, life had been normal. Three days ago, he would've been grading papers, looking for an hour to sneak away to the gym. He might've gone over to Liam's lab. Maybe Dylan would have been there, and Jake and the boy would have tried to teach the Crawlers some new trick. Now Liam was dead, tortured by those very same Crawlers. Jake was in a backyard bio lab, waiting for a guy named Harpo with fright-wig hair to decipher Liam's final message. A message Liam had left hidden inside the genome of a fungus under a pile of rocks in a forest.

He pulled out his phone and called Maggie. Six rings, then voicemail. He left a message and tried again. Same result. *What the hell?* He'd talked to her a half-hour before—she said she was making progress, had found an entry in Liam's field notebooks that was almost certainly about the Uzumaki. So where was she now?

He called information, got the number for her work. It rang four times, then clicked to voice mail: a woman's voice, not Maggie's, saying he'd reached the Cornell University herbarium, offer-

ing a phone tree of options. Jake chose "0" and left another message, telling Maggie to call him right away.

Damn it. Where was she? And if she had left the herbarium,
why didn't she call? The only thing he could think of was that
something had happened, maybe something back at home.

He called Rivendell.

The phone rang and rang and rang. No answering machine. No
voice mail.

What the hell was going on? Maggie's roommate Cindy was
supposed to be there, watching Dylan.

He thought about calling the police, then glanced again at
Harpo's gun collection, to the Beretta M9. Jake could be at the
herbarium in fifteen minutes. He took down the M9 and unhol-
stered it. Range of maybe fifty meters. History of slide problems
but a good weapon. Checked the magazine. Full. Fifteen rounds.

He sought out Vlad and Harpo, the M9 in hand. "Harpo, I
need to borrow this."

"You plan on committing a felony?"

"No jokes. I can't get Maggie on the phone."

"Did something happen?" Vlad asked.

"I don't know. Call my cell the minute you have the rest of the
sequence. And if you don't hear from me in the next half-hour, call
the cops."

ONCE OUTSIDE, JAKE CALLED LIEUTENANT BECRAFT AT THE
Cornell police department. Becraft sounded surprised to hear from
him. "Professor Sterling? Where are you? The Detrick people—"

"Can you do something for me? Can you send someone out to
Maggie Connor's place? No one's answering the phone. A woman
named Cindy Sharp is supposed to be there. Watching over Dylan.
Maggie's son."

"Jake. Where are you? Is there some kind of problem?"

"I'll be in touch. Send a car out to Maggie's."

"What's going—"

Jake hung up.

· 25 ·

ORCHID CHECKED THE PHONE NUMBER WITH A FEW QUICK
taps of her fingers. The heads-up screen in her glasses gave the response: LT. BECRAFT. CORNELL UNIVERSITY POLICE.

She listened to the conversation between Jake Sterling and Becraft. Orchid had taps on both Jake Sterling's and Maggie Connor's
cells, allowing her to hear all conversations, control all functions.
She'd installed the modified SIM cards in both phones weeks ago,
long before she had taken Liam Connor hostage. She had wanted
complete control of the communications environment. The taps
had proven invaluable. Minutes before, Maggie had tried to call
Toloff at Detrick. Orchid had shut her phone down.

Orchid checked the latest GPS location from Jake's phone. He
was moving, driving away from the address on Buffalo Road.

Toward Maggie, she was sure.

Good.

Orchid backed the FedEx van up to the front door of Rivendell,
thinking it through. The police would likely be here in minutes, but
she still had time. She went inside the house and dragged the dead
woman, Cindy Sharp, through the front door. She threw Cindy's
body in the back of the FedEx van. Orchid had stolen the van a

week before from a storage garage in Pennsylvania. She closed the door carefully, locked it, then walked around to the driver's door.

She got in, started the engine, and checked Jake's location again. He was retracing the path he'd taken, heading back to the Cornell Plant Pathology Herbarium. He was fifteen minutes away from his destination. Orchid was five.

She turned the FedEx van around, started down the gravel road. She heard a squeaking sound in the back of the van.

She glanced over her shoulder into the storage area. Dylan Connor was cuffed to the wall, tape on his mouth. He'd started to write HELP in the dust of the tinted back window with the tip of his shoe.

Clever boy. Just like his great-grandfather.

She pulled to a stop, then took a length of rope and secured his legs. "No more tricks," she said. She wiped away the boy's message with a brush of her fingers.

She turned onto the main road. Maggie's call to Toloff still worried her. What if Maggie had used another phone? What if she had gotten through?

Orchid typed a series of commands on her leg.

Time to make sure everyone at Detrick was very, very busy.

· 26 ·

XINTAO LU WAS EXHAUSTED. HE'D BEEN UP ALL NIGHT, working his way through the final part of the processing run. He was a graduate student in physics at the University of Maryland, College Park, but he was pretty sure he was going to switch to electrical engineering.

He dipped the wafer cartridge into the etching tank, letting the hydrofluoric acid perform the final step in the fabrication of his device. The little silicon chip he was etching had an array of microscopic holes, each barely larger than a virus. When superfluid helium passed through the holes, it would exhibit coherent oscillations that were sensitive to the absolute motion of the earth with respect to the stars. That's what his thesis adviser said, anyway. But he was beginning to wonder about that. It all seemed too wild. Etch some holes in a piece of silicon, cool it to near absolute zero, and you would detect your rotation relative to the entire universe.

It made his head hurt to think about it, especially after twenty-four straight hours in his white bunny suit in the cleanroom. The dust-free environment was kept so by a ceiling full of HEPA filters constantly chugging away, creating a low roar that crept into your bones.

He scanned the rows of equipment, seeing only a couple of

other users. A seminar was going on about a new kind of solar cell based on carbon nanotubes that had everyone jazzed. In a few more minutes, the seminar would end and the cleanroom would begin filling up again. The electron beam lithography machines were running—the demand on those was relentless. People were also camped out on the various other machines—the evaporators, ion millers, and etchers. They were all in their anti–dust bunny suits, conducting a defensive war against particles of dust and flecks of skin.

Xintao began to gather everything up. He was nearly done.

He heard a beep.

Strange. Near the RF plasma cleaning chamber. That was when he spied it. He'd sat before the machine time and time again, waiting for his sample to be finished. The wall behind the chamber was imprinted on his memory. Two brass pipes running vertically, delivering water to the cooling head.

Now there were three.

He approached the third pipe, touched his hand to it.

The pipe was vibrating ever so slightly.

Xintao wasn't sure why, but he immediately panicked. He stared at the pipe for a few seconds, then quickly glanced around, looking for one of the staff.

To his surprise, the pipe beeped again. Quietly, like an alarm clock sounding in another room. He pulled his hand back, walked away briskly, certain that he had to find someone from the staff.

He didn't get far before the blast hit him.

LEON SOLOMON, THE FBI'S CHIEF COUNTERTERRORISM SPE-cialist, arrived in the back of an unmarked van after a short ride over from the J. Edgar Hoover Building. A barricade of cruisers, orange cones, and yellow police tape kept the crowd from getting too close to the wreckage. Twelve FBI men were already on-site in addition to hundreds of local firefighters and police. The crowd was big and growing, drawn by the irresistible lure of destruction. Some were slack-jawed, frozen in shock. Others had a strange kind of energy about them, an almost giddy excitement. Something had *happened.*

Solomon had a straight visual line to the carnage. The windows of the building were blown completely out, glass and concrete littering the street. A section of wall midway up the building was torn loose, tenuously hanging in space by a few strands of rebar. The TV vultures were everywhere, all three networks. Two helicopters circled overhead. The media were jumpy, hyped up, and ready to pounce. The press in New York were told that the shutdown of Bellevue was because of an outbreak of SARS. Total bullshit, and a few of the reporters were smelling it. You don't send in the Chemical Biological Incident Response Force for SARS. And now, a day later, an explosion at the University of Maryland.

Solomon was anxious as hell. By design, a university campus was a hub of dissemination, full of people from around the world—people who would seek to return home in a time of crisis. Rescue workers, students, professors rush in, breathe the pathogen, and you've got an outbreak that sweeps across the campus, then the city, then the country, then around the world. If you wanted to spread a pathogen, this was a hell of a way to do it.

There had been a wild shouting match when the anonymous email had arrived in Sadie Toloff's inbox, claiming credit for the explosion. The FBI director demanded they seal off the whole university, evacuate the entire College Park area. But they had dodged a bullet in Manhattan, and everyone was feeling lucky. The results had come in from Toloff's lab at Detrick fifty minutes before. The kid in Times Square had been loaded with LSA—d-lysergic acid amide—one of the primary psychotropic alkaloid products produced by the Uzumaki. But the LSA was pharmaceutical-grade, likely administered by injection. All the genetic markers were negative for the actual fungus. The kid did not have an Uzumaki infection. He was going to make it. The Times Square incident was an elaborate ruse.

As for the mysterious Asian woman's profile, the CIA thought she could be a member of one of the ultranationalist, anti-Japanese groups, such as Sunshine 731 or Black Sword. These radical groups were furious that the United States would not turn over Hitoshi Kitano for prosecution as a war criminal. She was playing games, seeking publicity, that's what the profilers said.

Solomon wasn't so sure.

Inside, he met up with the local fire chief and the shell-shocked director of the facility. The main atrium was utter chaos. Debris—

wood, glass, chairs, railings, piping—was strewn about the floor. One of the skylights overhead was shattered. The fire chief pointed inside. "It's in there. That's where the bomb was."

Solomon went in, going straight to the epicenter of the explosion, scanning the wreckage for the item mentioned in the email. The fire chief filled in the details. As best they could tell, the explosive was fitted inside a fake section of piping. Thankfully, the student who saw it had survived, though he'd lose an arm and sight in both eyes. He'd told them that it had started to make a noise. It had likely been set off remotely.

But it wasn't the details of the bomb that interested Solomon. It was another item, one that no one else had yet noticed, partially obscured by a piece of plaster. Just like the anonymous email had said, right there on the floor, glinting in the rescue spotlights.

A goddamn brass cylinder.

MAGGIE WAS BEGINNING TO UNDERSTAND HOW *FUSARIUM spirale* could be turned into a devastating biological weapon.

During World War II, genetics was still a new science. No one was even sure that DNA was the basis for genetic information until the Hershey-Chase experiments on T2 viruses in 1952. Even with today's techniques for splicing and dicing genomes, creating a successful genetically modified organism was a huge undertaking.

But the scientists at Unit 731 had chosen well.

Fusarium spirale was relatively harmless when it lived in your gut, viciously dangerous when it infected a corn plant. If you want to make a monster out of it, all you had to do was scramble its genetic programming. Turn off a few genes, turn on a few others, get its signals mixed. Make it pump out toxins when it was living inside you. Maggie shuddered at the thought. You'd have a chemical weapons factory killing you from the inside out.

Maggie could guess how they'd done it. They could have used chemicals or radiation to induce mutations, then test them on human subjects. Cultivate the ones that killed the quickest. If you were a sadistic monster willing to use live human subjects, you didn't need biotechnology.

Maggie felt the mysteries shrouding her grandfather dissolving away, the pieces of his life coming together. Her grandfather had gone to work at Detrick right after the war. Liam never talked about it, but she had gathered threads from what her grandmother Edith had told her. In the months before she died, Edith and Maggie spent a great deal of time together. Maggie loved to get her talking, to tell the stories of her life. It made Edith happy, distracting her when she was in great pain from the treatments. Edith said that Liam had insisted that they move to Maryland so he could continue his work at Camp Detrick. "He never was quite the same after the war," she said. "He had nightmares. It must have been terrible. I can't imagine."

Maggie was willing to bet that those nightmares were about *Fusarium spirale.*

Bam! Bam! Maggie nearly jumped out of her skin at the thudding noise. Someone was banging on the front door.

She started toward the reception area. Could it be Jake?

Bam!

But why wouldn't he have called?

She stopped, pulled out her phone, and flipped it open. The main display showed no messages. But she hit the key that took her to her voice mail. To her surprise, there were seven. All from Jake, all in the last half-hour. Why hadn't her phone rang? Something was wrong with her phone.

The banging grew louder, a steady *thump, thump, thump.* She retrieved the gun that Vlad had left her, suddenly thankful to have it.

"Jake?" she asked, standing across the reception room from the front door, gun pointed toward it. Her hand was shaking. "Is that you?"

The banging stopped.

Complete silence. Her heart was pounding.

She forced herself to check the window. The parking lot was empty.

She leaned in close to the glass, trying to see the front door, but the angle was wrong. The window frame blocked her view.

Then she heard a voice: "Mom?"

"Dylan?"

No answer.

"*Dylan?*" She quickly flipped the deadbolt, turned the knob. He sounded scared. Really scared.

The door exploded open, catching Maggie square in the chest. The next thing she knew, she was on her back, stunned, staring up at the ceiling. The back of her skull screamed in pain, her right arm bent behind her. She shook her head to clear her thoughts, pulled herself up.

The gun barrel was less than six inches from her forehead.

JAKE PULLED TO A STOP ON THE ROAD LEADING TO THE herbarium, a good two hundred yards away. He picked up the Beretta from the passenger seat, released the safety.

He jogged to the building, staying out of sight of the front door. When he got close, he felt his heart jump into his throat. The front door was ajar.

Maggie would not have left that door open.

His pulse raced as he slid through the open door and into the waiting area, gun in the lead, ready to shoot. A weapon always upped the stakes. If you showed deadly force, you had to be willing to use it.

The room was empty, the phone off the hook. Beyond it, through a windowless metal-reinforced door, was the herbarium proper, with its rows of storage cabinets. A tough space to enter unnoticed. He'd have a target painted on his chest.

No choice. He had to go there.

Jake opened the door slowly. The main lights were out, the only illumination coming from the back of the room. One brown cabinet after another, each maybe seven feet tall and four feet wide, arranged in four rows like giant dominoes. He listened closely for any sound, then stepped inside. He took up a position against the closest cabinet on the left, keeping his breathing even and slow. If someone was here, they would have heard him enter. Better to play dumb.

"Maggie? You in here?"

Nothing.

"Maggie?"

A rustling came from somewhere in the middle of the room. He peered around the cabinet, gun ready, his finger half-squeezing the trigger. He saw a human form standing in a shadowed space between the two rows of cabinets.

Jesus. It was Maggie. Her mouth was taped closed, her hands behind her back. Bound and gagged.

Jake kept the gun up, worked his way carefully along the left wall.

Then Jake's phone rang.

Jake pulled it from his pocket and glanced down. The caller ID said ANS OR SHE DIES.

Jake edged around until he could see Maggie again. He accepted the call.

"You're going to do something for me," the woman said, her voice calm and low. She had an accent—Chinese, Jake was pretty sure. He picked up a slight echo, probably from her voice carrying across the warehouse-sized space. The acoustics of the room were complex, sounds ricocheting off the walls and cabinets. He couldn't yet tell where she was, but he was sure she was inside. And therefore not more than a hundred feet away.

Jake tried to think it through. She was most likely across the room, on the other side of Maggie. His best bet was to go left, circle around. Outflank her. "Who are you?" he said into the phone, listening for the echo.

"You can call me Orchid."

"What do you want?"

"In time. Now. Look at your phone."

Jake saw the numbers of his phone appear one by one, as if he was dialing. The dialing stopped on the second-to-last number. He recognized the number. It was Vlad's cell.

"Here's what you will do. You'll tell him everything is fine. Tell him that Ms. Connor's cellphone batteries were dead. You understand? Then ask him how his search is going. He'll tell you. You'll respond appropriately. Then you'll hang up. Do you understand?"

"What do I get in return?"

"Nothing. You fail, I kill her. I'll be on the line. I'll cut you off if you try and say anything wrong. You understand?"

Jake kept moving, hoping the confusing acoustics would mask his forward progress. He swung around the next cabinet, gun in one hand and the phone in the other.

Nothing.

Jesus Christ, where was she?

The last number appeared. Then the phone was ringing.

Vlad picked up on the second ring. "Jake?"

Jake approached the next cabinet, gun drawn.

"Jake? Everything all right?"

He whipped around, ready to fire. Nothing. "Everything is fine. Where are you with the sequencing?"

"What was wrong with her phone?" Vlad asked.

"The battery was dead."

Jake stepped around another cabinet, gun drawn. Nothing.

"What about the landline?"

"I don't know. Maybe she didn't answer it."

"You didn't ask her?"

"No. Vlad. It's fine. Tell me about the sequence."

Vlad didn't respond. Then, "You sure you are fine?"

"Vlad. Leave it. It's been a tough couple of days." Jake continued his progress along the left wall. Only three more cabinets to go.

Jake was close. The next row was the one that was his best guess. "We've almost got it, Jake. Another half-hour."

He heard the slight squeak of rubber. A shoe. It came from the other side of the cabinet he was now facing. He looked to his right. He could still see Maggie. The shoe wasn't Maggie's.

Moment of truth. He'd come around it quickly, firing.

He took a breath, held it. He muted his phone, then tossed it across the room. The phone struck the far wall with a clang. Jake turned the corner, gun held in both hands, ready to blow Orchid's head off.

Standing there, staring right at him, was Dylan, eyes big as moons. Jake's legs went rubbery, hands shaking at what he'd almost done. He'd come to within a fraction of a second of shooting.

He eased the pressure on the trigger, his knees almost buckling.

From behind him, a voice very close: "Put down the gun. Slowly."

· 28 ·

INSIDE OF AN HOUR, THEY HAD THE BRASS CYLINDER AT DE-
trick.

Dunne watched by video hookup from a nearby secure room as
Toloff picked it up and turned it over in her gloved hands. She was
inside the USDA class-4 Uzumaki facility, in a full pressure suit
with external air. She looked like an astronaut on the moon. The
facility had a bunch of cameras, always on, but they were typically
used only for archiving. They'd been tapped into, were being
broadcast live, with power players up and down the security food
chain watching every move. The head of Detrick, a general named
Arvenick, was certainly watching, as was the FBI director. Dunne
assumed the President was linked in as well.

A team of weapons experts and forensic materials scientists
had already poked and prodded the cylinder every way they could.
It had identical dimensions to the ones that had been recovered
from the Japanese submarines. Something slid around inside when
you tilted it, like a marble. They couldn't do an MRI because the
metal shielded out the radio waves. X rays didn't show anything. A
quick and ferocious debate followed about what to do, but in the
end they'd simply decided to open the damn thing, and Toloff got
the task. On the video, Dunne saw her hand shaking and the

rivulets of sweat on her face as she twisted open the cylinder. The camera zoomed in on her gloved hands. "It's resisting," she said. Her hand jerked slightly. "All right," she said. "The threads are sliding past one another. Here we go."

Dunne braced himself as if he were in the room with her. The cylinder might be booby-trapped. They'd checked the mass against the thickness of the walls, which they had evaluated with ultrasound. It could be an explosive.

She unscrewed the cylinder, then carefully set the upper section on the table. She looked inside the other half.

"Holy crap," she said. She studied it for a few seconds, then looked up at the camera. "You're not going to believe this."

She laid a Texwipe on the table, gently shook the cylinder over it to disgorge the contents.

You've got to be kidding, Dunne said to himself.

It was a bone. A human finger bone. The significance of the finger bone was not lost on Dunne. She had probably taken it from the finger she cut off of the man in Times Square.

Toloff said, "There's writing on it. Zoom in."

Etched in letters so small that they were barely readable was a message.

KITANO MUST PAY 兰花

Dunne recognized the Chinese characters at the end of the message. They were the characters for *Orchid.*

SHE DID EVERYTHING RIGHT. ORCHID MADE JAKE TAPE HIS own mouth closed, then put him in the lead, where he could see nothing but the way ahead. She directed him out the back door, a path that would take them nowhere near the gun he'd tossed aside. Her exit route was secure and hidden—through a stand of woods behind the herbarium. It was still light out, but the sun was low, the branches casting shadows that cut across the patches of snow like streaks of black paint.

They were hundreds of yards away from the nearest road. If anyone caught a glance from afar, they'd look like a group of hikers.

Maggie was behind him, holding Dylan close. Jake heard her crying. Orchid questioned her as they walked, asking where the Uzumaki was hidden. Maggie kept repeating, "I don't know."

Jake's nerves were on high alert. He was thinking it through, and he didn't like where his thoughts were leading. If Orchid was after the Uzumaki, Jake had to end this. No matter the cost.

Orchid spoke. "Up there," she said. "To your left, twenty degrees."

A white FedEx van was parked on the side of the road.

"The back door," she said.

The door screeched as Jake opened it.

Maggie screamed, shielding Dylan from the grisly sight. A young woman was curled up on the floor of the van like a discarded doll. She'd been shot in the head. The bottom of the van was sticky red.

"Inside," Orchid said. Jake obeyed, the smell of iron thick in his nostrils. He recognized her from the red curly hair. Cindy. Maggie's roommate from Rivendell.

Orchid pointed toward the right wall. "Put that on." A belt was hanging on the wall, thick and black with a plastic box on the back the size of a paperback book. Jake strapped it to his waist. He had a pretty good idea what it was for.

She tapped a sequence on her leg.

The belt on Jake's waist hummed as fifty thousand volts shot up his spine. It knocked him to his knees, hands in fists, groaning. "That was a warning," she said. "At full strength, it will kill you." Orchid pointed to the woman on the floor. "Get her out. Put her in the woods. Make sure the body's out of sight."

Jake did as he was told, carrying Cindy's lifeless body. He tried to block out the cold, clammy feel of her skin, the terrible whiteness of her arm. A memory hit him from the bulldozer assault, the Iraqi soldiers buried in the sand, cat shit in a litterbox. Afterward he'd seen a sunburned arm sticking out of the sand, clutching a boot. The poor bastard must've been asleep, then took off running, grabbing what he could.

Stop it. Jake focused on the situation, sorting it through, *click, clack.* Jake knew it, the soldier in him knew it. You do what you have to do. And what he had to do was stop this woman.

He laid Cindy down among the leaves. He looked around. He was far enough away. He could make a run for it, might make it or at least get noticed. The other side of the woods led to a major road. He glanced back toward the van. Dylan was crying, Maggie trying to console him. Orchid stood, watching Jake. She had the gun pointed at Maggie's head. She spoke, just loud enough to be heard: "Let's go."

· 30 ·

"HE'S BEEN SITTING LIKE THAT FOR ALMOST TWO HOURS," said Stan Robbins, the man in charge of Kitano's surveillance. Robbins and Dunne were in a secure National Security Council conference room in the Eisenhower Executive Office Building, the six-hundred-thousand-square-foot monstrosity across the street from the West Wing. On the screen before them was an overhead view of Hitoshi Kitano's cell, a real-time feed from the surveillance cameras at the United States Penitentiary in Hazelton, West Virginia, a maximum-security facility.

DUNNE HAD FIRST MET HITOSHI KITANO MORE THAN TWO decades ago, when Dunne was still a relatively unknown professor at Yale. Dunne's Ph.D. treatise, then still speculation, on the downfall of the Soviet Union and the subsequent rise of China had caught the old man's attention. Kitano was by then one of the richest men in Japan. Their relationship had ended twenty-two months before, when, at eighty-three years old, Hitoshi Kitano had been imprisoned at Hazelton. The previous sixty years had been a circular journey for Kitano, starting and ending in an American jail. Dunne had insisted that the FBI closely monitor Kitano since his imprisonment. It had been a mess of paperwork, not to mention demanding the more or less full-time attention of Robbins. But the FBI had more than twelve thousand agents—they could spare one. Where Kitano and the Uzumaki were concerned, Dunne took no chances.

The camera shot of Kitano's cell was from a light fixture in the ceiling. Kitano sat stock-still, staring into space. The time stamp said four-forty-one p.m. What the hell was wrong with him? Dunne wanted to crack open his skull and peer inside.

Dunne scanned the rest of the cell. On a small shelf on the wall were three books. "What's he reading?"

"One's a book on pigeon racing."

"He's a fanatic," Dunne said. "Specializing in long-distance races. Two years ago, right before he was put in, one of his pigeons won the twelfth Sun City Million Dollar in South Africa, the most prestigious pigeon race in the world."

"Good for him. Book number two: *Institutions, Industrial Upgrading, and Economic Performance in Japan: The 'Flying Geese' Paradigm of Catch-up Growth* by Terutomo Ozawa. I read it: the author advocates something called *gankou keitai*."

"Kaname Akamatsu's 'flying geese' model of Asian cooperation," Dunne said. "The economies of Asia would develop in the mythical pattern of flying geese, with Japan at the lead and the other nations—China, Korea, Malaysia, and the like—following behind."

"And book number three?"

"Yukio Mishima. *Sun and Steel:* art, action, and ritual death."

Dunne nodded. "Kitano idolized Mishima."

"Why would he idolize a Japanese novelist?"

"Because of how he died. Mishima killed himself in 1970. He was only forty-five and a huge cultural figure. He took the commandant of the Japan Self-Defense Forces hostage, then gave a speech from a balcony in Tokyo, demanding a return to rule by the emperor. He was trying to incite the Japanese military. Then he went inside and disemboweled himself."

"Why?"

"He thought Japan had been emasculated at the end of the war. He was a fanatical believer in Bushido—the way of the warrior. Kitano bought the sword that was used by Mishima's second to cut off his head. Kept it hung on his wall of his study." Dunne watched the old man. Kitano had fought for a victorious Japan but over the years he had come to believe in wealth as much as in force. He helped rebuild the Japanese industrial base and pushed for an expanded role of the military in Japanese society. The way to a reemergent Japan was through both the yen and the sword. But Japan had slipped beneath the waves of history. China was the new dragon.

Dunne knew Kitano's history like he knew his own. Sixty-four years before, after the events on the *Vanguard*, Kitano had been held in a military brig in Honolulu. The Pacific Command had launched a furious search for the other submarines, each purported to have a brass cylinder containing the Uzumaki. Over the years they'd recovered five of those original seven cylinders, four right after the war, including the one found by the *Vanguard*, and a fifth in the 1970s in a wreck off the southern California coast. The final two, assuming they existed, were never found.

Kitano had been held in a cell no larger than a closet for months on end, a beast in a cage, furious and raging. He had been questioned mercilessly, threatened repeatedly with trial and execution for war crimes. He claimed to have told them everything he knew—names of the Tokkō, information on their targets. They kept squeezing him until MacArthur cut a deal with Shiro Ishii. In May of 1947, Ishii turned over some ten thousand pages of records documenting the "research findings" obtained at Unit 731 about biological weapons, including the Uzumaki, in exchange for immunity. The prosecutions of all Unit 731 personnel were terminated, and Kitano was freed.

After his release, Kitano became part of a network of Unit 731 veterans who took up positions of authority within the Japanese medical and pharmaceutical industries. He was a cofounder of Green Cross, a Japanese pharmaceutical company that rose to prominence after the end of World War II. Green Cross ran one of the larger blood banks in Japan, and Kitano profited handsomely. Kitano abruptly left Green Cross in the early 1980s, selling his stake for in excess of two hundred million dollars. Soon after, Green Cross became enmeshed in controversy for knowingly selling HIV-tainted blood. Approximately a thousand Japanese contracted the disease and eventually died.

Kitano took his money and moved to the United States. He bankrolled various biological start-ups, both in La Jolla and north, in Silicon Valley. A few of these hit it big, and by the mid-1990s Kitano's net worth was approaching the five-billion mark. Through the 1990s, Kitano amassed even more with investments in a number of health-related dot-coms, clearly seeing both the promise and the hype of the Internet. In 2000, he divested from Silicon Valley just before the bust. He was flush with cash, looking for the next wave.

After the events of September 11, he saw it. The Kitano Group, his investment firm, poured money into military-related start-ups, correctly predicting that an administration unwilling by temperament to expand a federal bureaucracy would be dumping money into the private sector. They invested in companies that provided the military with everything from data-mining services to personnel. Kitano himself had personally overseen the group's investments in biotech ventures, particularly those aimed at bioterrorism countermeasures. They had large positions in most of the major players, from Genesys to DNA Biosystems. Kitano had also begun acquiring biotechnology companies in Japan, Korea, and China, constructing a pan-Asian network that would be the cornerstone of economic progress in the region as synthetic biology replaced silicon microelectronics as the dominant growth technology.

Kitano was not just involved in business ventures. He had also carefully cultivated relationships with a number of prominent American foreign-policy hawks, Lawrence Dunne among them. Kitano funded a trio of neoconservative, pro-Japanese think tanks, including one where Dunne had camped out between posts in Washington and stints teaching. They were a formidable team, working in concert to build a bulwark against the rising power of the Chinese. Their greatest achievement being, of course, the election of the current president of the United States, a pro-America, anti-China crusader.

Kitano had also helped Dunne take a modest nest egg and turn it into a not-so-modest nest egg. He'd also introduced Dunne to some of the other pleasures to be had by those of great wealth and power. Most of Dunne's colleagues did their best to keep Kitano at arm's length. Stories still surrounded him, rumors about his role in the Japanese war effort in World War II. This history drew Dunne like a moth. For almost two decades, the two men forged a professional and personal relationship based on their mutual distrust of China and their love of expensive scotch and women.

Kitano had it all—an enormous economic empire, and the ear of the most powerful government on the planet.

Then the old man fucked up.

KITANO WAS A STATUE, COMPLETELY MOTIONLESS AS HE SAT dead in the center in his cell.

"Does he know he's being watched?" Dunne asked.

"He's never shown signs. Never looks up. Nothing." Robbins shook his head. "I don't get it. His routine was normal this morning."

"Show me."

Robbins hit a few keys and an image on a second screen appeared, the time stamp showing seven-twenty-two a.m. Kitano was doing some kind of knee bends. "Every morning he performs a half-hour of calisthenics. After that he reads until the gates open and he's allowed to visit the common room. There he watches television. Give me a second. We've got a camera in there, too. I'll bring up the video from this morning."

The image shifted. The time stamp said eight-oh-four a.m. Kitano sat alone in a chair, watching television, rapt. The rest of the prisoners sat as far away as possible, clearly avoiding him.

Dunne knew why. Soon after arriving at USP Hazelton, a prisoner stole Kitano's lunch, thinking him to be a powerless old man. Kitano didn't react. But two days later, the guy's wife, a waitress in East Fishkill, New York, was bludgeoned almost beyond recognition. They had to use DNA to make the identification. The next day, the prisoner himself was found dead, bled out from a massive cut across the belly. Kitano's alibi was unassailable: he was locked in his cell. There was no evidence connecting Kitano to any of it, but after that the other inmates avoided Hitoshi Kitano like the plague.

Dunne focused on the screen. Kitano was watching the television with great concentration.

"What's he watching?"

"Just a second." He hit a few more keys, and the screen split, the right showing a feed from CNN, with a time stamp that matched the one from the camera showing Kitano.

CNN was showing footage of Bellevue. The reports ran on, a talking head, pretty and blond, with a little curl to her lips. "Can you get audio?"

"Sure."

Her voice came on, too loud until Robbins turned it down: ". . . is denying that this is connected to a case earlier in the day of a crazed young Japanese man found in Times Square, but an unnamed source who is an employee at the hospital challenges this assertion. The Japanese man, who sources identify as an undergraduate at Columbia University named Hitoshi Kitano, was missing his right middle finger. . . ."

Kitano stiffened at the mention of his name. The other inmates looked toward him.

"Hey, that's you!" someone said. "Kitano! Your name's on the TV!"

Kitano stood, but he seemed shaky, holding on to the chair a moment, steadying himself. He watched the news piece to the end. Then he walked purposefully out of the room, the other prisoners parting before him.

"And that's that," Robbins said, and clicked them back to the live view of Kitano's cell. "He came back to his cell, turned on his radio to a news site, sat down, and hasn't moved since."

Dunne kept thinking of a conversation with Kitano, almost ten years ago now. It was one of the most important conversations of Dunne's life, before or since. The thirty-six-year-old foreign-policy wonk and the seventy-five-year-old billionaire were discussing the geopolitical consequences of biological weapons, drinking a very fine scotch, as was their custom. Both men believed that biological war was a near inevitability. The technology was moving so fast, sooner or later biological attacks could become commonplace between adversaries.

It was unlikely that Europe would ever attack America with such weapons, nor would Japan. The Soviets had a huge biological-weapons program, but they had the good grace to collapse.

The Chinese wouldn't hesitate, both men agreed. Not if they felt threatened. Dunne believed the only way to avoid it was Pax

Americana. To decapitate the Chinese Communist leadership and replace them with others woven into the U.S. tapestry.

But how? How could one derail the China juggernaut before it became unstoppable?

They'd danced around it for quite a while before Dunne finally said it: the Uzumaki.

With the Uzumaki, they both agreed, it would be straightforward, once the United States had developed a cure.

Although a decade had since passed, Dunne could remember the conversation word for word. "Where would you release it?" Kitano had asked.

"One option is Harbin. Like construction stirred it up. Or near one of the Chinese agriculture ministry's biological research facilities south of there. Make it look like the incompetent fools were working on the Uzumaki, accidentally released it themselves."

"Like the Soviet anthrax incident at Sverdlovsk in '79?"

"Exactly."

Together they'd sketched out how it would go from there. The Uzumaki spreads, the country is isolated. Every other nation, fearful of a pandemic, shuts off travel, closes down trade with China. The Communist Party's hold on power was already tenuous, propped up by the twin sticks of nationalist pride and the promise of economic growth. Robbed of that prosperity and angry at a leadership impotent before the spreading horror, the people would riot, first in the countryside, then in the cities. The State Council would collapse within weeks, the country plunging into chaos. The stage would be set for a joint United States–Japanese force to step in and restore order, backed by a cure and a bayonet.

If the United States developed a cure, Kitano and Dunne speculated, it could bring down China anytime it wanted. The two men shared a secret bond, one that deepened as China continued to rise in power. The Uzumaki, the Japanese superweapon, might still change history. It was almost a game with them: two men planning the downfall of the most populous nation in the world.

But then Kitano changed the game.

The first report that something was amiss had come to Dunne from the CIA. A consortium of Central American and Asian agricultural investors had purchased ten thousand acres of Brazilian farmland about four hundred miles from where Toloff had discovered *Fusarium spirale*. On it they built a multimillion-dollar agricultural genetics research institute and agricultural experiment station called SunAgra. It was staffed with dozens of Ph.D.-level scientists with expertise ranging from crop science to fungal genetics, all living and working on-site. Their stated goal was to develop new strains of genetically modified maize for Far East markets. On the face of it, quite reasonable: corn had become a key crop throughout Asia. China was the number-two producer and consumer of corn in the world, and North Korea had become completely dependent on the crop under Kim Il-Sung. A little digging, however, turned up a number of alarming details. For one, scientists at the SunAgra Institute published no papers, wrote no grants, and filed few patents. Furthermore, one of the species they studied was a rare fungus known as *Fusarium spirale*, a strange choice, since it was unknown outside of a four-province area of Brazil and had no apparent relevance to the Far East markets. And most alarmingly, the investor group was largely a shell. More than ninety percent of the money behind the project came from a single Japanese investor, the billionaire Hitoshi Kitano.

Kitano was running his own private Uzumaki program.

DUNNE HAD NO CHOICE BUT TO TAKE ACTION. BUT HE WAS in a bind—Kitano could burn him. Much of the information Dunne had shared over the years during their China conversations was classified, putting him in violation of the State Secrets Protection Act. It was treason, sharing NOFORN classified information with a foreign national, not to mention plotting the overthrow of a foreign government. Such a thing could get you a very long prison term, possibly even a death sentence.

Dunne had provided Kitano with classified information, and in turn Kitano had shared insider information about certain publicly traded Japanese companies. Kitano could reveal this to federal prosecutors, how Dunne, while sipping Kitano's expensive scotch, had indiscreetly shared sensitive state secrets and subsequently made a small personal fortune in the Asian stock markets.

Dunne had one thing in his favor. The U.S. government under

no circumstances wanted to draw attention to the Uzumaki. The Japanese doomsday weapon was still unknown to all but a tightly held group in the security establishment. Toloff's program at USDA was top secret, no foreigners. If word of it got out that the United States was tinkering around with a biological weapon of that magnitude, not to mention the connection to Unit 731 and the tests on Chinese civilians, Beijing would go ballistic.

But Dunne also knew that no organization as large as Kitano's could stay entirely on the correct side of the law. He ordered some digging done, and the next time Kitano arrived in the United States, federal marshals arrested him for tax evasion. The trial was quick and antiseptic. Kitano remained silent throughout the trial, and never took the stand in his own defense.

Dunne had made sure of that. In a private meeting at Kitano's estate before the trial, Dunne had threatened Kitano with the biggest weapon he had. "Tangle with me at your peril. We'll disappear the Uzumaki program and then turn over everything on you to the Chinese Ministry of State Security: the records from Ishii, the photographs, the transcripts—anything and everything that implicates you in the torture and genocide of Chinese civilians. And after they're good and worked up, we'll turn *you* over to them for prosecution of war crimes."

That had shut Kitano up. Neither man spoke for almost a minute. Finally Kitano had said, "You have no fear that I will tell the Chinese everything?"

"You don't seem to realize that you lack any sort of credibility— a Japanese war criminal and mass murderer trying to save his skin? Listen closely. Beat the tax charges if you can, but close down SunAgra *immediately*. And stay far away from the Uzumaki."

ROBBINS PERKED UP. "LOOK. HE'S MOVING."

Kitano stood and went over to his small desk. He took down one of the books from his shelf, tore out a blank sheet from the back, then picked up a pen and set about writing.

"Can you read that?" Dunne asked.

"It's too far away. Let me see if I can—"

Kitano pulled his chair to the center of the cell, directly under the camera, and grabbed the page on which he had written. Then he stepped onto the chair and held up the paper so the image filled the screen.

"Shit. He knows about the camera," Robbins said.

Dunne barely heard him. He was transfixed by the message.

I CAN TELL YOU
WHO SHE IS

31

VLAD GLAZMAN TYPED AS HARPO READ OFF THE SEQUENCE
from the gel. The two had finished the second round of PCR and
dielectrophoresis a half-hour ago, and were recording the genetic
sequence of the glowing fungus. Harpo read off the bands, calling
out a sequence of A's, C's, T's, and G's that Vlad dutifully tran-
scribed.

Harpo halted, took a great big sigh.

"That's it?" Vlad asked.

"That's it."

Vlad stared at the string of letters:

GACTCGACTAGCTAGCAATTACTGATCAGCATTTTSCCCAAT
GCAGCATTTTCGACTGACCCGACTCGACTAGCTAGCAATTA
CTGATCAGCATTTTSCCCAATGCAGCATTTTCGAGCAAATCA
GACTCGACTAGCTAGCAATTACTGATCAGCATTTTSCCCAAT
GCAGCATTTTCGAGACTCGACTAGCTAGCAATTACTGATCA
GCATTTTSCCCAATGCAGCATTTTCGA . . .

It ran on for three pages.

"Run it through the translator."

Vlad hit a sequence of keys, shipping the data to a simple script translator called BabelGene, which rendered it in alphanumeric form. Each three-letter codon corresponded to a letter of the alphabet, AAA for "a," ACA for "b," and so on. Connor had been the one that had originally proposed the standard.

BabelGene did its job, and the screen filled with text.

The Uzumaki is an extraordinarily dangerous weaponized version of the species known as *Fusarium spirale*. It is highly virulent, spreading by spores that can survive in human, avian, and agricultural hosts. . . .

"Christ," Harpo said.

Vlad barely heard him, stunned as he read paragraph after paragraph detailing everything Connor had learned about the Uzumaki and everything he had done to try to defeat it. Not only that, but Connor said that he *had* one of the Uzumaki cylinders. Included in the message were the GPS coordinates of the location where it was hidden.

"Shit," Vlad said. "Double shit."

Vlad pushed Print. A LaserJet next to the computer fired up, spitting out a sheet of yellow paper with Connor's revelations.

Harpo grabbed the printout. "We should send this to someone. Now. CDC. FBI. CIA. Someone."

Vlad flipped his cellphone open. He hit Jake's number. It rang once, then clicked off.

He tried it again. Same result.

He checked the bars. Plenty of signal. So what was wrong?

Then he heard a pop, felt a splash of liquid on his cheek.

Vlad turned.

Harpo was falling, the back of his head gone.

JAKE HEARD TWO SHOTS, THEN A QUICK BURST OF FOUR more. He pulled at the cuffs, trying desperately to get loose. He was in the passenger's seat of the FedEx van, held by a ring and chain welded to the floorboard. Maggie and Dylan were tied up in the back. A strap of flesh-colored tape covered his mouth.

The cuffs holding him were virtually indestructible, brushed stainless steel with a rubberized lining and connected by a flexible band made from some kind of reinforced plastic. His bones would break before the cuffs would.

He watched Harpo's house, alert for any movement inside. Then another gunshot. Jake yanked with his arms, trying to pull loose the ring in the floor, but it was no use.

Jake saw movement. Vlad shuffled around the corner of the house, dragging his right leg behind him. He looked to be badly hurt, hopping forward, holding a yellow printout in his hand. He looked desperate, focusing on his goal, each hop deepening his grimace.

Jake tried to yell. Tried to warn him.

He had no idea Orchid was right behind him.

"VLADIMIR," ORCHID SAID, AND WAITED FOR HIM TO TURN.

She put the first bullet in his neck, just above the Adam's apple. His mouth formed an O, but no sound came out. He went down straightaway, no fuss, gurgling and spitting up blood.

She stood over him. The yellow printout was still in his grasp, jittering with the firing of his dying nerves.

She knelt, put the silencer directly to his temple, and put in a second bullet to finish it.

She waited until he was still, then pried the printout from his fingers.

She stood. Her own hands were shaking. This was it. Success or failure.

She read the message. By the fourth paragraph, she knew the answer.

She glanced up. Jake was staring at her, hate in his eyes.

No matter. He would be dead soon.

Orchid folded the sheet of paper carefully and tucked it in a pocket. Within hours she would have the Uzumaki. Within days it would be done. Kitano would be dead, the Uzumaki would be free, and she would have all the money. She did something she hadn't done in a long time.

Orchid smiled.

32

DUNNE STARED ACROSS THE TABLE AT KITANO, AND KITANO stared back. The only other person in the room was an FBI interrogator named Felix Carter. No lawyers were present, no aides, no security personnel. Any information gained would have no criminal relevance, could not be used in a court of law. Kitano had demanded this in writing. He had something to tell them. He would do so only if he was granted blanket immunity.

Age was destroying Kitano, but he was putting up a hell of a fight. The man was nothing but bone and sinew. His eyes had yellowed, the pupils dark and cold, a contrast to his bright orange prison jumpsuit. Dunne was in a three-thousand-dollar blue pinstriped suit by H. Huntsman, one of four by that Savile Row tailor that hung in his closet. When Dunne had first met Kitano, his most expensive suit had come from Brooks Brothers. Their individual fortunes changed, a role reversal for the billionaire and the up-and-coming wonk, one ascending spectacularly, the other falling dramatically.

Kitano had three further stipulations. The first was that Dunne be physically present. Dunne knew why. Kitano had leverage on him and was prepared to use it.

The second one was unusual. Kitano kept a large pigeon rookery at his house in the Maryland countryside, north of Washington, D.C. Even in jail, he'd made sure the pigeons were attended by a full-time caretaker. Hitoshi Kitano demanded full and regular access to his pigeons.

Requirement number three was perhaps the most visceral, in that it demonstrated the primitive survival instinct. Dunne could tell by the videos of Kitano talking to the FBI. He knew Kitano's body language like he knew his own father's. Kitano said the woman was after him. She wanted to kill him, he was certain. Kitano's whole body had stiffened when he'd said it, his hands held in tight fists. He was scared to death.

Demand number three: under no circumstances, no matter what happened, no matter what pressure she applied, could they turn him over to her.

IN THE ADJOINING ROOM WAS A TEAM OF INTERROGATION experts analyzing the spectrum of Kitano's voice patterns, the fluctuations in his pupil size, the electrical conductivity of his skin. The FBI interrogator would be getting real-time updates on Kitano's stress levels.

The interrogator began by reading a summary of events pertaining to the woman. Dunne took no pleasure watching Kitano's shocked reaction to the details of the victim taken to Bellevue, the "731 Devil" symbols carved into his chest. A similar reaction when Kitano learned of the finger bone in the cylinder with the words KITANO MUST PAY.

Before today, Kitano couldn't talk about their cozy and highly improper relationship without getting himself in at least as much trouble as Dunne. But now the duplicitous rat had blanket immunity.

THE QUESTIONS STARTED EASY, QUERIES ABOUT KITANO'S personal information, his business interests, all for the instrument boys to get baseline readings. From there it moved into more interesting territory, questions about the man dropped off in Times Square. Dunne watched closely, attentive to Kitano's every gesture. He appeared calm, answering in simple declarative sentences.

Finally the interrogator nodded to Dunne.

"All right, Hitoshi," Dunne said. "Talk. Do you know who the woman is? Or are you just jerking us around?"

Kitano's eyes met Dunne's. "Did you find a tattoo on the victim? An Orchid flower? Anything like that?"

Dunne said, "Yes."

Kitano nodded. "She goes by the name Orchid."

"Orchid," Dunne said. "How do you know?"

"I saw the photo. I recognized her."

Kitano was correct. They'd picked up their first real information on the woman less than an hour ago. The name tattooed on the finger bone had set off alarm bells with the CIA station chief in Beijing.

"Who is Orchid?" Dunne asked Kitano.

"She is a kind of specialist. Known in the Chinese right-wing circles. It is rumored she was behind the bombing of Japan's Yasukuni Shrine. Last year. And the murder of Kabawi."

"Kabawi?"

"A conservative member of the Japanese legislature. He led the movement to purify the textbooks of anti-Imperial rhetoric. What your newspapers would call a *revisionist*. Denying the Rape of Nanking. The Korean comfort women."

"Why does Orchid want you?"

"Many know of my past, what happened at Harbin. Her benefactor wants revenge."

"Who does she work for?"

"There are rumors of a billionaire Chinese backer. Rabidly anti-Japanese."

"No names?"

"Billionaires in China are a cancer. In 2003 there were none—now there are hundreds. It is very dangerous, such sudden power, sudden wealth. It amplifies one's secret desires, secret prejudices. Such men are very dangerous."

You should know, Dunne thought. "Why did Orchid torture Liam Connor?" he asked.

Kitano's demeanor changed at this question. Dunne saw it in his face, his body language. A chink in the man's confident armor. Now they were getting down to it.

The room was silent. Dunne began to wonder if the old man had suffered a stroke.

Finally he spoke. "Do you know what happened after they destroyed the USS *Vanguard* back in 1946? About the confrontation I had with Connor on the USS *North Dakota*?"

A knock, and the door to the interrogation room opened. It was Dunne's attaché. He passed Dunne a note. It said one word: IMPORTANT.

DUNNE STEPPED OUT INTO THE HALL. HIS DEPUTY WAS WAIT-ing. "What now?"

"In Ithaca. They found a woman shot dead near Maggie Connor's workplace. No one can find Ms. Connor. Or her son. The police said there was a fire. And a second fire that was even stranger. Out in the sticks with the rednecks. Firemen found what looks like the remnants of a state-of-the-art biotech lab. The firemen also found two bodies inside, both with gunshot wounds. One of the victims was a Cornell professor, a friend of Jake Sterling's."

"Sterling? Has anyone spoken to him about this yet?"

"They can't find Sterling, either."

"What? But he should be at Detrick by now."

"He never showed."

"And why wasn't I told?"

No explanation.

"Is everyone around here goddamned incompetent? Why didn't Sterling show up?"

"No idea, sir."

DUNNE WAS SHAKEN AS HE STEPPED BACK INSIDE THE INTER-rogation room. He sensed a malevolent pattern, a dark web of danger just outside his reach. Now he wanted answers. "No more stalling, Hitoshi. Why did Orchid kill Connor?"

Kitano raised his right hand, highlighting his missing finger. "She is looking for a small brass cylinder. The length of the medial phalange finger bone. At Unit 731, I had it implanted in my finger. I was extracting it when Connor stopped me. He took it. I had no intention of bleeding to death, not before I released it. I am the seventh Tokkō."

The light went on in Dunne's head. "Connor kept the cylinder? He was holding on to a specimen of the Uzumaki all these years?"

"Yes."

He leaned back, stunned. He thought of the reports from Ithaca, Maggie Connor going missing. The pieces snapped together, a cold knot growing in Dunne's chest.

· 33 ·

JAKE DROVE THE FEDEX VAN ALONG ROUTE 96A, THE SAME road he'd taken the morning before. FedEx vans were like telephone poles, part of the landscape. The President could put on a FedEx uniform and no one would notice him.

Orchid crouched behind him in the storage area, gun drawn. Dylan and Maggie were tied up in the back, mouths wrapped in packing tape. Orchid was guiding them by Liam's message, the yellow sheet of paper she had taken from Vlad. Jake didn't know what the text said, but he had a damned good idea where it was leading them. There wasn't much else out here but the Seneca Army Depot. They were just a few minutes away now.

In the rearview mirror, Jake caught glimpses of Maggie and Dylan in the shadows. Orchid had secured them to the wall with the same kind of high-tech handcuffs she'd used on him. The cuffs opened and closed electronically, and Orchid controlled them by tapping a sequence on her leg with her right hand. The same kind of tapping also controlled the electric shocks that came from Jake's belt. There must be some kind of transducer built into Orchid's gloves. She used them to control everything.

He paid close attention to the patterns of the taps of her fingers.

. . .

UP AHEAD THE FENCING STARTED, VISIBLE IN THE VAN'S headlights. On Orchid's command, Jake parked the van near a locked gate. He turned off the headlights.

"Put these on," Orchid said, tossing him the cuffs.

Jake obeyed, closing the latch down loosely.

Orchid tapped a pattern on her leg and the cuffs came alive. The shackles tightened, pulling in close, to the edge of real pain.

She tossed him a small army shovel. He caught it with one hand. She tapped another sequence on her leg, and Jake jumped. A bolt of electricity shot through him, emanating from his waist belt, and just as suddenly stopped.

Jake was practically hyperventilating, his heart beating *rat-a-tat-tat*.

"Don't forget," she said.

THEY WALKED DOWN AN ENDLESS ROW OF BUNKERS, EACH one an ominous, hulking shape in the growing darkness. Jake was in the lead, Orchid forty feet behind, Dylan just ahead of her. Maggie was still in the van, unconscious—Orchid had stuck a needle in her that knocked her out in less than a minute. Orchid had placed a handwritten sign in the window that said, TOW TRUCK ON ITS WAY, and they'd left her behind.

Jake had taken a careful inventory of Orchid's tools. He had been watching her closely, both in the van and now, catching looks when he could. She had on a small black backpack and carried a Glock in her hand. She'd put on thick, wraparound goggles that Jake was pretty sure were equipped with night vision. And she had her gloves. She could shock him with a few taps of her fingers. She could similarly control their cuffs. Jake was pretty sure that two taps of her index finger, one with her ring finger, followed by three with her thumb caused the cuffs to tighten. The opposite sequence caused them to loosen.

If Jake could get to her, knock her out or kill her, he thought he could release the cuffs. But he had to get past that gun. And he had to do it without getting Dylan killed.

Every few hundred feet was another concrete bunker, all long out of use. They'd passed twelve of them so far. He was alert to everything, every sight and every sound. In the distance he heard squawking. Liam had told him there was a pond on the other side of that tree ridge, a stopover for the geese.

A WHITE DEER CROSSED THE ROAD UP AHEAD, A GHOSTLY apparition seeming to float in the darkness, its body as luminous as the moon. When the fences went up around the periphery in 1941, a decent-sized population of deer were trapped inside, and a few rare white deer were among them. Over the years, the depot guards hunted the brown deer, but they left the white ones to graze among the bunkers. Seneca Army Depot now had the largest white deer population in the world. The simplest rule of evolution, of ecology, of ethics. You reap what you sow.

Liam had brought Jake here ostensibly to show him the white deer. Liam put out salt licks, then collected the DNA that scraped off the deers' tongues when they licked them. It had always seemed a bit odd to Jake: Liam wasn't a population biologist. The deer were visually striking but nothing special genetically, simply rich in the genes for white fur.

Now Jake understood: the deer were not what had attracted Liam to Seneca Army Depot. The real reason was its isolation and the bunkers. Miles of nothing. Liam had told him that a single guard was responsible for patrolling the whole damn thing.

If Liam wanted to hide a dangerous pathogen, this would be a great place to do it.

"Stop," Orchid called from behind. She ordered him to veer right. The visibility was better now, the moonlight bathing the white concrete bunkers in an eerie glow.

Jake glanced over his shoulder, saw Orchid herding Dylan before her, the boy scared half to death. She checked a handheld GPS, triangulating in space and time by four satellites flying over twelve thousand miles overhead. Liam must have left a latitude and longitude reading that told where to find the Uzumaki. Orchid's footsteps slowed regularly each time she checked the GPS. She was checking it all the time.

"Take a forty-five-degree right turn."

Jake turned. There was nothing. Only empty grass, waist-high. A few chunks of concrete sticking up through the weeds.

"In there?"

"Twenty meters," she said.

He counted them off, twenty strides, pushing through the tangle of brush and weeds. He stopped when the count was done.

At first he saw nothing but grass and brush, but then he spied a dinner plate–sized chunk of concrete. In the moonlight, he could just make out a rough design etched in the concrete, three lines spinning outward from the center. A spiral.

"That's it," Orchid said, glancing down at the page with Liam's message. "Move it aside and dig."

Jake held up his hands, still shackled together.

With the gun, she gestured to Dylan beside her, his hands cuffed before him. "Get cute and I shoot the boy." She tapped her fingers on her leg and the cuff on Jake's right wrist popped open.

Jake was careful to note the sequence of taps she used.

Jake took the spade and went to work.

After ten minutes, at a depth of maybe three feet, his spade struck concrete. He brushed away the dirt.

"Dig it out," Orchid said.

Five minutes later, he had it free of the earth. It was a cylindrical plug of concrete, maybe a foot in diameter and two feet long. It weighed about fifty pounds. A piece of rebar stuck out of the top, like a handle.

Orchid said, "I was sure it was in one of the bunkers. I checked nearly every damned one."

Jake understood. The bunkers drew your attention, but they were decoys. Liam had hidden the Uzumaki in a nondescript patch of weeds. Orchid couldn't have found this spot in a hundred years. This is what Liam had been hiding, and what he had died trying to protect.

"Give it to me," she said.

THE ENTRANCE TO THE BUNKER WAS SEALED BY A MASSIVE iron door, ten feet tall and thick as a safe's door. A larger metal bar sealed it closed, locked by a simple combination padlock. Orchid read him the combination from the sheet of yellow paper. Jake opened the lock and lifted the handle. To his surprise, the door swung open easily, the hinges barely squeaking. The interior of the bunker was dark, but Jake detected a kind of odd glow inside, brightening and fading with the rhythm of a heartbeat.

"Inside," Orchid ordered.

As Jake entered, the source of the glow became clear. Bioluminescent patches of red, green, and yellow all along the walls, pulsing slowly on and off. The glowing fungi that Liam had left in the letterbox—there were rows and rows of it here.

"Go to the back," Orchid said.

Orchid flipped a switch, and an overhead light turned on.

The bunker was a half-cylinder, twenty feet high in the center and maybe a hundred feet long, like a submarine cut in half. The floor was swept bare concrete. But it wasn't empty, like the one that Jake had visited when he came here with Liam. Rows of lab benches lined the walls, some covered with beakers, pipettes, and a few larger pieces of equipment, others with trays of glowing fungi, pulsing red, yellow, and green. It was a smaller, stripped-down version of Liam's lab back at Cornell. He must have brought it in bit by bit over months. Maybe years. Assembling it on his trips to supposedly observe the white deer.

Orchid directed Jake to set the concrete plug down. Orchid held Dylan close, the gun to his head.

Dylan was wide-eyed, staring at a strange chair in the center of the space. It was made of black reinforced carbon struts, almost like a high-tech electric chair. There were straps on the arms and legs, and there was a terrifying head assembly of bolts and clamps.

Next to the setup was a small metal table. On it, Jake saw a MicroCrawler.

It took him a moment to realize.

This is where she had tortured Liam.

Dylan was transfixed by the chair. He looked scared to death. He seemed to grasp what it was for. He was shaking, in full-blown panic.

He broke for the door.

Orchid caught him with one arm and tossed him back, smashing him into one of the cases holding the glowing fungi. The boy fell to the ground, pulling trays of fungi down on top of him.

Jake took a step toward her. "If you hurt him, I'll—"

Orchid tapped on her leg and a lightning bolt ran up Jake's spine. He fell to the ground, quivering, seeing white.

Finally it stopped. After a few seconds he managed to sit up.

Dylan had backed against a wall, patches of glowing fungus clinging to him. His face was empty, hollow, as if the boy Jake knew and loved had disappeared.

"Stay still," she said to Dylan, "or I'll shoot you."

Orchid pointed to the chunk of concrete. "Break it open," she said to Jake.

Jake slowly stood. He lifted the plug of concrete and threw it down hard on the concrete floor. A corner broke off, but nothing more. The second time was no better. The third time it hit at an angle and split open cleanly, revealing a hollow, spherical cavity inside. Inside the cavity was a large child's red balloon.

An old builder's trick. You want to leave a cavity inside concrete, help keep the weight down, you embed an inflated balloon when you pour it.

Jake picked up the balloon. Something was inside it.

Jake ripped the balloon away, the rubber old and brittle. Inside, he discovered a rectangular metal box the size of a paperback book. Jake guessed it was made of titanium. The box was featureless except for a thin, almost invisible seam at its midsection and an index card–sized display panel on top. The panel sprang to life, turning a soft white in response to Jake's touch.

Words appeared on the screen.

ENTER #1

Orchid stared at the box for a long moment, then said, "Touch your right index finger to the pad."

Jake did as ordered. The words on the screen faded, then said:

IDENTITY #1 ACCEPTED
ENTER #2

Orchid said, "Take it to Dylan."

Jake understood. Liam had programmed it so that only Jake and Dylan could open it. Jake guessed that Maggie's prints would open it, too. Any two of them.

He carried the box to Dylan, the boy's hands still cuffed together.

Dylan looked terrified.

"Hang in there," Jake said. "You never know when the blueberries will come."

Dylan seemed to understand. It was one of his elephant jokes. It wasn't blueberries that would be coming. It would be elephants.

Jake held the box out. Dylan touched his finger to the pad.

The screen changed again, said:

IDENTITY #2 ACCEPTED

Jake stepped back. He heard a click. He opened the lid.

Inside was a layer of gray clay. Pushed into it was a thin brass cylinder, perhaps an inch long and thin as the ink cartridge in a ballpoint pen. Jake guessed what it was. Liam had told Jake how on their missions the Japanese Tokkō had carried the Uzumaki in small brass cylinders.

"Put it down," Orchid said. "On that table."

Jake ignored her. He carefully removed the cylinder from the box. The thickness changed slightly midway along, where there was a seam. The two halves were threaded, then screwed together. Unscrew the two halves, release the contents, and millions of people would die.

"Professor Sterling."

He glanced up at Orchid. He saw the excitement written on her face. This was it. This was when she was most vulnerable.

"Put it down on that table. Then reconnect your cuff," Orchid said.

Jake turned to face her. He held the cylinder tight in his right hand.

"Put it *down*," she said, raising the gun to point it directly at his skull.

Jake said, "No."

EVERY GOOD SOLDIER KEPT A THREAD, A LIFELINE TO THEIR larger self. The lifeline was a rock-solid anchor, a fixed point that would allow them to act for the greater good no matter what the cost, to put aside any fear or hesitation. For some it was a connection to a particular person: a wife, a parent, or a child. For others it was an idea, a belief in the rightness of their task. For Jake, it had been his belief that a soldier's suffering, given or received, prevented a still larger suffering. That had been his anchor during the Gulf War. It let him come back from what they had done.

Soldiers without an anchor were time bombs. Once they left the military, once freed from the structure of regimen and hierarchy, these souls became lost. The darkness in Orchid's eyes said she was capable of anything. She had killed Vlad at close range, without a thought. She had tortured Liam Connor in an unimaginably gruesome fashion. She would set off a pandemic as easily as another might kill a fly.

She could not be allowed to have the cylinder.

Jake glanced at Dylan. He was watching everything closely, intently. He was terrified but still very aware of his surroundings. He knew something was coming. He was ready.

"Give it to me," Orchid said to Jake. "Or he will pay."

"All right," Jake said, swinging his arm back. "Here. Catch."

Jake tossed the cylinder.

For Jake, the world slowed to quarter speed. Orchid reached out with her free hand. She couldn't help it, the desire to catch from the air what she most desired. But the cylinder was outside of her grasp. Jake had not tossed it to Orchid. He tossed it toward Dylan.

Orchid lost her focus for just a split second. Her gun hand drifted slightly. Jake was already moving toward her. She was off balance now, trying to recover, and she overcompensated. She tried to do two things at once. She tried to bring the gun back to Jake and fire. And she simultaneously went to tap out the sequence on her leg to shock him.

Twice meant neither. Both were slowed by a split second. The split second that Jake gained was enough. Out of the corner of his eye, Jake saw Dylan catch the cylinder. At the same instant, Orchid fired, but the bullet missed, screaming past Jake's right ear.

Jake caught her square and they both went down, the gun skittering away across the concrete. Jake landed a blow on her cheek. He felt the crunch of bone, and she seemed to go limp, her hands at her sides.

Zap! The electricity hit him like a hammer, every nerve in his body firing at once. He fought it, forcing himself to focus through the fireworks going off in his head. He felt as though his entire body were on fire.

He grabbed her right hand and pulled her fingers back, breaking at least one of them. He gritted his teeth, growling through them to keep focused, and tapped her broken hand against her leg, trying to reproduce the sequence that would stop the electric shocks. He smashed her hand again and again against her leg, losing his ability to think. He held on to her tightly, but she was like an eel in his grasp, twisting and turning.

"Dylannn, ruhhh! Ruhhhh," he dribbled out, the words barely understandable, his teeth chattering, his stomach convulsing. He threw up.

Jake held on and Orchid fought, Jake's thoughts reduced to a single command: *Squeeze, squeeze, squeeze.* In the strange contours of his electrified mind, he had become a python, choking his prey to death.

They were like this, Jake holding her, the shocks hitting him in waves. He had no idea how long this went on. Seconds? Minutes? All he was aware of was the continuous chatter of the impulses running up and down every nerve in his body.

Then suddenly Orchid was free of his grasp. He reached for her, but his arms curled up like a dying spider, every muscle contracting, every nerve firing at once. He could no longer see Orchid. He could no longer see anything but burst after burst of searing white light.

He could form only one thought: *Run.*

· 34 ·

DYLAN RAN.

He bolted out of the bunker, brass cylinder in his hand. He ran as fast as he could down the middle of the road, back the way they'd come, heading instinctively to his mother.

After a few hundred yards he realized that is exactly what Orchid would expect him to do. He turned right, running as fast as he could between two of the bunkers. The weeds sliced and grabbed at him, his side already starting to ache. He knew he was making all kinds of noise, but he had to get away. He would reach the next road, then turn back in the direction of the FedEx van. Was it better to run down the road? Or stick to the grass?

He heard a slam in the distance, what he took to be the closing of the bunker door. He stopped and listened. Who was closing it? Jake? Orchid?

Please let it be Jake. He wanted to run back, to Jake.

But it might not be Jake.

He started forward again, running fast. He'd heard footsteps. In the weeds.

It had to be Orchid. Jake would call out.

He looked down at the brass cylinder in his hand. Dylan understood. This was the most important task that he'd ever faced. Maybe that he would ever face.

She couldn't get it. No matter what.

He had to hide.

The big metal door on the bunker to his right was open a few inches. He was drawn to it, a primordial instinct, seek shelter in a cave. He ducked inside, just able to slip through.

It was dark inside, pitch-black. Not like the other one with the glowing *Fusarium*.

He wanted to pull the door closed behind him, but that would make a noise. *Go all the way in.* He'd be safe. There was no way she could check them all.

He stepped deeper into the bunker.

The darkness swallowed him.

The bunker was in bad shape, damp and leaky. The smell of mold was strong. He walked with his hands in front until he found the back wall. He moved as far as he could from the strip of moonlight that leaked in through the partially open door.

He crouched down, cold and scared. He listened carefully for any sound, trying not to breathe. All he heard was a steady drip of water. He wanted to go inside himself, to hide far away.

The blackness was absolute. Darker than anyplace he'd ever been.

Otherwise, he would have never noticed them.

On his shirt sleeves were tiny pinpricks of glowing light, slowly pulsing on and off. Bits of glowing fungus were still clinging to his clothes.

ORCHID SCANNED LEFT AND RIGHT, LOOKING FOR ANY SIGN of the boy with her night-vision goggles. She cradled her gloved right hand in her left. The son of a bitch Sterling had broken two of her fingers. She'd kicked him senseless, then had grabbed her backpack and filled it with Connor's fluorescent fungus, scraping it off the metal trays as fast as she could.

She'd tripped the electronic controller near the main door that activated the self-destruct mechanism, a series of incendiary devices she had placed in strategic positions inside the bunker. She had always planned to destroy Connor's hideaway. In two minutes, there would be no traces left of anything inside, all of Connor's work turned to ash. And now Jake Sterling would be ash, too.

She just had to deal with the boy.

He had a head start, and the Seneca Army Depot was a huge damned place. If he decided to hide, she would never find him in time. It would take days to search all the bunkers. And she didn't have days. She had only minutes. Soon the explosion would go off and this place would be crawling with people. She had to get the cylinder, get back to the FedEx van, and head to the border.

Stick to basics. Keep looking.

Orchid checked up and down the empty road between the bunkers. *Which way?*

Then she saw something odd. She almost missed it, thought it was a flicker in the noise in her infrared CCDs.

But there it was again. A tiny blinking light. She took off her glasses, and it vanished. It was so faint, she could see it only with the goggles.

She jogged over to investigate. It was a tiny piece of fungus, stuck to a blade of grass. The blinking fungus.

She wiped it onto the finger of her glove. It must be on his clothes.

She scanned the weeds around her. In a few seconds she saw another little glowing patch. Then another, like bread crumbs.

The trail was almost too easy to follow.

JAKE REGAINED CONSCIOUSNESS SLOWLY. HE FELT AS THOUGH he'd been beaten with a hammer, every muscle aching and pulsing as he sat up. The room was dark, save for the glowing fungi and a flashing red light near the door.

How long had he been out? He had no idea. He tried to remember what had happened. At first his memories were jumbled, like a jangly, disjointed dream. But after a few seconds his thoughts popped into their proper place. The digging. The cylinder. The struggle.

Dylan.

He jumped to his feet and tried to open the door. He pushed on it hard, looking for a handle but finding none. He threw himself against it. The massive thing didn't budge an inch.

It must be locked from the outside. He'd never get through it.

He turned to inspect the blinking red light next to the sealed door. A timer. Fifty-four seconds and counting down.

Oh, shit. Jake had been in the 46th Engineer Battalion. They worked with explosives all the time. He recognized the box for what it was: a timer counting down a destruct sequence. Three dots below the numbers told Jake there were three explosives.

He picked up the timer, looking for wires. None. It was wireless, he was sure.

"Damn it!" he yelled, the sound echoing in the sealed bunker. He knew the design—the timer had a fail-safe mechanism so it couldn't be disarmed once the destruct sequence had begun. Once started, the timer put out a steady signal to the bombs. When the signal terminated, the explosives detonated. If you disabled or destroyed the timing unit, the signal would cease and the bombs would go off immediately.

His only chance was to find the bombs.

The first one was easy, taped into a corner near the door. It was sealed in a plastic shell. There was no way he could disarm it without setting it off.

Jake scanned the place, looking for cover. The only light was from the glowing fungi.

The numbers in the corner counted down.

Forty seconds.

There must be ventilation in these bunkers. Jake scanned the walls, up high. On the back wall, and the end of the chamber, was a HEPA filter unit designed to remove any particulates. He pulled over a table, jumped up, and ripped out the unit. Beyond it was a thin passageway in the concrete, maybe wide enough for him to crawl through, maybe not. At the far end he saw a metal grating— cast iron, he guessed. No way he could get through that in time.

He'd have to let the explosives do it for him.

He tossed the first explosive into the vent, then searched for the others. The second one he found in the back corner of the room. He grabbed it and tossed it into the vent with the first. But where was number three? He checked the timer. Ten seconds left.

Nine, eight . . .

Damn it, where?

Jake turned over tables, looking everywhere. Then it hit him.

She'd want an explosive in the ventilation passageway. An explosion there would create a pressure wave that pushed inward, sealing in the roiling heat and pressure from the other two bombs. The three explosions together would turn the bunker into a high-pressure, high-temperature inferno, incinerating everything inside.

There was only one problem. He hadn't seen a bomb in the vent passageway.

Five seconds. Four . . .

Jake ran to the HEPA filter on the floor. He ripped off the back panel.

Three.

Two.

There it was. Jake grabbed it, did a hook shot with the bomb into the vent chamber, and dove behind a table.

DYLAN HEARD THE BLAST AS HE COWERED IN THE CORNER.

His whole body was shaking. He wanted more than anything to cry out, to scream and holler and draw the attention of someone. Anyone. But his mother was tied up and drugged. Jake? He didn't know about Jake. He prayed that Jake was out there, but he knew that he wasn't. Jake would be calling his name. The only person who would be searching for him without calling his name would be the woman. Orchid.

There it was again. Footsteps outside.

He looked at the cylinder in his hands. He had to get rid of it. Jake had trusted him. He tried to figure out what Jake would want him to do.

Why hadn't he thrown it in the bushes? There was nowhere to hide it here. If she found him, she would get it.

Dripping water. He heard dripping water. Where did it go?

He thought of the other bunker. It had a drain in the floor, in the middle of the room. Maybe this one did, too.

He crawled on his hands and knees in the direction he thought was the center of the bunker.

What could he do? Swallow the cylinder? No. If she knew what he'd done, she could . . . The thought made Dylan shudder. *Then how?*

Then Dylan realized he didn't have to keep the cylinder from her. The dangerous stuff was *inside*. What if he emptied it out? Gave her an empty cylinder? How would she know?

He tried to twist it open, felt the threads give. The rectangle of light at the door to the bunker flickered. *Be brave, Dylan,* he told himself.

The shadows at the door shifted. Orchid was out there.

He rapidly unscrewed the cylinder. Turned it upside down over the grating to dump the contents.

What?

He was pretty sure nothing came out.

He took half of it, tapped it on the floor.

Nothing.

The other half dinked onto the concrete and rolled away.

Was it empty? Could the cylinder already be empty? Why would Pop-pop hide an empty cylinder?

Surface tension. Pop-pop had taught him how bugs could slide along the surface of the water, held up by surface tension. He also told him how hard it was to get liquids out of small spaces in rocks, for the same reason. He'd demonstrated with a thin little straw, about the same size as the cylinder. You get water inside, you couldn't get it out by shaking.

There was only one way to get it out. Negative pressure.

Suck it out.

Be brave.

Dylan saw Orchid's shadow in the doorway. "Don't move," she said.

Dylan placed the half-cylinder to his lips and sucked on it. The liquid hit his mouth, salty. He spit it out. Into the drain, spitting and spitting, trying to get it all out.

He was shaking, scared to death. He looked around him. Where was the other half of the cylinder?

WHEN JAKE CAME TO, HE COULDN'T HEAR A THING.

The blast had left him dazed, ears ringing, with a brutal aching in his skull. He tried speaking, but his voice sounded muffled, barely audible.

But he was alive.

He coughed, tried to stand. The air was searing hot, the chamber full of smoke. He couldn't see anything, couldn't breathe without his lungs burning. He found the ventilation shaft, grabbed it and pulled himself into it, his hands burning from the heat. Unable to breathe, he crawled forward, then pushed out the remnants of the grating and fell out headfirst, dropping ten feet to the earth like a bag of rocks.

The first gulp of air was the sweetest he'd ever tasted.

He coughed and spit, his lungs still on fire, his hands covered with blisters. He staggered around to the front of the bunker, but he saw no one.

He called out, "Dylan!" But he barely heard his own voice.

He started running down the middle of the road. "Dylan!"

He saw nothing at the first juncture. Just rows and rows of bunkers. He couldn't hear anything. He felt as though his head were full of bees.

A shadow in the weeds on the road to his right. A shape emerged, started running toward him.

Dylan!

He ran toward the boy, scooped him up in his arms. Dylan was crying.

"Are you all right?"

Dylan answered, but Jake couldn't hear him through the buzz in his skull.

"Are you all right?"

Dylan nodded yes.

"Where is she?"

He spoke, but again Jake couldn't understand.

"Where? Point!"

Dylan kept speaking, but he also pointed. Back toward the edge of the depot, where they had parked the FedEx van.

"Stay here!" Jake yelled.

DYLAN WATCHED JAKE RUN AWAY.

He was again alone in the darkness.

He was suddenly very cold, shivering, his teeth chattering. He could still taste the salty liquid on his tongue.

DAY 5

■ FRIDAY, OCTOBER 29 ■

VECTORS

· 35 ·

LEVI BROWN LOVED THE QUIET. IT WAS BEFORE SIX A.M., the sky deep blue-black and empty, save for the scatter of stars. The lights from a lone street lamp stippled the old playground near the Genesee River, just outside the Rochester city center. Levi had a good half-hour before the early-morning mothers arrived, kids in tow. The neighborhood wasn't the best, but there was little reason to fear a mugging this time of day. No gang-banger was crazy enough to be out at this time. Not in this cold. No one would interfere with the coming transaction.

Levi spotted his customer approaching from the north. The customer was well dressed, about forty, probably upper management at Kodak, an overachiever looking for something to fill the void.

No words were spoken. Levi handed over the two vials of small multicolored pills and took the cash in exchange. He quickly counted it, eight hundred dollars.

Transaction done.

Levi waited until the customer was out of sight, enjoying the feel of the money.

A siren started up in the distance.

He had turned to leave when he spied it, sitting on a bench, plain as you please. A woman's purse.

The purse was red leather, small, with a thin shoulder strap. The kind the young girls carried.

He picked it up. The zipper was open. He looked inside, saw a fold of money. A lot of money.

He reached in to get it and was rewarded with a sharp sting. "OUCH!"

He jumped, dropped the purse on the ground.

He looked at his finger. Two pools of blood were rising on the side of his finger. He wiped it off and saw two thin cuts before the blood rose to hide them again.

What the hell?

Levi knelt before the purse, carefully picked it up. He shook out the contents.

The sirens were getting closer.

The money was there, along with a few pens, a tube of lip balm, and a condom in its wrapper. He picked up the money.

Something slipped from between the bills and lay on the concrete, sparkling in the first rays of the morning sun. At first he thought it was some kind of crystal, or a piece of glass, but it had metal strips on it. More like a little computer chip.

"Are those *legs?*" Levi said aloud.

He prodded it with the end of a pen. It skittered backward, then raised up on its hind legs as if to put up a fight.

The sirens were getting louder. He saw the spinning lights playing across the buildings.

One thought took over: *Get the hell out of here.*

THE UH-60 BLACK HAWK CAME IN LOW. ARMY CAPTAIN JAMES McNair, 10th Mountain Division, was at the stick. Major Arthur Ricks, 2nd Battalion, 10th Combat Aviation Brigade, was at the open door. This was his baby. They had scrambled out of Fort Drum, a straight shot over Lake Ontario, running full out, covering the distance in less than twenty minutes. The orders had been clear but undeniably odd. They were after a robotic spider. And if they found it, or if the locals found it, Ricks and his men were to seal it in a biohazard box and get that little robot spider out of there as soon as goddamn possible.

Ricks spotted the park. It was tree-lined, square. It was also empty. The local police had established a perimeter. Ricks counted eight squad cars.

"Major. Over there."

Ricks saw it in infrared. A man running along the river, away from the park.

Ricks tapped his headset and spoke to the brigade commander back at Drum. He watched his language. Higher-ups were also on the line. "We've got a civilian, fleeing. On foot."

"Jesus Christ" came the response, a voice Ricks didn't recognize. "Get him. *Now.*"

LEVI WAS RUNNING NOW. HE DIDN'T UNDERSTAND WHAT WAS happening. Something big was happening, something bad. That's when he heard it. A low *swish, swish, swish,* barely audible over the sirens in the distance, but then louder.

He looked up. A helicopter popped into view over the trees, hovered directly overhead, huge and violent, the wind tearing at them, stirring up huge swirls of leaves.

He froze, tossed the money on the ground. The helicopter wash tossed the bills to and fro.

A voice boomed from above. "Do not move!"

· 36 ·

THE NEWS OF THE SUCCESSFUL INTERCEPTION REACHED Lawrence Dunne as his Town Car pulled into the gates of Camp David. Forty minutes before, they'd received an untraceable satellite phone call from Orchid, with GPS coordinates for a park in Rochester, New York. She claimed a Crawler infected with the Uzumaki was there. A Black Hawk out of Fort Drum had taken the man who found it into custody. Local law enforcement was cordoning off the surrounding neighborhood, and a CBIRF squad was on its way.

The officers at the guardhouse did a complete car search before waving Dunne's car through. On the insistence of the head of the Secret Service, the President and his crisis team had relocated to Naval Support Facility Thurmont, as Camp David was officially known. The reason was simple: thousands of people passed within a few hundred feet of the White House every day, any of whom could release a burst of spores that might find their way into the building's ventilation ducts. Camp David, on the other hand, was an isolated one-hundred-eighty-acre site in the Catoctin Mountains, sixty miles north of Washington, D.C., one of the most thoroughly guarded sites on earth. All of the staff were the Navy's finest, trained at the highest level and specially selected, all with

Yankee White clearances, the most rigorous possible. There was no way anyone could get close to Camp David.

The deputy director of the FBI, a cocky little bastard named William Carlisle, was waiting for Dunne as the car door opened at the main compound. He had a sealed 9x12 envelope in one hand and a handheld video display in the other.

He handed Dunne the envelope. "We know who Orchid is," he said. "Her name's Lanfen Wong."

Dunne took the file, opened it, pulled out the photo. The woman was young, pretty, dressed in a military outfit Dunne recognized as Chinese, People's Army.

"There's a file on her at FBI," Carlisle said. "We're working it hard. I've got maybe fifty agents on this full-time, pulling records, looking for credit cards, phones, anything. So far it's mostly history. Foreign national, came from Shanghai, spent time in the Chinese army. She came to the U.S. in 2000, went to college at Wayne State, in engineering. She was off-scale bright, made straight A's in her freshman year. But she had a habit of hurting people. Sophomore year she broke the arm of one of her instructors in a dispute over getting a B.

"After that, she signed on with Blackwater."

"Blackwater? They hire foreign nationals?"

He nodded. "For their non-U.S. operations. But they couldn't handle her. Lasted a year there, ended really ugly. Apparently a few of her fellow employees tried to rape her in 2003 while on assignment in Africa. She killed one, broke the spine of the other. She returned to China before she could be arrested. After that, the trail goes cold."

"When did you get this?" Dunne asked Carlisle.

"Twenty minutes ago."

"Why didn't anyone spot her on U.S. soil sooner?"

"Facial recognition didn't pick her up. That's what the scars are about. She changed her face. She's unrecognizable to the computers. An entirely different eigenface, as the NSA boys call it."

"And you've got nothing since 2003?"

"Four years ago, she canceled her credit card with Bank of America."

"Then nothing?"

"Nothing. We're hitting everyone who ever knew her. Focusing on her entire life here. We might get lucky. Maybe someone's seen her. Or she's using an old haunt."

"Anything about her being political? Anti-Japanese?"

"Here's the thing. She's actually not entirely Chinese. She's one-quarter Japanese."

"You're kidding."

"Yup. She is from Nanking. Her grandmother was raped by a Japanese soldier before the war. So her mother was half-and-half. Apparently that was a no-no after the war. Her mother was treated like a third-class citizen. The granddaughters, too. They had the stigma of Japanese blood in them. That was why she came to the United States.

"There's something else. Even bigger. An email with a video attached came in a little over a half-hour ago, delivered to an FBI office in Kalispell, Montana. We traced the email to an Internet site called Time Cave. You compose an email, they send it at a later time."

"And?"

"One of the geeks at the NSA just hacked the site. The communication was paid for using a stolen credit card. The email was entered late last night. Couldn't tell from where. No way to trace it. The account name was, get this, *testicle.*"

"Testicle?"

"She's being cute. *Orchid* is from the Greek *orchis.* Which means testicle. Apparently the bulbs of the flower look like a hanging pair of balls."

"Which she has us by."

"That she does," Carlisle said. "She wants three things. Number one: absolutely nothing in the press. Number two: money. Ten million dollars now, more later. And number three: she wants Hitoshi Kitano. She included an indictment of Kitano for war crimes against the people of Harbin, China. Murder, torture, biological experimentation, everything. She said nothing was negotiable. That if anything went wrong, that Crawler in Rochester loaded with the Uzumaki was only the beginning. She says she has an army at her command."

"What army?"

"You're not going to like it," he said. He clicked on the video display, and an image appeared of an Asian woman dressed entirely in black. You could see her face clear as day—Orchid. Next was a close-up of her gloved hand, palm open. In the palm were two halves of a small brass cylinder.

"That's likely the cylinder she took from the Connor kid," Carlisle said. "The one Sterling told us about." The camera shot lingered for a few seconds, then zoomed out. The wider view again showed Orchid. In her other hand, carefully balanced, was a large, almost perfectly transparent glass sphere about the size of a beach ball.

"What the hell is that?" Dunne asked.

"Hang on. You'll see."

Small black specks decorated the wall of the glass sphere. Dunne noticed that the dots were moving.

The camera zoomed in.

"Oh, Christ," Dunne said. "You've got to be kidding."

Inside the sphere, crawling all over one another like bees in a hive, were thousands of MicroCrawlers.

37

THE QUARANTINE WING AT DETRICK WAS CALLED "THE SLAMMER."
There were seven rooms, each with a bed and a window that looked out on an observation room. A telephone allowed visitors in the observation room to talk to the quarantined person. From what Jake had been told, they sat empty almost all the time, reserved for the rare accident in the BSL-4 facility, where a cut on a glove or an improperly seated seal could expose an individual to a level-4 pathogen, such as Marburg or Ebola.

Jake was in one of the quarantine rooms, had been since four in the morning. Dylan was in the next one over. Where Maggie was, no one knew.

THE EXPLOSION AT SENECA ARMY DEPOT HAD BROUGHT everyone from the Geneva Fire Department to the CIA. Jake was half deaf as he tried to answer the questions yelled at him by authorities ranging from the local police to the FBI. He kept yelling back, demanding they put every man on the search for the FedEx van with Maggie tied up in the back. They assured him that roadblocks had been set up, helicopters were scouring the region. But the searchers found nothing.

By secure linkup, Jake had told Dunne and General Anthony Arvenick, the head of Detrick, everything he knew. Within an hour, Jake and Dylan had been placed in containment suits and airlifted out. As soon as they were airborne, a series of bombers swept in and dropped incinerating explosives on a mile-wide stretch of the depot. The sky was an orange hell. Jake saw the white deer running for their lives, trying to stay ahead of the flames.

They'd landed at Andrews Air Force Base in the middle of the night. From Andrews, it had been a ride in a convoy to Detrick, where they had been ushered into the slammer, Jake and Dylan in separate rooms. A steady stream of tests had followed: Jake was poked and prodded, and had a huge amount of blood drawn and saliva samples taken, along with a painful procedure during which they scraped tissue from his lung using a long arthroscopic device. They had also loaded him up with Amphotericin, an antifungal medicine.

After that came the debriefings. He told his story again and again, enduring question after question, his hands in bandages, his lungs still raw. He hadn't had a moment to think until a half-hour ago. The DNA marker tests that they were running next door in the BSL-4 lab would be done by eleven a.m.

It was ten-fifty.

Jake paced the cage. His ears still hurt like hell, but his hearing was coming back in stages. According to Albert Roscoe, the head physician, a wiry, mid-fifties man with leathery skin and clear blue eyes, another day would be needed to see if the damage was permanent.

Jake didn't care about his hearing or the burns on his hands. He fixed his thoughts on Dylan, thinking about how that brave little kid had tried to dump the Uzumaki. He had opened the cylinder, sucked out half of it, spit it on the floor of the bunker. But Orchid had gotten to him before he could do the same with the other half.

Dylan was asleep now, finally. They let Jake talk to him by telephone about two hours ago. They were only a few feet apart, but they might as well have been across the country.

Dylan and he had talked quite a while, mostly about Maggie. Dylan was so worried about her. Jake tried to keep some distance from that. He was already thinking too much about her, more than was good for him. There was nothing he could do about Maggie right now but try to help her son.

Dr. Roscoe told Jake what symptoms to watch for, what the Uzumaki would do to a human being. They had the records from what had happened on the USS *Vanguard,* as well as from the files recovered from Unit 731. Apparently there had also been some tests run on American prisoners in the late fifties, lifers willing to trade risk for a shot at a bigger cell and better food. The symptoms would show up inside of a day, the low temperatures, the sweats, the nervous energy, the itchy skin. From there, the visual hallucinations would start, the general deconstruction of the personality, leaving a raving, dangerous maniac.

Jake felt fine. No hint of a symptom. But Jake had a terrible feeling in his chest. Dr. Roscoe had Dylan's medical records retrieved from his GP in Ithaca. Dylan had been on penicillin antibiotics twice in the last six months, most recently five weeks before. Just before Dylan went to sleep, he had said that he was feeling light-headed. And that he was sweating.

A RUCKUS IN THE HALL. JAKE WAS ON HIS FEET, WATCHING the action in the main hallway through two sets of windows. They ushered in a man in an isolation suit identical to the ones Jake and Dylan had worn. Jake caught a glimpse of his face: good-looking, middle-American boy, scared half to death, looked like he couldn't be more than thirty.

Roscoe showed up in the observation room soon after. He picked up the phone, motioning for Jake to do the same.

"What happened?" Jake asked.

"He found one of your Crawlers in a children's park in Rochester. It bit him. They think it had the Uzumaki inside it."

"She's using them as vectors."

Roscoe nodded. "We're proceeding worst-case, even though we got to the guy within ten minutes of contact with the vector. We've also quarantined the team that picked him up."

"Wait. Ten minutes? How did you get there so fast?"

"I don't know. Look. Let us worry about him. I have news. Your tests are back. The DNA arrays and the cultures are negative. No signs of the Uzumaki in your lungs, in your stomach. You're completely clean so far. We'll keep you in quarantine the next few days, just to be sure. But the odds are you're clean."

"What about Dylan?"

Roscoe hesitated. "We're not finished with his."

"Why? Why are mine finished and not his?"

"There was an issue with contamination with Dylan's lung sample. We have to run it again."

"Contamination? In a BSL-4 lab?" Roscoe was hiding the truth. "You know something, tell me."

"There are people here to see you."

"Goddamn it. Tell me."

"Let us finish the tests, Jake. We'll know for sure soon. There are people here to see you."

JAKE'S VISITORS WERE IN UNIFORM, A MAN AND A WOMAN.

"I'm Colonel Daniel Wheeler, USAMRIID. This is Major Melissa Larkspur."

"I'm an electronics expert out of Wright-Patterson in Dayton. I've been studying your Crawlers, exploring ways to stop them. Orchid," Larkspur said, "programmed the Crawler at Rochester to respond to a thermal signal and strike. We checked the registers on the flash drive. The last program she entered was there."

"Orchid appears to know a great deal about your Crawlers," Wheeler said. "We're looking to see if she hacked into your computer system."

"She wouldn't have to. We had a kind of owner's manual on a Wiki. Open access. My student made it. Joe Xu."

"Xinjian Xu?" Wheeler said. "The FBI has him in custody."

"Custody? *Why?*"

He brushed off the question.

Larkspur asked, "How sensitive are your Crawlers to electromagnetic pulses? Do you ever blow out the electronics?"

"On occasion. Why?"

"We're trying to figure out if we can knock them out with an electromagnetic pulse."

"An EMP weapon? You've got to be kidding. You're contemplating setting off a nuclear explosion in the upper atmosphere? It would knock out a decent fraction of the nation's communications infrastructure."

"We have smaller versions. Non-nuclear. Ones that can take

out all the electronics in a fixed area. Anything from a single building to an entire city."

"You really think you can disable the Crawlers with an EMP?"

"That's what we hoped to find out from you."

"This Wiki," Wheeler said. "It had the plans to build the Crawlers?"

"Sure. It had everything. The CAD files for all the mask levels. Detailed procedures."

Larkspur looked pained. "That's where she got them," she said to Wheeler.

"Got what? We're a federally funded academic research lab. Everything is open access. There's nothing illegal about that. Now. Why is Joe Xu in custody?"

"He's a Chinese national."

"So?"

"He could have shared the designs with—"

"I told you, it was all available. There's nothing to . . ." Jake suddenly put the pieces together. "Why are you worried about the designs for the Crawlers?"

Larkspur said, "Because two months ago a woman matching Orchid's description placed an order with a Taiwanese silicon foundry called Unafab. It specializes in custom electronic and microelectromechanical systems. The CIA has had them under surveillance since 2007. They're known to take any work they can get, including from military and even terror groups. Two weeks ago, that order was picked up, supposedly by a Chinese company called Star Technologies. We haven't been able to find out anything on the company. But we do have a photo from the pickup."

She slid the photo across the table. The shot was from a distance, but Jake recognized her easily. "Orchid," Jake said. "You think she ordered a manufacturing run of Crawlers."

"We know."

She showed Jake the video of Orchid and the glass sphere filled with Crawlers.

AFTER AN HOUR OF QUESTIONS, JAKE WAS LEFT ALONE WITH his thoughts.

They'd gone over it from every angle. The Crawlers used a standard silicon foundry chip set. They were not particularly vulnerable to EMPs because they had no external wires to act as antennas. The Army had, over the last decade, run an extremely thorough set of EMP tests on handheld devices and laptops. Now they were about to run a series using Crawlers from Jake's lab at Cornell. If they were lucky, they would find a strong electromagnetic resonance, a frequency where the Crawler acted as a particularly good antenna. Then they could engineer the EMP bomb to hit it hardest at that frequency.

They had their plans. But as Jake knew, sometimes things didn't go as planned. And if they failed—if the Crawlers released the fungus, the results could be catastrophic.

Jake remembered a quote by William Osler, one of the forefathers of modern medicine: "Humanity has but three great enemies: fever, famine, and war; of these by far the greatest, by far the most terrible, is fever."

Osler had seen the ravages of a world war. Sixteen million people had died in World War I, including three hundred thousand at Verdun alone. Sixteen million in four years. But the influenza that followed in 1918 killed many times that number in a matter of months.

And it wasn't only the number of dead. A biological threat tore apart a society. War, for all its horror, galvanized a nation, pulled it together against a common opponent. But fever was a different kind of enemy. It struck from within, driving everyone into paranoid isolation, afraid of touching anyone around them. Jake had experienced it firsthand during the Gulf War. When the chem/bio weapons alarms went off and you put on your suit, you were alone and powerless inside that sweaty cocoon.

No honor, only suffering. Courage was useless against a bacterium, a fungal spore, a virus that slipped into you by water, by touch, by breath. No way to be brave in the face of danger when the danger was beyond your ability to see. There were no war memorials to influenza victims in towns across America. Those people just suffered and died, and everyone tried their best to forget any of it had ever happened.

An Uzumaki epidemic would be much worse than the 1918 flu

pandemic, both in numbers and in the nature of the illness itself. The flu attacked only your body, but the Uzumaki turned you into a raving maniac, suicidal at best, homicidal at worst. An Uzumaki epidemic would be like hell on earth.

Jake paced his cell, wanted to punch the Plexiglas window separating him from the outside. Thousands of Crawlers. She could release them in waves, at hundreds of locations simultaneously. If only a few succeeded, that would be enough. He had seen a map once, showing the travel patterns of people, tracked by their cellphones. Dense mats of lines connecting the major hubs of L.A., Chicago, New York, Boston, and Seattle. Smaller lines fanning out everywhere else. Infect just a few people, let them spread out, go to work, go to school, stop by the local Walmart, get on a plane for California to see a friend. In a matter of days the Uzumaki could be everywhere. At that point, there was no way to stop it.

Game over.

DOCTOR ROSCOE KNOCKED AT THE WINDOW. HE LOOKED beaten down.

Jake picked up the phone, his heart racing. He thought of Maggie, wherever she was, so far away from her son. "Tell me," he said.

Roscoe took a deep breath, looked down at the floor, then back to Jake. He met him head-on, one man to another. "It's Dylan's tests. I'm sorry. The news is bad."

38

MAGGIE FLOATED IN DARKNESS, COOL AND BLACK. SHE TRIED to will herself out of the darkness, into being. But she felt nothing, not even the movement of her arms.

Dylan. Memories of Dylan. He was six years old, and they were looking for arrowheads at Taughannock Falls.

Dylan had asked who Taughannock was, and she told him he'd been a Delaware Indian. The Iroquois had captured him and threw him over the falls.

Dylan had stood at the waterfall's bank for a long time, looking into the gorge, as if he saw the chief plummeting downward. "If I were falling, would you save me?"

"You can count on that, buddy."

A SPARKLE, A SENSATION, LIKE A SILVERFISH IN MOONLIGHT.

Pain.

Her leg ached, the left one, for a reason she couldn't remember. Her breathing was labored, her lungs constricted, unable to get enough air.

Dylan. Where is Dylan?

She jerked awake, eyes open, wincing at the onslaught of bright light. A wave of nausea hit her. She closed her eyes and clenched her teeth, breathing hard, fighting it off. The nausea crested, faded. She opened her eyes just a slit this time, let the light in slowly, titrating the light, until she could take its full force.

She was strapped to a table tilted about thirty degrees from the horizontal. Above her was a high ceiling, round, a half-dome, I-beam struts holding up what looked to be sheets of painted white metal. She tried to sit up, but she was held by a gray elastic band tight across her chest. She was handcuffed at the wrists to the table on which she lay.

Maggie looked around the room. In front of her were a pair of workbenches, one covered with electronic equipment: an oscilloscope, soldering irons, and spools of wire. The second was empty. Hanging above the workbench on a pair of hooks were two masks. Gas masks, she realized.

Maggie strained at her bonds, looked as far to the left as she could manage. She saw a pistol on a cabinet ten feet away with an unusual, larger-than-normal barrel. Next to it was a pair of cylinders the size of a roll of mints, each with a needle protruding from the end. A tranquilizer pistol. Beyond it she could see the top half of a large transparent sphere that looked to be made of glass, perhaps two feet in diameter.

She turned to the right and immediately froze. She could just make them out from the corner of her eye. On a metal table not a foot from her head.

She stared at them, fear like a hand slapping her. Five Micro-Crawlers.

Next to them was a pair of tweezers, the objects laid out on a square of white cloth like dentist's tools.

Maggie pulled at her bonds, fighting off panic.

A door opened and closed, the sound coming from the direction of the stairs. Then footsteps.

Maggie felt a chill run through her as Orchid came into view. "You're awake," Orchid said flatly. She wore a skintight black outfit, with black gloves. Her hair was cut short, like a man's. She looked beaten up. The side of her face was black and blue. The fingers of her right hand were taped together.

"Where's Dylan?" The words came out like a croak, her throat parched.

Orchid grabbed a water bottle. "Open," she said. Orchid poured in half a mouthful.

Maggie swallowed, coughing. But the water was soothing.

"Where is my son?"

Orchid didn't respond. Instead she stood and went to a bench across the room. She returned with one of the gas masks Maggie had seen hanging on the wall. Orchid laid the mask on Maggie's chest. It had a large, clear faceplate and dual particulate filters emerging from each side, like truncated tusks.

She leaned over Maggie, looking directly into her eyes. "How much do you know about the Uzumaki?"

"Screw you. Where is my son?"

Maggie saw a flash of rage cross Orchid's eyes. She raised her arm and struck Maggie brutally hard in the chest with the base of her open palm, driving it into her sternum. Maggie gasped, the pain radiating outward as though she'd been cracked open. She saw spots before her eyes and was afraid that she would vomit.

Orchid said, "A word of advice. This is not going to be pleasant for you no matter how it goes. It's your choice how bad it has to be. Now answer my question. How much do you know about the Uzumaki?"

Maggie was still breathing hard, her breastbone throbbing. She couldn't come up with a good reason not to answer. "Look, before yesterday, I'd never heard of it."

"Do you know the pathways of infection?"

"Ingestion," Maggie said. "From what I know, it's by ingestion."

Orchid nodded. "That's right," she said. "Through the stomach. That is one possibility. But there is another one. Do you know what it is?"

"Inhalation," Maggie said. "Spores."

"Correct."

Orchid picked up the gas mask and placed it on Maggie's face. She pulled the straps around the back of Maggie's head, tightening them, making the fit snug. She was methodical, careful, checking the seals with her fingers.

"Blow out," she said. "It's important that this fits properly. Exhale as hard as you can. Quickly."

Maggie quickly exhaled, sending a fresh wave of pain through her chest. The mask swelled slightly but held its seal.

"Again. Harder. First breathe in."

Maggie slowly inhaled. She smelled the rubber and plastic, heard the underwater sound of the air hissing through the particulate filters.

"Now. As hard as you can."

Maggie exhaled hard. Again the mask swelled, but the seals held.

"Good."

Orchid grabbed the table with the Crawlers and pulled it close. She sat down on a stool next to Maggie. Orchid raised her damaged right hand, cupped her fingers, and moved them back and forth. One of the Crawlers, the farthest from the right, skittered forward, bumping into the tweezers laid out in front of them.

Maggie watched, a cold, slack terror sweeping over her.

Working carefully, deliberately, Orchid picked up the Micro-Crawler with the tweezers. With her free hand she carefully lifted up the edge of Maggie's gas mask. She slid the tweezers through the opening, placing the Crawler on Maggie's cheek. Maggie tried to shake her head, to knock it loose, but she couldn't. The Crawler's legs hooked her skin.

No, no, no, no . . .

Maggie was shaking, her whole body quivering. "Oh, God, no. Please. Stop this. What do you want from me?"

"No. That's not it at all. There's nothing you can tell me."

"Then why?"

"I want proof."

Maggie was hyperventilating. "Proof of what?" She tugged as hard as she could at her restraints, unable to move. The Crawler loomed over her left eye. She tried to will it away.

Orchid twitched her hand. The Crawler skittered right a fraction of an inch, its legs catching the skin like barbs of a fishhook. Maggie squeezed her eyes shut, tried to brace herself for the pain she knew was coming. She had seen Crawlers tear through leather—her skin would be like paper.

"Ready?" Orchid asked.

Maggie forced herself to open her eyes. She said, "Screw you."

Orchid smiled, then closed her hand into a fist twice in rapid succession.

Maggie winced, but there was no sharp bite of pain. Instead a slight sound, like a perfume mister. The air inside the mask was suddenly cloudy.

Maggie blinked, coughed inside the mask. The Crawler was motionless on her cheek, its legs holding on to her skin.

What just happened?

Maggie looked to Orchid. Their eyes met. Orchid smiled again.

The mask on her face. The filters were designed to catch particulates. Normally it was to keep dangerous agents out. But here it was meant to keep them in.

"Inhalation," Orchid said.

The Uzumaki.

The mist was full of Uzumaki spores.

· 39 ·

THE PRINCIPALS OF THE NATIONAL SECURITY COUNCIL AS-
sembled in Camp David's Laurel Lodge conference room. The
mood was serious, no small talk, no joking and jostling. Lawrence
Dunne took a chair along the back wall.

The room was long and narrow, with a sloped ceiling and
wood paneling on all four walls. A thirty-foot-long wooden table
ran down the center. The vice president, the President's chief of
staff, and the national security adviser were on one side, talking in
quiet tones. The secretaries of State, Treasury, and Defense, and the
chairman of the Joint Chiefs sat directly across. Clustered at the far
end were the directors of National Intelligence and Homeland Security, along with the FBI director, the head of the CDC, and the
commander of Fort Detrick. Normally a ring of lesser functionar-
ies would occupy the chairs against the walls, but not today. Today
no one was let in the room who wasn't absolutely essential. Dunne
was the only deputy-level staff member present, in the room at the
President's behest.

The POTUS himself entered solo, exuding authority, making it
clear to everyone who was in charge. With his Hollywood looks
and background as self-made CEO of a billion-dollar Internet services empire, he had run as an agent of change, loyal to no one but

the American people, promising to restore the nation to its former glory as the undisputed economic leader of the world. He was addicted to Butterfingers and was a serial sports fanatic, his current obsession being handball. He liked to project a calm, laid-back persona to the public, but he could stand up and dominate a room when he had to.

He worked his way around the table, calling for updates one by one. The Homeland Security chief, Mike Reardon, spoke first, a heavyset man with flat features and weathered skin, more truck driver than bureaucrat. "We've got the media under control for the moment. We're leaking stories that the ATF found marijuana fields at Seneca Depot, and the bombing was a burn. All part of a major drug ring roundup. We told them to expect more arrests soon."

"No one has connected this to Rochester?"

"We're connecting the dots for them. The cover story is that the Rochester event was part of the roundup, stopping a shipment to Canada across Lake Ontario."

Alex Grass, the head of the CDC, spoke next, a dapper man with sleepy eyes. "Dylan Connor is showing symptoms. His temperature dropped. He's still alert, but he's having auditory hallucinations."

"What about the guy from Rochester?"

"Positive. Also, one of the soldiers from Drum that picked him up looks like he has it. The rest we don't know."

"We're absolutely sure it's the Uzumaki?"

"Three labs independently ran the samples, all with different protocols. I personally supervised the tests at CDC. Toloff at USDA. Arvenick's people at USAMRIID. Every assay came back positive, three sigma. It's the Uzumaki."

The room was quiet except for the background clatter from the displays on the walls.

The President called upon the commander at Detrick, Anthony Arvenick. He was in charge of the operational response in case of a large-scale outbreak. "There's no doubt, Mr. President," the general said, his voice grave. "She's got the Uzumaki. And thousands of those Crawlers. The scenarios range from bad to worse to nightmare."

"Start with bad."

"She's already shown us *bad*. She leaves the Crawlers in a public place, they bite whoever happens by. But at least we know we've been hit. It's bad, but in this scenario, at least we know. We can do our best to contain it, have a shot at limiting the damage to a small geographic area. The difference between a few deaths and a few thousand might boil down to the direction the wind is blowing.

"*Worse,* she releases it in a major population center but *quietly.* Say, sending in a Crawler to expel spores in the ventilation ducts of a building. The unsuspecting occupants come and go, and a whole city could be infected within days. If we picked it up in time, we might be able to shut it down. But to quarantine a city would be hell. It would start a panic like you can't imagine."

"Give me *nightmare.*"

"She hits us a thousand places simultaneously. She cultures enough Uzumaki to load up all those Crawlers, disperses them across the country any number of ways. Hell, she could mail them to every major city, have them pop out of ten thousand envelopes all at once. She does something like that, we don't have a chance."

The room was silent. "Lay out our options."

"Other than giving her what she wants, not much. Our best chance is to stop her before she releases it."

"And if we don't catch it?"

Arvenick said, "Antifungals don't seem to work. A private company, Genesys, has a prototype vaccine. It's not ready, but we're going to run human tests. It's a vaccine, not a cure. It does no good if the fungus has already spread. Maybe we could prevent a second wave, but that's it."

The President nodded, his hands on the table before him. Dunne tried to read his face. "Mr. President," Dunne said, standing.

"Lawrence."

"The health consequences are only the start. However bad they are, they pale in comparison to the broader implications. The entire country would be cut off, isolated. No airline flights. No one would get in or out. The stock market would crash in a way that would make 1929 look like a walk in the park. Within days, we would have shortages of all kinds—food, medicine, water—as trade shut down. We would become a Third World nation. The financial center of the world would move to London, or more likely Hong Kong. The United Nations would—"

"I'm aware of what would happen," the President snapped. Then to Arvenick, "We've got nothing else?"

Arvenick shook his head. "Nothing good. We know that antibiotics make you vulnerable. We could ban antibiotic use, but in doing so we'd be signing thousands of death sentences. Not to mention we'd have a whole series of bacteriological epidemics sweeping the country. And even after all that, it might not help."

"Why not?"

"We've assumed that those people who'd taken broad-spectrum antibiotics within the last few weeks would be at risk. That gives a maximum number of dead in the hundreds of thousands. But it might be much, much worse. If you believe Sadie Toloff at the USDA."

Dunne jumped to attention at this. He'd heard nothing about revised estimates.

"Toloff's piecing together what Liam Connor knew. She's got a team of over forty scientists—fungal biologists, epidemiologists, gastrointestinal specialists—going through his notebooks. His published papers. It's clear he was looking to find a cure for the Uzumaki."

Dunne lost his patience. "Get to it."

"Mr. President," Arvenick said, pointedly ignoring Dunne. "We've known a long time that the Uzumaki infects humans after an antibiotic regimen. After the bacterial populations in the digestive tract are knocked down. But—and this is what Sadie Toloff is piecing together from Connor's notebooks—he maintained we have in our appendix a specific bacterium that feeds on the Uzumaki. Like a parasite, the bacterium knocks the Uzumaki out, almost like a natural bacterial immune system."

"And most people have this bacterium?" asked the President.

"Not quite, sir. Most people *had* it. But we've been using antibiotics for decades now. The bacterium might well be nearly wiped out in the human population. Once it gets killed by a course of antibiotics, it looks like it's slow to come back."

No one spoke. No one moved.

"General Arvenick, give me your best guess on casualties. How high?"

"Say on day one we have one person infected. And every day each infected person infects one more. At the end of one month, that adds up to over five hundred million."

It was as if the air had been sucked out of the room.

THE JUMBO BOX OF MALTED MILK BALLS ARRIVED IN THE hands of Wally Atherton in his morning food package. Wally was a long-termer, had been in for twenty-two years, with only four to go. He ran a number of small businesses within the Hazelton prison. He was a middleman, making a living on the spread, trading cigarettes for junk food, and contraband booze for skin mags. He could even get you a cellphone if the price was right. Most of what he did was penny-ante, but on occasion he came across an opportunity to make some real cash.

This was far and away the biggest opportunity yet.

He'd first been contacted two months before, and he had been laying the groundwork since. The money was already flowing, building up in an account in a bank in Toledo, Ohio, his hometown. When he got out, he'd be a millionaire.

Atherton took the carton of malted milk balls, wrapped it in a bedsheet, put the buds from his iTouch in his ears, and started for the laundry room. Marvin Gaye's "What's Going On?" serenaded him as he walked.

Once alone inside the laundry room, he placed the carton of malted milk balls on a folding table, opened it, and poured them out. They clattered and rolled, but the table had a little lip that kept them from falling to the floor. What the hell was malted milk, anyway?

He checked the chocolate balls until he found the specific one he was looking for. No malted anything here. It was a plastic sphere dipped in chocolate, designed to look and feel like all the other milk balls, but it was slightly larger. He popped it in his mouth and sucked off the chocolate. Then he wiped it down with a rag, took a razor blade he had stashed in his shoe and carefully cut the plastic shell open.

It split like a tiny egg. Inside was an amazing little thing.

A little mechanical spider, just as he'd been told. Glued to its back was the smallest damn camera he'd ever seen. The size of the dots on dice, no bigger. He leaned down to face it, then checked his iTouch. He could see his own face on the screen.

Wally hopped up on the table and set to work unscrewing the cover from the overhead vent. As he worked, he wondered if machines had a basic understanding of the world. They move, they respond, they move again. No free will, but an intelligence nonetheless. Wally was interested in free will. Someday a machine would have it, begin to carve out its own kind of meaning, he was sure. Not yet, but soon maybe.

This little bugger had no free will. It took its orders from the rich, faceless SOB who'd paid Wally one-point-four million dollars. This little bugger was an instrument of his will. Not that different from Wallace Atherton.

He did as ordered, placed the little Crawler in the duct, pointed it in the right direction. Then he hit the app on his iTouch and the Crawler took off down the vent, skittering away, Wally guiding it by running his finger across the screen. The sound of its legs was a delicate, almost lovely clitter-clatter.

To Wally it sounded like the echo of future coins of gold.

KITANO REMINISCED, FLAMES BURNING BRIGHT IN HIS MIND. Dunne was not due for another hour. In the meantime, Kitano had his memories. As he grew older, he found that the present became hazier, more like a dream, but the past became clearer and clearer.

It was as if the past was real, the present only a shadow. His true self lived there, still watching, still waiting, still reliving the events of 1945.

By summer, the war against the Americans in the Pacific was lost. Tokkō was Japan's doomed, romantic last-ditch effort to change the tide of the war against the imperialist Westerners. Machines of steel had failed. The machines of flesh were the last hope. Thousands of young Japanese soldiers, bravely piloting planes, boats, and human-guided torpedoes on one-way missions aimed at the heart of the enemy. In the West, they would be known by another Japanese name, a word that translates as "God-wind," after a pair of typhoons that destroyed a Mongol invasion in the thirteenth century.

God-wind. *Kamikaze.*

But even this could not stop the Americans.

August had arrived hot and bleak in northern China. The Soviets were amassing to the north. All was in chaos. An entirely new kind of bomb had been dropped on Hiroshima and Nagasaki, reducing them to rubble in seconds. The Soviets launched their attack, cutting through the lines of the Japanese Kwantung Army with ease. All was nearly lost. They would overrun Unit 731 within days.

The order came. All remaining prisoners killed, all records destroyed.

Eight men assemble in the room. The oldest was General Shiro Ishii, then fifty-three years old, his city of terror soon to be reduced to dust. Kitano stood beside him. The other six are Tokkō volunteers, none older than twenty. Ishii has been their commander and father, has supervised their training personally for months. He was usually brusque with them, almost cruel. But today he is solemn. Ishii opens the hinoki box, and to each Tokkō soldier he gives a cylinder, bowing respectfully.

These six would carry the last, most terrible breath of the God-wind. They are the breathers of Uzumaki.

They were the last hope.

Each Uzumaki specimen was contained in a small canister the size and shape of a cigar, bronze metal, two pieces threaded to lock and then sealed with wax at the joint. There were six of these canisters, contents identical, arranged in a polished hinoki cypress wooden box with inlays cut especially for them. The brass cylinders and hinoki box were constructed by the best craftsmen that the Japanese Imperial Army had to offer. Once a month, the cylinders were removed, and new ones put in their place. Unit 731 scientists were still working, improving, testing. This box contained the high-water mark of their achievement.

For Kitano, the seventh Tokkō, they had made a special cylinder, small enough to be implanted in his finger bone.

He would lie in wait as the submarines carried away the other six. If they failed, he would succeed. Slip into the world of his enemy and wait for the right moment. Confess everything, earn their trust. Then find his way to the right spot, somewhere in the north. He'd memorized the bottlenecks for all the major flyways. Migratory birds were almost perfect vectors for the Uzumaki. They could have spread the deadly fungus over the entire country in a matter of days.

He would have succeeded. Had it not been for Liam Connor.

WALLY STOPPED THE CRAWLER OVER THE FIFTH VENTILATION duct it passed, the one over crazy-old-man Kitano's cell. He made the little robot spider tilt so the camera looked down through the vent. The image wasn't much, like a thumbnail, but you could clearly see the old bastard on his bunk, staring off into space.

This better work, Wally thought. Kitano was one bad old Jap. This went right, he was rich. But this goes wrong, Wally Atherton was a dead man.

Wally moved his fingers. The little spider dropped through the grate and fell like a tiny little leaf, the camera shot spinning, spiraling down and down to the target below.

· 41 ·

THE DEPUTY DIRECTOR OF THE FBI SAT ACROSS FROM DUNNE in the reinforced-steel-and-bulletproof-glass limo, but the two hadn't spoken in more than fifteen minutes. There wasn't much to say.

The vehicle sped down I-68 at more than ninety miles an hour, a West Virginia state trooper escort in front and behind, lights on but sirens off. The Morgantown airport was ten miles behind them, and the federal United States Penitentiary in Hazelton was another six ahead. On the seat next to Dunne was a Lucite box containing two of Kitano's pigeons. More birds were in the trunk.

Kitano was waiting in his cell. Kitano had been told. He'd demanded to see Dunne.

Dunne's job was to get Kitano to agree to turn himself over.

The plan that the Army settled on was simple: give Orchid the money, give her Hitoshi Kitano, and then blow them both to hell.

DUNNE THOUGHT OF THE LAST TIME HE HAD SEEN KITANO out of prison. It had been at the old man's estate in Maryland, west of D.C. Kitano's compound was relatively modest by billionaire standards; set atop a hill, a shed-roofed clutch of modernist buildings were linked by glass walkways.

An assistant, Japanese, had led Dunne through the main house. The inside was spare, bamboo floors and white walls with only a few abstract paintings and a collection of Japanese swords interrupting the emptiness. Historically, samurai warriors had tested the quality of a sword by cutting through the stacked corpses of executed criminals. Kitano was a fanatic for swords—like most Japanese nationalists, he fetishized the blade. Dunne remembered a quote by Nietzsche, he thought: "Every murderer loves the knife."

The entire back wall of Kitano's home was glass, looking out on ten acres of pristine lawn and landscaped gardens. Dunne could picture him clearly that day, standing outside, looking down the hill, stroking the breast of one of his pigeons.

By then Kitano was already in deep trouble. He was forbidden from leaving the country, had been charged with federal tax fraud. His empire was bleeding. Investors were withdrawing their money, and his business partners were shunning him. Kitano's entire world, his carefully constructed reality, had been slit open, and Dunne knew the hand on the knife had been his own.

Dunne had stepped through a sliding glass door. The weather that fall day was cool but sunny. On a teak table next to Kitano were two glasses and a bottle of scotch, along with a plate of pâté. Dunne recognized the scotch. It was Macallan, Special Reserve, 1945. A ten-thousand-dollar bottle.

"Please," Kitano said.

Dunne poured a glass. Kitano tossed the pigeon upward. "Watch," he said.

The bird flew in a tight circle, then performed what amounted to a backflip in the air. The bird did the aerial somersault twice more before returning to Kitano's arm. "No good for racing, but they are a pleasure nonetheless, no?"

"Is it a new breed?"

"Heavens, no. This is an English short-faced tumbler. They've been around for centuries. Charles Darwin wrote about them." Kitano headed toward the coop, and Dunne followed. *Coop* didn't capture the sense of the place. It was a miniature pigeon palace. Seated on glass shelves were nests, each like a little apartment, with separate food and water. Kitano returned the English short-faced tumbler to its home, then went back outside, another pigeon in tow. "This is a racer. There is a red string on that tree, the large one at the end of the field. Watch."

Kitano tossed the pigeon upward, and it shot off in the direction of the tree.

Kitano said, "Try the matsutake and hazelnut pâté. It is the perfect season in the pine forests of Japan. My chef has a special preparation. He marinates them in blood." Kitano used a small metal spoon to scoop the mushroom pâté onto a cracker. He took a bite, then prepared one for Dunne. Dunne found its sharp taste seductive. Many of his sophisticated, expensive tastes could be traced to this man. Kitano had opened up new worlds.

Dunne noticed Kitano watching the sky.

Dunne followed his gaze, spotting a large bird circling high above. "Is that a hawk?" Dunne asked.

"Falcon. I also keep birds of prey."

The pigeon flew toward them, the red string in its beak, oblivious to the danger. The falcon hung in the air high above the pigeon, practically motionless. Neither man spoke.

Finally, Kitano said, "We had plans."

Dunne kept his face neutral, taking another bracing sip of the alcohol. "That was a long time ago."

"Time has not diminished the necessity of action."

Kitano appeared calm, placid, but Dunne knew better. "Hitoshi—"

"You and I were going to change the world. Instead you are sending me to jail."

"That was your own fault."

"Don't insult me. You had those charges brought against me. You can stop this at any time."

"Hitoshi, you left me no choice."

Kitano kept his eyes on Dunne. "How close are you to a cure?"

"We don't have it. Let it go. It's over."

Kitano turned his gaze back to the falcon. "It can dive at one hundred eighty miles an hour. It comes down so fast that its prey cannot see it, cannot respond."

Dunne watched as the falcon pulled in its wings and plummeted downward, picking up speed as it neared its prey. It was over in a fraction of a second. The falcon struck, and the pigeon almost exploded in midair.

Kitano said, "Make these charges go away. Or I will kill you."

Dunne had put down his scotch carefully, looked Kitano directly in the eyes. "You think this impresses me? A falcon killing a goddamn pigeon?" He shook his head. "If you can beat these tax evasion charges, do it. But the Uzumaki is a national security issue. You say one wrong word, and I'll have you locked up without a trial so quick your head will spin." Dunne paused. "Another option would be to turn you over to the Chinese for prosecution of war crimes."

Dunne had laid it out in detail.

"You need me," Kitano said. "Once I have the Uzumaki—"

"But I don't need you, Hitoshi, not anymore. I have the President now. And once Detrick develops the cure, we can take down China anytime we want."

"You've discussed this with him. The President of the United States."

"When the time is right, I can bring him along."

Kitano changed direction. "Japan will oppose any unlawful—"

"We've already spoken to the Japanese government. They will be best pleased if we make you disappear. You are an embarrassment, a relic that they'd prefer to forget. Listen closely. I'm the falcon here, not you."

And that had been the end of it. Kitano had kept his mouth shut. He had lost his case, gone to jail. SunAgra was shuttered.

Kitano had become nothing more than an old man in a cage. Soon he would be dead. No matter what happened to Orchid, Kitano would not survive—on that, the President had clearly agreed with Dunne.

TWENTY MINUTES LATER, THEY WERE OUTSIDE KITANO'S cell. The old man stood stiffly in the small room's center, head held high and clearly angry. From behind Dunne, they wheeled in the cart with the pigeon cage. Kitano barely glanced at them, keeping his focus on Dunne.

"Leave us," Dunne said to the warden.

When they were alone, Kitano pointed to the pigeons. "I expected to go to my estate. To see them fly again."

"Clearly impossible at this point, you must know that. You wanted to see your pigeons; here they are." Dunne pushed on. "Now let me tell you how this will play out: You'll lead us to Orchid, you and a Marine. Special Forces. He'll be carrying the money. In the money are carbon trackers—completely undetectable. We'll hit first with an EMP weapon, knock out any electronics, including the MicroCrawlers she's collected. After removing that major threat, we hit her. We take Orchid down, and that's that. It's over. You ride away in a Black Hawk helicopter." Dunne laid his hand on the pigeon crate. "We put you on a flight to Osaka with your birds. You're a free man."

"Why should I trust you?"

"Because I'm telling the truth."

One of the pigeons in the box fluttered its wings. Kitano said, "I want a signed presidential pardon. For any and all crimes committed."

Dunne didn't look away. "It's already arranged. If you make it."

"When?"

"We're waiting for another communiqué from Orchid. We're assuming first thing in the morning."

Kitano studied the trapped birds, running his fingers over the lock on the door. He stepped forward. His face was only inches from Dunne's.

"You sicken me, Mr. Dunne."

Dunne didn't look away. He wouldn't give him the satisfaction.

Kitano surprised him. He spit in his face.

"You son of a bitch!" Dunne said.

Kitano attacked. He dove for Dunne, on him like a monkey, hands scratching at Dunne's face. The ancient prisoner was remarkably strong. Dunne couldn't shake him, and yelled for help.

A giant guard came through the door and grabbed Kitano by the neck. The old man was thrown backward and fell in a heap against the far wall.

A second guard stood over Dunne, eyes wide. "You hurt?" Dunne shook his head no, though he tasted blood. He was in shock. His neck was bleeding. The other guard, the giant, had Kitano in a headlock. The pigeons screeched, flapping their wings wildly inside the cage.

Dunne got his wits about him and stood. Wiping blood off his face with his jacket sleeve, he said, "I hope Orchid slices you open, like you sliced all those prisoners at Harbin."

He left the old man to the screeching of his birds.

· 42 ·

THE ROOM WAS PITCH-BLACK. MAGGIE AWOKE, DRENCHED IN sweat and hyperventilating. She had been trapped in a horrible, horrible nightmare. She was standing in an empty field, Dylan at a distance and walking away from her toward a cliff. She tried to run after him, to save him, but she couldn't move. She tried to yell, to warn him, but it was as if her throat were made of stone. She was frantic and panicked, unable to warn her son, unable to stop him.

Maggie tried to calm herself, to erase the terrifying image of her endangered son. The air was sticky and humid inside the claustrophobic gas mask. The tears on her cheeks were cold. From not far away, she heard the sound of geese, their cries echoing in the chamber.

She knew what was happening. The toxins of the Uzumaki were chemical cousins of LSD—hallucinogenic but much rougher. The alkaloids exploded like a bomb in your mind, causing a wild hallucinatory mania. Outbreaks from infested rye in Massachusetts in the 1600s had led to the Salem witch trials, where infected women were put to death. Outbreaks in France in the summer of 1789 had incited the manic, crazed riots that catalyzed the French Revolution.

Even though Maggie knew what to expect, the truth of it, the awful plunge into it, was much more frightening than she could have imagined. She was alone inside her head, alone in the dark.

The hallucinations kept coming. A scratching noise, like fingernails on concrete. She knew what the sound was, even though she couldn't see it. The room was full of corpses, crawling like spiders. They were all over the floor, dozens of them. The floor was far below. The corpses wanted her, but they could not reach her.

Maggie pulled and pulled with her right arm, working to free her hand from the metal cuff, fighting to keep her thoughts under control well enough to focus on her task. She always had small hands, and after a car accident when she was sixteen, the bones in her right hand had broken in two places. Her thumb was never quite right. It would slot into her palm as if it were made to go there. She could form her hand into a small pointed cylinder and slide it in almost anywhere. She'd been fighting to pull it out of the cuff since she'd been imprisoned.

Pull, Maggie. Pull.

The skin grabbed against the metal, the pain like an ice burn but good because it helped her concentration.

Nothing else is real. Keep pulling.

THE SOUND OF METAL.

Jake was at the boundary of sleep. He'd finally slipped under, but it had been light, too much worry in his head to let him go deep.

The sound again. It took Jake a second to identify the metallic screech. When he did, he was instantly awake.

It was the hatch, the metal, submarine-like door separating Jake in his quarantine room from the outside.

It swung open. Dr. Roscoe was there, in the flesh. They'd broken Jake's quarantine.

"Is it Dylan?"

"No. Nothing like that. You're to come with me."

"Why? What time is it?"

"Four a.m."

. . .

TWO MEN WERE WAITING, BOTH IN MILITARY FATIGUES.

"We'll have to talk while we walk," said the one on the right, a tall African American, clearly the ranking officer. "I'm John Lexington, Air Force colonel, on loan to the Defense Intelligence Agency. This is Major Robert Altair, Army. We're part of the operations team. What did they tell you about Orchid's demands?"

"Nothing."

"She has two. She wants Hitoshi Kitano, and she wants money. As much money as a man can carry. This morning, we are supposed to deliver Kitano to a specified location. Accompanying him, carrying the money, was to be a Marine."

"You said *was*."

"Orchid changed it up at the last minute," Altair said. "She's trying to throw us off guard. She chose a new money hauler. Someone with a vested interest in Maggie Connor. Someone whose decision making might be compromised."

"She wants you," Lexington said. "We have to get you ready. We don't have much time."

LAST DAY

■ SATURDAY, OCTOBER 30 ■

TOKKŌ

· 43 ·

"EACH BILL WEIGHS ABOUT A GRAM," MAJOR ALTAIR SAID, holding a hundred-dollar bill in his hand. "A thousands bills, a kilogram. You'll carry one hundred times that, a hundred thousand bills, about two hundred pounds." Jake looked down at the stack of cash and did the math. Ten million dollars. It didn't seem like enough money. Not for all this.

"We have trackers implanted in one hundred of them," Altair said. "Needles in a haystack. Every hour, one will go off, sending a pulse that will be picked up by the satellite system. Once an hour. One hundred hours. Over four days of coverage."

"Won't she be able to detect them?" Jake asked.

Altair handed Jake a bill. "There's one in here. See if you can find it."

Jake ran his fingers over the hundred, folded and unfolded it. He held it up to the light. He saw nothing.

"It's a beauty. No silicon. No metal. The antenna is a weave of carbon nanotubes, a thread no bigger than a strand of spider silk. It runs along the edge of the bill, invisible to nearly any form of imaging technology. X-ray machine, RF scanner, you name it."

Jake understood. Electronics based on carbon had begun to invade the territory that was once the exclusive purview of silicon. "The logic circuits?"

"Pentacene transistors. Low performance but good enough. An RF graphene transistor drives the antenna. The whole thing runs on an electrochemical power source consisting of a bag of ATP. Carbon. Carbon everywhere. All right," Altair said. "Now we just need to take care of you."

TEN MINUTES LATER, JAKE WAS ON HIS BACK IN A SIMPLE operating theater. A doctor stood over him, holding a metal syringe with a four-inch needle. "Left or right?" the doctor asked.

"Left."

"This may sting. Whatever you do, don't move your head."

He inserted the needle in the space between his left eyeball and the socket. He slowly dispensed the plunger, implanting the tracker.

Altair watched closely as the doctor worked. "The basic platform is the same as the trackers in the money, with a few little twists. The antenna runs along the optic nerve. The sensor and power supply look like blood vessels.

"We used to put them in your arm, but sometimes you could see them in an MRI. This is better. The eye is a region of complex imaging contrast. There's a lot going on in there, lots of fibers and tissues behind your eyeball. No one is going to notice our little tracker."

Jake suppressed the desire to flinch. He felt the needle rattling around in the space beside his eye. He thought of Isaac Newton, who pushed sewing needles behind his eyes in order to understand the optics of vision. Newton was insane.

The needle popped out, and Jake took a deep breath. He sat up slowly, blinking rapidly. Needle or no, he was just glad as hell to be out of the slammer. He thought he might have gone mad if he'd had to sit in that little room doing nothing while Maggie was missing and Dylan deteriorating a few feet away. He had a deep burn going, a desire for retribution. He wanted more than anything to save Dylan and Maggie, and he wanted to punish Orchid for what she'd done.

"Run your finger over the spot," Altair said. "You feel that? That little stiff thing? That's your tripwire. You pull that, the pulse triggers. You'll feel it, like someone kicked you in the head. Might lose your vision for a little while."

Major Altair went over it in detail, Colonel Lexington watching from the other side of the room. "You understand? It's right up against the blood vessel, nice and warm. Only two ways that's going to happen. Number one: you pull the tripwire out, or—"

"Or number two: I'm dead."

"You got it. Your heart stops, your epidermal tissues cool fast. A sensor will go off if the temperature drops below ninety-two degrees. It triggers somewhere between one and five minutes after you expire, depending on the thickness of the fat in the surrounding tissues. It'll go off even faster if you pull the tripwire. Maybe ten seconds. In either case, we triangulate from the satellites, and we'll be there in minutes."

"How many minutes?"

"You let us worry about that. Just as soon as everyone is together, do it. We'll hit the area with an EMP pulse. Then we'll be there. We got your back. Jake, you with me? Orchid's there, you're there. You pull. Then we come in."

"Got it."

"One more thing. You pull it, you be sure and make Orchid stay put for the next few minutes. Make sure she doesn't wander off. No more than, say, two hundred meters. You understand me?"

Jake caught the look in Altair's eyes. Jake nodded. He understood. In case they wouldn't be putting boots on the ground. In case they'd be sending bombs.

"You understand? No mistakes, soldier. No excuses."

"No excuses, sir," Jake said, an Army man's reflex.

· 44 ·

DUNNE WAS SWEATING LIKE CRAZY AS HE SAT WITH THE President and the NSC principals in the conference room at Camp David. The chairman of the Joint Chiefs stood, a rail-thin Marine named Stanley Narry: "Mr. President, it's go/no go time. We either send Sterling and Kitano, or we hold back."

The FBI director, an African-American ex-senator from Illinois, also got to his feet. "Mr. President, his psychological profile checks out. Sterling is ex-military. Good mental discipline. Scores low on rebellion scales. The only caveat is that he knows Maggie Connor well, has some involvement with her family, though, of course, that's why Orchid wants him."

They were silent. Dunne watched them trying to come to terms with a world suddenly on the brink of devastation. He couldn't think straight, had barely slept the previous night. It had to be the stress. He'd never reacted to pressure this way before—he thrived on pressure. But then again, no one in this room had ever faced down a danger like this.

He caught himself scratching at his arm. His skin itched, as though ants were crawling underneath.

The President turned to the chairman of the Joint Chiefs. "Stanley? Where are we?"

"Every EMP weapon in the arsenal is in the air, full coverage except for some remote areas. And if you want something burned, odds are we can do it in under twenty minutes. We pulled all the MK-77 incendiaries that we could, including all the old Vietnam-era stuff that was mothballed at Fallbrook Detachment. And we've got the MOABs. Biggest non-nuke in our arsenal, blast radius of a couple of football fields. That's what I'm recommending, Mr. President. If it comes to it. No mistakes with a MOAB. The Mother of All Bombs."

"What about boots on the ground?"

"That'll take longer. Depending on the location. Hour, half-hour at best."

The head of the NSA cleared his throat. "If I can interrupt. The first tracker is set to go off in ten seconds. Nine, eight, seven . . ."

Dunne watched the screen displaying a map of the eastern United States. When the tracker in the money blipped, satellites would record the signal and the location, and have it on the screen in less than a second.

"Five, four, three, two, one." A moment of silence, then a blue blip appeared along the coast, north of the tendril of Cape Cod. The satellite perspective zoomed in, the coastline magnified, the grid of human cities defined, along with the tangled web of the Boston road system.

Dunne recognized the Charles River, the haphazard buildings of the MIT campus on one side, Back Bay Boston on the other. He felt nauseated. Finally the zooming stopped, the screen at maximum resolution.

The blue blip was on Beacon, two blocks from Mass Ave.

"They're waiting for the go."

The President said, "All right, folks. Look sharp. You gotta take a piss, it's too late. This is about to get hot."

IT DIDN'T TAKE LONG FOR THINGS TO GO WRONG.

Jake Sterling was behind the wheel, Kitano in the passenger seat. The car was a silver 2006 Toyota Camry, just as they'd been told. It wasn't lost on Jake or his handlers that the Camry was the most popular car in America, and silver was the most popular color.

It was a quiet Saturday morning in Boston, the sky clear, only a few clouds. A cold front was predicted to move in by the afternoon. Leaves swirled off a maple on the side of the road.

They arrived at the parking lot on Boylston, following Orchid's instructions emailed hours before. They had with them a cellphone that had been mailed to Fort Detrick the previous day. The Langley spooks had studied it as though it was the Rosetta stone, looking for anything that would reveal the nature of their quarry. They took it apart, checked every component, every diode and RF filter, but there was not a damned thing special about it. It was a cheap cellphone with a phone number. Nothing else.

As expected, the phone now rang. Jake answered. The synthesized voice on the other end told him to leave the garage they were in and drive to another garage across town. The phone went dead. Jake did as commanded, sure that the call had been intercepted and a surveillance crew was on its way to the new location.

Jake kept glancing at Kitano. The old man's features were dead. He had a bandage on his face from his fight with Dunne. He was sweating like hell, a rank odor coming off him. Jake didn't bother with small talk. Instead he simply drove.

The Air Force guy, Lexington, had told Jake to keep a close eye on the old man. Kitano was here under duress—a sheep offered to the predator—and he might try to run for it. Lexington wanted to cuff Kitano to Jake, but Orchid's instructions forbade any weapons, ropes, watches, anything at all.

Ten minutes later, they reached the garage. Jake took the little parking ticket from the machine, entered, began ascending the slow spiral upward.

They were on the third level when the phone rang again. Jake answered, and the voice said, "Take the next available slot." Jake and Kitano did as ordered. "Go to the fourth floor. There is a Red Taurus with Michigan plates. Get in it. Pull down the visor."

In they went. Jake pulled down the visor.

The card said:

GET OUT.
GO TO THE FIRST LEVEL.
ENTER A GRAY VAN THROUGH THE REAR DOORS.

The interior of the van was outfitted like a cross between a Geek Squad van and an ambulance. Two video cameras looked down from mounts in the corners. A laminated sheet of paper dangled in the center of the van's storage bay. On it were a series of instructions, to be followed sequentially.

Step one was to strip to the bone. Jake and Kitano did as ordered. Jake soon was naked except for his hands. He slowly unwrapped the gauze covering the burns, the air stinging the wounds.

Per step two, they put all their clothing and possessions in a pair of metal boxes, then stored them in a locker at the back of the van and locked it with a Yale padlock.

On to step three. As instructed, Jake took the battery-powered clippers and trimmed his hair short, tight against his skull. He handed the clippers to Kitano, then turned around before the camera. Kitano trimmed his wisps of hair, his face showing the indignity of being old and naked, a body in decay. Jake felt a twinge of compassion for Kitano, his shrunken arms barely anything, just bits of skin and sinew. But then he thought of Harbin, Unit 731, the torturing, the experiments.

Jake turned away, studied his short-haired reflection in the back window of the van. He felt as though he were nineteen again, a soldier-to-be, not yet schooled in the currency of death.

Step four. Stand before a white panel on the side wall of the van. Some sort of full-body scan, Jake guessed. Altair had assured him that the carbon tracker they'd put in him was invisible to almost anything, but Jake couldn't help but worry. Engineers always believed in the infallibility of their latest technology, like Icarus, right up until they fell from the sky.

Steps five through seven, according to the laminated sheet: get dressed—jeans, sunglasses, and red shirts for both. Leave the van. Bring the money. Get in the VW Golf with tinted windows parked three spaces down. Instructions on the visor.

Jake and Kitano got in the Golf. Jake pulled down the visor.

OPEN THE GLOVE BOX.

The glove box was completely empty, save for an iPhone.

Jake picked up the phone, and the display lit up. On screen were driving instructions. The first direction said:

LEAVE THE MONEY
IN THE PARKING SPACE.

"Leave the money"?

Jake got out of the car and placed the backpack containing the money on the asphalt, Kitano watching closely from the passenger seat. Jake got back in, put the Golf in gear, backed out, started down the spiral ramp to the exit.

One hundred tracers were now sitting in an empty parking space.

· 45 ·

ORCHID WALKED ALONE TOWARD THE CABIN. THE SUN CUT
through the trees, the snow bright. The air was cold and fresh, a
break from the underground shelter. Soon Orchid would be free of
that place—it smelled like something had already died down there.
Minutes before, she had left Maggie Connor in the shelter. Tied up,
her prisoner was shaking uncontrollably and had been for the last
half-hour. The hotshot granddaughter looked just as pathetic as the
hotshot grandfather had looked at the end . . . and Orchid wasn't
done with her yet.

Orchid entered the cabin, carrying with her a laptop computer
and a folded white robe. She placed the items in the center of the
dusty floor. She unfolded the white cloth to reveal a short *tantō*
sword and a World War II vintage Papa Nambu pistol. She rechecked
the pistol's magazine, then pulled back a loose floorboard and hid
the handgun underneath. She carefully replaced the board and
arranged the folded robe and the sword to cover the spot.

Sitting cross-legged on the floor of the cabin, she fired up the
computer, a Lenovo netbook with a built-in wireless card. The reception was better up here. She logged into her mainframe and
checked the GPS reading coming from the Volkswagen Golf. The
vehicle had left Boston, and it was heading north, following the

route she'd laid out. The mainframe also had a piece of voice-recognition software running that had been monitoring all the police bands, but it had picked up no relevant APBs yet.

So far, so good.

She then clicked on the Zip file, a digital information package revealing everything about the Uzumaki. She scanned through the memos with large letters stamped on them. TS. NOFORN.

They were copies of classified documents collected over the years, at considerable expense and risk, all about the U.S. acquisition of the deadly fungus after the war. Documents proving that Fort Detrick had an aggressive countermeasures program under way, all with the imprimatur of the deputy national security adviser. Documents that made it clear that once the United States had finished developing the cure for the Uzumaki, it would have in its possession a devastating biological weapon.

Orchid hit a key and an audio clip played, the most damning of the evidence. The recordings of Dunne and Kitano. "It's Connor's law. The Uzumaki will be the perfect weapon. Once Detrick creates a cure." Dunne's voice. The voiceprint was incontrovertible. The son of a bitch was caught.

Then a second voice—Kitano: "Where would you release it?"

Dunne: "One option is Harbin. Like construction stirred it up. Or near one of the Chinese agriculture ministry's biological research facilities south of there. Make it look like the incompetent fools were working on the Uzumaki, accidentally released it themselves."

Kitano: "Like the Soviet anthrax incident at Sverdlovsk in '79?"

Dunne: "Exactly."

That would seal it. The Chinese government would go ballistic.

She typed in the private email addresses of the ambassadors of China and Japan, along with the top-ranking military officers at the Chinese Ministry of State Security and the Japanese Defense Intelligence Headquarters, then attached the Zip file containing the documents.

She hit Send.

46

DUNNE STARED AT THE MAP ON THE WALL. AT THE ONE-HOUR mark, the position signal came in. Center of the garage. Nothing.

The money hadn't moved.

Now the two-hour mark was seconds away.

Bing! The dot appeared on the map. No one said a word.

The FBI director was first to break the silence. "I don't get it. The money hasn't moved. It's been two hours and the money hasn't moved. I say we go in."

"Yes," the President said. "Do it now."

Dunne tried to focus but couldn't think clearly. *It's been two hours. Why should I trust you?* . . . Some moments he felt as though he were above the room, floating, watching the proceedings from a distance. Other times he felt frozen, paralyzed, his thoughts acidic, eating away at the tissues of his brain. What the hell was wrong with him?

The President's chief of staff entered the room. "Mr. President. Something strange is happening. At the Chinese and Japanese embassies."

"What?"

"The Chinese ambassador is livid. He says he must talk to you. Immediately. The Japanese ambassador as well."

"George, we're a bit busy here. Send somone over to babysit them."

"Both ambassadors claim we are in violation of the 1972 UN Biological Weapons Convention. With our development of an offensive weapon called the Uzumaki."

The room went silent. Dunne felt as if his skin was burning.

"They used that word?"

"Yes, Mr. President. Sometime in the last hour, Orchid sent both the Chinese and Japanese governments a message. We don't know what's in it yet, but it's clear she informed them about the Uzumaki."

The President was silent for nearly a minute, anger and worry etched on his face. "Goddamn it. I don't understand. Why would she do this?"

"Mr. President. One other thing. A number of the staff from both embassies are said to be leaving work, scrambling to get on flights to Beijing and Tokyo. The rumor is that she's already set the Uzumaki loose."

47

JAKE AND KITANO DROVE NORTH. THE IPHONE DISPLAY TOLD them where to go. On its face was a map, with a little circle showing their location. Below it were written instructions, updating as they progressed. Jake put the phone on the dashboard where he could easily see it.

They were approaching the Canadian border now, just east of Lake Ontario, an area called the Thousand Islands. Here, the Saint Lawrence River widened and fragmented, wandering among the eighteen hundred chunks of land isolated by the river, each a moored ship in the slow-moving flow. A light snow was falling. It was still October, but winter was knocking at the door. This far north, snow could come at any time after September.

After leaving Boston, they'd traveled in total silence. The instructions on the iPhone told Jake exactly which roads to take, a series of state and county highways passing through western Massachusetts, cutting the corner of Vermont, then into New York and through the Adirondacks and on to Watertown. Jake had hit the radio a couple of times, tuned to a news station in case anything happened. But Kitano turned it off, without a word, each time.

Four days. Four days since the psychopath Orchid had started her rampage. Liam was dead, Vlad was dead, Maggie was a prisoner, and Dylan was mortally ill.

Four days.

Jake was sore all over, an aftereffect from his near electrocution a day and a half ago. His right ear still ached, his hearing still bad on that side. Roscoe said it might never come all the way back.

Jake had his game face on, but he was weighed down with worry and guilt about Dylan. It killed Jake how brave Dylan had been, running from Orchid, risking his life to get rid of the Uzumaki. It broke Jake's heart that Dylan's bravery had been repaid in such a horrible fashion. Jake felt responsible. He'd filled Dylan with ideas about being brave and conquering fears. And now Dylan was paying for it. A nine-year-old kid. Their last meeting had been tough, right before Jake had left for Boston. Jake had stood outside Dylan's containment room, looking through the glass, phone to his ear. "I don't feel right," Dylan had said, his voice thin. "I can't think right."

Jake had promised Dylan the moon. "I'll get your mom. I'll bring her back. We'll get through this." He tried to believe it as he said it, so that Dylan would believe it, too. "Hang in there, little guy."

The doctor was ready with a hypodermic. They planned to sedate Dylan as soon as Jake left. It was the only thing they knew to do. It took all Jake had to hold back the darkness. He had never in his life felt so powerless.

Jake was haunted by a truth he'd been circling for months. More than anything he'd wanted since the war, he wanted a life with Maggie and Dylan. He couldn't picture any other future. But his fantasy was shattered before it came close to coming true, replaced by a reality where Maggie was Orchid's prisoner, Dylan was gravely ill, and all Jake could do was chauffeur an old war criminal to his death.

He tried to shake it off. He was beat up, adrenaline-burnt, but itching for action. The combination of frustration, anger, and anxiety made him dangerous, possibly prone to mistakes. Every soldier knew that danger the way he knew his rifle. Unreleased pressure ate at you, chewed you up. Jake had seen it, the slow, creeping toll of unreleased pressure. Months in the desert, staring across the sand, waiting to kill or be killed, putting on the damned bio-weapons suits, taking them off again. It was a relief when the final orders came down and they were moving. Once that happened, the air changed. Everything was sharp, like a knife, the contrast suddenly turned up. You could do anything.

"THERE IS A CRISIS," KITANO SAID SUDDENLY, JUST AFTER they left the town of Hammond, a few miles from the Canada border.

Jake jumped so hard he swerved. The back wheels slipped before catching the road again. The road was empty, nothing but forest on either side. He hadn't seen another car for a couple of miles. "What're you talking about?"

"In Japan. A crisis with the men. Approximately two-thirds of the young men. They have become *soshoku-danshi*."

"I don't know what that means."

"*Soshoku-danshi.* Herbivorous males. Grass-eating men." Kitano shook his head. "They are soft. Weak. No longer interested in war. They are not even interested in women. They garden. And buy trinkets for their homes. A marketing report from Matsushita maintains that forty percent of them sit down when they piss."

Kitano went silent. Jake glanced over. The old man's face was drawn, eyes narrowed. His hands scratched at his skin. Kitano said, "The Japanese defense ministry is calling it a crisis. The grass-eaters are taking over, and soon there will be no men left to fight. The ministry is forced to spend billions developing robots that will fight to defend Japan." He glanced at Jake, his jaundiced eyes dark. "I am ashamed to be Japanese."

Jake turned back to the road. An old police cruiser sat in the driveway of a shuttered bait shop to his right, unoccupied. He felt Kitano's gaze like a shadow on him. "It's a phase. A fad. Next year they'll all be taking up kickboxing."

"No. You are wrong. It is not a phase. It's the war."

"What war?"

Kitano smirked. "What war? The *only* war. Not these skirmishes you have now. They are children's games."

The sky overhead was slate-gray. Everything was old, the

houses, the cars they passed. A cellphone tower peeked above the trees on a nearby hillside, the only evidence that they were not in some kind of time warp, taken back two decades.

The only war. World War II. The last full-on, all-out, winner-take-all struggle for survival. A war where the most powerful nations in the world fought for their lives. Not a strategic skirmish. No arguments about dominoes or oil. A war of survival. The world had seen nothing like it since.

The war had left its mark on America. Given America the swagger, the confidence to rule the world for more than half a century. Japan had experienced the other side, what it felt like to be conquered.

Jake pulled up to an intersection with a four-way stop sign. No other cars were in sight. "That was a long time ago," he said.

Kitano shook his head. "A few decades are nothing for Japan. We are a nation that does not forget easily. We are held together by our memories." He closed his eyes. Jake could see stains growing around the armpits of Kitano's shirt. The guy was scared to death.

"After the war," Kitano said, "we were nothing. The Americans emasculated us. They defiled the emperor, made him a man. They imposed their laws, re-created Japan in America's image. They even confiscated our fighting swords. To keep our traditions alive, we fought with blunt, dull metal." Kitano smirked, spat on the floor. "They would have us be children." Kitano returned to his scratching, hands working furiously. Red streaks appeared on his arms. If he scratched any harder, he'd draw blood.

"Take it easy," Jake said. "You all right?"

Kitano stopped suddenly, tilted his head, listening carefully. "Do you hear that? The sound? Like a steady knocking?"

Jake listened. The road was two lanes, poured concrete laid down in sections, with seams between the sections. The tires made a repetitive knocking noise as they passed over. "What about it?"

"How much did they tell you about me?"

"Enough."

"I was no great warrior. I was a technician. An engineer. Like you, Jake. You drove bulldozers, correct?"

Startled, Jake asked, "Who told you that?"

Kitano ignored the question. "There is a story I will tell you. Not my own. A tale told to me by one of the other Tokkō. He said he would hear a sound. He even described it as the sound of tires on a road. Regular. *Thump, thump, thump*. The Tokkō. They were to travel to the United States, carried by some of the last remaining submarines in the Japanese fleet. They were to attack with the Uzu-maki. These were the most important men in Japan, proudly serving the emperor. They were selected from existing Tokkō squads. Chosen for their dedication. Do you understand?"

"No."

"Seigo Mori and I were both from the University of Tokyo. Almost all of the kamikaze were from the University of Tokyo. The best and the brightest. The soldiers would come and line us up. 'Who will volunteer?' they would ask. 'Who will sacrifice for Japan?' Seigo was a French literature major. He was a romantic. He stepped forward.

"Seigo was assigned to Tokkō Squad 232. His kamikaze squadron was ordered to attack the Americans at Okinawa. They were all young, flying dreadful planes, dregs left over after everything valuable was shot down. He had on his *senninbari*, a belt stitched by the hands of a thousand women. His mother sat on a street corner for days to get the necessary hands. He also had his *hanayome ningyo*, his bride doll."

Jake tried to follow what Kitano was saying, but he kept jumping around, barely making sense.

"Seigo left a letter addressed to his older sister, describing his last day. I read it later, in 1954. She showed it to me. His squadron, the letter said, had spent the previous night at a tea house, drinking and smiling and laughing. In the morning they faced their hometowns and sang patriotic songs. Though they all had been racked with doubts, all uncertainty vanished as they taxied their planes down the runway. The local girls came out, waved cherry blossom boughs. Sent them on their journey. They were to die, they were proud. They were the only hope.

"Seigo said he was happy. He said he was alive in a way he had never been before. He longed to fly into the arms of death, on a mission to save his country. 'To save my father and mother, my sister from the white devils.'

"They took off after dawn. Then Seigo heard it, coming from the front of the plane, the thumping. His heart sank. It was the engine. He'd been carefully attending to it for a week, trying to make it run on the terrible fuel that they were given. He tried, but in truth he was doomed from the beginning. The plane would not make it the last hundred and fifty miles to the target. It would be lucky to make it back to the base.

"He told me that he cursed and screamed, beat his hands against the controls. His fellow Tokkō pilots began to pull ahead, disappearing into the clouds. These men were the closest brothers he'd ever had. They were to die together. The thought of leaving them behind was too much. But he had no choice. So he returned.

"After he landed, he ran to his barracks. Thankfully, no one was around. He was alone with his shame. It was the worst moment of his life. He had let down his family, his country. And most of all, his fellow Tokkō. He said that he felt as though he were already dead. His family thought that he was dead. The only idea that brought him comfort was that soon he would be in another airplane, pointed toward another American warship. But that was not his fate. Instead he was called to Harbin. Do you understand now? Why he was chosen?"

"No. I don't."

"He had proved he was willing to die. He was very brave, Seigo Mori. He wanted to get in a plane and attack right away. But as a Tokkō, he was willing to wait, to be one of the walking dead for as long as was required. He was no *soshoku-danshi*. No grass-eating man."

A NARROW ASPHALT ROAD BRANCHED OFF TO THE RIGHT, and the arrow on the iPhone told Jake to take it. A few more turns put them onto a gravel road. Jake didn't like the way Kitano was talking. He felt the menace coming off the old man, in addition to the smell of sweat, a pent-up aggression that might boil over at any moment. And the scratching—he was going to tear through his skin.

Kitano was starting to panic, Jake reasoned. Cracking up. Jake would have to keep a close watch when they got out of the car. He might try to run, or even attack, as preposterous as that seemed. Jake didn't blame him. Orchid had viciously tortured Liam. She'd killed Vlad and Harpo, murdered Maggie's housemate. She'd tried her best to kill Jake. What would she do when she got her hands on Kitano?

Kitano was distracting Jake with his anger, his stories about the war. It was dangerous, keeping Jake from focusing on his real adversary. Orchid was his target. He needed to keep his mind on Orchid, not on Kitano. Another hundred miles north and they'd enter a huge swath of nearly uninhabited wilderness and into what was known as the "north hole" in GPS satellite coverage. Satellites were predominantly over the equatorial regions: coverage got worse and worse the farther north you went.

Jake touched the trigger they'd implanted, the tiny thread next to his eye. All that was left to connect them to the outside world was the tracker, and soon even that might not work.

THE ROAD TOOK A SHARP LEFT, THEN BEGAN TO WIND THROUGH a forest of bare trees. Jake checked the time: they'd been driving now for almost eight hours. The clouds were thickening.

An address appeared on the iPhone: 23 Giles Street. Soon after, they came upon a series of cottages tucked back from the road, all empty for the winter. The windows were shuttered, the doors already blocked by small drifts of snow. Behind them, Jake glimpsed stretches of blue water through gaps in the woods. The slow-moving Saint Lawrence, here more a lake than a river, peppered with islands by the thousands. The border was halfway across. On the other side lay Canada.

Jake checked the addresses of the cabins on the right, the ones on the side of the river. Soon he saw 23 Giles, a nondescript saltbox with deep brown wood siding and an incongruous bright blue door. He pulled into the driveway, tires marking the snow, stopping in front of a two-car garage.

Kitano spoke. "If the other six Tokkō failed, I was to be the last to strike. Holding back the Uzumaki until it was time."

"Too bad Connor took it away from you," Jake said. He got out of the car, approached the front window of the house, all the while keeping tabs on Kitano. Jake glanced though the glass pane. The interior of the house was empty and dark.

Kitano joined him on the porch, his movements jerky and

quick. His eyes darted around, as though he sensed danger just out of sight. He was freaking out.

Jake left the porch and checked the garage. Inside was the FedEx van, the back door open. No sign of life.

He returned to the car and grabbed the iPhone. The arrow on the screen pointed through the house and toward the water, the word *rowboat* underneath it.

He walked around to the back of the building, and Kitano followed. The wooden rowboat was pulled up into the middle of the yard, upside down to keep out the snow.

Two parkas were stored underneath.

Jake gave one to Kitano and put on the second himself. He prepared the boat for the journey, rolling it over and dragging it down to the edge of the water. Kitano excused himself, taking a piss over by the bushes. Jake watched him carefully.

MINUTES LATER, JAKE WAS ROWING ACROSS THE RIVER. HIS hands ached, from both the burns and the cold. The snow was still falling, cloaking them in a world of white. It was perfectly quiet. All except for the sound of the oars, the strain and creak of wood on wood, the small splashes as he pulled the oars through the water.

In the back of the boat, directly in Jake's line of sight, was Kitano. The old man was silent now, huddled inside his parka. Jake was glad for the chance to focus. He was hyperaware of every shift of Kitano's body movements.

The screen on the iPhone flickered. The map was gone, the display blank. Then two words appeared: *Stop. Wait.*

Jake lifted the oars, and the boat drifted in the current. They were in the middle of the vast, slow river, hundreds of yards from any of the islands. It was cold as hell. Kitano's lips were moving, but no sound was coming out.

Jake took in his surroundings. The water. The gray-and-white clouds. The snow white on the shoreline, muted shadows cast by the empty trees. What were they waiting for? A boat? He played the oars back and forth in the water, keeping his muscles warm. He prayed that Dylan wasn't suffering. Maggie would go crazy when she found out. She would be inconsolable. Assuming she was still alive. Jake tried to picture a way out of this, a scenario in which everything turned out all right. But it was impossible to imagine.

Kitano spoke again: "When Japan was conquered, our souls were imprisoned. We denied it. We managed to re-create ourselves within the matrix of the conqueror, like a bird living in the rib cage of the beast. The bird wakes up every morning and goes about its day. But soon the bird understands its fate. It lives in darkness. It lives in slavery. It serves no purpose but to digest the food of its host. It becomes a parasite."

The old man's eyes were lit up like coals. He had bits of white spittle in the corners of his mouth. "When this realization occurs," Kitano said, "the bird first acquiesces. Accepts its fate. That is what I did. That is what the modern men of Japan have done, these grass-eaters. They are little birds, living inside the cage America built for them. They have never known any other life. They have never fought. They have never tasted blood.

"But the bars of the cage are rotting away. Soon America will be too weak to protect itself, let alone Japan. So the bird must act. The bird must fight its way out of the darkness, and back into the sun. Japan must break free. It must retake its position as a dangerous and proud nation."

A chill ran up Jake's spine. "What the hell are you talking about?"

"Do you know what we call you? You Caucasians? The *bata-kusai*—the men who smell like rancid butter. You are disgusting creatures who cannot even bathe yourselves properly. And you are cowards. You come and we defeat you. The Dutch came and conquered, but in the end we defeated them. The French, the British, the same. In the end our courage, our willingness to die, is your undoing. Your century is over. Ours has begun."

"You're insane. Japan doesn't even have a real army," Jake said. "Your constitution forbids it."

"*Your* constitution," Kitano said. "MacArthur wrote it. It has no authority over *me*. The armies of the east, of China and Japan, already equal in number those of the United States, and we can raise five times that number. Our military spending is doubling every five years. In a few short years, it will exceed America's. China's economic growth is outstripping yours by a stunning margin. You falter, China rises, with Japan leading her forward. You are not stupid, Mr. Sterling. You must know it. Soon we will dwarf you. China will be the body. And Japan the head."

"China and Japan hate each other."

"Waters ebb and flow. The nations of Europe were mortal enemies for centuries. The Chinese and Japanese similarly fought, struggling for the upper hand. But now we will join together."

Jake felt an incredible heat coming off Kitano. The man was on fire. Jake heard a humming noise coming from far away. After a minute, he spotted it gliding over the water, too small to be an airplane.

It passed directly overhead, then banked and circled. Jake recognized it—an unmanned aerial vehicle, or UAV, maybe one of the old RQ-2 Pioneers the Navy had flown in the First Gulf War. Jake had seen them up close on a number of occasions: they were human-sized, a few feet tall, with a wingspan of maybe fifteen feet, primarily used for reconnaissance. This one was sleeker than the old RQ-2s, probably one of the newer RQ-7 Shadows. What the hell was an RQ-7 Shadow doing out here?

"Do you know the history of the kamikaze?" Kitano said, completely ignoring the UAV. "They are named for a pair of giant typhoons, the winds of God, that destroyed Kublai Khan's Mongol fleets in 1274, and again in 1281. The Mongols came to invade Japan. They paid for their arrogance with their lives. Those not killed by the storm were slaughtered by the Japanese forces. For the next seven hundred years, no *gaijin* dared repeat that mistake. Not until the Americans, the *bata-kusai,* the latest incarnation of the rancid-butter men. When they are destroyed, when *you* are destroyed, no one will dare threaten Japan again."

The air was cold and still. Snowflakes fell slowly. "Cut the bullshit," Jake said. "What the hell are you talking about?"

"Let me ask you a question. What if you Americans discovered the Chinese had the Uzumaki since the war? And told no one? What if they had built a billion-dollar facility whose mission was to develop a cure for the Uzumaki? And then what if an extremely high-ranking Chinese official was caught *on tape* describing a plan of attack, a plan to release the Uzumaki in the United States, killing millions and millions of your citizens. What would you think then? Would you do anything to stop them?"

"Quit playing games."

"Answer me. Would you do anything to stop them?"

"Of course."

"And if someone else stopped them, if someone else made them pay? Would that person, that nation, become your ally? Even if in the past they had been your enemy?"

"Tell me what is going on."

"Hours ago, Orchid sent a series of encrypted files to the Japanese and Chinese embassies. In them are documents and audiotapes proving that the United States is preparing a biological attack against China. A secret, underhanded, despicable act. A plan to use the Uzumaki as a weapon to bring down the Chinese government. To kill thousands, perhaps millions, of innocent Chinese civilians."

The words were like an electric shock. Suddenly Jake understood.

"You son of a bitch. You hired Orchid."

A hundred connections appeared, images flooding his mind. Connor jumping off the bridge. Vlad shot in the head. Dylan alone in an isolation tank. All because of this man. "You're paying Orchid to get you out of jail. You did all this to set yourself free." Jake grabbed one of the oars, held it like a club. "Tell me where Maggie is."

Kitano ignored the threat. "The United States kept the Uzumaki secret for over sixty years. It covered up Japan's infamous Unit 731 to protect this precious secret. And now it is undertaking an aggressive countermeasures program that will allow it to use the Uzumaki as an offensive weapon. I have documents proving all of this."

"That's total bullshit. No one will believe you. Documents can be forged. You think China will love you after this? Be your friend just because you cook up some crazy conspiracy theory that the U.S. is going to attack China?"

"The Chinese will revere me for exacting revenge against the white devils."

"Revenge? What the hell—"

Kitano cut him off. "You still do not understand, do you? It is over. The Uzumaki is already free. It is already spreading."

48

DUNNE SLIPPED AWAY TO THE WOOD-PANELED ROOM THAT was his temporary office at Camp David, phone pressed to his ear, talking frantically to Paul Waller, his attaché. Reports had started coming in from the prison at Hazelton. "Seventeen guards called in sick," Waller said. "The prisoners are agitated. They started a riot."

"Why?"

"No one knows. Everyone is acting crazy. The warden said he's never seen anything like it."

"Find out *why*."

Dunne tossed the phone down on his desk, skin itching like fire. He tried to keep calm, but it was as if his thoughts shredded before he could understand them. Streaks of light shot across his line of vision.

He sat at the desk, poured a glass of water from the pitcher on the table. His hand shook as he tried to take a drink. "There's something wrong with me," he said aloud. Denying it was no longer possible. Now his thoughts were crawling everywhere, almost as if they were outside his head, like spiders on his scalp. One second he was Lawrence Dunne, sinew and substance, the deputy

national security adviser for the most powerful nation in the world.
The next second he was a loose collection of dust, water, and sand.

"Walking dead," a voice said.

Dunne looked up, shocked. It took him a minute to realize that
he had said it. He was sitting in a chair, at a desk, his BlackBerry on
the desktop before him, but he was also standing across the room,
watching himself sitting in the chair. *I'm having some sort of
breakdown.*

The other Dunne watched him. The other Dunne was now a
rotting corpse, bits of skin hanging down like peeled paint. The
other Dunne spoke, his voice sounding as if it came from the bottom of a well. "Walking dead."

Dunne closed his eyes. The other Dunne was still there, waiting
in the blackness.

I'm cracking up.

A wave of nausea hit. He shook his head, saw streaks of lights
like tracer bullets. The walls began to pulsate, as if the office were
a giant, breathing animal.

The prison. Everyone at the prison was going crazy.

He flashed to Kitano, the old man on the floor of his prison cell,
a drop of spittle on his lips.

His phone vibrated on his desk, wriggling like a living creature.
Dunne forced himself to pick it up.

It was Waller again. He sounded panicked. "They tore apart
Kitano's cell. He had a phone. A goddamn cellphone—one of the
guards admitted to smuggling it in for him. He'd been texting back
and forth with someone. Lawrence, *he knew.* He knew everything
that was coming. The demands, everything. But that's not the
worst. In one of the books he'd carved out a little space. Inside it
they found a MicroCrawler. It was wrapped in a note. The note
said, 'The falcon strikes.' "

Dunne dropped the phone. The room pulsed a dark red. Dunne
fought to keep control of his thoughts. The walls ran bloodred.
Looking up, he saw a falcon pulling in its wings.

Dunne ran out of his office, trying to get away. He stared upward, seeing not the ceiling but a sky on fire, flames tearing holes
in the world. From the center of the maelstrom came a Tokkō plane
diving, orange flames shooting as it fell, melting and re-forming, as

a falcon, as a burning sword. Yelling at the top of his lungs, Dunne heard nothing, screaming and running until the Navy guards grabbed him.

The next thing he knew he was on the floor, strong arms holding him down. The President, the cabinet, the Joint Chiefs, all stood over him. Men in their uniforms, the trappings of power. Bombs, missiles, satellites, all worthless, nothing. Today it ended. Kitano would end everything.

49

MAGGIE WAS RUNNING OUT OF TIME.

She strained against the cuffs on her wrists. Two feet away, on the little table, lay the pair of tweezers that Orchid had used the day before. They were a pitiful weapon, but if she could get her hands on them, it might just be enough.

The skin on her right wrist tore, rolled back. The blood was slick, acting as lubrication between flesh and metal. A few more minutes and she'd be there. If Orchid would stay away just a few minutes longer.

Maggie was very close.

If only Orchid would stay away.

THE LAST TWELVE HOURS HAD BEEN A TERRIFYING JOURNEY. A descent into madness, and then, incredibly, a return to sanity. Orchid had infected her with the Uzumaki, then left her overnight in complete darkness. For hour after interminable hour, Maggie had grown increasingly frantic, trapped inside the claustrophobic gas mask, trying to scream, trying to escape the corpses grabbing at her.

Hours later, Orchid had returned and switched on the lights, dispelling for the moment her ghostly attackers. Maggie had let loose with a string of curses like she'd never uttered. She'd howled, called Orchid a bitch and a whore, screeched all the ways she'd like to kill her. A demon possessed her that had little relation to the self that Maggie had known.

Orchid had opened her backpack on the bench, reached inside. Maggie had kept up the invective, only stopping when she saw what Orchid held in her palm. A glass vial filled with her grandfather's glowing *Fusarium* fungus.

Orchid had taken some of the multicolored stringy fungus and mixed it together with a liquid in a test tube. With a hypodermic, she'd pulled the liquid up inside, then injected it into Maggie's stomach.

Then Orchid had left.

Over the next few hours, Maggie's shakes had continued, with mad visions of Crawlers tearing apart her son and corpses grabbing at her. But after a while, she'd noticed a change. The hallucinations were lessening.

The crazy itching, the homicidal fantasies. The corpses. All retreated further with every passing hour. Orchid would return for a moment, closely observing her movements. She would take Maggie's temperature, as well as a blood sample, which she stored in a small refrigerator.

Maggie could tell that Orchid was pleased.

The glowing fungus.

"Your grandfather," Orchid had said.

Maggie thought of the glowing fungus on the piece of wood: the prize that Liam had left at the end of the letterbox trail. *That's* what they were meant to find. That's what Liam had left for them. Her grandfather had created an antidote for the Uzumaki.

He had created an antidote for the most dangerous biological weapon ever developed. Because of it, she wouldn't die here, unhinged and alone. The progress of the Uzumaki could be stopped. Because of her grandfather.

As that understanding took hold, Maggie was overcome with emotion. Profound awe, a tremendous respect and admiration for her grandfather, and a relief that soaked her entire body. He had succeeded in doing, all alone, what all the scientists at Detrick couldn't accomplish.

But soon enough, Maggie's relief dimmed. Slowly, a darker knowledge had taken root inside of her.

Orchid had the cure.

Connor's law: you have the cure, you have a weapon.

MAGGIE PULLED AS HARD AS SHE COULD, IGNORING THE searing pain. One last, vicious yank and her hand popped free. She opened her fingers, the muscles obeying, though she could barely feel them.

A noise. The door opened at the top of the stairs.

She grabbed the tweezers off the table and quickly put her hand back down, as if her arm was still handcuffed.

She forced her breathing to slow, nice and easy.

One chance.

Orchid came down with a gun drawn, as she always did. She saw Maggie, ran her eyes up and down her, then holstered the gun in the small of her back and flipped the snap closed.

Maggie tried to control her breathing as Orchid took a fresh needle from the plastic pack, attached it to the syringe. To draw Maggie's blood.

Maggie went over it again and again, rehearsing the moves in her head, trying not to completely freak out. Finally Orchid turned, needle in hand. She came toward Maggie as she had each time before.

Maggie watched her rhythm. *Get ready. Get ready. Get ready.*

Orchid stopped before her, syringe in hand.

Then Orchid hesitated, looking down to the floor.

Oh, shit. She had seen blood dripping off Maggie's wrist.

Orchid looked up, into Maggie's eyes. Maggie shifted her grip on the tweezers, holding them in her fist like an ice pick.

She went for it. With a great sweep of her arm, Maggie jammed the sharp end of the tweezers into Orchid's face.

Orchid screamed, twisted her head and body to the right. That sealed Maggie's fate. Maggie released the tweezers and reached for Orchid's handgun. But when Orchid twisted to the right, her body blocked access to the gun. Either by chance or instinct, Orchid had cut off Maggie's only hope.

Chance or instinct, it didn't matter. Orchid stepped back, the tweezers impaled in her cheek, leaving Maggie grasping at air with her one free hand.

"I'll kill you!" Orchid bellowed, blood streaming from the wound. She pulled out the tweezers and threw them across the room.

Orchid stepped back, wide-eyed and panting. She picked up a strand of rope and rushed Maggie, grabbed her free arm and tied it down. Maggie fought, but Orchid was much stronger.

Once Maggie was secured, Orchid picked up the glass sphere. Maggie was shocked to see that it was filled with Crawlers. Orchid tossed a spool of thin wire over a bar in the ceiling and rigged the ball so that it dangled over Maggie, inches from her face.

Orchid moved her gloved hand, and the Crawlers came to life. They were manic, running like a nest of crazed spiders. The noise was a high-pitched cacophony, thousands of razor-sharp legs scratching wildly at the glass.

Orchid roughly grabbed a hammer from a nearby bench and held it high, her eyes wide, her teeth bared. Her entire body shook with anger. "Your son is infected with the Uzumaki. Did you know that? He must be half dead by now. He'll be dead by the time I deliver the cure to the Chinese and Japanese. Your protector, Jake? I'm going to shoot him in the face."

Maggie fought against her restraints. Orchid loomed over her, snarling like a crazed animal. "Get ready for the moment. Your protector is dead. Your son is mad. The Uzumaki is spreading everywhere." She clacked the hammer against the glass sphere. "I break this open and they fall on you, cut through your eyes, crawl inside your goddamn skull, and feast on your brain. And I will enjoy watching you die. I will revel in it."

· 50 ·

"WHERE IS MAGGIE?" JAKE DEMANDED, HIS HANDS ON KI-
tano's throat. "Tell me, you son of a bitch—*where is Maggie?*"

"Kill me, but it will cost you Maggie Connor's life," Kitano
said. He pointed to the phone. "Pick it up."

"*Tell me now.*"

"I do not envy you," Kitano said, a sudden clarity in his eyes,
as if the demons had bizarrely departed. "You are a Tokkō, but
your sacrifice is hollow, nothing. It is your fate. Pick up the phone."

Jake pushed Kitano away and grabbed the iPhone.

The screen flickered, sprang to life. The image was like a kick
in the chest. A close-up of Maggie, her eyes darting, panicked, her
mouth taped closed. Above her head hung the glass sphere filled
with Crawlers. They were swarming inside, thousands of them.

Orchid's voice came from the phone. "You're the expert, Jake.
How long will she last?"

"You hurt her and—"

Orchid cut him off. "Get Kitano here in fifteen minutes. Follow
the UAV. Or in fifteen minutes she's dead."

· · ·

THE TRAIL STEEPENED, AND JAKE HAD TO HALF DRAG, HALF carry Kitano. The UAV shadowed them, turning in circles a few hundred feet overhead. They were on a large island, ascending from the water's edge up a thin, rocky trail. The rowboat was far below. Kitano's delirium had returned, worsened. He was now shivering, raving in both English and Japanese, half frozen from the cold.

"I have been dead for sixty years," he said, as Jake dragged him on. "My mother gave me the cloth, the death service. Since then I have been bones. I have been nothing. Wandering the earth for sixty-four years, desiring filth, eating filth, consuming filth. I have been a hungry ghost."

"Shut up," Jake said. Kitano refused to tell Jake anything more about Maggie or the release of the Uzumaki. His words occasionally made sense but more often were incoherent, rambling diatribes about the war.

Jake was increasingly certain Kitano had been infected. He had all the symptoms, the sweats, the smell, the manic delusions. But if he and Orchid were in league, then why would he be infected? Could Orchid have double-crossed him?

However it had happened, if Kitano was infected, there was a good chance Jake was as well. He didn't feel anything yet, but he'd been around Kitano for only a few hours.

The trail opened up on the left, the trees thinning and then gone altogether. Jake found himself on the crest of a long, U-shaped band of cliffs. A suspension bridge hung above river water rushing toward a dramatic waterfall, the water breaking into mist and spray as it dropped. The old slats creaked as they crossed the bridge. Hundreds of feet below was a marsh protected by steep walls on three sides and connected to the Saint Lawrence on the fourth. Geese were everywhere. A few hundred suddenly took to the air, a wall of flapping wings rising up, circling not a hundred feet from them, squawking and twisting as they rose. Kitano seemed hypnotized by the sight.

A wave of dread swept over Jake as he followed Kitano's gaze to the thousands of tiny shapes. Thousands and thousands of geese, more than Jake had ever seen. He felt as if the ground were about to give way beneath him. Kitano and Orchid had not randomly chosen this spot.

Faster, Jake. Go faster.

"No more filth," Kitano mumbled. "I am ready to die. To fulfill my destiny." He began to shake. Jake didn't know how much longer the old man would last.

Jake glimpsed a patch of red through a break in the trees. The door of a cabin.

Dragging Kitano with him, he sprinted for the building, heart in his throat.

The UAV was circling like a vulture.

He reached the cabin door and pulled it open. No lock. Just a simple latch.

The cabin was nearly empty, the corners full of dust and cobwebs. In the center of the room was a carefully folded garment, brilliant white. On top was a short Japanese sword with a carved wooden handle and a shorter polished steel blade.

Seeing the sword, Kitano pushed past Jake, but Jake shoved him back. Kitano fell to the floor in a heap.

Jake picked up the sword. It had a wooden handle with a black Japanese symbol stamped on it. What the hell was this doing out here?

Kitano's eyes were fixed on the sword. "Give it to me."

"Where's Orchid? Where's Maggie?"

"Give me the sword."

Weapon in hand, Jake stepped back outside, scanning every direction. At the clearing's edge was what looked like the entrance to an underground storm shelter. Jake spotted footsteps in the snow near the entrance.

"Give me the sword!" Kitano said from behind him.

Jake grabbed him and pushed him along the snowy path to the storm shelter entrance. He paused and grabbed the tiny thread implanted next to his left eye. Pulling the tripwire sent an electric shock through him, as though he'd grabbed a live wire. He momentarily saw spots but steadied himself.

He guessed he had ten minutes, fifteen at the outside, before the bombs started falling.

JAKE HELD THE SWORD AT KITANO'S BACK, SCANNING FOR Orchid as they made their way down the series of steps that ran at a steep angle underground.

A plaintive moan drifted up. His heart nearly stopped.

Maggie.

He saw her now, strapped down to a table, mouth taped closed. The glass sphere was suspended above her, inches from her face. Inside it, the Crawlers were a roiling silvery-black mass, filling the room with a noise like locusts in a field. The rest of the room was cloaked in shadows. There was no sign of Orchid.

Lifting her head and spotting Jake, Maggie tried to scream, then started kicking and twisting frantically.

IN THE DARK BEHIND THE STAIRS, ORCHID COOLLY WATCHED through a broken riser as they slowly descended the steps. Jake pushed Kitano ahead, using him as a shield. It would do him no good. Orchid was behind them.

She waited until Jake reached the bottom of the stairs, the back of his head perfectly framed in her small rectangular view, before she stepped out from behind the stairs and took aim. She preferred shooting her victims in the face, to observe their expression at the moment of death.

"Jake Sterling," she said.

THE INSTANT HE HEARD HER VOICE, HE DUCKED. AS HE PIV-oted, a bullet grazed his forehead.

He dove behind a small wood-and-Formica table a fraction of a second ahead of the second bullet. The sword clanged to the floor. She shot four more times, the table splintering.

From the floor, Kitano scrambled to his feet, retrieved the sword, and fled up the stairs.

Using the table as a shield, Jake rushed Orchid. She fired, pulling off two rounds at close range, the bullets fragmenting the wood and Formica as he continued toward her. The second shot caught him in the shoulder, but the table had taken most of its power. Jake crashed into her head-on, slamming her backward. Her gun fell and clattered across the floor. Jake dove for it, won the race.

He turned, rolling, aiming and firing at Orchid, who had pulled a snub-nose from an ankle holster. Her right upper arm erupted in a spray of blood. Incredibly, she held her position, firing three shots and sending Jake diving behind a cabinet. The last echoes of the shots settled, leaving only the noise of the Crawlers.

To his right, Maggie struggled against her bindings. The glass ball dangled above.

IGNORING THE PAIN IN HER SHOULDER, ORCHID WAITED FOR a clean shot. She knew she was the superior fighter, but Sterling had the better weapon and more rounds remaining. She had to change the rules.

The noise of the Crawlers' legs on glass was the only sound in the room. Seeing Maggie straining at her bonds, Orchid glanced back to Jake's position.

Let's give you something else to worry about.

She aimed her pistol at the glass and fired. Its glass shell cracked.

. . .

JAKE REALIZED HE HAD ONE CHANCE NOW TO SAVE HIM AND Maggie both. To pin Orchid down, he fired once more, then ran toward Maggie. Diving over her, he was in the air, propelled by rage and fear and sheer determination, grabbing the sphere of Crawlers, praying it didn't break. If it did, the Crawlers would rip him to shreds.

His momentum snapped the wire, and he and the sphere flew through the air, headed for the ground. Twisting so his back hit the floor first, he held the orb above him like a baby, the gun still in his hand.

Fighting to keep his breath, he didn't hesitate. With an arching hook shot, he launched the sphere at Orchid and then he fired.

The ball exploded.

Jake heard a cry of surprise, then, a second later, a scream.

Frantically trying to rid herself of thousands of razor-sharp Crawlers, Orchid bolted to her feet, screaming and writhing, firing wildly in Jake's direction until the trigger clicked, the chamber empty. She threw down the gun, grabbing at her face.

She was covered in blood from a thousand razor-blade cuts. She staggered and fell against the wall, sliding to the floor as the Crawlers sliced unceasingly. Her eyes were shredded, blood flowing down her face. Her screams diminished, her motions reduced to jerky spasms, then nothing.

Jake was at Maggie's side, gently pulling the tape from her mouth. Her first words were "Is Dylan infected?"

Jake nodded. "I'm so sorry. But we've got to get out of here. In a few minutes, this place will be blown to hell."

"Jake—there's a cure."

· 52 ·

OUTSIDE, JAKE SAW NO SIGN OF KITANO.

Maggie was in front of the cabin, trying to establish a connection to the outside world using Orchid's computer. "It's password-protected. I can't get through." She was scared and beat up, her right hand bruised and bloody, but she was also completely determined to save her son. They had gone through Orchid's backpack: no cellphone, but it was loaded with dozens of vials filled with the glowing fungus that was the Uzumaki cure. Jake still couldn't believe it—a cure. But any doubt was dispelled by the yellow sheet of paper they found in Orchid's backpack. It was the decoded message Liam had left them, the one Orchid had killed Vlad to get.

He let himself believe they were going to make it. Maggie was alive. Dylan would be cured. Kitano and Orchid had planned to deliver the cure to the Japanese and Chinese after the outbreak had taken hold in America. But now he and Maggie had the cure.

They ran, Jake carrying Orchid's pack, Maggie ahead of him. In just a few more minutes, they'd be over the suspension bridge, down the hill, and beyond the blast zone.

· · ·

KITANO TIGHTENED HIS GRIP ON HIS SEPPUKU SWORD.
It took every ounce of will to hold on to his thoughts, to keep
the madness from interfering with his mission. The soldiers had
been with him since the morning, floating above him. They had
watched silently at first. Thousands of ghosts, the spirits of the
young Japanese Tokkō who had given their lives to stop the Americans. Now they surrounded him, singing old songs, more real than
the bridge on which he stood. More real than the steel weapon in
his hand.

Kitano unsheathed the short sword, its silver blade blinding in
the sun. He wrapped the sword's upper part in cloth, then held the
sword by the blade, keeping an eye on the woods. Kitano took
three sharp breaths. The mind had to be clear, the body ready. Kitano would have no *kaishaku* to help. No assistant to decapitate
him when the pain became too great.

JAKE AND MAGGIE EMERGED FROM A COPSE OF TREES INTO
an open area. Twenty yards away was the suspension bridge.

Kitano stood in the middle of the bridge in white ceremonial
robes, sword in hand. Spotting them, he carefully set the sword
down and pulled a gun from a fold in his robes. Taking aim and firing, he drove them back into the woods.

"Is there another way down?" Maggie asked.

"I don't know. There's a fork in the trail about fifty yards
back."

Jake's eyes met Maggie's—both understood what Kitano was
doing. "Christ, Jake. The geese. This is a major migration flyway."

Jake thrust the backpack at her. "I'll stop him. You get as far
away as possible. Don't wait for anything."

"Jake—"

"Give Dylan a hug for me," he said, taking a last look at her
before turning back to face Kitano.

Behind him in the sky, Jake saw the approaching planes. They
were minutes away. He had to keep Kitano occupied for those crucial minutes. Otherwise, the old Tokkō would at last execute his
mission, sixty-four years after his first attempt. The sociopathic
monster was going to kill himself and set off the worst pandemic in
history. Infect the geese with the deadly spores and blanket the

Northeast with Uzumaki in twenty-four hours, the entire country within a week. In a month, it would cover the globe.

"It's over," Jake called, stepping into the clear, palms open before him. "Orchid is dead. She's not going to deliver the cure to Japan. You set the Uzumaki loose, the cure won't get anywhere near Japan, but the Uzumaki will."

Kitano took aim at Jake. "This is my destiny."

As Jake sprinted toward Kitano, the impact of the first bullet spun him around. The pain in his shoulder joint was ferocious, but he didn't halt his charge.

Kitano's next bullet missed, but the one that followed took Jake's leg out from under him. He staggered to the edge of the bridge. Another shot, this one in his side.

He went down.

THE SOUND OF THE FIRST GUNSHOT BROUGHT MAGGIE TO A temporary stop.

More gunfire.

Maggie started running again, barely able to see through the tears. Tripping on a branch, she fell, scraping her arms and face and dropping the backpack. She stared for just a second at the streaks of her blood on the snow before retrieving the pack. She had to get the cure off the island. To save Dylan.

She heard another shot.

The cure—Dylan would die without it. And maybe thousands, millions more.

She pushed on, but the trail suddenly ended at a sharp dropoff. Her heart sank. No way down. She was trapped. She couldn't go down.

She looked to the sky. The planes were so close. She wouldn't get far enough away. She was dead, she knew it, but could she still get the cure off the island?

Though comes the darkness, though the cold winds blow,
This will banish the worst, set the whole world aglow.

Recalling Liam's poetic message, hands shaking, she opened the backpack and stared at the vials of glowing fungus. She dug out the yellow page that Liam had left for them, desperately scrutinizing her grandfather's words.

"Liam. Oh my God, Liam."

JAKE FELT THE LIFE DRAINING FROM HIM.

His thoughts were disjointed, flashes of scenes. Jake was at the bedside of his mother on the day before she died, her lips on his cheek. He was in the trenches of the Iraq desert, watching bulldozers push mounds of dirt. He felt the rumble of the machine as it chugged through the earth, tearing it up, coming to bury him. He imagined hearing Maggie's voice, saw her running toward Dylan with Liam's cure, but then she was obscured by a wall of black.

Struggling to rise, Jake saw that Kitano was half off the bridge, his torso dangling over the water, a knife protruding at a right angle. The old man had eviscerated himself. A shock of bright red spread across his belly and the white silk robe.

Jake got to his feet and crossed the bridge. He reached for the blood-slick Kitano, but it was too late: the old man slid over the edge, splashing into the river. In an instant he was over the falls. Kitano had won.

Jake collapsed in pain. A white streak shot across the sky. With each labored breath, he felt his connection to the world slipping away. Closing his eyes, the pain flared, then dulled. His senses muted. The roar of the river receded to a background murmur.

MAGGIE TRIED TO GET HIM TO HIS FEET. "JAKE — PLEASE."

Jake could barely speak. "Go. Maggie. You have to . . ."

She looked up at the airplanes almost directly overhead now. How long did she have? Twenty seconds?

She frantically opened the vials and dumped their glowing contents off the bridge. Crying now, she longed to tell a barely conscious Jake about what she had found on the yellow sheet of paper, Liam's last message: ". . . the fluorescent fungus is a dispersal vector for the cure . . ." Liam had designed the cure to spread the same way the Uzumaki did. The geese would carry it.

The glowing strands drifted down into the water, blinking bits of red, yellow, and green. Within seconds it was all gone, swept over the falls. The last vial she put in her pocket, saving it for Dylan.

Grabbing Jake's arm, she dragged him to the edge of the bridge. Was he breathing? Oh, God, she couldn't tell. She lay down on top of him. His skin was so cold against hers, their faces inches apart. Rocking them back and forth, the next thing she knew she was underwater, still holding on to Jake. The brutally cold water dragged them toward the falls. Maggie held him as tightly as she could, harder than she had ever held anything in her life.

In seconds, they were at the falls' crest, then over its edge, locked together when the sky exploded, a shock wave like a giant hammer striking them down.

They were airborne, falling, a deafening hurricane roar coming from overhead. The sky above was red, swirling fire, a twisting maelstrom of flame. Then a violent slap like hitting a wall. They struck the bottom of the falls and were immediately sucked under the surface. Stunned and confused, Maggie was twisted and tossed by the churning water, unsure which direction was up.

She fought her way to the surface, spitting and coughing.

She couldn't see Jake. The white froth of the waterfall was churning around her, its roar drowning her voice, the orange flames overhead raging like the end of the world.

· 54 ·

THE FIRST SOLDIERS AIRLIFTED IN FROM FORT DRUM FOUND her wandering about in the shallows, shivering, her arm broken. She gave them the vial with the cure, explaining what Liam had done. She said again and again, "Where is Jake? Please, you have to find Jake."

They found him in the reeds near the river's edge, as if he'd dragged himself partly out of the water. His bullet wounds were washed clean, skin white, nearly drained of blood. They checked for a pulse. A tiny thing, then even that faltered. They went to work, pumping his chest.

"Oh, God, no," Maggie whispered. "Please. Please."

HIS HEART HAD STOPPED WHEN THE MEDICS LOADED HIM into the helicopter, Maggie piling in after them. Jake had lost more than forty percent of his blood, no vital signs, but they kept working on him to get a pulse. A decision was made to divert to Fort Detrick, where they had the containment facilities to handle them.

A medic tended to her wounds. She had a broken arm and a fractured bone in her wrist from pulling her hand from the cuff. After they had put her arm in a sling and secured it to her chest,

Maggie stayed beside Jake the rest of the way. "Hold on, Jake," she begged. "Please hold on."

WHEN THEY LANDED AT DETRICK, MAGGIE WAS TAKEN TO THE slammer. Two hours in, they let her talk to Dylan through the glass of his quarantine unit. The doctors administered the antidote she'd given them. She forced herself not to break down at the sight of her drugged and barely conscious son. In a moment of lucidity, he asked about Jake. "Is he going to be okay?"

"I don't know, Dylan. Let's you and I pray with every bit of hope that we have."

No one was sure of the final outcome for Jake Sterling, not the first day, not the next. On the third day, he'd opened his eyes. On the next, he'd asked for water. Not long after that, beside his hospital bed, Maggie held his hand while he slept. She sobbed like a baby for reasons she only half understood.

ONE YEAR AFTER

THE SMALLEST THING

THE UZUMAKI WAS A DISTANT MEMORY. ALMOST FOUR HUN-
dred people around the Hazelton prison and Camp David came
down with early symptoms. Hundreds of other clusters of cases appeared up and down the Atlantic and Mississippi flyways, but none
of these expanded into a full-blown epidemic, thanks to Liam Connor's last gift to the world, the fungus Maggie had released along-
side the Uzumaki. The cure had spread like a branching river from
the release spot, Liam Connor's fungal creation quickly taking root
in fields up and down North America. Later, spores had carried the
cure overseas, with the fungus turning up everywhere from Africa
to Australia, France to the Falklands.

Liam's cure came from the protective bacterium that lived in
the guts of people who were antibiotic-free. It flipped a genetic
switch that turned *Fusarium spirale* from its deadly form back to
the relatively harmless, single-celled version that Liam had first discovered in Brazil five decades ago. Liam had taken the genes and
inserted them in a fluorescent fungus that could spread just like the
Uzumaki. People merely had to ingest a small amount. Maggie
named the cure *Fusarium spero,* borrowing from the Latin phrase
Dum spiro, spero. While I breathe, I hope.

An FBI investigation into Kitano revealed that he had been spying on Liam for years. After he learned about Liam's labs at the Seneca Army Depot, he had hired Orchid. It had been her job to deliver the cure to the Chinese and Japanese governments. Hitoshi Kitano, the last Tokkō, would finally destroy America.

But Kitano hadn't counted on Jake Sterling. Or Liam Connor.

Liam's cure was not perfect. It worked reliably only when adminstered immediately after the infection. Of the three hundred and seventy-two known cases of the Uzumaki that occurred before the cure was widely available, twenty-nine had died, including Lawrence Dunne. The deputy national security adviser had lasted three weeks, completely mad the entire time, screaming and cursing and begging to die.

The UN hearings on the Uzumaki in the months after the crisis had held the world in thrall. Maggie's testimony, along with Jake's, was said to have drawn a worldwide audience of more than three billion. Pressure was building, and negotiations were under way for new limits on biological-weapons programs, with all the major powers participating.

THEY'D BURIED LIAM CONNOR AT A LITTLE GRAVEYARD IN Ellis Hollow, laid him to rest beside his beloved Edith in a quiet ceremony with no press. Life slowly returned to normal but with a few changes. Jake still taught at Cornell, still built microbots, but he had started a side project creating custom prosthetic limbs for soldiers returning from Iraq and Afghanistan. He would visit the soldiers, listen to their stories, fit them with their new limbs. It was therapeutic for him. Jake came back from the sessions at the Syracuse VA shaken but somehow more alive. Maybe one day Dylan would join him. He was calmer by the day, the panic attacks almost gone.

Maggie had started her own project, using the almost eighty million dollars that Liam had left her. On the site of the old Seneca Army Depot, she'd started construction on a living herbarium, a gigantic garden of decay, going after the entire fungal kingdom. Fungi were among the most remarkable, versatile, and powerful forms of life, yet they were also among the most mysterious. Ninety-five percent of all fungal species remained to be identified, their genetic makeup and their morphological variations still to be classified. She was going to change that. By the time they put her in the ground, the Kingdom of Fungi would no longer be a mystery.

There had been other changes, too.

JUST BEFORE DUSK, THE LITTLE EXPEDITION SET OUT TO SEE the colors.

Dylan and Turtle led the way, Maggie behind them. Jake was happy to bring up the rear. The best spot for viewing came at the end of a long walk through Treman State Park that had been one of Liam and Edith's favorites, a stretch of the Finger Lakes Trail that ran above Lucifer Falls.

They stopped at a spot on a small bluff. Turtle sniffed the earth. Around them was a stand of tall trees, leaves shimmering in daylight's last rays. *"Poplulus tremula,"* Dylan said, the budding taxonomist. "Pop-pop always liked them."

Jake reached his hand to Maggie's, their fingers intertwining. They'd married the month before, in a big outdoor celebration in the backyard of Rivendell. For a time, she'd resisted his proposals—but she never really had a chance after realizing that what had kept them apart for way too long was fear. Fear exposed is the weakest of emotions; love is so much stronger.

Jake had often wondered about himself. After the war, his marriage had fallen apart, and he'd never really been able to put himself back together. No one seemed to be able to touch him. Now he knew why. He was waiting for these two people. Maggie and Dylan had brought him back to the land of the living.

Together they looked out over the cornfield, waiting for the peak of the colors. At dusk, the sight was unbelievably beautiful. As the last sunlight faded, they began: a million little fungi, all flashing in reds, yellows, and greens, like multicolored stars. The cure had spread around the world, Liam Connor's fungal creation. As if the old man had taken one last, great breath and exhaled it all over the world.

Jake mussed Dylan's hair. "I wish Liam was alive to see this."

"He is alive," Dylan replied.

An old Irish saying came to Jake, one of Liam's favorites: "The smallest of things outlives the human being."

There were tears in Maggie's eyes. "Come on," she said to her son. "Count it down."

Dylan nodded. "Ready? Three, two, one . . ."

Together they all took a big breath, drawing in the memory of Liam Connor. They held on as long as they could, then exhaled Liam back into the world, ready for another go.

ACKNOWLEDGMENTS

My editors, Susan Kamil and Dana Isaacson, were brilliant—I cannot thank them enough for their patience, wisdom, and skill. Jane Gelfman made everything possible; she has been a steadfast advocate and all-around miracle worker. Also thanks to the rest of the team at Random House and Gelfman Schneider, especially Noah Eaker and Cathy Gleason, as well as Katie McGowan at Curtis Brown.

Kathie Hodge, professor of mycology at Cornell and curator of the Cornell Plant Pathology Herbarium, provided inspiration and endlessly fascinating facts about fungi. Paul Griswold gave an enlightening tour of the now-shuttered Seneca Army Depot, and Cornell Chief of Police Curtis Ostrander answered my questions about what would happen if a world-famous faculty member jumped off a campus bridge. Nina Shishkoff, Ph.D., of the USDA at Fort Detrick provided many helpful insights and facts. Captain Larry Olsen, U.S. Navy, assisted with matters nautical. Ed Stacker was a wonderful early editor.

My parents, Joe and Mary Lu McEuen, and parents-in-law, Robert and Judy Wiser, have been great readers and cheerleaders, as have been the rest of the McEuen/Arnevik/Wiser clan. My grandparents Buddy and Mary Jane Lorince, both sadly now deceased, were inspirations. Thanks to Cornell University for the freedom to pursue this quixotic quest, and to all my graduate students, post-docs, and colleagues who read early drafts. Many others have read, commented, encouraged, and criticized over the years, including Jessica Shurberg, Jayne Miller, Barb Parish, Debbie

Lev, Rob Costello, Elan Prystowsky, Lesley Yorke, Josh Waterfall, Kim Harrington, and the wonderful crowd at Backspace. Thanks to all.

Finally, this book is dedicated to my wife, Susan Wiser—devoted psychologist, enthusiastic editor, and dog rescuer extraordinaire (visit www.cayugadogrescue.org). Occasionally critical, always supportive, forever mine.

ABOUT THE AUTHOR

PAUL MCEUEN is the Goldwin Smith Professor of Physics at Cornell University. He has received numerous awards for his research, including the Agilent Technologies Europhysics Prize, a Packard Fellowship, and a Presidential Young Investigator Award. He lives with his wife and five dogs in Ithaca, New York.